ME BEING ME

IS EXACTLY AS INSANE AS

YOU BEING YOU

ME BEING ME

TODD
HASAK-
LOWY

IS EXACTLY AS INSANE AS

YOU BEING YOU

Simon Pulse
New York London Toronto Sydney New Delhi

SIMON PULSE

An imprint of Simon & Schuster Children's Publishing Division

1230 Avenue of the Americas, New York, NY 10020

First Simon Pulse hardcover edition March 2015

Text copyright © 2015 by Todd Hasak-Lowy

All rights reserved, including the right of reproduction in whole or in part in any form.

SIMON PULSE and colophon are registered trademarks of Simon & Schuster, Inc.

For information about special discounts for bulk purchases, please contact Simon & Schuster Special Sales at 1-866-506-1949 or business@simonandschuster.com.

The Simon & Schuster Speakers Bureau can bring authors to your live event. For more information or to book an event contact the Simon & Schuster Speakers Bureau at 1-866-248-3049 or visit our website at www.simonspeakers.com.

Jacket designed by Jessica Handelman

Interior designed by Hilary Zarycky

The text of this book was set in New Caledonia.

Manufactured in the United States of America

2 4 6 8 10 9 7 5 3 1

Library of Congress Cataloging-in-Publication Data

Hasak-Lowy, Todd, 1969–

Me being me is exactly as insane as you being you / Todd Hasak-Lowy. — First Simon Pulse hardcover edition.

p. cm.

Summary: Through a series of lists, a narrator reveals how fifteen-year-old Darren's world was rocked by his parents' divorce just as his brother, Nate, was leaving for college, and a year later when his father comes out as gay, then how he begins to deal with it all after a stolen weekend with Nate and his crush, Zoey.

[1. Family problems—Fiction. 2. Divorce—Fiction. 3. Brothers—Fiction. 4. Gays—Fiction. 5. Dating (Social customs)—Fiction.] I. Title.

PZ7.H26865Me 2014

[Fic]—dc23

2014011035

ISBN 978-1-4424-9573-9 (hc)

ISBN 978-1-4424-9569-2 (eBook)

For Ariel

ME
BEING
ME
IS EXACTLY
AS INSANE AS
YOU
BEING
YOU

4 Conflicting Parts of Himself Darren Jacobs Attempts to Ignore as He Tries to Ask a Particular Eleventh-Grade Girl for a Really Big Favor on Friday, April 25, at 10:38 a.m.

1. His reluctance to become a screwup/stoner/delinquent. Because he might be taking a step closer to turning into any or all of those things if he asks her this favor (and she agrees to do it). Or even just deals with someone like this particular girl, who (based on the cigarette and the all-black outfit and the piercings) is pretty clearly a screwup and/or stoner, but probably not an actual delinquent. At least, Darren hopes she's not, but who knows anything for sure at this point? Certainly not Darren, who keeps finding out that people aren't who he thought they were.

2. His curiosity to see what would happen if he did something that a screwup/stoner/delinquent would do. Just this once. Because overall he's been a pretty well-behaved kid his whole life, so then what's the big deal, seriously, with doing something maybe not so smart just this one time?

3. His desire to kiss her, and have her kiss him back, right here and right now. There's no way that's going to happen, even though all it would take is the two of them wanting it to. Because you see kids kissing and even totally making out at

North High pretty much every day, so it's not like he's fantasizing about walking on the moon or anything here. And it's not even such a big deal that Darren has thought about kissing this particular girl once or twice, because (if he's going to be totally honest about it) he's probably thought about kissing fifty or sixty different girls at North High. Maybe even more actually. He's pretty sure he hasn't thought about kissing any guys, but he wouldn't swear on it, because these kinds of thoughts just sort of pop up whether you want them to or not.

Like you're getting a drink from the fountain outside the cafeteria, and the next thing you know, you're wondering what it would be like to make out with Christie Banks, who isn't even that cute in the first place, and not only because of that thing on her nose. She just happened to be waiting to get a drink, that's all it took. This kind of stuff happens so much that if Darren is going to be really and truly 100 percent honest about it, then he'd have to admit that once or twice (okay, about fourteen times) he's thought about kissing Ms. Gleason. Who just so happens to be his English teacher. She's maybe his youngest teacher and has perfect skin, but still, what's up with that?

4. His failure to convince himself that this is just about him. Because he kind of feels it in the very center of his presently quivering gut: The whole thing might also be about this particular eleventh-grade girl standing about four feet away from him and giving him a half-curious, half-annoyed look, like,

Uh, can I help you? Or, more precisely, it might be about him *and* her most of all, as in the two of them as some kind of unit, some kind of thing. Not a couple, necessarily, but a thing of some sort. A him *and* a her. A them.

Because right now she is just this entirely separate person standing four feet away from him and waiting for him to stop standing there like a paralyzed idiot, but once he asks her this favor and she agrees to do it, then, even for just a little while, there's going to be a new "them." And who knows, "them" might only last like a half hour, but maybe for reasons beyond his control, this "them" will take on a life of its own. And so this "them" might be good, but it might be bad. It might even be very bad. Or very, very, very good. Which somehow freaks Darren out most of all.

Because Darren's had enough lately of the grief that being in a "them" can cause you. And so, in order to cut his future losses, maybe he should not do what he's actually doing right this very instant, which might bring about the creation of another "them" that he's a part of:

"Hey," he says. "Uh. Yeah. Look, could you maybe drive me to the El so I can get downtown to Union Station and then get on this bus to go visit my brother in Ann Arbor? Because . . ."

Oh well, too late.

1.
THURSDAY,
APRIL 24

6 Words His Mom Sounds Like She's Saying as Her Voice Travels through Walls and up Stairs Until It Reaches Darren, Who Wonders Why His Mother Is on the Phone at—What the?—5:24 a.m.

1. Malah
2. Snaff
3. Thuhn
4. Bechah
5. Inham
6. Geraflab

10 Sentences or Sentence Fragments Darren Has Heard Her Say through Walls and up Stairs So Many Times over the Past Two Years That He's Positive She's Saying Them Right Now, Even Though It Still Kind of Sounds Like She's Saying Stuff Like "Antfurlm" and "Waflevah"

1. Tell me why.
2. That's all I'm asking.
3. Ugh, you've *got* to be kidding.
4. Spare me.
5. Just this once.
6. Oh, give me a break.
7. Bull. Shit.
8. Whatever, Howard.
9. Whatever.
10. You're so full of shit.

3 Arguably More Accurate Ways Howard Could Be Described

1. Darren's father
2. Darren's mother's ex-husband
3. The person who used to live in and own this house but doesn't as of about twenty months ago. Though actually, he may still own half of the house. Darren's not totally sure what they finally settled on, because by the time they finally settled on whatever it was they settled on, he was so sick of hearing about it (sometimes through walls and up stairs, etc.) that he just tried to ignore whatever they told him they finally settled on.

4 Emotions Darren Identifies in the Sound of His Mother's Footsteps, Which Are Clearly Approaching

1. Anger
2. Contempt
3. Remorse
4. Sorrow

3 Names She Calls Him in Quick Succession as She Sits Down on the Edge of His Bed and Softly Pats His Shoulder to Wake Him, Even Though He's Pretty Much Totally Awake by Now

1. Honey
2. Sweetie
3. Darren

9 Names Darren Thinks Would Be Better Names for Him Than "Darren"

1. Gabe
2. Max
3. Sam
4. Noah
5. Adam
6. Jordan
7. Nate, if it wasn't taken
8. Mo, maybe
9. Jacob, if his last name wasn't Jacobs

6 Imminent Events, According to His Mother

1. Her cab's arrival, any minute now
2. His dad entering the house at around seven thirty
3. His dad making him breakfast and packing his lunch
4. His dad talking to Darren about something important
5. His dad taking him to school
6. Her cab's arrival, if the thing's on time for once

7 Reasons Darren Doesn't Do the Obvious Thing and Ask Her to Elaborate a Bit about Item #4 from the Previous List

1. He really doesn't want to know.
2. She might not know, which she'd be annoyed about.
3. She knows but has agreed not to say anything, which she's already annoyed about, so why make her get more annoyed and bitch about his dad?
4. He really doesn't feel like having a conversation with anyone right now.
5. The less he says, the faster she leaves.
6. Because maybe he can still fall asleep again.
7. And who knows, maybe this is all a dream, which it would be really good if it is; in fact, he wouldn't be that bummed if all of the past two years have been one big dream, though that seems extremely unlikely unless Darren is having an unusually long and vivid dream that isn't exactly a nightmare but does kind of suck about five times more than regular awake life should.

2 Additional and Unfortunate Facts Relevant to Understanding How Darren Got the Name "Darren"

1. It was some sort of compromise between his parents.
2. Meaning that "Darren" was nobody's first choice.

2 Objects Some Faint and Unclear Light Source Reflects Off of in the Moment Before His Mother Leaves Darren's Room

1. Her left boot, which is dark brown, leather, and fancy. She wears them a ton these days, especially on days she travels, and she travels a ton these days. She actually looks pretty good in them, especially when she tucks her expensive jeans into them. But more than anything, these boots remind Darren that his parents, around the time they got separated and later divorced, each just sort of quickly evolved into kind of different people, because she only wore fancy boots like three times throughout the first fourteen or so years of his life.
2. Her right boot.

3 Thoughts Darren Has as She Closes His Door Softly

1. In a couple of minutes I'll be the only one in the house.
2. Which still always feels weird whenever it happens.
3. But I guess it's just as well at this point, especially if there's no way Nate could be here right now.

7 Arguably Optional Activities Darren's Mom Spent the Most Time on during Each of the Previous Seven Years

1. ZUMBA

   Which is some kind of extremely strange dance fitness program.

2. RESEARCHING GRADUATE PROGRAMS

   Because she wanted to get a job but couldn't get any of the ones she wanted without going back to school.

3. AGONIZING OVER WHETHER OR NOT TO ATTEND GRADUATE SCHOOL

   Though it was clear that if she did, it would be in computers or marketing. Or computers *and* marketing. Whatever that means.

4. ACCUMULATING A GIANT LIBRARY ON WEB DESIGN AND E-COMMERCE

   So she decided not to go to school at all, since she somehow decided that she could get a good job without it.

5. LAUNCHING N.D. DESIGN

   As in "Nate and Darren Design." It was some sort of computer marketing company she ran out of the guest room.

6. SELLING N.D. DESIGN

   Apparently, some people with a lot of money really liked her company. The whole family went to the Caribbean for ten days afterward.

7. PACKING AND UNPACKING BEFORE AND AFTER TRIPS TO CALIFORNIA

Such as last night. And actually, this one has been going on for two years now.

12 Basic Bits of Information about Darren Jacobs

1. Fifteen years old
2. Five feet six and a half inches
3. 181 pounds
4. White
5. Brown curly hair
6. Brown eyes
7. November 29
8. 20/25 right eye, 20/20 left eye
9. Right-handed
10. Youngest of two boys
11. Jewish
12. Virgin

1 Fantasy That Darren First Had All of a Sudden One Night When He Couldn't Sleep but That He Now Thinks about a Lot on Purpose, Especially When He's Trying to Fall Asleep

1. Darren is lying down on the floor and takes a knife, or somehow there is just this knife moving through the air, and the knife pierces his skin right in the center of his forehead. It hurts, because the knife is cutting into his skin, but it doesn't hurt as much as you'd think, more like a very big pinprick, plus it doesn't bleed a whole lot either. Sort of like how a paper cut bleeds. And then the knife slowly starts moving straight down his forehead, cutting along the length of his nose and then over his mouth and his chin, cutting about a half inch into him. The knife is incredibly sharp, so sharp that the skin falls open without any real effort, which somehow makes it hurt a lot less, plus it turns out that right below his skin there isn't really anything, just air really, so the knife can keep going easily, down past his neck and straight through his gigantic chest.

By the time the knife gets to just below the level of his heart, he can feel the cut-open skin starting to fall away, or fall open. Like the way the travel bag his mom uses—the one with the zipper running right down the middle—folds open. This doesn't hurt at all; it actually feels incredibly good, like

21

he can now breathe for the first time in two or three years, and by the time the knife is cutting down below his belly button, Darren begins to sit up. He pulls his new skinny arms out from inside his old flabby arms and then removes himself from his old self. Like the way you get out of a sleeping bag. He stands up and looks down at the skin and all that fat still connected to it. New Darren stands there and looks down at old Darren motionless on the floor.

3 Pieces of Evidence Darren Quickly Gathers After Waking Up That Prove He Wasn't Dreaming Before

1. Someone is downstairs in the kitchen
2. Humming what sounds like "The Girl from Ipanema," which would mean it's his dad
3. Whose dark blue Morris Minor Darren can see parked in the driveway. It's kind of a sweet car, but there's something about the combination of it and his dad that embarrasses Darren but doesn't exactly surprise him, which only embarrasses him more.

6 Reasons Darren's Parents Got Divorced, If Darren Had to Guess

1. His dad got really weird and started talking differently until his mom just couldn't take it anymore.

2. Around the time his mom sold N.D. Design and started going to California a bunch, her work definitely became the most important thing in her life.

3. His mom probably hooked up with some guys out in California, because his parents probably weren't doing it together anymore, because that's what Nate told him, though Darren isn't sure if she probably hooked up with all those guys because his parents weren't doing it anymore, or the other way around.

4. Nate went off to college, so Darren was the only kid in the house, which made it really easy for his parents to see that pretty soon there wouldn't be any kids in the house, even though Darren was still only in ninth grade. And since he's pretty quiet and doesn't cause much trouble, it was already kind of easy for them to see what it would be like to have no kids in the house, and they could tell that they weren't going to want to be married anymore once that happened, so why wait?

5. One day his mom suddenly said they should all move to California. His dad said he didn't want to. His mom asked his dad to think about it, to please consider it. So he tried to, but in the end he said he didn't think he could. His mom wasn't satisfied with that response, meaning they kept talking about it on and off, for weeks and maybe even months. But not talking, actually, at least not when it got into months. It was more like arguing then. They argued about California and his dad's work and what would be best for Darren and Nate and the whole family until Darren started wondering if the pros of being deaf might actually outweigh the cons.

6. Their cats, Chick and Dell, got old and started peeing on everything and ruined the couch in the den and most of his mom's shoes and the rug by the entrance, until one day his mom said, "I swear to God, if they piss on one more thing I'm going to put them down."

To which his dad said, "You'll do nothing of the sort."

So Darren and his dad took Chick and Dell to the vet the next day, where for about three hundred dollars the vet gave them all sorts of medications and ideas that she said should help. And she was right, because for about three months nothing happened, until one night Darren heard his mom screaming about an outfit she left on the floor of the closet that cost her a fortune, and then there was a lot

25

more screaming, his dad yelling, "You will not!" and his mom yelling back, "Try and stop me!" and they kept arguing for what seemed like forever.

When Darren came home from school the next day, he noticed that Dell didn't come to the front door, which he usually did when Darren got home, so Darren checked the whole house but couldn't find him or Chick anywhere, which, even if his mom totally meant what she had said the night before was weird, because she flew to California early that morning. She was packing for her trip and that was why she found the ruined outfit, which she couldn't have worn anyway, since even if it hadn't been peed on would still have had to go to the cleaner.

But none of that really mattered now, because the last room Darren thought to check was his parents' bedroom. When he opened the door he found his dad lying on the bed, awake, his face red because he was still crying a little bit. He was just lying there with a glass of wine in his hand and an empty bottle on the nightstand next to him.

Even though Darren still would have found out eventually, he suddenly wished with all his might that he had gone over to Nicky Smith's house after school, because then at least maybe when he did get home his dad wouldn't have been drunk and crying and saying over and over, "I'm sorry, Darren, I'm so sorry," while Darren just stood there wondering how two cats, two parents, and one brother had so quickly become just one parent and him, despite the fact that he never really thought that much about the cats most of the time, though he did sort of like how Dell used to greet him at the front door whenever he came home.

1 Nickname Based on His Initials That Darren Tried Halfheartedly to Get People to Use Instead of "Darren" but That Even Nate Wouldn't Call Him Because It Might Be a Very Cool Nickname, but It Doesn't Fit Darren at All

1. DJ

7 Standard Ingredients in Darren's Daily Wardrobe

1. Dark blue low-top Chuck Taylor All Stars (size 10½)
2. White sweat socks with either one or two blue or green or red stripes near the top
3. Blue jeans (36W, 30L)
4. No belt
5. Boxers, typically with plaid pattern but sometimes they're just one color (38–40)
6. Gray or black XL T-shirt, usually with something on it, like the name of a place or a design, but he doesn't really care
7. Gray zip-up hoodie

4 Features, Mostly Weird, of the Scene Waiting for Darren in the Kitchen

1. His dad is standing there, placing a glazed doughnut on a plate. Which shouldn't be weird, since his dad has probably spent as much time as anyone in this kitchen from the time Darren was a baby up until a couple of years ago. Darren's probably even seen his dad put this kind of doughnut on this kind of plate in this very kitchen before.

2. But it is weird, because not only does his dad not live here, he's also kind of officially not even supposed to be in the house anymore.

3. And because it's his dad, the weirdness doesn't end there. This reappearing dad-who-isn't-supposed-to-reappear-here has a different appearance than the one he had back when he was allowed to appear here. Bald head and kind of fashionable outfit: expensive and pretty tight jeans; nice button-down shirt, but not the kind you'd wear with a suit; and dark black leather shoes that never seem even a tiny bit scuffed. The shoes are to Darren's dad like the boots are to his mom. And maybe the jeans and shirt are like her new hairdo and shiny lip gloss.

4. The feeling in Darren's stomach. In other words, the whole scene isn't exactly doing wonders for Darren's appetite. But still, this is a chocolate glazed doughnut we're talking about.

6 Unexpected and Fairly Odd Speeches Darren's Dad Has Delivered to Darren (or Just Said in His Presence) Since His Parents Got Divorced, Which Darren Is Thinking about Because He's Got This Feeling That #7 Is on Its Way

1. You would think people ought to give compassion more attention when they're discussing virtues. We hear so much about courage and honor and determination, but we have too much of those, if you ask me. Sometimes you'd think compassion belongs on the endangered species list.

2. I shaved it, Darren, because I had struggled for years with balding. But now I've taken ownership of the situation. My hair seemed intent on falling out, so I thought I'd save it the trouble.

3. If you are ever interested in smoking marijuana—pot, dope, weed, whatever you young people call it these days—you should feel free to do it here. If you'd like, you and a couple friends could smoke here one weekend. I'd strongly prefer that your first time be in a safe environment. I could even leave the house for a few hours if that's what you want. If you're interested.

4. It is a rotten world in many ways. In too many ways. But the world isn't only rotten, even if it's actively rotting right this very instant. Yes, I am quite certain

there are still some perfectly good spots, some ter-
rific people, some things utterly unrotted. They're out
there, I know it.

5. Your mother is doing her best, Darren, I'm sure of it.
   As am I. Oh, you know what I mean. We all are. Even
   if, well, even if our best has been so mediocre lately.

6. I love you, Darren. I love you more than you can possibly know. I love you for being exactly who you are. And
   I will always love you, no matter what. You are a much
   more wonderful person than I think you realize, and I
   am confident that in time you will be endlessly grateful
   to be Darren Jacobs and no one else.

5 Contributions Darren's Dad Makes to This Morning's Conversation Before Darren Makes Any Himself

1. Good morning, Captain America.
2. Wait, don't move. My God, I swear you grew since Sunday.
3. Fresh-squeezed OJ?
4. Isn't it delicious? It was still warm when I picked it up from Bennison's.
5. Oh, forty percent chance of light rain this afternoon. FYI.

2 Features of Tomorrow, Also Known as Friday, That Have Helped Darren Make It through a Kind of Lame Week, Which, Despite This Most Perfect Doughnut, Is Probably About to Get Lamer Yet

1. Driving to Ann Arbor (even if it will be with his dad)
2. Visiting Nate at U of M

12 Best Things about College, According to Nate

1. Girls.
2. Sleeping in every day of the week except Tuesday and Thursday, when he has Econ at nine thirty, which he actually has already missed a few times, because you get pretty used to sleeping in until noon, plus you can just watch all the lectures online anyway.
3. No parents, and definitely no divorced parents.
4. His roommate, Kyle, whose parents are totally loaded, so he and Nate have a giant plasma-screen TV and a sweet stereo.
5. Beer.
6. Parties, some of them anyway. Most of them. Actually, just about all of them.
7. Football games, even though U of M isn't as good as they used to be.
8. Going to the supermarket late at night and buying peanut butter crackers and then just walking around campus eating them and drinking Dr Pepper and checking everything out.
9. This Intro to Film Studies class, where they talk about *The Godfather* and *Taxi Driver* and cool shit like that.
10. Having around six bowls of Cap'n Crunch for break-

fast every morning, or at least on those mornings you wake up in time to have breakfast.

11. No one gives a shit if you're cool or popular.
12. Girls, because they deserve to be mentioned twice. Trust me.

4 Physical Distances Separating Darren and His Dad during the Three Minutes Immediately Before, during, and After the Moment in Which Darren Finally Learns Why His Dad Is Here This Morning

1. ELEVEN FEET

About three bites into his doughnut Darren can tell something very weird is up with his dad, who has been so weird so often since his parents split up that his dad must be acting extremely weird right now for Darren to even notice. The obvious thing for his dad to do would be to sit down at the table with Darren, but instead he's just standing there in the middle of the kitchen, kind of frozen. Plus he hasn't said a word since his pointless comment about the weather.

He's got this expression on his face, Darren's dad does, that is maybe him realizing how weird it is for him to be in this particular kitchen at this particular moment, only there's some little glint in his eyes that might mean his dad thinks it's good weird and not bad weird. Who the hell knows anymore. His dad's silence suddenly seems like the silence of a monk who has taken an oath of silence, like his dad isn't even close to talking. Plus he keeps raising his fist to his mouth and softly tapping it against his lips. But he's not avoiding Darren; in fact, right now he's looking straight at him and actually smiling, too.

2. ONE YARD

When Darren is about three-quarters of the way through the doughnut, which he has to admit is crazily delicious, his dad comes over and sits down across from Darren at the table.

He suddenly speaks. "Darren."

But then doesn't say anything else.

So Darren, still chewing, finally speaks his first word of the day. "Yeah?" He tries to keep his mouth mostly closed when he says it.

"There's something I need to tell you," his dad says, "something I've been wanting to tell you for many months, for nearly a year, in fact." Darren tries to listen and tries to keep chewing, but the doughnut and OJ now feel like paste in his mouth. "Darren," his dad says, "this may not be easy for you to hear. But it is something I absolutely must tell you."

Darren forces himself to swallow the newly disgusting chocolatey-orangey lump of paste and for a moment almost convinces himself that because he recently has had a lot of practice at hearing things that aren't easy to hear that maybe this one won't be so hard, whatever it is. Still, he wishes there had been some way for him to have known to get out of bed and go downstairs at 5:24, so he could have taken the phone out of his mom's hand and told his dad, without too obviously taking sides with his mom or anything, that this morning would be a bad time for him to come over and tell Darren something that won't be easy for him to hear.

"I am gay, Darren," his dad says. "Gay." He says the word again.

Darren slowly reaches out for the last bite and a half of doughnut and notices how the whole world seems to briefly shift its coloring, like everything blue turns to red and then to green and then back to blue again. Or it might be instead that the world instantly turns all the way upside down and then back around just as fast, and is now right-side up again. Though Darren can't be sure any of this actually happens, since whatever happens happens unbelievably fast. Meaning everything seems exactly the same as it seemed before, only it somehow seems different, too.

Darren puts the doughnut down and notices his thumbprint in the chocolate. He looks up from his breakfast and sees his dad, whose eyes are sort of glassy, trying to smile at him. His dad starts to say what sounds like "I still love you, Darren" or something along those lines, but Darren gets up quickly from his chair in order to cut him off, quicker even than he planned to get up, though maybe he didn't plan it at all. His dad stops talking, while Darren walks around the table toward him.

3. ZERO INCHES

Darren bends over and gives his dad a hug. He might be hearing in his head the words "I am hugging my gay dad" as he hugs him. His dad puts his arms around Darren, at first so feebly that Darren is reminded of what it felt like, eight years ago, to hug him immediately after his dad had his wisdom teeth removed. But then his dad hugs him more firmly, quite firmly, in fact. There's considerable strength and muscle mass in his dad's shoulders and upper arms. His dad has probably been lifting weights lately, something, Darren supposes, a gay dad might do on a pretty regular basis.

4. ONE TWO-HUNDRETHS OF A MILE AND GROWING
Once Darren retracts himself from their hug, he heads upstairs to his room, this being the extent of his present plan for absorbing his dad's announcement. At the top of the stairs Darren stops and notices some chocolate on the tip of his thumb, which he therefore inserts into his mouth, but only for a moment or two, as Darren was never a thumb-sucker, not even as a much younger child.

3 People Darren Has an Urge to Text but Can't. So He Just Texts Himself, *What the Fuck?* Which He First Did, a Little Bit as a Joke, around Two Years Ago

1. His old friend Bugs, who moved away the summer before high school started and now lives in the Pacific Time Zone, where it's not even six in the morning yet, meaning he's not awake unless his parents (who are still married and both straight, as far as Darren knows) are having an argument in the kitchen over whether or not today would be a good day for Bugs's dad to come on over and tell Bugs he's gay
2. Nate, also asleep
3. His mom, on a plane

1 Additional and Perhaps Actually Main Reason His Parents Got Divorced

1. Duh

16 Freestanding Messages on Darren's Phone That Together Add Up to the Closest Thing Darren Has to a Diary

1. Me: *What the fuck.* Sent: February 4
2. Me: *What the fuck.* Received: February 4
3. Me: *What the fuck?* Sent: March 26
4. Me: *What the fuck?* Received: March 26
5. Me: *What the fuck.* Sent: May 14
6. Me: *What the fuck.* Received: May 14
7. Me: *WTF.* Sent: July 4
8. Me: *WTF.* Received: July 4
9. Me: *What. The. Fuck.* Sent: October 11
10. Me: *What. The. Fuck.* Received: October 11
11. Me: *What the fuck fuck fuck.* Sent: December 20
12. Me: *What the fuck fuck fuck.* Received: December 20
13. Me: *What the fuck.* Sent: December 20
14. Me: *What the fuck.* Received: December 20
15. Me: *What the fuck?* Sent: April 24
16. Me: *What the fuck?* Received: April 24

3 Strategies for Avoiding His Father That Darren Briefly Contemplates Before Returning Downstairs with His Backpack

1. Climbing out his window and leaping to the ground, which he thinks about long enough to decide that even if he tossed his pillow and blanket out first, they wouldn't break his fall enough

2. Building a time machine out of his iPhone, a half-built solar-powered radio he got for his eleventh birthday, and maybe, who knows, some dirty underwear, so he can travel to the 1890s, which Nate once told him was probably the least-messed-up decade in the past 150 years

3. Hiding in his closet, which he considers the longest and most seriously, until he remembers that whole "coming out of the closet" thing, which, in significantly different circumstances, he might find funny, but right now not even a little bit

10 Subjects Darren and His Dad Do Not Discuss during Their Drive to School

1. Global warming
2. The chances of a musician making a decent living in the age of digital file sharing
3. The pros and cons of social media
4. The prospects for a peaceful settlement of the Arab-Israeli conflict
5. His dad's sexual orientation
6. Women's reproductive rights
7. What exactly will happen when the planet's oil reserves have been used up
8. The likelihood of complex life existing somewhere else in the universe
9. The fact that Darren and his dad are supposed to drive together for more than four hours tomorrow in order to visit Nate, which means, obviously, that his dad made his announcement this morning to give Darren some time to begin digesting the fact that Dad = Gay, all so that by the time tomorrow rolls around and they get back into his dad's sporty homobile, they'll be able to really talk about it at great length and without interruptions, oh joy
10. The possibility of a benevolent God existing in a world where people suffer needlessly

13 Conclusions Darren Reaches After His Dad Finally Comes to a Stop at 8:04 a.m. by the Edge of the Student Parking Lot, Where Darren Sees Fellow Tenth Grader Moe Whitehead Get Out of His 2002 Pontiac Grand Am

1. I am younger than pretty much everyone in tenth grade.
2. So I can't drive yet.
3. I used to think it was cool to be just about the youngest kid in my grade, because it meant I got to hang out with older kids all day.
4. Even though sometimes it kind of sucked. Like in PE.
5. Plus maybe if my parents hadn't decide that it would be okay for me to start kindergarten early, even though my birthday's in November, I'd have more friends and a whole different and maybe better life.
6. And for some reason, I still don't really understand why they decided to do that in the first place.
7. But so what, the point is I can't drive yet, even though pretty much everyone in my grade can by now.
8. Which sort of blows, because everyone acts like driving is the coolest thing ever.
9. But then again it doesn't completely blow, because I have a feeling I'm going be a lousy driver and maybe even one of those kids who gets into a nasty accident a month after getting his license.

10. And so why do I keep forgetting to ask Dad to drop me off on the other side of the building near the main office so I don't have to see idiots like Moe Whitehead driving themselves to school?

11. Moe's a dick, too.

12. But at least he distracted me from Dad.

13. For a little while anyway.

5 Hyperbolic Phrases or Idioms That Would Reasonably Describe the Speed at Which Darren Exits His Dad's Car

1. Faster than a speeding bullet
2. Like he was shot out of a cannon
3. As if his pants were on fire
4. Like he was dying to get to school
5. As if there was nothing he wanted more in the whole wide world than to get out of that car

People at School Darren Feels Like He Can Talk to about What His Dad Just Told Him

3 Girls Who Might Be Capable of Drastically Improving Darren's Life, Girls Darren Thinks about as He Heads to His First Class, Trying Really Hard Not to Freak Out Completely about You Know What

1. EMILY PRINCE

Member of Darren's lab group in first-period chemistry. Bright blue eyes and shiny blond hair. Little. Little feet, little hands, little tush, little boobs. Giggles every time Brian Spanelli lights things on fire they're not supposed to light on fire. Whenever Emily puts on her oversize safety goggles, and only then, Darren feels an urge to lift her up in his arms, carry her to the school gymnasium, lay her down softly on a red tumbling mat, smooth out her shiny hair with his thick hand, and tell her that he could love her forever, probably.

2. MAGGIE BLOCK

The best trumpet player by far in jazz ensemble, not just the best girl trumpet player (which wouldn't be hard, because she's the only girl trumpet player), but just the best overall, even better than Kurt Phillips, who thinks he's better than he really is. She has a much better sense of rhythm than Kurt and her tone is at least as good. Plus sometimes from behind his bass Darren can see her getting really into it, at which point her face turns dark red and the pimples she tends to have right at the edge of her cheekbones sort of change color too. She really isn't very good-looking, mainly because in addition to the pimples her almost black hair is so frizzy it makes him wonder if she's intentionally trying to be unattractive, but even so, her body is pretty great, especially her chest, which is huge but not too huge. Plus she actually talks to Darren, and even swears when she does it, but not the way most girls swear, like the time she told Asher Lipshitz to stop being a big dick already.

3. ZOEY LOVELL

They actually went to elementary school together and were even in the same first/second grade split class. In fact, Darren's pretty sure he was at her seventh birthday party. But then Zoey went off to private school for like eight years or something, so when she showed up at North High last year it took him a couple of weeks to even recognize her, because she was just a little girl back then but definitely isn't now, even though she's still pretty small.

He hasn't had a single class with her yet (she's in eleventh grade, which doesn't help), but they've sort of randomly wound up eating near each other in the cafeteria, and every once in a while he times his trip to the garbage can to coincide with hers. They've had maybe four conversations, or exchanges, just really brief things, like, he'll make a comment about the unopened yogurt drink she's throwing out. And she'll always say something that doesn't really mean anything, something like "whatever" or—well, she usually just says "whatever." But one time, before saying "whatever," she sort of looked at Darren, right at him, for a moment or two, her pale face either curious or confused, and it was then that he realized she may be the saddest person at North High, sadder than him, even. And so he would hug her if she ever asked.

13 Adjectives Darren Wouldn't Be Surprised to Hear His Peers Using to Describe Him

1. Chubby
2. Nice
3. Awkward
4. Smart, kinda
5. Vegetarian
6. Weird
7. Quiet
8. Slow
9. Lame
10. Curly haired
11. Cute, sorta
12. Unimportant
13. Whatever

1 Girlfriend Darren Has Had Since Fourth Grade

1. MELANIE RUBIN

At the end of middle school there was a big end-of-the-year trip to Six Flags for all the eighth graders. About a week before the trip, Jesse Desmond somehow decided that it would be cool for there to be couples, because then the couples could each ride all the two-person rides alone together. Like the Condor and the Orbit. The next thing Darren knew, there were like eleven new couples at school, not that the couples were really doing anything couply at all.

And it wasn't like Darren was super against being in one of these new couples, but that doesn't mean he was going to do anything to become part of one either. Only on the bus ride to Six Flags, right near the end actually, Ashley Reeves, who got paired up with Mason Nichols the day before, walked down the aisle of the bus and whispered to Darren, "Hey, Melanie would go out with you if you want." Darren said, "Okay," as in, "Uh, I don't really know how to respond to that information." But when he got off the bus, and Melanie was waiting for him and smiling a little, he realized that Ashley thought he said a different kind of "okay."

Anyhow, he and Melanie didn't even hang out that much. Because it's not like Darren is a daredevil, exactly, but Melanie pretty much wouldn't ride anything scarier than the

Little Dipper, which is this tiny little roller coaster that the other kids rode only as a joke. They did share some cotton candy, though, just him and Melanie. After which Darren held her hand for a few minutes while they walked to Buzzy Bees. Their hands were sticky and sweaty, but Darren didn't mind, and he's pretty sure Melanie didn't either. It was almost okay.

All the couples pretty much just dissolved before the first week of summer was over, which was just as well with Darren, because Bugs didn't have a girlfriend that day and was kind of mad at Darren for going off with Melanie like that. She moved to Deerfield that summer, so he hasn't seen her since. Not even once. Now that he thinks about it, Darren's not all that sure Melanie Rubin really counts.

2 Places on a Body-Weight-Distribution Graph (for Someone His Height) Darren Could Be Plotted, with 1 Percent Being Extremely Skinny and 100 Percent Being Extremely the Opposite

1. 76 percent: where Darren would plot himself.
2. 64 percent: where his doctor would plot him.

9 Actions, in Addition to Timing His Lunchtime Trips to the Garbage with Zoey Lovell's, Darren Has Taken in the Past Year That Might Be Construed as Him Trying to Do Something about That Whole "One Girlfriend in the Past Seven Years" Situation

1. Demanded that his parents take him to a place where haircuts cost more than eleven dollars, even though his fro still remains pretty out of hand most days.
2. Started paying attention to which shirts he puts on when, so that he doesn't wind up wearing the same one twice in the same week.
3. Asked Emily Prince for her phone number about three months ago, which was officially because they were paired up for a science project on titration, but was also secretly because he was going to find reasons to text her jokes, or whatever kind of texts might be understood as flirting without obviously being flirting. But he couldn't get up the nerve in the first few days, and now it would just be weird if he texted her out of nowhere.
4. No more cheese fries. Unless Nate's in town. Or someone else suggests it. Or he had a small breakfast and/or small lunch. Or they're at Edzo's. Or he hasn't had them in a while.

5. Smiled right at Jessica Brady three days in a row while walking into history class. She smiled back the first two days, but then just looked super confused the third time he did it.

6. Talked to Maggie Block the way Maggie talks to most everyone else. Meaning lots of kind of unpredictable swearing. But she just laughed at him, in a nice way, and told him not to be such a "ridiculous shit-ass."

7. Decided to sit closer to this almost cute group of ninth-grade girls during lunch, even though he doesn't know a single one of them by name.

8. For about three weeks in March, splashed on a little of the cologne he got for Hanukkah, until Nate noticed when he was back home during his spring break. Nate said, "Dude, you smell like a giant French douche bag." Nate went on to clarify that he has nothing against giant French douche bags, "per se," but that Darren pretty undeniably isn't one and so trying to smell like one might not be the best plan of action for him. Darren then thanked his older brother, which maybe wasn't necessary.

9. Stopped trying to do anything to get a girlfriend, because he saw some unquestionably cool guy in some unquestionably average movie say to his unquestion- ably uncool friend something like, "Hey, man, it ain't gonna happen if all you do twenty-four-seven is try to

nab yourself a honey. You just got to let it happen, bro, and it'll happen." But then Darren realized he couldn't *not* do anything, because how the hell could that possibly lead to him nabbing a honey, or even just having a girlfriend, so instead he started focusing on being nice to girls in a totally unselfish way, which meant really listening to them if they were talking to him or telling him a story. He also started thinking, pretty much out loud in his head, when they were talking to him or telling him a story, It's totally, totally okay if she's not my girlfriend. But this had the weird effect of causing a number of girls (Grace Zonder, Mia Deutsch, and Beth Maschino especially) to talk to him a lot, as in way more than he could deal with, but in the way a girl talks to a guy she has exactly zero interest in ever going out with.

4 Candidates to Replace Bugs as Darren's Best Friend, and Why They Haven't Panned Out

1. Sam Goldstein. Talks too much. As in, literally never shuts up.
2. Ray Campo. Just wants to blow stuff up. Or light stuff on fire. Or drop stuff out his bedroom window. Or put stuff in a blender (which was pretty cool actually, but only the first two times).
3. Jesse Aronoff. Impossible to get him away from his computer. Which would be bad enough all by itself, but got way worse a few weeks ago when Jesse said, "Oh man, you've got to see this," and then just started showing Darren one porn site after another. And it's not like Darren hadn't seen that stuff before, but, actually, he hadn't seen a lot of the stuff Jesse was showing him, stuff that just seemed kind of out of hand more than anything, to the point that it all made Darren sort of wish no one ever invented the Internet in the first place (especially the one with some guy in a gorilla suit—at least, he hopes it was a gorilla suit).
4. Nicky Smith. Super nice. And super duper dumb.

5 Specific Times since 11:00 a.m. That Darren Misses Nate, the Last One of Which Is Happening Right Now

1. 11:09 a.m.—After taking an extremely quick shower near the end of gym class (Coach Rakowski made them run and Darren could tell that he was pretty stinky by the end), Darren passed Roy Brooks on the way back to his locker. Darren could feel that Roy was looking at his boobs. Darren's pretty sure they're smaller than they used to be, but he still thinks of them as boobs. Either way, Roy didn't say anything like he would have a year or two earlier, because for some reason Roy is less of a dick lately, a fact that somehow made Darren feel even worse, which made no sense to him at all. He wouldn't have told any of this to anyone, not even Nate. But who knows, if Nate had been there—which Darren knows was never really a possibility to begin with—maybe Roy wouldn't have looked at him like that in the first place.

2. 11:16 a.m.—In between third and fourth period, Darren let himself fart pretty loud in one of the stairwells at school, because Nate told him that's the best time and place to fart, since because with all of the noise and people, you can get away with a pretty loud or even diabolically smelly fart there.

3. 11:17 a.m.—Nate also told him that a really loud fart will echo like crazy in the stairwell if no one else is there, and Darren really wishes he could get up the nerve to fart like that but knows he would only really enjoy it if Nate were there with him, which is pretty unlikely at this point, now that Nate is at U of M.

4. 11:46 a.m.—Darren thought again about going to visit Nate at school tomorrow, which at first made him happy, but then he realized that he's only going to see him for about forty-eight hours before having to say good-bye to him again, which he'll have to do like it's no big deal.

5. 12:48 p.m.—Darren goes to throw out his lunch at the same time Zoey Lovell goes to throw out hers. Or a split second after she goes, since that's why he goes when he does. Darren stands up from his lonely, marginal seat in the cafeteria right after Zoey gets up from her similarly marginal spot. They reach the garbage can about a half second apart.

He lets her throw out her stuff first, and right as she's dropping a Ziploc bag and a wrapper for what was probably a granola bar into the garbage can, Darren notices a ring on her left pinkie he's never seen before. It's silver and made up of about six or seven separate rings, all of them kind of crooked and somehow held together. Without thinking much about it, Darren suddenly says, almost to himself more than to Zoey (but definitely out loud either way), "Cool ring."

Zoey sort of freezes and gives him this look that might be her daring him to try and make her happy. But maybe she's actually asking him to and not daring him at all. Or begging, even.

For a moment this garbage can isn't such a bad place to be. Darren almost feels like it wouldn't be totally impossible for it to transform, in some kind of magical, special-effects way, into a fountain. And then, all around, the whole cafeteria would follow, turning into something not entirely unlike that place the kids get to pretty early on when they're visiting Willy Wonka's factory (in the first movie). Where all the candy and stuff is just growing out of the ground. Not that the candy would be necessary right now. Just the rolling paths and the green-park feel of the whole place.

"It's really cool," Darren somehow manages to say to Zoey, who doesn't thank him for saying this. She doesn't even directly acknowledge that he said it at all. But something happens with her eyes, the irises of which are almost perfectly black. The thing that happens lasts maybe two seconds, and as soon as it's over Darren knows he'll never be able to explain it to anyone, even though he might try later with Nate.

What happens is that her eyes do something that somehow tells him, or makes him feel, even, that there's an entire person connected to these eyes. Which isn't exactly a surprise, because obviously Zoey is an entire person, but so maybe what happens is that her eyes remind him of this. Or ask him to really think about what this means. That she's an entire person. Her eyes tell him, by opening a little more than normal and almost reaching out to his, something like, *I know I barely talk and pretty much act like I'm not even here, but I'm totally here and have a million things to say, and me being me is exactly as insane as you being you.*

Or something like that.

Zoey touches the ring with the fingers of her right hand, turning it back and forth. Then she walks straight out of the cafeteria. Darren's eyes follow her, not so much because he's trying to check out her butt or anything, but because he's trying hard not to lose his conviction that whatever just happened actually happened. And also, even though the garbage can is still just a garbage can, he sort of wonders if it might be possible for a small, uneven line of wildflowers to sprout out of the ugly linoleum floor along the path of her exit.

7 Variations on the Request *Please Call Me* That Darren Texts to Nate between the Beginning of Second Period and the End of Fifth Period

1. *Call me*
2. *Cmon dude call*
3. *Why wont you call*
4. *Call dick*
5. *Please just call please*
6. *Im serious you gotta call*
7. *Im gonna kick you in the nuts tomorrow if you dont call I mean it*

4 Months That Have Passed Since Darren Decided He Was No Longer Going to Contact Bugs Every Time He Wanted To, Which Might Explain Why Even Though Darren Really, Really, Really Wishes He Could Talk to Bugs Right Now, He's Not All That Sure He'd Tell Him If He Got Him on the Phone

1. January
2. February
3. March
4. April (most of it, anyway)

23 Text Messages Exchanged by the Jacobs Brothers After Nate Finally Responds

1. Nate: *Cant call at Stats review*
2. Darren: *Fuck*
3. Nate: *Whats up?*
4. Darren: *Dad*
5. Nate: *What about Dad*
6. Darren: *Did he say anything 2 u?*
7. Nate: *About what*
8. Darren: *Did he*
9. Nate: *What r u talking about*
10. Darren: *Forget it*
11. Nate: *Tell me*
12. Darren: *No*
13. Nate: *Tell me dickwad*
14. Darren: *Dads gay*
15. Darren: *Hes gay he told me*
16. Nate: *Bullshit*
17. Darren: *U didnt know?*
18. Nate: *Ur lying*
19. Darren: *Im not*
20. Darren: *He told me this morning*

21. Nate: *R gay dad. Funny psych prof talked about denial 2day*
22. Darren: *Huh?*
23. Nate: *Ill call you in a couple hours*

5 Events That Had to Take Place in Order for Darren to Become Oblivion's Bassist, Even Though the Band Sort of Broke Up When Nate and Phil Went Off to School

1. Nate bought a guitar with money he earned lifeguarding the summer after tenth grade.

2. Nate, Phil Reed (drums), and Ricky Chen (bass) decided to form a band, which they first called Showtime.

3. Sometimes Nate let Darren quietly watch their rehearsals.

4. Ricky (who sucked anyway) quit the band or got kicked out, and when he quit/got kicked out he pushed over his amp (but luckily didn't do any serious damage to it) and then just left without even bothering to take his equipment.

5. A few weeks later Nate and Phil (who kept jamming together anyway and now called themselves Protest) had a friendly argument that started when Nate asked Phil, "C'mon, seriously, how hard could it be to play the bass?" Which eventually led to Nate saying to Darren, who was sitting on a milk crate in the corner of the garage and wondering why he hadn't gone inside already to watch TV, plus he had homework, "Hey, Darren, come here."

The next thing he knew, the heavy instrument was hanging from a strap that ran between his neck and shoulder. Nate took his brother's left hand, held it under the bass's neck, and placed the index finger on a certain spot on the top string and said, "This is a G; just play that steady like this," and he showed Darren how to strum the thick string with the index and middle fingers of his other hand. Next Nate said, "Okay, so when I say so, move your finger to this string, that's a C, and then back to G, and then we'll go up here to D, then C, then G. You got it?"

Darren said yes, because he always listens pretty closely to whatever Nate says.

And even though it hurt the tip of his index finger, playing the bass was pretty easy, which wasn't nearly as surprising as the fact that Darren kind of knew beforehand that it would be easy, he just knew, so the three of them jammed for about five minutes, Nate smiling at Darren in this way that made Darren ten times happier than he had been in a long, long time. Phil nodded his head like Darren was his new hero, and when they stopped, Nate said to Phil, "See what I mean?"

9 Other Names Showtime/Protest Had Before Becoming Oblivion, and the Person Who Named It That

1. The Elements (Phil)
2. Acid Bath (Nate)
3. Electric Eye (Nate)
4. Colonel Punishment (Phil and Nate)
5. Ax and Hatchet (Phil, and a little bit Darren (the Hatchet part))
6. Sequoia (Nate and maybe Phil)
7. The Ozones (Phil)
8. Zero Gravity (Matt or Marc or Max Brodsky, some guy from Nate and Phil's grade)
9. The Meds (Nate)

5 **More Times Today That Darren Misses Nate, and This Is Getting Ridiculous Already, but Every Once in a While Darren Has a Day like Today, When Everything Makes Him Think of His Brother, and It's Not Like Today Is Just Another Day Anyhow, So the Whole Thing Isn't All That Surprising**

1. 1:35 p.m.—Darren correctly completes twelve of Mr. Gibbs's sentences. The guy has this strange habit of pausing for a moment or two before saying the last word in a sentence, something Nate told Darren about when Darren told him he was going to have Mr. Gibbs this year. The record, held by Nate of course, is a will-never-be-broken seventeen, but twelve is still pretty good.

2. 2:54 p.m.—In English class, as part of a poetry unit, Ms. Gleason has them read and discuss the lyrics to Bob Dylan's "Visions of Johanna." The first thing they do is just go around the room, everyone reading two lines at a time. One of Darren's lines is "The ghost of electricity howls in the bones of her face," and even though it was obviously just luck, he has this odd feeling that Nate would be proud of him for getting what is clearly the greatest line in any rock song ever, something he could tell by the way Ms. Gleason, in her red scarf, lights up when she calls his name and asks him to read it.

3. 3:26 p.m.—Darren tunes his bass and wishes again that he had done a better job convincing Nate to come home for tonight's concert, even though he understands what it means that Nate has an exam in Stats tomorrow morning that he can't miss.

4. 3:29 p.m.—Maggie, probably for the concert tonight, has done something drastic to her hair, which for the first time looks normal and even good. She now has thick, beautiful curls that fall almost to her shoulders. Eight-elevenths of the remaining ensemble members make fun of her in this way (playful and giddy) the group tends to make fun of anything unexpected. Maggie, not blushing even a little bit, instructs her ensemble-mates to eat her. Darren definitely belongs to the three-elevenths of the ensemble that wisely keeps its mouth shut, in part because he immediately starts trying to think of a way to change the position or angle of his chair so that it will be harder to look at her while he's playing, because now Maggie is attractive in a way that would be much easier to explain to Nate and therefore is very distracting.

5. 3:59 p.m.—When the ensemble finishes a pretty solid version of "Take the 'A' Train," Mr. Keyes looks at Darren and snaps just for him, because Darren finally agreed last week to take a short solo at the start of "Footprints," but only because Mr. Keyes kept telling him that he thought a great bass solo right then would really "knock everyone's socks off." Only Darren forgets to start playing, and then, when he does start, it just doesn't sound very good at all. He bets that everyone is looking at him with what Mr. Keyes calls "encouraging eyes," but Darren just stares at his own feet and thinks about how he would never blow it for Nate in a situation like this.

3 Parts of What Could Be Considered a Single Phone Conversation That Darren Has with His Frazzled and Apologetic Mom, Who Has to Keep Calling Him Back, Because Cell Phone Reception in North High Totally Blows and They Keep Getting Disconnected

1. Darren's walking from ensemble rehearsal to his driving lesson when she first calls, and the timing doesn't really surprise him, because it's totally like her to know exactly when there's a five-minute opening in his schedule.

"Hi," Darren says, like the worst receptionist in the history of the planet.

"Hi, honey," she says, a little singsongy. "I'm so sorry I couldn't call you earlier; my flight was almost ninety minutes late."

"Oh."

"Some kind of 'mechanical problem with the aircraft.' Whatever that means. Completely screwed up the whole day, which was going to be crazy to begin with."

"Bummer."

"The day's a total disaster at this point. I swear, I'm not exaggerating." She's talking superfast, which somehow happens when she's in California. "Complete and total disaster, I mean—"

"Mom?"

"Yeah, sweetie?" She slows down. "How ya doing?"

"Did you"—there's no one anywhere in the long hallway, but Darren still wanders to the nearest corner and kind of mumbles—"know about Dad?"

"Yes. Of course I did."

There's a bunch of black-and-white charcoal drawings hanging on the wall nearby. Of shoes. "How long"—a couple are pretty good, but most of them aren't—"I mean, when did you . . ."

"I've known for a while."

"A while?"

"I wish your father hadn't elected to tell you this today. I mean, of all days—"

"What do you mean, a while?" She doesn't answer. "What the hell does a while mean?" No answer.

Darren looks at his phone. They've been disconnected. He stands there, trying to decide if he should start walking again, until his phone vibrates again.

2. "Hey," Darren grumbles.

"Hi."

No one says anything for two or three seconds.

"He told me around the time we decided to separate."

Darren has started walking back toward the band room, not that he plans to go back inside. "But what? You didn't, you didn't, like, know before?"

Long pause. Darren looks at his phone. Still connected.

"I wasn't completely surprised when he told me."

"What does that mean?" Darren asks quickly.

"It's complicated."

"Complicated how?"

"Why don't . . ." He can hear her exhale. "When I get back, you and I can have a long talk about this. Why don't we do that? If you want to."

"But what's so complicated? Wasn't he gay the whole time? It's not like you just wind up gay all of a sudden." Darren somehow finds himself in what might be considered an alcove located between a bunch of lockers and a large column, painted blue. "Right?"

"For a number of years"—pause—"I was under the impression he was bisexual." Darren adjusts his pants, which feel very hot. "But, I believe it is his intention going forward to date only men."

"What?"

"I know," she says softly.

"He's bisexual?"

"I believe so. Yes."

"Why'd you marry someone bisexual?"

"Darren, it's—"

"Or did you only find out later?"

"I'm sorry, Darren."

"Sorry? You're sorry?" Now Darren's talking like he's in California. "What are you talking about?" Plus, somehow, he's back by the shoe drawings.

"I promise, when I get back, I promise to tell you . . . most everything I know about the whole thing, and—"

"What do you mean, most everything?"

"Most everything. Because there are certain things that are not for me to tell you."

Two girls, giggling and carrying lacrosse sticks, are heading his way. So he starts walking toward them, trying to look normal. "Whatever," he says as neutrally as he can. He looks at the girls as he passes them, but they don't seem to notice him. "And then he tells me without Nate. I mean, seriously?"

"I agree. I would not have told you and your brother separately."

"I mean, what the hell?"

"But it wasn't my choice to—"

Stupid-ass cell phones.

3. Now he's outside. Not far from the ugly minivan he has to drive in about two minutes. When she calls back, he might not even answer. The phone vibrates.

"Yeah."

Then again, he might.

"Darren." Nothing. "Honey. You should ask your father whatever you want about all this. I'm sure he'll be honest with you."

"Awesome."

"I'm sorry, sweetie."

"So this is why you got divorced. Not all that other stuff you told us about."

"Sort of, but not . . . It's not the only reason we got divorced." Darren's pants are not cooling down. "But it's obviously—well, it's a big part why. A pretty big part."

If Darren had a bazooka, he'd take out that minivan. Actually, he'd set the bazooka down, walk over to the minivan, place his phone on the roof, go back to the bazooka, and then take out the minivan. He'd hope for the kind of hit where the minivan doesn't just explode, but also lifts in the air and then flips over and comes down on its back.

"It's very complicated."

"Fine."

Long pause. Pants possibly beginning to cool down.

"How was the rest of your day?"

Darren elects to ignore this.

"Well. The weather here, today, it's so magnificent. It's such a shame . . . Oh wait, damn it. If this is who I think it is . . . Yep, damn it, I've got to take this. But listen, honey, I'm so sorry I'm not there. I promise, we'll talk about this after your concert. Which I can't believe I'm missing. And, and I'm so excited for you that you're going to see Nate tomorrow. You two will have a blast, I'm sure. Even after all this, I'm sure you will. I love you, okay?"

"Yeah, okay."

"Bye."

12 Words That Darren Was Able to Guess Today Before Mr. Gibbs Actually Said Them

1. Germans
2. Appeasement
3. Surprise
4. Well
5. Sudetenland
6. Situation
7. Sure
8. Idea
9. Mussolini
10. Chicken
11. Inevitable
12. Monday

4 Unpleasant Feelings or Thoughts Darren Feels or Thinks (Often More Than Once) during Today's Driving Lessons

1. In general he already feels bigger than he wants to feel, and when he buckles himself into the driver's seat and starts making the car move, he feels how the car is an extension of himself, which is actually, for some stupid reason, how Mr. Faber, the driving teacher, tells him to think about the whole thing. Plus he's driving a Chrysler Town & Country minivan, which seems like a pretty fat car to him.

2. Whenever he's had a bad day, Darren likes to be in the car with one of his parents or Nate driving, because then he can just stare out the window and not even really bother moving his eyes. And so today, which is obviously a total shit day, has him worried he'll stare out the window, not move his eyes, and accidentally kill someone, including maybe himself.

3. Even though all the kids his age can't stop talking about how awesome it will be once they can drive, Darren just doesn't want to drive, not yet, anyway. He a little bit tried to put off going to driving school, but Bugs was right that his parents definitely wanted him to be able to drive as soon as possible, meaning that every time

he drives, like right now, he realizes just how much his parents can't deal with each other anymore.

4. He knows that sooner or later he'll run over an animal, which in fact he nearly does just before the end of today's lesson, when an idiot squirrel darts halfway across Lake but thankfully changes its mind a split second before Darren and the minivan would have squashed it. Even so, Darren just about pukes right there in the minivan.

10 Significant Implications of the New Situation Darren Considers While Staring out of a CTA Bus Window, Which Causes Him to Totally Miss His Stop and Have to Walk More Than Half a Mile to Get Home

1. There must be a lot of kids who have a mom or dad who is actually gay but who (the kids, or maybe even the mom or dad too) don't know it yet (and maybe never will?).

2. So that's why Mike and maybe that guy Gary are at his dad's place all the time, not because they like the Cubs, or not only because of that (since Mike at least does seem kind of fanatical about them).

3. His dad has probably had gay sex. Maybe even last night or this morning. Probably not this morning, though, since he got up pretty early to come over to the house.

4. Darren might be a total moron for having absolutely no idea about any of this, even though he's pretty sure Nate and maybe even his mom didn't either.

5. Unless Nate and/or she did have some idea, which would then mean he/she/they decided not to tell Darren.

6. It's completely unclear if the whole concept of bisexuality, whatever that means, exactly, would make any of this any better at all, assuming it could be applied to his dad.

7. Darren's pretty sure he's not gay himself, but if homosexuality is inherited—which he's pretty sure it isn't, but still, it could be, who the hell knows—maybe he'll only realize he's gay thirty years from now, unless his dad has known for a really long time, which would be pretty pathetic.

8. Darren will probably have to discuss all this with his dad and Dr. Schrier (his dad's therapist, who his dad basically worships) at least a couple times, since his dad is always trying to get Darren to come with him to Dr. Schrier's anyway, which maybe in this case wouldn't be so bad, since his dad pretty much invites Darren to be mad at him, or at least complain, whenever they're at Dr. Schrier's office.

9. Maybe this explains why his mom started being extra impatient with and sometimes even mean to his dad about a month after they officially split up, because before then they were at least very polite with each other most of the time, but then that sort of just stopped being the case with his mom, who it's kind of impossible to know what she even thinks about the whole thing, because it's not like she'd want to be with him anyway at this point, but still, it's got to feel pretty weird to know you were married to someone for so long who doesn't (and maybe even didn't ever really) like your gender, in a sexual way, in the first place.

Even though you definitely had sex, maybe a lot of times, even.

10. It's probably hard to be gay (or at least to admit that you're gay and then have to deal with people about it), but then his dad has seemed happier recently than he used to, and this likely has something to do with admitting and accepting it.

6 Items or Sets of Items or Even Absent Items in His Dad's Apartment That Somehow Look Totally Different to Darren Than They Did Before

1. The elephant-headed Hindu statue thing sitting on top of the stereo

2. About ten books on the small shelf near the stereo, with titles like *Being Present in the Darkness*, *Self-Compassion: Stop Beating Yourself Up and Leave Insecurity Behind*, *Radical Self-Acceptance*, *When Things Fall Apart: Heart Advice for Difficult Times*, and *Suffering Is Optional: Three Keys to Freedom and Joy*

3. An elaborate, slanted wooden candle holder resting on the windowsill in the living room that looks like the kind of thing you'd see on the most boring page of the *SkyMall* magazine

4. A photograph on the refrigerator of his dad and three other guys (Mike, Gary, and some guy wearing a fanny pack whose name Darren can't remember) at the end of some wooden pier with the sun setting off to the right of his dad and the water totally still and smooth and dark, dark blue, with everyone looking not so much happy as just really, really content

5. Top-of-the-line wheatgrass juicer sitting on the kitchen counter, which his dad uses pretty much every day Darren is with him but somehow looks pretty much brand-new anyway

6. Total lack of any dirt or dust or mess anywhere, even though his dad was kind of sloppy sometimes back when he lived at home, especially in terms of leaving his shoes everywhere and being pretty bad at cleaning up the kitchen

5 Objects Darren Begins to Imagine That He'd Definitely Find Somewhere on the Other Side of His Dad's Bedroom Door That Keep Darren from Opening It

1. A journal sitting right there on his nightstand
2. Various half-empty tubes of lubricant in the drawer of this nightstand
3. Some hair on one of the pillows (though his dad is totally bald these days)
4. An iPod docking thing with an iPod next to it that's filled with playlists called things like "Just Us" or "Sweet and Slow" or "Come to Me"
5. A small, locked wooden chest on the floor of the closet that Darren would pretty easily figure out how to open with a screwdriver and that would be filled with books and photographs and even DVDs that would basically scar Darren for years, or at least freak him out so much that he's kind of freaked out already and so there's just absolutely no way he's going in there

7 Mentions of the Word "Fuck" (or Related Forms) during (or Immediately after) Darren and Nate's Phone Call, Which Takes Place in Darren's Room at His Dad's Apartment, Where His Dad Thankfully Isn't

1. "What the fuck?" Darren asks.

    "Dude," Nate says.

2. "Seriously, man, what the fuck?" Darren asks, or maybe he just says it this time.

    "Ditto," Nate says.

3. "No," Darren says. "I'm serious. What the fuck?"

    "I'm sorry, but could you rephrase that in the form of a yes-or-no question?"

4. "Nate, man, c'mon. Our dad's gay. Dad's fucking gay!"

    "That does appear to be the case. Assuming he's not trying to fool us. But wait, what if it's all a strange ploy designed to—"

    "Stop it, man, I'm serious. Why aren't you freaking out?"

    "Who says I'm not freaking out?"

    "Are you?" Darren asks.

    "Maybe. A little."

    "Dad's gay."

"This is true. Dad is, it turns out, a BJ machine—"

"Shut up, Nate. Do not—"

"You're right. It's quite possible that some gay men, like some of the supposedly straight women here at the University of Michigan, are not great fans of the BJ."

Darren almost laughs.

"I talked to Mom," Darren says.

"Lucky you."

"She said she's known for a while."

"And I thought she couldn't keep a secret."

5. "Nate, man, what the fuck?"

6. "What the fuck, indeed, little brother."

"Have you told anyone?"

"No, I figured posting it on Facebook would spare me the effort."

"Ha. I'm serious. Have you?"

"Not yet. I'll maybe tell Kyle tonight. Look, my study partner, whose sexual orientation I'm suddenly not so sure of, is pulling up. I'll call you later."

Darren hurls his phone at his bed and stands in the middle of the room for eleven long seconds with no idea what he should do next.

Eventually he removes an enormous green, cylindrical bin from his closet, a bin he's had since he was four. It's filled with about two thousand Lego pieces and was Darren's favorite and most-used toy for over six years starting in first grade. Still, it was almost given away a half-dozen times over the past couple years.

When Darren was sitting on his bed back at the house one Sunday afternoon trying to figure out what things he should keep permanently at his dad's new apartment, his mom, who was standing just inside the doorway, suggested, "Hey, why don't you keep your Legos there?"

"Uh," Darren said, "because I don't play with Legos anymore."

A couple weeks later he noticed that the bin had somehow materialized in the closet in his room here at his dad's place, but he didn't say anything about this to anyone.

This is definitely the first time he has touched it since then, which is definitely one time more than he thought he'd ever touch it since it showed up here.

7. "Fuck me."

8 Additional Implications of the New Situation Darren Considers While Building Absolutely Nothing out of Legos

1. He should probably see *Brokeback Mountain* now, which maybe wouldn't be so bad since that guy from the Batman movie was in it.
2. His dad doesn't seem very gay to him, but then again he's only been with him for about ten minutes since he's known; maybe he just didn't know what to look for beforehand. No, that's stupid. But his dad really doesn't seem all that gay.
3. Which, among other things, means that pretty much anybody could be gay.
4. Maybe he should go check out the LGTB club, or whatever it's called, at school, which he's seen flyers for a couple of times and which he's never really thought much about at all. But there's probably no way he's going to check it out, because if you even just stepped into the room where they meet, everyone would instantly think you're gay, so forget that.
5. There's nothing wrong with being gay, but there is at the same time, even though Darren's pretty sure he doesn't think there's anything wrong with it himself.
6. There's no way in the world he'll survive driving back and forth to Ann Arbor with his dad this weekend.

7. It's other people who make it a problem, because they think there's something really wrong with it, to the point that they sort of make it unfortunate even if you yourself think it's okay.

8. His dad is actually gay.

8 Best Things Darren Ever Built out of Legos, in Chronological Order

1. THE TOWER

Built during winter break in first grade. Two and a half feet tall, eleven inches wide at the base. Gradually narrowed toward the top, sort of like the Empire State Building. Red on top of yellow on top of black on top of green on top of blue on top of white. No mixing of colors. On the wall near the bottom of the stairs at the house is a framed picture of six-year-old Darren sitting cross-legged next to it and smiling with his teeth exposed.

2. THE RAT-DOG

Built Memorial Day in first grade. Was supposed to be either a dog or a bear but wound up looking like what Nate dubbed the Rat-Dog. In the right light was actually pretty scary. Was kept on display in the living room for almost a year until Darren needed the pieces for the pyramid.

3. THE PYRAMID

Built, with some help from Bugs, over the course of the last week of summer vacation before second grade. Four-sided pyramid. Eighteen inches tall, eighteen inches wide. Each layer is exactly one row narrower on all sides than the layer below it. Built from the top down. No color was allowed to touch itself, which is harder than it sounds. His mom called it the Rainbow Pyramid, but no one else did.

4. THE *MILLENNIUM FALCON*

Built on the first three days of summer vacation between second and third grade. All white. Even Darren's mom recognized what it was, though it was a lot more circular than the real *Millennium Falcon*. Nate took a picture of it and sent it to the website of this guy who posts pictures of things people have built from *Star Wars*, but it never got posted, probably because the guy stopped updating the site around then.

5. EXCALIBUR

Built near the end of fourth grade. White and red blade. Black and yellow handle. Wound up having to make the blade shorter than he wanted to, because it kept breaking when he swung it. Nate smashed it over Darren's shoulder after Darren accidentally stabbed Nate in the stomach with it harder than he meant to.

6. MOUNTAIN RIVER

Built Thanksgiving weekend of fifth grade. Two small mountain ranges, two peaks on one side, three on the other, with a thin river winding between them. Everything on a 2' x 2' green platform. River blue, mountains black. Two were snow-capped. Some green bushes near the river, plus a yellow animal that was either a small bear or a large beaver. His parents' all-time favorite.

7. GUITAR FOR NATE

Built Labor Day right before sixth grade. The day before Darren and his mom went with Nate to shop for actual guitars. Nate wanted a red Gibson, but it was about three times as much as he could afford. He bought a tan Ibañez instead. So Darren made him a Gibson out of Legos. Red body, black pick guard, some white dials, and a black neck. The neck had to be shorter than Darren wanted it to be, because it kept breaking. Nate called it "totally sick" and kept it in his room until he went off to school. It's actually still in his room; he just didn't take it with him to college, obviously.

8. THE CUBE

Built in the spring of ninth grade, the night after his parents told him they were getting separated. Just a small white cube with a single black piece near one of the corners. Darren sort of knew it would be the last thing he ever built out of Legos, at least for a long time, maybe even forever, unless he somehow has kids of his own someday. Still sits on his dresser back home.

10 Things Darren Does with a Particular Book After Putting Away the Legos Bin and Changing into His Outfit for the Concert but Before Showing Up at School

1. GRABS IT

After leaving a note for his dad, Darren was planning to just walk right out the door, only something stops him near the shelf by the stereo. He scans the titles quickly and for some reason grabs *When Things Fall Apart: Heart Advice for Difficult Times*.

2. STICKS IT IN HIS BACKPACK

He buries it pretty deep inside, below some papers and folders and a sweatshirt that's been in there for about two weeks now. Then he's out the door and waiting for the bus again.

He gets on the bus and thinks about looking at the book but doesn't. Though he does sort of realize that it might mean something that the book is even in his backpack at all.

He gets off one stop before school and walks half a block to Super Burrito. Orders a vegetarian burrito and a Sprite. Sits down at a table near the back. Looks around to make sure no one is watching and

3. TAKES IT OUT

and

4. STARES AT THE FRONT COVER

Which is just of a bunch of perfectly straight rows of slender trees with bright yellow leaves that have started to fall, so the ground is bright yellow too. It's beautiful in a sort of impossible way.

5. STARES AT THE BACK COVER

In particular, the picture of the author, who is a middle-aged woman but who looks more like an old boy, and whose expression is kind of friendly and sad and neutral all at the same time, and whose name is somehow Pema Chödrön, even though she's American.

6. HIDES IT UNDER HIS BACKPACK

When they call out that his burrito is ready. But then, when he gets back to his table, he

7. TAKES IT BACK OUT

and

8. STARTS LEAFING THROUGH IT

Darren is pretty determined not to actually read it. He's just holding the edge of it with his right thumb (his left hand is busy with the burrito) and flipping through the pages. Maybe he's hoping for a useful summary of his dad or his own situation or the whole entire world to appear to him highlighted in very simple language on page seventy-four or something.

But despite his mostly purposeless flipping, he can't help but read various phrases. Stuff like "we automatically hate them" and "to live fully" and "willing to die" and "save the world" and "a very vulnerable and tender place" and "as human beings" and even one entire sentence: "The student warrior stood on one side and fear stood on the other."

Darren chews and swallows and lets his eyes pass over fragments of whatever it is this Pema woman has to say. He's not sure he really learns anything in particular by reading it this way, but this one thought comes to him very clearly when he finally

9. STOPS LEAFING THROUGH IT

Which is that he's fifteen and sitting all by himself in Super Burrito, having a burrito. With this book. This book that belongs to his gay dad. Which feels like a meaningful thought to him.

10. RETURNS IT TO HIS BACKPACK

And throws out his can and the last third of his burrito, because his appetite isn't all that great right now, and walks the rest of the way to school.

2 Lies in the Note Darren Left for His Dad

1. Mr. Keyes told them they had to come in a half hour early to rehearse a couple of songs some more.
2. Edie Ross is going to pick him up and take him back to school.

12 Members of the North High Jazz Ensemble

1. Daniel Waxman, drums
2. Edie Ross, piano
3. Darren Jacobs, bass
4. Chris McMaster, trombone
5. Timothy Marx, trombone
6. Maggie Block, trumpet
7. Kurt Phillips, trumpet
8. Asher Lipshitz, alto sax
9. Kelly Meyer, alto sax
10. Noam Levitsky, tenor sax
11. Ariel Berger, tenor sax
12. Bella McMutely, baritone sax

3 Elements That Every Single Caricature Artist in the Entire World Would Focus On in His/Her Drawing of Mr. Keyes

1. Thick head of black, almost curly hair
2. Round glasses, top half of lenses tinted
3. Well-trimmed mustache

6 Songs Played by the Ensemble during Their Spring Concert

1. "MOANIN'"

Mr. Keyes snaps them in with some syncopated snapping, his snapping hand up by his head. The crowd isn't that big, but Darren doesn't care. Plus seeing everyone in the ensemble wearing black pants and a white shirt almost makes him happy. Because it really does help everyone focus, something he could tell a couple of minutes earlier just by the way Chris McMaster sprayed lubricant on his trombone and then moved the slide back and forth quickly to see if he sprayed enough.

They open with "Moanin'" because Maggie always plays an awesome solo on it. And so of course Darren watches her when she solos; everyone does. Only this time, even though he's playing right along with her, he isn't paying much attention to the actual music. Because she looks even better now than she did at rehearsal, and she must know this, which has Darren wondering, why did she wait so long to do whatever she did to her hair? Plus she must be using some new skin cream, because there's barely any acne on her cheeks.

All of which means that she's now actually hot and not just kind of attractive in a weird way.

Not to mention, she's playing extremely well, even for her.

2. "OLEO"

A lot of people wouldn't want to play the bass, because you wind up playing a lot of the same notes over and over. Plus no one pays any attention to you. But Darren doesn't care much about that second part. And as for the first, there's actually something cool about it. Because Darren can just stand there, moving only his fingers, his left hand, and his right foot, which he taps at the exact same rhythm Mr. Keyes snaps them in at, and still be able to think about other stuff.

Only in this case, that other stuff is pretty much just: The guy near the aisle in the fifth row is gay.

And: The guy near the aisle in the fifth row is my dad.

3. "LESTER LEAPS IN"

Darren's trying really hard not to keep thinking those thoughts, but it's tough. Especially when his dad is sitting right there smiling at him and looking so damn happy.

Darren tries focusing on Daniel Waxman's foot, which is bouncing up and down on the bass drum pedal. He tries focusing on Ariel Berger and Noam Levitsky soloing back and forth, the two of them almost giggling for some reason.

But nothing works, because Darren can't avoid realizing that he really doesn't want to go to Ann Arbor with his dad tomorrow.

He really, really, really doesn't.

4. "TAKE THE 'A' TRAIN"

Finally, out of almost nowhere, something gets him to stop worrying about having to go to Ann Arbor with his dad tomorrow. It's that Darren is stupid for telling Mr. Keyes that he doesn't want to take a real solo at the beginning of "Footprints." Because he could totally solo as good as most everyone here, except for maybe Maggie, who is totally on fire.

So Darren starts trying to get Mr. Keyes's attention, which is pretty impossible, considering Darren can only use his eyebrows and head for this purpose. Daniel Waxman does take a short drum solo near the end, but it's not long enough for Darren to actually walk over to Mr. Keyes.

As soon as the song ends, Darren quickly puts down his bass and hurries over to Mr. Keyes, who doesn't see Darren until he's right next to him.

"Hey," Darren sort of whispers, "can I have eight measures?"

Mr. Keyes slowly smiles and nods his head a couple times.

"Thanks," Darren says, and pretty much runs back to his bass. He lifts up the instrument and puts the strap over his head and onto his neck and shoulder.

And waits for Mr. Keyes to snap him in.

5. "FOOTPRINTS"

About two notes into his solo, Darren's eyes are closed. Not that he decided to close them. Still, he can feel everyone else's eyes, including Mr. Keyes's, his dad's, and Maggie's, looking at him. Which is kind of cool.

Not to mention, he got off to a really good start by playing these ascending notes that are not the actual ascending notes of the song, and this, combined with everyone's eyes, somehow helps him play even better.

Better in the sense of Darren suddenly doing things he's never done before, like going down near the pickups with about three measures left. He's almost playing the actual opening, but not yet, which he can tell the rest of the ensemble thinks is unbelievably cool. He can picture, without even trying to, Mr. Keyes giving him a big slap on the back after the concert ends.

These last two measures are pretty insane, because Darren both knows and doesn't know exactly how the next few seconds are going to sound, which might mean that part of him knows and part of him doesn't, and that definitely means that every note is somehow exactly the right note, even though he didn't really know it was going to be until he played it.

Right as he ends, the rest of the ensemble jumps in and the crowd goes absolutely bananas. Darren feels what a tightrope walker must feel when he gets to the platform at the other end of the tightrope (if he had just walked on a wire over a pool of alligators and wasn't allowed to breathe the whole time and there were a dozen people waiting on the platform to hug him with all their might the second he arrives because they were worried, truly worried, that he was going to fall off and be eaten alive by the alligators).

Darren opens his eyes. His dad is even happier than before.

6. "COTTONTAIL"

Darren experiences the last five minutes of the previous song and the first six minutes of this one in a "holy crap" post-solo fog.

At some point the song ends.

People whistle loudly.

Someone shouts, "Whooooo!"

A number of people scream, "Encore! Encore! Encore!"

Someone, maybe the "Whooooo!" person, shouts, "Yeah!"

The horn players are giving one another high fives.

Edie Ross's baby brother is crying.

Mr. Keyes gives them the signal to bow.

They bow.

2 People Who Volunteer, in This Order, to Move the Piano Back to the Band Room After the Concert Ends

1. Darren Jacobs
2. Maggie Block

11 Interesting Seconds That Pass Both Slow and Fast Immediately After Maggie Accidentally or on Purpose Puts Her Right Hand on Darren's Left Hand Just Before They Finish Pushing the Piano against the Wall

1. Kissing, mouths closed
2. Kissing, mouths open
3. Kissing, with tongue
4. Kissing, with tongue, and hugging
5. Kissing, with tongue, hugging, and Maggie leaning her chest into Darren
6. Kissing, with tongue, hugging, and Maggie leaning her chest into Darren, who takes a half step back until his butt hits the piano
7. Kissing, with tongue, hugging, and Maggie pushing her hips into Darren, who moves his right hand off Maggie's back while pushing his hips into Maggie
8. Kissing, with tongue, hugging, Maggie lowering her left hand down Darren's back and pushing her hips into Darren, who reciprocates and also touches Maggie's hair with his right hand
9. Kissing, with tongue, hugging, Maggie gripping and squeezing Darren's right butt cheek and pushing her hips into Darren, who reciprocates and moves his right hand to Maggie's left boob, which he cups and squeezes

10. Like #9 but more of everything
11. Like #10 but more of everything, plus Maggie moving her left hand around to Darren's front until she suddenly moves back a couple of steps

4 Run-on Sentences or Sentence Fragments Spoken in the Band Room a Few Moments Later While Maggie Is Exiting the Room by More or Less Skipping Backward

1. Maggie: "My parents are waiting to take me out for pie, they always take me out for pie after concerts and stuff, since I was like six, they think I still like it, I guess I do, so, um, we should get pie together sometime, I gotta go."
2. Darren: "Yeah, okay, sure."
3. Maggie: "Kick-ass solo on 'Footprints.'"
4. Darren: "Thanks, uh, you too. On 'Moanin',' I mean."

17 Conclusions Darren Reaches on His Way Back to the Auditorium, Which He Walks to Very Slowly in Order to Give His Boner Time to De-bonerize

1. I liked that.
2. I am not gay.
3. Maggie is not gay.
4. I hope we can do that again, but for about seventy-five times longer.
5. Eating pie with her and then doing that, for about seventy-five times longer, would be perfect.
6. Even though she isn't exactly the most popular twelfth grader, it would still be pretty cool to go out with her.
7. I don't really like pie, except for chocolate cream, but so what?
8. I could even wind up going to the prom with her.
9. Actually, I think I'd want us to have the pie second and do the other stuff first, because otherwise I might feel gross if I ate too much.
10. Nate probably won't believe me.
11. But maybe he will if I tell him her breath tasted like almonds.
12. Best of all would be maybe somehow doing the other stuff and eating the pie kind of all at the same time.
13. I should remember not to tell anyone I just thought that.

14. I can't believe I have to drive with my dad to Ann Arbor tomorrow.
15. Though then I'll be able to tell Nate in person.
16. Just the part about kissing her and stuff, I mean.
17. But he still probably won't believe me, not even if I tell him about her breath.

8 Pictures of All-Conference and/or All-State North High Athletes Hanging on the Wall of the Hallway Darren Stops to Look at for No Particular Reason (Except for the Last One) during His Walk Back to the Auditorium

1. Mike Powell, All-State, Baseball, 1976
2. Becky Cellini, All-Conference, Volleyball, 1979
3. Diane Corbin, All-Conference, Volleyball, 1981; All-State, Volleyball, 1982
4. Carl Simpson, All-State, Football, 1984, 1985
5. Marge Wallace, All-Conference, Softball, 1989; All-State, Soccer, 1989
6. Ben Nicholson, All-State, Swimming, 1996, 1997
7. Kip Webster, All-Conference, Wrestling, 2005
8. Nate Jacobs, All-Conference, Diving, 2013

2 Somewhat Surprising Developments or Sudden Realizations Darren Has during the Car Ride Back to His Dad's Apartment

1. His mom calls him, which is fine, even good, but then she tells him, "Your dad told me that you played an amazing solo. That's wonderful!" This means, obviously, that his dad told his mom something that wasn't absolutely necessary or part of an ongoing or new fight, and does this mean they might be nicer to each other from now on, and why do they even let him get his hopes up?

2. Maggie is going to go off to college soon.

3 Ways of Measuring the Amount Darren Finds Himself Missing His Mom While Talking to Her on the Phone, Even Though She Sort of Ruined His Good Mood and Seemed Pretty Distracted Herself, Too

1. 7.28 on a scale of one to ten, one being not at all, ten being can't be without her
2. This much (hands held apart at around shoulder width)
3. More than he missed her after saying good-bye to her this morning, but less than he misses Nate

5 Rather Uneven Exchanges between Darren and His Dad That Take Place Back at His Apartment in Front of the Fifty-One-Inch HDTV, Which Is the Only Feature of His Dad's Apartment Darren Prefers over Its Counterpart from the House

1. "Have you finished packing yet?" his dad asks during a commercial.

"Yeah, pretty much."

During the next commercial break, after Darren returns from the kitchen with a bag of popcorn, his dad says, "I was thinking we should leave tomorrow around two p.m. I can take you out of school early. That way we can beat rush hour and get to Ann Arbor in time for dinner."

"Okay," Darren says.

2. Their show is back on, but it's that very last part of the show that isn't even really a part, the part that only exists so they can get you to watch the last batch of commercials Darren and his dad just watched. So his dad says, "The concert was really wonderful, Darren. Especially your solo. I had no idea you could play like that! It's a shame Nate and your mother couldn't make it. Oh well, their loss."

Darren can feel his dad looking at him.

"Yeah, it was pretty cool," he says.

3. And then, during the first commercial of the next show, his dad asks, "I need to visit CVS tomorrow morning. Do you need anything?"

"Nah."

4. This commercial break seems unusually long. Or maybe it's just his dad, who says, while Darren watches an ad for an airline, "Look, Darren, I know that what I told you this morning was not easy to hear. I'm sorry that . . . I'm sorry that, well, that—that you must confront this now as well. I know it won't make tomorrow's ride much fun, but just so you know, we certainly don't need to talk about it if you're not ready yet. I just, I—well, I felt like I couldn't hide this from you any longer, because I love you and lying to someone you love . . . Well, I could no longer lie to you about this. I simply could not. Okay?"

"Yeah, okay."

5. Darren lets his dad kiss the top of his head, then gets up and goes to his room for the night.

7 Random Memories That Involuntarily Surface While Darren Is Trying to Fall Asleep

1. The picnic they had one summer when Darren was around five or six in the dunes near Lake Michigan. It was windy and everything kept blowing around, so the picnic didn't last very long, but it was still kind of fun when his mom and his dad sat leaning into each other watching Nate and Darren climb this one very steep dune that seemed like it was going straight up.

2. The way Nate was kind of distant and even a little bit mean the day they dropped him off in Ann Arbor for the first time, until he made up some lame excuse when the four of them were getting ready to go out for one last dinner together. Meaning that in the end, just Darren and his parents had dinner together, which, even though it was at Zingerman's, was incredibly depressing, because everyone was tired and no one could seem to think of anything to talk about.

3. This fight Bugs sort of had with Marc Burgess on the last day of school in fifth grade, which happened while they were lining up to go inside and wasn't really a fight; it was just Marc hitting Bugs in the face with his math textbook, which gave Bugs a bloody nose, but that Bugs said didn't really hurt much at all.

4. The time they went to Nate's swim meet his junior year at some school out in Des Plaines. Darren was super bored so he asked to go back to their car to get his homework, which his mom had told him to bring inside with them when they first got there, meaning now she wouldn't go get it. So Darren went himself, got totally lost in the hallways, and wound up missing most of Nate's dives, including the first one-and-a-half he totally nailed.

5. His grandma's funeral and how uncomfortable he felt when his mom, who held his hand for probably 70 percent of the time they were at the cemetery, gave him this weird smile and sniffled just before two of his uncles, one of his cousins, and Nate brought the coffin over to the giant hole they were standing in front of.

6. Lying on his back and looking at the stars in this empty field one night at summer camp when he was twelve years old. There was no moon or clouds that night, and his counselor, Lyle, had actually woken up their bunk in the middle of the night and made them all walk in total silence to this field, where he gave them doughnuts, told them to lie on their backs, and then started talking about the stars and how far away they are and the fact that some of them are probably dead by now but that they're so far away, their light is still reaching Earth.

   This was by far Darren's favorite experience from

camp, which he didn't like overall, because everyone in his bunk just wanted to play sports all the time, plus the food was heinous, but that night, listening to Lyle's voice, which was so deep and gravelly Darren thought he could feel it float across his face, Darren somehow found himself glad to know that the universe might be infinitely large, whatever that means.

7. Something from when he must have been just three or four, that maybe was actually from a dream, riding in a station wagon, holding an orange ball, and arriving at a park they used to live near, where his mom dropped him off, told him to be a good boy, and hugged or didn't hug him.

2.
FRIDAY,
APRIL 25

5 Mothering Strategies Clearly Informing His Mom's Morning Text Message

1. Be enthusiastic and positive, especially when your child is going through a tough time.
2. Show your child that you are extremely excited about things he could or should be (but isn't yet) excited about him- or herself.
3. Apologize for not being there when you can't be there.
4. Make it clear that the lines of communication are open, in part to encourage your child to initiate future communication.
5. Don't make your child guess whether or not you love him or her and are thinking a lot about him or her.

4 Terms for Whatever It Is Darren Is Clearly Suffering from Not Ten Minutes After Waking Up

1. Anxiety
2. Nerves
3. *Shpilkes*
4. Weak kidney energy

7 Manifestations of This Anxiety/Nerves/*Shpilkes*/ Weak Kidney Energy in Darren's Typically Uneventful Morning Routine

1. Waking up eleven minutes before his alarm was set to go off
2. Barely even reading his mom's brief, predictable text message
3. Showering longer than normal (mostly standing motionless under the water)
4. Inability to select T-shirt (eventually settles on black "The Who—Maximum R&B" shirt Nate bought him for his fourteenth birthday)
5. Difficulty not just paying attention to his dad, but also even pretending he is paying attention to his dad
6. Hurried consumption of two bowls of Rice Krispies with vanilla rice milk, with one heaping tablespoon of sugar scattered over each
7. Forgetting around three different times what he was looking for when opening a drawer in his room during the final stages of packing for his trip

2 Maggie-centric Fantasies Darren Explores Intently during the Bus Ride to School

1. Darren visits Maggie at school next year (unclear exactly where this will be, but Darren bets she'll be at an urban campus). Maggie, not surprisingly, will be playing in a jazz quintet. She'll have a gig the Friday night of his visit, and it will be during this gig that Darren will for the first time realize what a truly fantastic musician she is, since, he'll understand in retrospect, she was being held back by the overall mediocrity of the North High Jazz Ensemble, even if they're a pretty solid group as far as high school jazz ensembles go. She won't be the strongest link in this quintet, not at all, but she will be the youngest, and there will be an unmistakable excitement in the quintet and among the audience as well, stemming from everyone's awareness of her vast potential.

Watching her from his seat near the back of the bar, Darren will be overwhelmed by the newly feverish pace of her development, which he'll somehow realize is not so much her getting better as it is just her allowing herself to demonstrate how good she already is, as if she had been hiding huge parts of her ability until now. And this overwhelms Darren, because even from the back of the room he can't help but see just how much Maggie there is in Maggie, how much she has effortlessly shed or gotten over all the parts of her that allowed Darren and everyone else at North High to not exactly take her all that seriously.

Maggie, in short, is going to be ten times the adult than she was a teenager—she already is, such that people meeting her for the first time this evening could not possibly have any idea just how awkward and strange she often appeared only ten months earlier, because she's radiant right now, maybe even literally. Because, sure, there are bright lights pointed at her, but it's almost as if she is more than just reflecting the light; it seems like she's luminous all on her own, because Darren can swear she's brighter than the rest of the other lit-up musicians next to her onstage.

And so Darren is overwhelmed, because even though she invited him to get on a plane and fly to New York (of course she'll be in New York) to visit her (she even coordinated his visit with her roommate's trip home so the two of them— holy crap—will have her dorm room all to themselves), he strongly doubts that he can compete with the dozens of guys who are surely lining up to date or even just talk to this amazing woman.

But just as Darren is getting ready to go hide in the bathroom and plan his escape in order to cut his devastating losses, a song ends ("My Funny Valentine"). At which point Maggie walks up to the microphone, where she says, "We have a special guest in the audience tonight. My boyfriend, Darren, flew in today from Chicago to visit me this weekend."

Darren is so terrifically embarrassed just two short sentences into her announcement that his face feels heavy with all the blood rushing up to it. "And not only is he cute and funny"— Maggie sort of laughs here—"but he's a kick-ass bassist."

Darren feels like he might now die, especially once he sees the quintet's bassist, who is probably twenty-five and has an actual adult beard, carefully set his bass (his massive, hollow, acoustic, stand-up bass) down on the stage, which he then steps off from, smiling. Maggie has her left hand, the one not holding her trumpet, up against her brow, shielding her from the bright lights aimed at the stage. "C'mon up here, Darren, no hiding!"

Darren is at this point saying and doing all the things a person says and does when wanting to appear intent on declining a public invitation, waving Maggie off with his hands, muttering, "No, no, no," but of course, this is not a polite act on Darren's part. He does not in any way want to go up on that stage. But Maggie, the rest of her quintet, and the crowd simply will not take no for an answer.

Still, the applause and the chanting of "Dar-REN! Dar-REN! Dar-REN!" are not enough. It takes a smiling and mildly exasperated Maggie stepping off the stage, walking all the way to him, reaching down to take his hand, and, most of all, whispering warmly in his ear, "Please, Darren, for me, please," for him to agree. And it wasn't even the words of her request, it was feeling her breath on his skin as she spoke that somehow cured him of his fear. As if she blew a magic spell onto him. Or into him.

So he ascends to the stage, familiarizes himself as best as he can with the instrument, this being the third time he's so much as touched a stand-up bass, and looks over at the group's bassist, who nods casual encouragement Darren's way. Maggie turns to him and says, "'Footprints,' whenever you're ready," and then tells the other guys, "He'll take eight measures." And he does, he takes eight measures, and his solo is ten times better than it was in the jazz ensemble concert. In fact, he feels like a real jazz bassist for the first time, because, let's face it, unless you're playing fusion or something, you don't play jazz on an electric bass.

2. They have loads of sex. Tons of it. An absolutely immense amount of full-on sexual intercourse. All the time. Multiple times a day. Around the clock, even. And a lot of this fantasy isn't really a single fantasy, it's just a bunch of images of them doing it, or Maggie in a state of being ready to do it, which means naked or getting naked. For some reason he keeps picturing her sweaty, or glistening—no, it's sweaty, supersweaty, in fact, like she just finished a long workout at the gym, who knows why. And though it's tough for Darren to concentrate enough to come up with a single scenario to develop, he finds himself getting pretty interested in a couple of related settings: a grassy field and a forest. Honestly, it's the forest that really excites him, even though he has to admit it's not exactly the most conducive setting for really getting it on. For making out, sure, but ultimately—at least, he's pretty sure of this—you are sort of going to want to be on the ground, and the kind of forest he's thinking about, with trees pretty close together and fallen braches strewn all over the place, even with a blanket it wouldn't really work.

Why in the world logistics are so stubborn in this fantasy but not the other he has no idea, but he's nothing if not determined. So he creates for the two of them a small forest clearing, an intimate and smooth grassy patch surrounded by massive trees, magically mowed in the recent past, a place that not only offers a little bit of both settings, but also addresses the main shortcoming of the field, which was the way it just sort of had them doing it right out there in the open where pretty much anyone could see.

1 Additional Maggie-centric Fantasy Darren Has as He Enters School

1. Holding hands with her and walking quietly down a tree-lined city street. Preferably in the fall.

6 Particular Places Darren Searches for Maggie during the Eleven Minutes Before First Period Begins

1. Her locker, even though he doesn't know exactly where it is, but he's pretty sure it's right off the math hallway over by the elevator
2. Edie Ross's locker, which is definitely right around the corner from
3. His locker, because maybe she's actually looking for him
4. The English hallway, since he's pretty sure she's in AP English, which he's pretty sure Nate had first period back when he had it
5. The drinking fountain at the end of the English hallway
6. The library, and most of its aisles, though he gives up at around 500 in the Dewey decimal system, because what the hell would she be doing looking for a book on magnetism at 8:19 in the morning?

1 **Place He Finally Finds Maggie, Who Might Have Actually Been Holding Hands with Tyler Weintraub, or Whatever the Fuck His Name Is, and Who Then Sort of Tries to Hide This, but Not That Much, Meaning She Doesn't Really Care if Darren Saw, Which Either Means That It Doesn't Actually Mean Anything to Her That She Was Holding Tyler's Hand, or That It Does and So Too Bad for Darren, and He Kind of Gets the Sense It's the "Too Bad for Darren" One, Since She's Just Not Being Very Friendly with Darren at All, to the Point That Darren Can't Even Get Himself to Ask in This Kind of Joking/Friendly/Intimate Way, "Hey, So How Was the Pie Last Night?" Which He Had Been Looking Forward to Asking Maggie Ever Since He Entered the Building, So Much So That He Was Already Picturing It Becoming Some Kind of Inside Joke between the Two of Them, Even If He Wasn't Sure What Exactly It Would Mean or in What Situations It Would Be Used**

1. Tyler Weintraub's locker, or whatever the fuck his name is

8 People or Things Darren Wants to Pulverize by the Time He Retreats, Sweating and Red in the Face, from Tyler's Locker, Even Though Right at the End There Maggie Gave Him This Little, Little Smile That Might Have Meant She Was Sorry or Even That She Might Still Want to Have Pie with Him

1. Maggie, but really her trumpet for some reason, which he'd like to flatten over and over with a steamroller he himself is driving
2. Tyler and his stupid teeth
3. Tyler's locker, if he could somehow dent it without breaking his own hand
4. Adrian Levy, who just stood there the whole time, repeating over and over some asinine line he probably heard on TV the night before
5. The first row of computers in Ms. Dunlop's class, which he could see into over Maggie's shoulder, and he'd want to throw at least one of them out a window
6. Ms. Dunlop, because you can just tell she hates everyone at this point, the way she shut her door as the bell was ringing like she's surrounded by animals
7. The stupid bell
8. Wayne Shorter for writing "Footprints" or Mr. Keyes for convincing him to take that solo, or John Lennon

and Paul McCartney for getting Nate into music, which led him to buying a guitar, which led him to forming a band, which led him to getting Darren to play the bass, which led to him joining the jazz ensemble, which led to last night

15 Words on Señor McLaughlin's Vocabulary Quiz, Which Darren Totally Forgot to Study For

1. *baño*
2. *limpio*
3. *entrar*
4. *toalla*
5. *lavar*
6. *hacía*
7. *conclusión*
8. *sucio*
9. *cajón*
10. *calcetines*
11. exit
12. toiletries
13. repeat
14. bed
15. pants

2 Main Components of Darren's Still Pretty Nebulous Plan, Which Begins to Form Less Than Three Minutes into a Stupid Animated Video Narrated by a Sultry-Sounding Woman and Showing a Happy Spanish-Speaking Family Getting Ready for School or Work in the Morning

1. Skip the rest of school today.
2. Go to Ann Arbor without his dad.

5 Text Exchanges between the Jacobs Brothers That Take Place While Señor McLaughlin Is Busy Correcting the Quizzes and Pretty Clearly Not Paying Any Attention to the Class

1. Darren: *What if I come by myself?*
    Nate: *?*
    Darren: *To visit u*
    Nate: *Bold*
    Darren: *Should I?*
    Nate: *Yea*
    Darren: *Really?*
    Nate: *Mom and Dad will be pissed but fuck them*
    Darren: *I kinda want to go now*
    Nate: *Yes fuck skool 2*
    Darren: *Fuck everything ever*
    Nate: *Nothing will happen to u anyway*
    Darren: *You think?*
    Nate: *Yea*
    Darren: *Cool. But how?*
    Nate: *Hold on*

2. Nate: *Yo theres a Superbus to ann arbor leaving union station at 1145. Another at 1. Costs $18*

Darren: *Wheres that?*

Nate: *Hold on weenus*

3. Nate: *Corner of Jackson and Canal. Take red line. Switch to the brown. Get off at quincy*

Darren: *ok*

Nate: *You got the $?*

Darren: *Sweet yea I have over $22*

Nate: *Right on*

4. Darren: *What about clothes and stuff?*

Nate: *We'll figure it out*

Darren: *k*

5. Darren: *Shit how do I get to el?*

Nate: *Go to patio. Derek Schramm. Offer him $3*

Darren: *k*

4 Words Darren Got Right on the Pop Vocabulary Quiz

1. bathroom
2. enter
3. conclusion
4. *pantalones*

12 Items in Darren's Backpack

1. Cinnamon gum
2. Wallet
3. One pencil, no eraser
4. One pencil, tip broken
5. One pen
6. Keys to his house and his bike lock
7. Spanish folder
8. Two quarters, one dime, three nickels, and eleven pennies
9. Brown bag lunch
10. Dark green metal water bottle, two-thirds full
11. Program from last night's concert
12. His dad's copy of *When Things Fall Apart: Heart Advice for Difficult Times*

24 Gerunds (and Gerund Phrases) Various Parties Might Employ to Describe Life on the Patio, Which Is What Everyone Calls This One Stretch of Extra-Wide Sidewalk Containing Ten Cement Benches and a Half-Dozen Trees Near the Student Parking Lot

1. Smoking on the sly
2. Ruining your life
3. Taking it easy
4. Sticking it to the Man
5. Playing a little hacky sack
6. Chilling
7. Kicking it old-school
8. Daring you to say a word about it
9. Just hanging
10. Blowing it
11. Subverting the dominant paradigm
12. Going through a difficult phase
13. Getting a head start in the race to lung cancer
14. Rocking in the free world
15. Giving the world the middle finger
16. Falling in with the wrong crowd
17. Being a druggie
18. Dropping out
19. Hating life

20. Exhibiting defiant behavior
21. Keeping your parents up at night
22. Maintaining
23. Not giving a fuck
24. Keeping it real

1 Citizen of Patiostan Who Is the Obvious Second Choice Once Darren Can't Find Derek. Hint: She's Wearing That Ring with the Six Rings in It

1. Zoey Lovell

4 Techniques Darren Employs to Get Up the Nerve to Approach Zoey Lovell in Order to Ask Her to Take Him to the El for $3

1. Says "Fuck it" to himself
2. Just starts walking
3. Reminds himself that he is a bit of a badass for cutting classes and going to Ann Arbor without his dad (or at least planning to)
4. Looks straight down at his shoes until he can see her boots, which appeared way off to the right, because apparently he wasn't exactly walking in her direction

7 Objects or Groups of Objects That Would Equal the Difference in Weight between Darren and Zoey

1. A rather large bag of concrete mix
2. A week of groceries for the Jacobs family, pre-divorce and pre-Nate-going-off-to-school
3. Sixteen toy poodles
4. The combined weight of all the bowling balls eight young children would use at a bowling birthday party for a seven-year-old girl, plus the bowling-ball cake
5. Zoey Lovell, age thirteen
6. A 350-watt bass combo amplifier
7. The four boxes/crates of his own belongings (plus the lamp and iPod docking system his dad bought for him) that Darren himself carried into his dad's apartment when he set up his new room there

Acts That Are Cooler and Maybe Sexier Than the Way Zoey Exhales Smoke off to the Side While Still Looking at Darren, Who Says, "Hey . . . Uh. Yeah. Look, Could You Maybe Drive Me to the El So I Can Get Downtown to Union Station and Then Get on This Bus to Go Visit My Brother in Ann Arbor? Because . . . Because, Well, There's Some Stuff That Happened and So I Can't Really Go with My Dad Like I'm Supposed To. I Just Can't. Okay? Do You Think You Could? I'll Pay You Three Dollars."

10 Adjectives Darren Might Use to Describe Zoey Based on the Slightly New and Muddled Sense of Her He Somehow Gets Just from Following Her to Her Car

1. Freaky
2. Decisive
3. Quick
4. Mysterious
5. Awesome
6. Dangerous
7. Thin
8. Unhealthy
9. Quiet
10. Pure

4 Distractions That Keep Darren from Noticing That Zoey Is Driving in the Opposite Direction of the El, at Which Point He Asks, "Isn't the El in the Other Direction?" And to Which She Answers, "I'll Take You to Union Station If You Want," This Being the First Full Sentence Zoey Has Spoken to Darren Since She Was Seven Years Old

1. This is the coolest thing Darren has ever done, so screw Maggie.

2. He's not even sure how much of a big deal his dad being gay is. It's clearly not *not* a big deal, but it's not like his dad died or anything. But being gay is weird, even if it isn't bad weird. Because it's not exactly a coincidence that it's also called being "queer." But then maybe not telling Darren for so long is what made his dad weird more than anything else, meaning maybe his now-officially-gay dad will actually be less weird from now on. And so maybe Darren's stupid for ditching his dad like this, who is going to be more hurt than pissed.

3. He thinks Señor McLaughlin said he'll drop everyone's lowest vocabulary quiz at the end of the semester, so it's not such a big deal he forgot to study, but it still kind of blows.

4. Zoey's car is cleaner than he expected, even though it reeks of smoke, but at least the music sounds good.

5 Streets or Highways They Drive on to Get to Union Station

1. DEMPSTER STREET

There's some pretty fast indie-rock tune sung by a rather upset woman coming through the speakers of Zoey's car. Darren almost recognizes it, but only almost. He's trying to think of something to say and considers:

a) Cool song.

b) Who is this?

c) Hey, thanks for taking me. Seriously.

d) You skip class a lot?

e) What happened to you that you started dressing like that and everything? Not that I don't like it.

f) Did the one above your eye hurt?

g) Gross day.

h) Can I have a cigarette?

i) So, uh, what's up?

But then Zoey asks first, "Going to see your brother?"

2. THE EDENS EXPRESSWAY

Though maybe she just said it.

Either way, Zoey's an extremely good driver. It's kind of weird how good. Something about the way she merges onto the expressway. It's like she's a really calm professional race-car driver. Darren's pretty sure she's an even better driver than his mom, his dad, or Nate, all of whom seem like very good drivers to him.

"Hey," Darren says a couple minutes later. "Are your parents divorced?"

Zoey's head starts turning toward his, but then it stops. She doesn't answer for a while. The new song, sung by some British dude, is exactly 50 percent angry and 50 percent bummed. Darren steals a couple of looks at her, and her expression is something like 18 percent bummed and 82 percent refusing to give a shit.

"No," she finally says.

"Oh."

"But they should be."

She says this 100 percent deadpan.

Darren laughs but then stops himself, because maybe she didn't mean that to be funny. Only then she smiles. Or does something close to smiling.

3. THE KENNEDY EXPRESSWAY

"My parents are going to kill me," Darren says.

Zoey doesn't say anything. Darren notices—maybe he noticed it before, but not really—that there's a lot of writing on her right hand. Some numbers, maybe some words. And then some designs, too. Lines and stuff. Some of it's smudged. All of it's black.

"My dad especially," Darren says. "No, actually, my mom is going to kill me more. Shit. I don't know."

"You piss your parents off a lot?" Zoey asks, a little bit like she expects the answer to be yes—not that she would think it's such a big deal.

Darren wonders how to answer this. Lying is one option.

The Willis Tower, which everyone in Darren's family still calls the Sears Tower, has come into view. If it wasn't so overcast and he wasn't such a coward, maybe he'd ask Zoey to go up to the top with him. Forget Ann Arbor. Forget everything.

"No. Not really," Darren says.

The rest of the skyline starts showing up through the clouds or the fog or whatever that is.

"You'll be fine," Zoey tells him, like being fine isn't all that much better than the alternative. There might be more writing on her wrist, but it's hard to tell, since it's pretty much covered up by her sleeve.

"Do you piss your parents off a lot?" he asks.

They exit the expressway.

4. WEST JACKSON BOULEVARD

Maybe she didn't hear him. Some new song that sounds a lot like electric mud had just come on, but Darren's pretty sure he asked it clearly. He doesn't feel like asking again.

"Ann Arbor," Zoey says, maybe just to herself.

"Yeah," Darren says. "Yeah."

They're waiting at a stop sign. She looks at Darren and nods her head, maybe because she approves of his plan, but who knows, she could be approving something else.

He a little bit wishes Union Station was still another two hundred miles away. If he had a lot more money, he'd offer her a bunch of it and see if she'd drive him all the way to Nate.

5. SOUTH CANAL STREET

They've arrived. Or Darren has. Whatever. Zoey's car is done moving for now. He should get out. But he doesn't want to, not exactly. The last, totally horrible song is over and thankfully nothing else has come on. He's trying to think of something to say and considers:

a) Hey, it's really awesome you brought me all the way down here.

b) Maybe instead of me giving you that three dollars, we could go out sometime.

c) You know, Zoey, you're a really good driver. I mean it.

d) Thanks for the ride. It's the coolest thing anyone has done for me in, like, forever.

e) You should totally come with. Ann Arbor is pretty cool.

f) So, I'll see you around.

But what comes out instead is, "Sweet! I still have like twenty-five minutes before the eleven forty-five bus leaves. Thanks."

Zoey puts the car in park and turns all the way to look at him. Her face looks like it might want to actually say something. Like a whole, normal sentence that might lead to a whole, normal conversation. This possibility excites Darren a great deal.

But instead of saying anything, this little spot on her lip right below her nose twitches or something. In a good way. Like her face just said something kind and friendly that her mouth wouldn't. Or can't. Darren almost says, "What?" in the way you say it when you're trying to get someone to say whatever they're thinking and probably really wanting to say but aren't saying for some reason. She nods slightly. Happy, sad, maybe both.

"Say hi to Ann Arbor for me," she says. Actually, she just whispers it.

"Okay," Darren says, nodding his head. "I will."

He walks toward the station, the back of his neck desperately trying to figure out if she's still watching him, the rest of him praying that she is.

4 Authority Figures inside Union Station Who Darren Is Suddenly Worried Will Bust Him

1. Hefty security guard just inside main entrance
2. Bespectacled guy at the information desk whom Darren decides not to ask, "Where do you get tickets for the Superbus?"
3. Female police officer buying a sub sandwich
4. Old man who sells Darren his ticket for the bus, which actually picks up just down the block from Union Station

2 Compliments Nate Bestows upon Darren After Darren Texts Him, *Gonna Make the 1145!*

1. *Stud.*
2. *Total stud.*

6 Feats That Have Ever Been #1 on the List of Darren's Gutsiest Feats of All Time, the Last of Which Has Just Been Bumped Down to #2

1. Agreeing to have his picture taken with the terrifyingly enormous Mickey Mouse at Disney World when he was three
2. Attending this gymnastics sleepover party at Twisters Gymnastic Center when he was only four and a half and definitely the youngest kid there without an older sibling, since Nate decided the morning of the sleepover that he was sick of gymnastics and didn't want to go
3. Going down the Point of No Return waterslide at Noah's Ark water park when he was only eight, which wasn't actually that scary, though his bathing suit did go super far up his butt
4. Riding his bike when he was ten off the skateboard ramp that Bugs's neighbor Carl Getz built, which was maybe two or two-and-a-half feet high, and that actually wasn't that fun to go off, since Darren's bike didn't really go up at all; it just sort of went straight down off the end of the ramp, which wound up bending his front rim
5. Going with Nate and Ricky Chen just after Darren's eleventh birthday to put three M-80s in the Culligans'

mailbox, the front of which blew open so hard that the left hinge broke off, plus it might have been the loudest thing Darren had ever heard

6. Shoplifting a Baby Ruth from CVS when he was thirteen and then feeling so bad about it that he went back the next day (he couldn't get himself to eat it anyway) to sneak it back into the box he stole it from

8 Travelers Already Waiting for the Same Bus as Darren

1. Sort of chubby college-age girl with brown hair, chewing gum and playing with the handle of her red and black plaid roller-suitcase

2. Middle-aged heavy black woman whose right earlobe is super puffy for some reason

3. Short guy in black acid-wash jeans and a Pearl Jam tour shirt who either is growing out a Mohawk or just has a very strange haircut

4. Almost-old woman with big glasses, yellowish-gold hair, fake leather purse, and pale blue pants made out of a material Darren is unfamiliar with

5. Tall young guy with his hand in the pockets of his shiny Detroit Tigers jacket, with a pair of big headphones covering his ears and listening to music so loud, Darren can almost identify the song

6. Short Hispanic guy (even shorter than the Pearl Jam guy) who has a sort of kind, round face, except for the pale finger-length scar running from his jaw to his forehead

7. Nearly pretty woman in her forties (maybe fifties) with dyed light brown wavy hair that is growing out noticeably and who appears responsible for

8. Much older and absolutely not pretty woman who actually looks like an angry duck and who's clutching a small paper bag tightly with both hands

1 Justification Darren Would Give for Sitting in the Upper Deck of the Bus, Which He Didn't Even Know the Bus Was Going to Have and Which Makes Him Feel Like That Much More of a Total Stud

1. Duh.

6 Features of Darren's Seat That Could Be Improved and in Fact Should Be Addressed by the Good People at Superbus

1. It doesn't go back.
2. The armrests are so narrow that you can't really distribute your arm weight over them properly, meaning that the armrests actually seem to press pretty hard into your forearm.
3. The angle of the seat cushion and the seat back is more acute than it should be, even if it's technically obtuse and not acute.
4. The seat seems too narrow, almost like it's squeezing Darren from the sides.
5. There isn't that movable footrest thing attached to the seat in front of him that Darren remembers liking on a bus in New York once.
6. There is clearly a broken spring or random piece of metal sticking out a little right around the height of his shoulder blade on the left side, and he'd move, only he wants to sit next to the window.

17 Conclusions Darren Reaches by the Time the Bus Pulls onto the Highway Twelve Minutes Later

1. Cities are ugly.
2. People who ride buses are overall less fortunate than people who don't.
3. This seat is super uncomfortable.
4. I shouldn't have sat so close to the front window, because it's a little scary sitting so close to it without a driver in between, since without a driver you sort of feel like you're responsible for the bus, or at least the top half of it.
5. It doesn't really make sense that there are this many cars and trucks on this highway pretty much all the time.
6. The bus smells a little like sour milk and a lot like not very good vegetable soup.
7. My parents are going to be extremely upset by this, but it isn't my fault they got divorced or that Dad is gay and just decided to tell me yesterday out of nowhere, so they shouldn't get that upset.
8. The guy sitting at the other end of the aisle must think I can't see him picking his nose, but at least he's not eating it.
9. In terms of how Dad is going to find out what I'm doing, I can either text him, call him, ask Nate to do

either of them, or just wait for Dad to get to North High, which will pretty soon lead to Dad calling me. It might not be a bad idea to not have it be the last one. Or the one involving Nate.

10. If these seats were more comfortable and it was sunny and we were out in Colorado or Montana or somewhere prettier and I weren't almost running away, it would be kind of fun to take a trip on a bus like this, though obviously it would be more fun to take a trip like that in a car, which is something I'd like to do someday, preferably with a girlfriend, maybe even Zoey, because at least she drives really well, even if she probably isn't the kind of person who would want to take a road trip out west, but maybe she is, who knows. Maybe all she needs to not be so weird is a boyfriend who would want to take a road trip with her out west.

11. I could just call Nate and ask him to decide how Dad should find out, but for some reason that doesn't seem like the best idea in this case. Mom, even though she's going to be mad, might actually be the one to call.

12. If you eat your boogers near the front of a bus, you must not care what anyone thinks about you.

13. I'll get drunk with Nate if Nate offers to get me drunk, but I won't suggest it myself.

14. When I'm older my life better be better than it is now.

15. I'll eat lunch once we get to Indiana.

16. Maggie probably isn't a bitch, even though I wish she was.

17. It's very unlikely anything all that bad would have happened if I put my hand on Zoey's hand when she put it on the stick shift back at Union Station. Maybe then I could have asked her about all that writing on it too.

4 Pointless Phrases Spoken by Darren After His Mom Answers before the Second Ring, Which He Wasn't Expecting Her to Do at All

1. Nothing much
2. It's all right
3. Yeah, sure
4. You know, whatever

6 Considerably More Pointed Phrases Spoken by Darren's Mom Once He Spills the Beans, Which He Only Does After She Asks Him, "What's All That Noise in the Background?"

1. You what?!
2. Oh, Darren.
3. Your father is going to be extremely upset, you do realize that.
4. And Nate helped you, didn't he? He probably encouraged you.
5. This is really unbelievable.
6. Just unbelievable.

9 Arguably Childish Accusations Darren Finds Himself on Occasion (Such as, Uh, Right Now) Wanting to Hurl at His Mom

1. You think you're so perfect or whatever, but you're not.
2. You think you understand me, but you totally don't.
3. Computers are stupid, when you get right down to it.
4. And so is California.
5. You're mean.
6. Dad killed the cats because of you, and you still made him get a divorce, and that was before he was even officially gay.
7. It's not my problem you guys have so many problems.
8. You always think you get to decide how everything's going to be, but now I get to decide. I do.
9. You're always bossy. You are. Just admit it.

1 Two-Word Phrase That His Mom Has of Course Used
a Lot for Years and That Has Evolved Considerably during
the Past Eighteen Months and That Recently Darren Really
Hates to Hear Her Say, Because She Now Tends to Say It
with Contempt, Impatience, Bitterness, and/or Disbelief,
Except for When She Says It Just Now, Because Now It
Almost Seems Like She Still Loves His Dad, or at Least Can
Still Feel Bad for Him When Someone, like Darren, for
Instance, Does Something Really Lame and Inconsiderate
to Him, Such as, for Example, Ditching Him and Going to
Ann Arbor by Himself

1. Your father

2 Possible Sources of Courage That Allow Darren Not Only to Persuade His Mom Not to Drop Everything Right Now and Get on the Next Plane to Detroit, but Also to Say, and Pretty Firmly at That, "I Want to Visit Nate Alone; I Don't Want You or Dad to Come, Okay?"

1. Her tone is kind of all over the place during the conversation. Anger, disappointment, bewilderment, but then some guilt, too. Which sort of makes sense since, had the family not broken apart, it seems much less likely that things would have gotten to the point that Darren would be skipping school and taking a bus by himself to Ann Arbor. And so who's to blame for the family breaking apart and things getting to this point? Not Darren, that's for damn sure. He didn't ask for his mom to go to California twice a month, or for his parents to split up, or for his dad to be gay. Okay, so maybe that last one makes it his dad's fault, but it wasn't like his mom exactly stepped in to make that any easier to hear. And Darren didn't even ask Maggie to suddenly kiss him yesterday, not that his mom or dad can be blamed for that, either.

2. The bus started picking up speed as it finally left Chicago behind. And then, a couple of miles later, just around the time his mom started talking about flying

out there, it went over that bridge that, when you're traveling on it in the other direction, comes right after the sign that says WELCOME TO CHICAGO with the name of the current mayor below it. It's a pretty ugly bridge, just a lot of steel girders, not one of those cool suspension bridges, but for some reason this part of the highway itself arches way up in the air at a pretty steep angle, which nearly makes up for the lameness of the bridge itself, because it almost turns the bridge into a ramp, like you should be able to blast off into the air when you get to its highest point, which feels like it's got to be two or three hundred feet up in the air. And so the speed, and the bridge/ramp, and the going up, plus Darren sitting right near the front of the upper deck of the bus, feeling a little bit, or deciding to try to feel a little bit, like the bus is an extension of him, even if it's a smelly bus filled with losers—this made him feel like he might be able to do all sorts of things he couldn't normally do.

5 Stages of an Exercise in Imagining His Future, Which Darren Undertakes After Talking with His Mom, but Before Calling His Dad like He Promised

1. He'll take a gap year after high school and go on some program far, far away, in like Bolivia or Kenya or even Mongolia, where you dig ditches for some village that is getting running water for the first time. The food will be totally awful and he'll be pretty lonely most of the time, but Darren will lose a bunch of weight and get super tan and somehow learn to handle just about anything, so that when he comes back to go to college he'll almost be brand-new and not such a total wuss all the time.

2. By then his mom will have officially moved to California and arranged for him to have residency there too, something that will allow him to get into Berkeley or UCLA, schools he probably wouldn't be able to get into otherwise.

3. He'll join or even help form a band that will get pretty big around campus, so big that they'll tour one summer up and down the West Coast and open up a couple times for some indie group that everyone's crazy about. Maybe they'll even get a record contract or tour in Europe the next summer.

4. It'll take a while, but he'll eventually find a major that's totally perfect for him, psychology or art history or architecture, who knows, and there will be this one professor that gets super into him without making a big deal about it, and he'll come to graduation, where he'll shake Darren's hand really warmly and hand him a book on Freud or Van Gogh or Frank Lloyd Wright in which he wrote some extremely kind note, something like: *To a wonderful student, the future is yours!*

5. He'll go to Chicago for a few weeks near the end of the summer after graduation to visit Nate (who is living in the city, where he and a friend opened a successful café/bar that has live music at night) and his dad (who is living with Gary, who is actually pretty cool, plus somehow the whole gay thing somehow miraculously stopped mattering so much after Darren went to Mongolia, not that he hung out with tons of gay people in Mongolia or anything). His first night there he'll be drinking a beer at Nate's café/bar, and Zoey will walk in.

It will take him a moment to recognize her, because she let her hair (which is now natural light brown instead of dyed almost black) grow out, plus she is dressed totally different (just these really cool jeans and this funky, sort of loose tank top, which lets everyone see the sentence tattooed just below the nape of her neck that says in a perfectly half-elegant, half-casual handwritten font, *Love saves the day*), not to mention she took out the piercings over her eye and around her lip, but kept the one in her nose, where she now wears a thin silver ring that looks kind of sophisticated and bold at the same time.

She'll join him at the bar, and they'll catch up but also just sit there in silence a lot, both sensing how the two of them and this night of theirs are sort of gradually peeling away from the rest of the city here on a Thursday near the end of the summer. Once the band starts, they'll check out a few songs (after all, that is why Zoey came to the bar in the first place), until right at the end of the third song they'll both turn to each other and say, almost at the exact same instant, "Hey, do you want—" and neither of them will even have to finish the question.

They'll slowly wander around the neighborhood for a while, catching up, checking out the cool houses, sniffing the occasional wildflower, feeling like almost actual adults, until suddenly they're making out on a picnic table in a small park. They were both sitting on top of it, talking and looking out into the night sky dotted with silent planes. He made a little joke and they started laughing, something that for some reason compelled them to turn their heads toward each other and kiss.

Meaning they'll have this intense fling the rest of the time he's in Chicago, so he'll pretty much not see Nate or his dad and Gary. They'll barely sleep, falling totally in love, the way you can fall totally in love with the help of Chicago near the end of the summer, the whole thing so intense and steadily spontaneous that a couple weeks will go by before the future resurfaces as a thing the two of them might want to think about.

And so it isn't until the last three or four days that he and Zoey will start trying to figure out how to not just have to say good-bye to each other when he leaves, because he's already been accepted to a Master's program in architecture in L.A., not to mention she's moving to New York in late September because she got this amazing job at an art gallery, so there's just nothing either of them can do right now, which somehow makes those last three or four days the craziest of all, no sleep, long talks, plus, of course, marathon lovemaking (not sex, lovemaking) sessions that seem to take place halfway to another planet.

When they hug good-bye at the airport (she drives him there, of course), Zoey totally breaks down, burying her face in his chest and half-soaking his shirt, and for a while, maybe because he's completely exhausted, he feels sad but not like he's going to lose it, until she gives him this kiss with lips that are cold and wet from her tears, and that does it, meaning he cries a little too, maybe even more than a little, but still, the whole good-bye almost feels great, even though it hurts like hell most of all.

4 Terms of a Possibly Lopsided and Partially Conditional Quid Pro Quo Darren Agrees To Near the End of a Pretty Short Conversation with His Dad

1. Darren will be allowed to visit Nate by himself.
2. Darren will not do this kind of thing again. Ever.
3. His dad may come to Ann Arbor on Sunday morning to see Nate for a bit and return Darren to Chicago, though this doesn't need to be decided yet.
4. Darren and his dad will commit to finding ways to have difficult conversations, as there are clearly a number of difficult conversations the two of them ought to have.

3 Parts of His Lunch That Darren Starts Eating Quickly Once He Thinks the Conversation Is Over, Only Then He Suddenly Finds Himself Asking His Dad Another Question

1. CHEESE AND MUSTARD SANDWICH ON WHEAT

In fact, Darren had already said "Bye" to him, but then this came out:

"When did you know?"

"When did I know?" his dad asks, maybe confused.

"Yeah, you know. When did you know? About . . ."

"Well," his dad says, and then doesn't say anything for a while. Darren doesn't say anything either, just chews. "I knew many years ago—"

"How many?"

"—but then, then I thought perhaps I didn't know. Then I did again, then I didn't."

Darren swallows a large bite with some difficulty. "What?"

"Because I didn't want to know."

"Huh?"

"Until about two years ago. Then I knew again. And this time I knew that I knew, whether I wanted to know or not."

"Oh."

"Though I still didn't know when to tell your mother. Or you and your brother. Or how."

"Oh." Darren takes a sip from his water bottle.

2. SALT AND VINEGAR POTATO CHIPS

"Does that make sense?" his dad asks.

"But so why didn't you tell us sooner?"

"Well," his dad says.

"Seriously, once you told Mom."

"Well."

"Why'd you wait so long to tell me?"

"Darren."

"Huh?"

"Where are you right now?"

"On a bus. I already told you."

"And why might that be?"

Darren stares into his nearly empty Ziploc bag of potato chips. He switches the phone to the other side of his head. Then back to the first side again. He almost stands up. He feels, in addition to everything else he feels, a bit like a moron. Or an idiot. Or maybe even an asshole.

"Yeah, okay," Darren says. "I get it."

"We can talk more when you get back."

"Okay."

And then they really hang up.

3. A PEAR

1 Person Darren Did Not at All Expect to Find Lighting a Cigarette Right outside the Bus, Which for Some Reason Has Come to a Stop at the Edge of a Gas Station Parking Lot in Paw Paw, Michigan

1. Zoey Lovell

2 **Highly Processed Food Products Darren Purchases for $2.78 inside the Gas Station Food Mart After for Some Reason Saying, of All Things, to Zoey, "Hey, You Should Sit Upstairs. It's Kind of Cool There."**

1. Mr. Pibb
2. Snyder's of Hanover Honey Mustard & Onion Pretzel Pieces

7 Theories, Not All Plausible, Darren Comes Up With to Explain Zoey's Presence on This Bus, While They Silently Share the Pretzels and Mr. Pibb

1. Back at Union Station he actually did say to her that Ann Arbor is pretty cool and that she should come with, so she decided to.
2. She figured out pretty easily that he was sort of running away from home, which she's been pretty close to doing for a while, and if Darren can sort of run away, then why can't she?
3. She has a good friend or close cousin she's been meaning to visit who goes to Michigan.
4. She is thinking about going to Michigan for school, but hasn't yet had a chance to tour the campus.
5. She does this kind of thing all the time.
6. She likes, or even secretly loves, Darren, and this is her chance.
7. She is insane, more or less.

7 Brief Conversations Darren and Zoey Have While Zoey Plays This Game on Her Phone, Which Is Just Distorting the Faces of Random People by Using Your Finger to Pull Their Features Apart or Mush Them Together

1. D: You like North High? Z: Nah, not really. D: Me neither.
2. D: When did you get the one over your eye? Z: Last Thanksgiving. D: Cool.
3. D: Mr. Pibb is pretty excellent. Z: And nasty. D: Well, yeah. Z: Good nasty. D: Yeah. D: Great nasty.
4. D: Do you know Maggie Block? Z: Not really. Z: Why? D: No, nothing.
5. D: What are your parents going to do? Z: Do? D: When they find out. Z: About? D: About, you know, this. Z: Who cares. D: Are you scared? D: Are you? Z: (shoulder shrug) D: You should call them. I did already. D: Mine, I mean. D: They were mad, but not that mad, actually. D: You should. Z: (shoulder shrug)
6. D: Do you know where you're going to stay? Z: (noise he's pretty sure means no) D: You can probably stay at my brother's place. D: But it might be on a couch or something. D: He'd be okay with it. Z: Okay. D: He's cool.
7. D: That one's awesome. Z: Thanks. Z: Your turn. D: Sweet.

5 New Thoughts Darren Has about Zoey, Now That He Can Just Stare Right at Her, Because While He Was Playing the Game on Her Phone, She Crossed Her Arms, Rested Her Head to the Side, and Fell Asleep, Which Is Maybe One of the Advantages of Being Small, Since There's No Way Darren Could Ever Get Comfortable Enough in His Cramped Seat to Fall Asleep

1. Her haircut (sort of shaved on one side but long and almost poufy on the other) is kind of stupid. Almost cool, but mostly stupid. He'd never in a million years have the guts to get his hair cut that way, or in some other kind of way that would be equivalent for boys.

2. Her nose and mouth are pretty small, and the way her nose curves around or below her nostrils (right where the bottom of her nose meets the rest of her face), along with the plumpness of her top lip in the middle, where it juts up and out a bit, this being the one part of her face that isn't little and thin, are probably the best parts of her face, which is maybe a little plain overall, but is definitely pretty in those places. Plus her skin looks super smooth, not to mention really pale.

3. She smells like a cigarette, which is gross, but there's another smell too, which is either a hair product or some perfume, or some combination of them, and the

185

smell isn't that strong, but it's really distinct and steady, almost like it's in her clothes, too. He has absolutely no idea what the name of the smell is or how even to describe it, except that it is a smell that makes you want to keep smelling it, which is probably the overall point of perfume, if you think about it. So it's kind of interesting that Zoey puts something on that makes you want to keep smelling her, because if you asked her, "Do you want people to want to keep smelling you?" she'd almost certainly say no; in fact, she probably wouldn't even answer the question.

4. You can do all that stuff to your hair and face, but then when you're asleep you still look just like pretty much anyone else when they're sleeping, because there's no sleeping expression that only sad or defiant or bitter or mysterious people (or whatever Zoey is) have, and so there's something extra pathetic about looking at her like this, to the point that he's almost embarrassed for her right now.

5. If it were somehow the right or appropriate thing for him to do, he'd lean over and kiss her neck, maybe two inches below the place where her jaw curves up toward her ear. Just a little kiss, not even very long and definitely not juicy or anything. And it's not like he's thinking about some kind of frog/princess situation here, but he almost has the sense that the world would

be a much better place if it were somehow the right or appropriate thing for him to kiss her on the neck, because, again, it's not like she'd turn into a princess, but he does think it would make her life much better, change it somehow, assuming he could kiss her neck in just the right way, which he would definitely try to do and wishes he could.

10 Questions Nate Texts to Darren during an Exchange That Starts with Darren Texting, *Im Bringing Someone OK?*

1. *Someone?*
2. *???*
3. *Who dat?*
4. *Toby Lovells sis?*
5. *She hot?*
6. *U bonking her?*
7. *So wtf?*
8. *She gonna stay here?*
9. *U want to be bonking her?*
10. *Whatevs. Was Dad cool?*

4 Possible Translations of the Startlingly New Expression That Briefly Passes over Zoey's Face When She First Starts Waking Up but Before She Is Totally Awake, an Expression Darren Gets a Pretty Good Look at, Because He Was Still Staring Right at Her

1. Oh, I forgot you were here. Glad you're here.
2. That was a strange but not entirely unpleasant dream I was just having.
3. Good morning, sweetie.
4. If this crappy world were exactly the same as it is right now, exactly the same in every last way, except I knew that you'd always be next to me and watching over me while I slept, then I'd be much happier about living in this crappy world.

4 Mostly Trivial Events That Together Quickly Ruin the Moment

1. Zoey presses the palm of her hand against her mouth while kind of squinting one eye and then looks at her palm, maybe because she was expecting to find some drool there, though Darren's pretty sure there wasn't any.

2. A couple of college-age guys sitting a few rows back have a pretty loud and brief conversation about Superbus's unreliable Wi-Fi service, a conversation that could pretty well be summed up in the phrase, "This is bullshit, man," which is said more than once during this conversation.

3. Zoey quickly stands up, grabs her worn-out canvas backpack, and starts walking toward the back of the bus before turning around and saying "Bathroom" to Darren.

4. It starts raining lightly, the small drops stretching out into thin lines along the side windows but just sort of turning into deformed rings on the front window, which has no windshield wiper, which seems perfectly reasonable but still makes Darren a little nervous.

6 Instances of Physical Contact Involving Darren and Zoey That Take Place between Battle Creek and Ann Arbor

1. Zoey returns to her seat. Darren had raised the armrest to make a little more room for himself. When she sits down, her side, especially her shoulder and upper arm, momentarily push into his upper arm. And then sort of keep pushing. Not that hard, but still. So Darren softly leans back into her to see what will happen. The answer is nothing, meaning they sit there, pretty much leaning into each other and watching Michigan roll past.

2. Darren looks down at the back of her right hand. The number 827 is written on her thumb. Small circles are drawn around each knuckle. "Hello," "Bye," and "Hello" are written below the place where her pinkie and ring finger come to an end. Her sleeve is pushed up just a bit and Darren can see that there's more writing there. So he lets the index and middle fingers of his left hand reach down to this sleeve and push it up an inch or two more. She doesn't stop him.

The end of her forearm is covered by some sort of design. Curvy lines and straight lines and little colored-in rectangles. It looks a bit like fish scales, a bit like medieval chain mail, a bit like waves. The lines are incredibly intricate and have been drawn so steadily that Darren assumes it's all a tattoo.

"Is that . . . ," he starts to ask.

"I drew it," she says.

"Can I . . ." But she just pushes the sleeve up herself.

"Holy crap," Darren says. The pattern covers the entire top half of her forearm and reaches almost all the way to her elbow. It looks weird, but it looks awesome, too. It's almost scary at first, but then, somehow, it isn't. "How did—"

"Left-handed," she says, like that explains anything.

"No, but . . . ," Darren says.

He really can't decide what he feels about it. When he thinks about what it looks like (fish scales and all that), he's not so crazy about it. But then when he just looks at and kind of lets himself get lost in the pattern, he totally loves it. Maybe because the pattern is almost perfectly consistent. Like a machine did it. Or maybe because it's just a killer design that kind of turns her arm into something other than an arm.

"That's sick," he says. "But how—how can you do that?"

Zoey shrugs her shoulders, but this time Darren's pretty sure it doesn't mean what it's meant all the other times. Now it's more like she's a little embarrassed that he's so impressed, even though she's glad he is.

"Totally sick," he says.

The next thing Darren knows, Zoey reaches into her bag and pulls out one of those fine-tip Sharpies. For a second Darren figures she's just showing him what she drew it with. But then she takes off the cap.

Her small, dark eyes grow a little wider. The white is really white next to the black, which is really black. Darren's not exactly sure what his face does, but it must do something, because her eyes shrink and she asks, sounding ready to be disappointed, "You don't want me to?"

"Huh?"

"It's cool," she mumbles, puts the cap back on, and leans down toward her bag.

3. "No, wait," Darren says, and grabs her shoulder, which is small and muscular.

She freezes and looks at him quite seriously.

"You can," he says, but her expression doesn't change. "I want you to. For real."

4. Zoey softens a bit, including in her shoulder.

"Yeah?" she asks.

"Yeah."

She looks at his hand, which is still on her shoulder. He decides it's probably time to remove it. She sits up straighter.

"Okay. First . . ." She reaches over and pretty much takes off his zip-up hoodie for him. Then she puts the armrest down and sets his arm on it. She turns her whole body to face him and tucks her right leg under her butt.

Darren's glad she's not mad at him or anything, but otherwise he's not so sure how he feels about all this. The more he looks at her arm, the more he thinks it looks like a tattoo. Maybe it actually is, and maybe she's just screwing with him and will laugh once he's done letting her draw all over his arm.

5. But too late, because she takes hold of it with her right hand and starts drawing with her left. The ink flows out of the Sharpie and onto his skin. She begins with small waves, with these little bumpy lines running across the width of his forearm. When she finishes one line she goes back to where she started, but moves maybe a quarter-inch up his arm. Each line is identical.

The tip of the marker on his skin, he can't figure out what it feels like, but something between the feel of it and just watching her hand steadily hovering over his arm, it makes him close his eyes. Darren pictures the design slowly spreading over his arm. He wishes Zoey had three hands so he could hold one of them. The more he sits there, the more he has trouble figuring out where he ends and Zoey begins, which feels like the answer to a question he's been trying to ask himself for a while.

He opens his eyes about ten minutes later. Was he sleeping? At some point she finished the waves, and without him noticing, switched to longer lines running down the length of his arm. He can't tell if they're straight or not, because it's like one of those optical illusions, or at least it could be. And it doesn't make any sense, because he swears the bus ride is bumpy, but all the lines are straight. Like even the wavy lines are somehow straight, whatever that means.

He really wants to say something, but it's way better not to. Which is good, because he has no idea what he'd say. Part of him is ready for her to finish already, but part of him wishes he was lying on an operating table, wearing only his boxers and a T-shirt, so she could do his other arm and both legs.

When she finishes the longer lines, she starts filling in some of the curvy rectangles created by all the intersecting lines. Darren tries to figure out the pattern she's using, like how is she deciding which rectangles to color in? After a while he decides it's random. But good random. The fingers of her right hand have been pressing hard into the area above his elbow this whole time. He might be able to feel a pulse in her fingertips. Though maybe it's his own pulse she's helping him feel.

6. Zoey sits up but continues looking at his arm. The stretch of skin she drew on is now about three-fourths black. She turns her head this way and that, checking something. Then she pushes her right sleeve all the way up and presses her forearm firmly against his.

Even though his arm is bigger, the patterns are identical. The waves in the shorter lines. The weird bends in the longer ones. Even the colored-in rectangles. All the same. They press their matching arms into each other. His skin is a little darker than hers.

"Holy shit, that's crazy!" he says.

"Do you like it?" she asks with what sounds like absolute and unguarded sincerity.

"I love it," he says, "seriously," at a volume the drone of the bus just about swallows up.

He looks at their arms, pushed together firmly, until they stop looking like arms to him. Zoey and he are members of some gang. Or superheroes. Or cyborgs. Or aliens. There's something weird and important and awesome about the whole thing.

"Zoey," Darren finally says about two minutes later.

"Huh?" Zoey asks.

"Aren't Sharpies permanent?"

"Yeah," she says.

"Oh," he says.

"Pretty much."

"Cool." He flexes his forearm. "Cool."

6 Manifestations of Darren's Sudden Nervous Excitement to See Nate, All of Which Intensify as the Bus Turns Left into a Parking Lot in Ann Arbor

1. Right leg bouncing up and down
2. Nodding his head over and over
3. Needing to pee like crazy
4. Wanting some gum to chew
5. Wishing Zoey would either disappear or finally hold his hand
6. Which is sweating

5 Components of Nate's Outfit

1. Black suede Puma sneakers
2. Jeans, torn slightly above left knee
3. Mickey Mouse T-shirt
4. Plaid flannel (mostly blue, green, and red), unbuttoned
5. Red winter hat

3 Words Nate Greets Darren with, Warmly

1. Yo
2. Yo
3. Bitch

4 Suppositions of Varying Certainty Darren Reaches While Hugging Nate for Five/Six Seconds

1. I am taller than Nate.
2. I am much heavier than Nate.
3. Hugging Nate is good for me.
4. Nate smells like an Italian spice.

2 Follow-up Questions Darren Doesn't Even Have to Ask, Because Nate Sort of Points to His Own Face/Head and Says/Asks, "Kind of Sick, Right?" as Soon as They Stop Hugging and Each Take a Step Back to Look at Each Other

1. When was the last time you had it cut?
2. Is that a beard?

4 Times in Jacobs Brothers History That the Two of Them Considered Someone Else from a Possibly Safe Distance with a Combination of Awkward Confusion (Darren) and Baffled Amusement (Nate)

1. The weekend of their mom's very first business trip to California, their dad said, "Hey, how about us men head downtown? Lunch at Eleven City Diner and then we can hit the Shedd Aquarium. What do you say?"

Darren looked at Nate. "Yeah, sure," Nate said.

Only finding a place to park before lunch was a pain, so their dad just dropped the two of them off in front of the restaurant, where they waited for him outside. Nate and Darren, then ages sixteen and eleven, were just standing there, pretty much doing nothing, when some older guy appeared out of nowhere.

"Young men," he said to them, like being young men was really crucial to something. Nate and Darren said nothing. The man was not particularly clean.

"God. Bill Gates. Steve Jobs. Who's it gonna be?"

"Okay," Nate said with slight sarcasm, while Darren took a half step closer to his brother.

"Bill Gates. Steve Jobs. Evil magic." Without moving, Darren tried to look at Nate. The man stuffed his hands into his pockets. Darren could tell they were fists. "Evil. Magic."

"Okay," Nate said again, this time more sarcastically.

The man closed his eyes tightly for a moment, like he was trying to remember something. Or was in pain. Then he turned and started walking off. Not only were his pants ripped down the back, but a small slice of what appeared to be his right butt cheek was plainly visible as well.

Darren didn't think it was funny; in fact, the sight of the man's discolored flesh made him feel kind of what he'd felt when he'd seen a bloody, car-flattened squirrel a week earlier. But the next thing he knew, he had joined his brother in a very brief and very audible burst of laughter, which, not surprisingly, caused the homeless and/or crazy man to turn around.

For a moment, Darren feared a showdown, but just then their dad showed up and, without even noticing the other man and the slice of his exposed ass, patted both his sons on the back and said jovially, "Gentlemen, let's do lunch!"

2. Their cousin Eli, who's exactly between Nate and Darren in age, clearly has some sort of something. He's probably not autistic, but Asperger's, to the extent that Darren even knows what that is, seems like a very distinct possibility.

The main symptom, or weird thing he has, renders Eli totally clueless when it comes to understanding what constitutes an appropriate speaking volume in almost any situation, meaning he'll often scream in restaurants while other times whisper as a train approaches. And when talking loud, he also tends to lengthen each word, riding out the vowels for seconds at a time and at a rather high tone. They used to see him a lot when they were younger, but the year Darren started middle school, Eli's family moved to Boston.

A couple of months before Darren's bar mitzvah, Nate started yelling for him from his room. Darren hurried down the hallway and found Nate sitting in front of his computer.

"Oh my God," Nate said.

"What?" Darren asked.

"Holy shit," Nate said.

"What?" Darren asked again.

"Check this out," Nate said, and clicked on a black-and-white YouTube clip, which looked to be from some old movie. A guy, Jerry Lewis according to Nate, was sort of talking and singing about, of all things, enchiladas.

"What the—?" Darren started to ask.

"Shh, just listen," Nate commanded, and moved it back a few seconds.

And then Darren got it. "Dude," Darren said.

Jerry Lewis, decades prior to their cousin's birth, appeared to have perfected an imitation of Eli. Needless to say, the Jacobs brothers spent more than a few minutes watching this clip over the next couple months.

Eli and his family arrived on the Thursday before Darren's bar mitzvah in order to have an evening alone with Darren's family. After dinner, Nate and Darren, under some pressure from their parents, invited Eli upstairs so the adults could talk downstairs. Hugely excited by this plan, Eli raced upstairs, well ahead of his cousins. As Eli neared the top of the stairs, Nate sang out, quite loudly, "Enchiladas! I don't know. Enchiladas! Oh, hello."

Eli froze and turned around.

Nate and Darren just smiled, while Eli screamed, much as Jerry Lewis would have, "What? Wha-at? Whaaaaaat?!"

The Jacobs brothers stood silently at the bottom of the stairs for a few seconds, until Eli turned around and continued toward his younger cousin's room.

3. Three years ago the Jacobs took what would turn out to be their last major family trip (a cruise in the Caribbean, which was pretty cool overall). Their mom, because it was the kind of thing almost all the women seemed to be doing, decided to get cornrows at their stop in Jamaica (while Nate and Darren went snorkeling). Snorkeling took much longer than getting cornrows, so their mom was already lying in the sun when the boys returned from their time in the water.

Nate and Darren, both dripping wet, stopped simultaneously about eight feet from her towel. And stood there speechless, staring at the rows of hair and pale scalp now on display. The shape of their mother's head surprised him. After about ten seconds she somehow sensed their presence and opened her eyes. Actually, she only opened her right eye, because of how bright the sun was.

Just then their dad, holding a purple, umbrella-decorated blended drink in each hand, walked up to them.

"Pretty cool, huh?" he asked.

The boys said nothing.

Their mom undid her braids prior to dinner that evening, but not before giving her sons a lecture on manners.

4. In a parking lot in Ann Arbor, on an overcast afternoon in late April of this year, just as a Superbus is pulling away, the Jacobs brothers finish greeting each other and turn to face Zoey Lovell, who stands a couple of car lengths away and almost appears to be hugging herself, while looking down and to the side, a cigarette burning slow and steady in her right hand.

"Nate," Darren says, "that's Zoey. Zoey, this is my brother, Nate."

"Greetings, Ms. Lovell," Nate says.

Zoey appears to scratch her upper arm.

7 Reasons Darren Concludes That He Is, in Fact, a Stud, or at Least Much Cooler Than He Usually Considers Himself to Be

1. He's about to get into a black BMW 325i, because Nate's roommate, Kyle, let Nate take his car to go pick them up.
2. He got to Ann Arbor all by himself.
3. And with some help from Zoey Lovell.
4. Who for some reason decided to join him.
5. And he didn't even bring a change of clothes.
6. And neither did she.
7. Plus Nate has a beard, which is pretty patchy, but still.

8 Quintessential College Scenes Darren Observes from Inside Kyle's Black BMW 325i, Which Also Smells like Some Sort of Italian Spice, as They Drive across Campus toward Nate and Kyle's Apartment

1. A huge guy in sweats walking across an empty field, with a sports bag hanging off one of his massive shoulders
2. Two girls with giant backpacks walking down a sidewalk, talking excitedly and using their hands a lot
3. Three guys tossing a football back and forth in front of an oversize frat house
4. A nice steady stream of people walking up and down the stairs of a huge, old gray stone building (with columns and everything)
5. Four or five students gathered around what has to be a professor, since the guy's old and holding a few books
6. A skinny dude with glasses and a thick beard sitting cross-legged at the base of a tree and reading a book
7. A packed coffee house (not Starbucks) where every table is taken up with books, laptops, and mugs
8. A half-dozen housemates sitting on crappy lawn furniture set up on the roof of the awesome wooden porch of their massive Victorian

5 Comments Nate Makes during the Drive That Are Funny but Also Make Darren a Little Uncomfortable, Especially the Ones That Have Anything to Do with Zoey, Who Darren Can't Believe He Actually Forgot about Entirely for a Few Minutes, but She's Sitting Silently in the Back, and during the First Part of the Ride Nate Played the Fourth-Best Song of All Time Really Loud on Kyle's Insanely Good Car Stereo, Plus Darren Is in Ann Arbor with Nate but without Either of Their Parents, Holy Crap

1. Hey Darren, guess what? Your dad's totally gay.
2. Zoey, congratulations on winning the first annual "Run Away to Ann Arbor with Darren Jacobs" contest. With so much competition, you must be beside yourself with excitement.
3. Seeing how the two of you have no clothes, and seeing how my little brother is now bigger than me, and seeing how Zoey is a female, we probably should do some shopping. I was thinking this is a pretty good excuse to pick yourselves up a trademark Michigan sweatshirt, though I can't promise they make them in black, Ms. Lovell.
4. We're still finalizing the weekend's activities. Let me know what you think: Get wasted and puke and *then* lose your virginity, or the other way around? Any preference on that one, kids?

5. Zoey, not that we're anything but tickled to be hosting you this weekend, but I would be interested in hearing what your parents think about any of this. I guess I just want to know when to expect the police to show up.

17 Inhabitants of Nate and Kyle's Refrigerator, Which Darren Opens Up, Partially Because He's Pretty Hungry

1. Three carry-out containers, contents unclear
2. A quarter loaf of white bread
3. Four bottles of Miller Genuine Draft and one bottle of Natural Light
4. Seven individually wrapped slices of American cheese
5. Blue-lidded translucent Tupperware, about the size of a fast-food hamburger, contents unclear
6. A carrot, wilting
7. A pink Styrofoam carton of eggs
8. Half an onion, mostly covered in Saran wrap
9. Approximately one-third stick of butter, half covered by its mangled silver wrapper
10. Plochman's mustard
11. Skippy peanut butter, crunchy
12. Heinz ketchup
13. Smucker's concord grape jelly
14. Hershey's syrup
15. Seven AA batteries
16. A quart of orange juice, one-third full
17. A half gallon of organic 2 percent milk, two-thirds full

5 People Nate and Darren Briefly Discuss in the Kitchen While Zoey Checks Out Kyle's Records in the Other Room

1. THEIR DAD

Nate sits on the kitchen counter while Darren makes himself a PB&J sandwich and keeps an eye on Zoey.

"Hey," Darren says after licking the knife, "I played a sick bass solo last night at the concert. It was crazy. You should have been there."

"Gaydad said it was pimporiffic."

"No he didn't."

Nate opens a nearby cabinet, removes a glass, and gets some water from the sink. "My Stats exam was not pretty."

Darren takes two and a half bites before he bothers to start chewing.

"So, like, have you and Gaydad talked about the whole thing since he dropped the gay bomb on you?"

"Stop it."

"What?"

"The 'gay' everything."

"Why? Because it's gay?"

"Ha-ha."

"Have you?"

"What?"

"Talked about it with him?"

Darren drinks some milk. "A little."

"I can't fucking believe he told you first. Like he couldn't have guessed you'd tell me right away. I'm sorry, but that's some gay shit right there."

2. MAGGIE BLOCK

Darren walks right up to where Nate is sitting. "Hey," he whispers. "Do you remember Maggie Block?"

Nate, with an expression of mild displeasure, says, "Yeah."

"I made out with her after the concert."

Nate says, "Nice," and offers his palm for a hand slap. Darren slaps it. "Any boob action?"

"Yeah," Darren says, half smiling. "But only for a few seconds."

"How big?"

"About like this," Darren says, placing one of his curled-up hands over the other.

"Right on."

Darren finishes off the sandwich.

3. THEIR MOM

"Hey," Darren says. "Did Mom call you or anything?"

"Yeah," Nate says, "but we only talked for a couple minutes. Miss California had an urgent meeting to attend."

"What'd she say?"

"You know"—Nate takes a long drink—"all her typical

bullshit: you're the adult, don't do anything stupid, promise you'll let me know if you think anything is seriously wrong."

4. KYLE

"Hey," Darren says. "Where's Kyle?"

"Picking up some stuff from this guy across campus. Should be back soon."

5. ZOEY

Nate softly kicks Darren, who was checking out Zoey in the next room, right below the ribs. "So what's up with Lady Darkness? You into her or something?"

"I kind of like her," Darren whispers. "I don't know. What do you think?"

"I think she's half-freak, half-show. All freak show. But that could be okay for a little while."

"She's a really good driver," Darren says. "I swear. I mean, it's weird how good of a driver she is."

"Sweet. Hopefully there's an as-yet-undiscovered correlation between driving and BJ skills."

Darren blushes. "Hey, so, like, what are we going to do tonight and stuff?"

"I got some ideas, we'll see," Nate says, and hops down from the counter. "Ann Arbor is our oyster, you oversized vegetarian pussy."

"I eat seafood, dickwad."

3 Characters Kyle Could Convincingly Dress Up as with the Proper Costume/Makeup/Facial Hair

1. Mario (of Nintendo fame)
2. Bluto (from "Popeye")
3. Ralph (from *Wreck-It Ralph*)

6 Minutes That Pass After Kyle's Arrival Until a Bong Is Taken Out

1. 5:52
2. 5:53
3. 5:54
4. 5:55
5. 5:56
6. 5:57

14 Seemingly Random and Possibly Meaningless Sayings Kyle and Nate Begin Tossing Back and Forth around 5:54, the Gist of Which Is Pretty Clear by 5:58

1. Shall we take it to another level, Mr. Jacobs?
2. Friday, Friday, got to get down on Friday.
3. I believe the time has come.
4. This time it's personal.
5. Do you think they'd like to say hello to our little friend?
6. I'm personally quite eager to thank the Academy.
7. We'd best mobilize our forces.
8. Or flirt with disaster.
9. We could just settle down for the evening.
10. As long as you show me how you really feel.
11. Is your seat belt securely fastened?
12. My tray table is in an upright and locked position.
13. We've been cleared for takeoff.
14. Time to renew our pledge.

1 Inhabitant of the Refrigerator Whose Contents Are Now Quite Clear

1. Blue-lidded translucent Tupperware, about the size of a fast-food hamburger

6 Drugs and the People Darren Associates Them With

1. METHYLIN AND CONNOR DAVIDSON

Connor was Darren's best friend for most of second and part of third grade, a friendship facilitated by Connor's family moving in two houses down from the Jacobs' house during the summer before second grade. Connor was a pretty crazy kid, but funny and kind too. In fact, he was great at sharing his toys. But he did have a lot of trouble at school, especially during the second half of second grade, by which time their teacher (Ms. Barelli) had decided and more or less announced to the entire class that Connor was no longer really the "new kid" and thus should no longer expect special treatment for his unacceptable behavior.

Connor sort of disappeared for most of that summer, and when Darren saw him again just a week before school was supposed to start, Connor seemed pretty different. Slower more than anything. Plus he didn't seem to want to eat much. They wound up having different teachers for third grade (though their classes got together for reading), and then Connor's family moved again over winter break.

Darren sort of remembers asking his mom back then about what exactly happened to Connor, and Connor may have even told Darren himself, but it was only a few years later (he and his mom were looking through old pictures

219

on her computer and saw a photo of Connor) that Darren finally got the full story about Connor's ADHD and his meds. Darren's mom had, to her almost-instant regret, befriended Connor's mom as well, a needy woman who told Darren's mom much more than she cared to know about her marriage and her children.

2. NITROUS OXIDE AND CRYSTAL OR CANDICE

During a routine checkup in fourth grade, two cavities were discovered in Darren's teeth. The following week his father brought him back to Dr. Mauer's office, where Crystal or Candice, one of Dr. Mauer's dental hygienists, informed Darren, as she tilted backward the elaborate chair in which he was sitting, that he'd be receiving laughing gas.

Crystal or Candice, blond, rail-thin, and pretty (but only at first glance), placed a ring of rubber tubing around Darren's head and rested some sort of inhaler over his nose. She seemed kind of distracted up to the moment her eyes noticed Darren's, which were, despite the word "laughing," not at all amused by what was about to happen.

So she stopped (stopped setting up her work station, stopped humming some song to herself, stopped chatting with a coworker on the other side of the nearby partition) and smiled at Darren. She addressed him as "honey," told him he had nothing to worry about, and then, possibly as part of her effort to adjust the inhaler, ran the back of her fingers down one of his cheeks. Darren was instructed to close his eyes, breathe deeply, and think about something that makes him happy. So he did, thinking about Crystal or Candice's fingers on his cheeks.

3. PINOT NOIR AND HIS PARENTS
Darren's parents were never big drinkers. But around the middle of eighth grade, Darren began noticing a lot more wine bottles in the kitchen, dining room, and den (he even saw bottles a couple times in their bedroom).

His parents didn't make a big deal about it, and truthfully they still didn't drink all that much. In fact, he saw a lot of bottles, around a third full, being poured down the kitchen sink, because they weren't good anymore. But for whatever reason, his parents pretty much only drank a kind of red wine called Pinot Noir, to the point that they would often ask one another, "Hey, you want some Pinot?"

In the fall of ninth grade, the two of them started talking seriously about his dad joining his mom on one of her business trips so they could take a vacation up to wine country afterward. But it never happened, because they wound up getting divorced instead.

4. BEER AND BO GRIFFIN
Bo and Bugs were sort of friends, even though Bo is kind of an idiot when you get right down to it. Still, he convinced

Bugs and Darren to come over one Saturday about two years ago, because Bo's parents were out of town and his older sister, Ashley, told him she didn't "give a care" what he did as long as he left her alone and stayed out of her room, where she and her boyfriend, Blake Haines, were going to be (having sex, probably).

Somehow Bo got his hands on four beers, which he had set out on the kitchen table, along with three short White Sox glasses. Bo told them they were going to play a game called "quarter-bounce," which involves trying to bounce a quarter off the table and into a beer-filled glass. If you get it in, you pick someone else and that guy has to drink the entire glass.

At first Bugs and Darren were kind of excited, but it took about ten minutes before anyone could get a quarter to go in. Plus the beer tasted, as Bugs put it, "like rooster piss." Still, Bo really, really wanted to play, so he told them he'd drink whenever anyone got the quarter in. By this point Bugs and Darren just wanted to leave, but they both felt kind of bad for Bo, who they could tell thought this night was going to be the best ever. They kept playing until Bo was totally drunk. For a while it looked like he was going to puke, because he kept burping, closing his eyes, and sort of tucking his chin down. But all he did was fall asleep on the floor in front of the TV, so, during a commercial, Bugs and Darren just let themselves out and ran back to Bugs's place.

5. ZOEY LOVELL AND CIGARETTES

It's not like he hasn't seen a lot of other people smoke cigarettes before, but Zoey's really the first person he feels like he knows (even though he doesn't know her that well) who smokes, or the first person he knows who seems like they almost were meant to smoke. It just seems like she really likes to smoke, or really needs to, and not just because she's addicted, which she probably is, since cigarettes are supposedly super addictive.

The truth is, Darren totally can't decide if he likes it that she smokes or not. He knows, somehow, that he's not supposed to let himself think it's cool, but it kind of is, at least when she does it. Who knows, maybe she's just really good at it. But then, it is a pretty dumb thing to do, not to mention the smoke is gross and definitely must cover up her smell to some extent, which is too bad, because he's starting to really like being able to smell her. And the smoke must be on her breath, too, which means that if they ever do wind up kissing—which he has no idea if they will or even how much he wants them to (he does a lot in most ways, but it might be a bad idea, especially after Maggie)—he'll have to taste the smoke, which he'd try not to be bothered by, but what if he can't help it?

6. MARIJUANA AND NATE

Just like with cigarettes, Darren has definitely seen people smoke marijuana before, even if it's mostly in movies. And he's seen it before in person (Bugs found some in his mom's underwear drawer, though he wouldn't tell Darren what he was doing in there) and even smelled it being smoked once (Nate convinced their parents to let him take Darren to see Steely Dan at Ravinia last summer, which was a pretty cool concert, even if Darren felt ten times younger than normal there).

But he's never really seen anyone actually smoke it, especially not his brother, who seems not so much good at it (the whole bong thing looks pretty ridiculous) as just having had a lot of practice, if there's a difference between the two. Plus, it's hard to explain, but Darren can tell pretty quickly that marijuana is hardly a trivial part of whoever his brother is now but wasn't just a couple of years ago. Meaning the hair and the beard and the flannel shirt and the silly way he talks with Kyle—it's not that any of those things really make much sense now, but Darren can sort of tell where they came from or what they're connected to, or even what Nate would say they all have in common.

7 Stages of an Awkward Exchange between Guests and Hosts

1. Zoey takes out her cigarettes and lighter, gets up off the floor by the stereo, and walks toward the door.
2. Kyle, laughing for maybe a second, asks, "Where ya off to?"
3. Zoey holds up the cigarettes.
4. Kyle looks at Nate and the two of them crack up as if this is the single funniest response in human history.
5. Nate eventually calms down, wipes his nose with his sleeve, and says (from the top of the couch where he's sitting), "It's cool, Zoey, you can smoke in here."
6. Zoey shrugs her shoulders and leaves anyway.
7. Darren, who almost started laughing with Kyle and Nate, because it was kind of funny (though not even a tenth as funny as they thought it was), gets up to follow her, sort of half saying to himself (and trying not to look at Nate), "I think I'm going to have one too."

6 Features of Darren's New Reality That He Tries to Wrap His Head around While Sitting Next to Zoey on the Steps in Front of Nate's Building and Smoking His Very First Cigarette Ever

1. Nate is a pot smoker and I am a cigarette smoker, at least right now.
2. There seem to be few if any actual adults in Ann Arbor.
3. I'm not nearly as good at holding my cigarette as Zoey is at holding hers, probably because I'm too preoccupied with knowing when to tap the end with my thumb so the ash will fall off. Still, I feel pretty cool.
4. I'm more comfortable with Zoey than with Nate, at least right now, even though Zoey barely talks.
5. The clouds have pretty much disappeared, and it's really, really nice out, both because of the shade of blue the sky is and because Ann Arbor is just way mellower than Chicago, including, somehow, the suburbs. Ann Arbor is just really nice. Nice as in peaceful.
6. Kyle's not annoying or mean or anything, but it would still be better if he just went away.

1 Response from Darren, Which Concludes a Brief Exchange between Him and Zoey, an Exchange Establishing That Zoey Has, in Fact, Smoked Marijuana Before and Probably Will Later Today but Just Didn't Feel Like It Right Now

1. Oh.

2 Possible Types of Sentences That Zoey Speaks to Break the Silence about Thirty Seconds Later, When She Says, "Your Dad's Gay"

1. Question
2. Statement

6 Mostly Silent Minutes That Pass While They're Finishing Up Their Cigarettes

1. 6:21

Darren is probably supposed to respond to her question/statement, but he focuses on his cigarette instead. His cigarette, plus Zoey and her cigarette.

Zoey takes a big drag and exhales a ton of smoke.

"I found out yesterday," he finally says.

"You didn't know?" she asks him.

"No," Darren says slowly, maybe checking with himself that he really didn't. Yep, he had precisely no idea. Darren's looking straight ahead, but he can somehow tell that Zoey is thinking about this. About what that kind of surprise might do to you.

"That sucks," she says.

"Yeah."

He turns to her. She's looking ahead and nodding slowly.

2. 6:22

"Yeah, I guess it does," he adds. He has about half a cigarette left, but he's kind of gotten the point for now. Still, he keeps holding it.

3. 6:23

4. 6:24

He steals another look at Zoey. She's got her arms wrapped around her knees, which are up by her chest.

"So . . ." She looks at him, and he doesn't look away. This almost makes him feel better. Her eyes are smarter than he realized before. Would he want a girlfriend smarter than him? And what kind of smart girlfriend is stupid enough to smoke? "That's why they got divorced?"

"Probably."

"And why you wanted me to take you to the train."

Darren nods.

5. 6:25

"Zoey," he says.

"Yeah?"

"Why'd you get on the bus?" Zoey puts her cigarette in her mouth and lets go of her knees. "I mean I'm glad you did and everything. But, you know, it was kind of . . ."

Darren can hear her breathing, maybe a bit louder than normal. He almost feels bad about asking, but it sure seems like a pretty reasonable question.

"Where'd you even put your car?"

6. 6:26

Zoey pulls Darren's sleeve up a bit, exposing some of the design she drew on him.

1 Faraway Planet Zoey Tells Darren About

1. "There's this other planet," Zoey says. "It's really far away. But it's still a lot like ours."

Darren fights off the urge to ask, "What?" like she's insane, but his face probably says as much.

"There is," she insists. "I swear."

"Okay," he says slowly. "What about it?"

"Well," she says, "there's this one way it's different."

"Yeah?"

"Guess."

"Uh, no idea."

"C'mon, guess."

"I don't know. The people are green."

"No," she says, like she's embarrassed he actually guessed that. "What's different is that one in every million people, they have this special mark somewhere on their body."

Darren can feel his face smiling. "A special mark?"

"Yeah." She doesn't smile back. "Around the time you hit puberty it shows up. *If* it shows up. Because for most people it doesn't."

"So it's part of puberty for some people?"

"Sort of. But not exactly. And it can be anywhere. On your back. Your legs. Even your face."

"Can it be on your forearm?"

231

"Yeah, it can be there, too." She says this like she has no idea why he asked about forearms of all places.

"Cool."

"Only one in a million people get a mark."

"What else?"

Zoey starts to say something but stops.

"And?" Darren asks.

"That's it." Zoey nods quickly. "That's all I know. All anyone knows."

Darren looks up at the sky for a bit.

"Seriously?"

"Yup."

Maybe he should be an astronomer. He wonders what the hell Zoey is talking about and why she suddenly got quiet. Wonders if he should ask her again about why she got on the bus or where her car is or what the hell. Wonders if she seems more weird or less weird now that he knows her a little better. Wonders if he actually knows her a little better and if he's going to keep wanting to touch her like he wants to touch her right now.

7 Predictions That Darren Makes After Zoey Leans Over to Put Out Her Cigarette on the Underside of the Bottom Stair, Because Immediately After She Does That and Sits Back Up, She Smiles at Darren in This Impossibly Straightforward/Friendly/Kind/Open/Supportive/Sympathetic/Reassuring/Optimistic Way

1. Darren will fall in love with Zoey.
2. Zoey will welcome this development.
3. Meaning she will too (fall in love with him).
4. Darren will smoke cigarettes with some degree of regularity for the last couple years of high school.
5. Zoey will remain a bit unusual, but Darren will learn that she's not really such a freak overall.
6. Darren's running off to Ann Arbor with her will prove to be the best decision he ever made.
7. Everything will be different from now on.

2 Possibly Additional Features of This Faraway Planet

1. "Do you think . . . ," Darren says. "Like what if everyone who gets one—a mark—what if there's someone else who gets that one too?"

"The same one?"

"Yeah, the exact same one. And they both get it around the same time."

"Maybe," Zoey says. "Yeah, maybe."

"And then if you have one, that means you have to find the other person, right?"

"Right," Zoey says with quiet conviction. "You have to leave your home and your family and your friends and everything and go find them."

"The other person."

"Yeah."

2. Darren can feel himself blinking a lot, trying to think. "And then, when you do, when you find them—"

"If you do."

"Right, because some people don't—"

"Most people don't."

"But if you do, when the two of you are finally together"—Darren pauses, and suddenly wishes he had a cigarette, which terrifies him a little, but whatever—"then you have to stay together. Once you find each other."

Zoey crosses her arms and nods these small, little nods, like she's verifying his theory against all the other information she has on the subject.

"Together," she says, as if she's suddenly unsure if she knows what the word means.

"Yeah, well, but not necessarily *romantic* together."

"Not necessarily."

"Because sometimes the other person with the mark, they're the same gender."

Zoey looks at him like he is the very opposite of intelligent.

"Oh, yeah, right," he says. "Whatever. The important part, it's just, you know, being together. You have to stay together. If you have the same mark."

"Like the planet or the people won't survive unless you do," Zoey says.

"Right."

"But it's hard"—she says this like it's actually much harder than you might think—"because if you get a mark, it basically means that the whole life you thought you were going to have for the first twelve years or whatever, you're not going to have it at all."

Darren thinks about this, really wishing his cigarette hadn't gone out.

"So," he says eventually, "having a mark means you're super special, but it kind of sucks a little too."

"Yeah," Zoey says.

"It's kind of cool, but it kind of blows, too."

"Until you find the other person."

Darren puts his cigarette back in his mouth, but then feels stupid for doing that. "But, so, do other people understand the whole setup? People without marks. On that other planet, I mean? Do they get it?"

Zoey doesn't say anything. Maybe she shrugged her shoulders and he missed it.

Darren obviously has a pretty big urge to push his sleeve up, and Zoey's, too, because then who knows what would happen. But instead he just sits there until the urge passes. Which somehow makes sitting there with her even better.

"So," he says about a minute later, "that's why you got on the bus?"

Darren is about to repeat his question when she looks at him and says with just about complete seriousness, "Bus? What bus?"

Darren nods his head, wishing it was dark outside and they had a telescope.

2 Knees, the Sides of Which Meet and (Despite the Limited Communication Skills of Most Knees) Somehow Inform Each Other (Along with the Bodies and People Connected to Them) That They Are Now Officially and Definitely Friends, and Maybe Even on Their Way to Becoming More Than Friends, Though Let's Not Get Ahead of Ourselves (We're Only Knees, After All)

1. Zoey's right knee
2. Darren's left knee

4 Elements That Could Be Front and Center in a Perfect World

1. These knees, like this.
2. These stairs and their distance from the sidewalk and street, because the sidewalk and street are nice to look at from this height and distance.
3. The weather, right now, especially the breeze, which is soft and cool.
4. The half-dozen or so mostly invisible birds nearby and their chirping, especially the one that sounds like it's saying, "Hello, hello. Hi, hi, hi, hi, hi, hi. Hello."

7 Honks of Increasing Duration from an Old Red SUV That Pulls Up in Front of the House across the Street

1.

2. Zoey winces.

3. "I hate horns," she says.

4.

5. Zoey sits up straight, her knee leaving Darren's without saying good-bye. She snorts a little, or just exhales loudly. Maybe she even laughs, though not like anything's funny.

"He did you a favor," she says. "Your dad did, telling you and everything." Her voice is quicker and sharper than before.

"He did?"

"Things aren't the way they made us think they were when we were little. People aren't either." She kicks a twig off the stair where her foot's resting, though not violently. "Being an adult, like a real adult, not just someone who, you know, happened to go through puberty—that just means figuring out a way to not break, like, some major law once you realize that your childhood was a big lie. Basically."

Darren nods his head in agreement, though he's not sure he agrees. He really, really doesn't want that SUV to honk again.

6. Zoey continues, her voice picking up speed. "Because what do they expect us to do? Like we're supposed to say, 'Awesome, it's all right that, that Mom wished she had been working the whole time. And that Dad loved her a lot, but loved about three other women too. And that, that most of all—" Zoey kicks away another twig, with way more force this time. "Forget it. Whatever. Most people don't figure it out until later. That's why adults are so miserable. Now you know. You've got the rest of your life to figure out what to do about it. So, yeah, might as well thank him."

Darren turns to look at her, squinting even though it's not bright outside. "Forget what?"

"Huh?"

"You said, 'Forget it.' You were about to say something else."

"Nothing."

"C'mon, tell me," Darren says.

"Never mind."

"Seriously. You said 'most of all.' What was it?" He tries really hard with his face to tell her that he'll understand and keep it to himself and all that. And it might be working, as long as that SUV keeps quiet.

7. Oh well. Zoey stands up, turns to go back inside.

"Fine." Darren gets up too. "Your choice. But it's, it's not like you don't know about my dad, so you can tell me, whatever it is."

But Zoey is already back inside.

Darren brings his hands up toward his mouth, planning to yell, "Asshole!" at the SUV. Only it drove off when he wasn't looking.

8 Signs That Nate and Kyle Are Rather High, Some of Which Might Just Be Darren, Since He's Definitely Feeling a Little Different Himself after That Cigarette

1. Nate is lying belly-up with his pelvis and abdomen stretched over the armrest of the couch. His head is about a foot from the floor, which his dangling hair nearly reaches.

2. Nate and his red face greet Darren and Zoey by saying, "Well, hello, brother; hello, brother's traveling companion."

3. The air, while not exactly smoky, seems less transparent than normal.

4. Kyle is sitting cross-legged by the records and does not appear to register Darren and Zoey's return in any way.

5. Kyle is holding up a record cover opposite his face, but his eyes are closed.

6. Darren doesn't recognize the music, but it sounds like music any high person would totally love, since it's pretty much just a soft, almost funky groove without any words.

7. Nate requests a glass of water from Darren, which is no big deal, except that he says it as if there is some-

thing fundamentally confusing about making this request.

8. Without moving from his position on/over the couch, Nate attempts (with impressive focus) to take a drink from the glass Darren has brought him.

1 Impassioned Monologue Nate Delivers After He (in More or Less a Single Motion) Soaks His Face and Hair, Twists off the Couch, Falls onto the Floor, Bounces Back up, and Jumps onto the Middle of the Couch, Where He Now Stands with Arms Outstretched and Toes Hanging over the Front Edge

1. "Here's the thing about diving," he says, "the greatest thing about diving: You can't think about it. Not really. Because of gravity. Which won't let you. You can think about it before the dive. You can. You have to. But once you get on the board, that's what I figured out. I remember, at the New Trier meet, I was like, either this is going to happen or it's not. Either I'm going to nail this fucker or I'm not. The one-and-a-half with a twist. Remember that, D? I kept fucking it up, because I thought I needed to remember, to *remember* to do the twist. The one-and-a-half I had down. And so there'd be that moment in the dive, happened at ETHS and Highland Park, when I'd be like, *Now! Twist now!* But then I'd fuck the whole thing up. Because you can't think it, you've got to just do it. And then I was like, *Holy shit.* I was like, *Eureka, bitches!*

"Because I got it, I finally got it. Don't think it, just do it. But it wasn't even that simple, because then I got more than that too, because even after I got it, I fucking *un*-got it.

Un-fucking-got it. Because two weeks later, where was it, at Glenbrook South, I blew it again, not because I was thinking about it, or not because I *wanted* to think about it, but because I got scared and my brain, my *brain*, thought about it. It said, 'Don't be scared, just remember what you need to do.' And I was like, 'No, you—you brain.'

"Because, whatever, forget my brain, because that meant it wasn't just a problem of thinking or not thinking, it was also a matter of being scared. Or that thinking and being scared are kind of the same thing, when you think about it. You know? Damn, I should write that down. That was the heart of the whole thing. Because I knew what I needed to do. I *knew*. I knew way more than whether I might remember, you know? But diving is scary; it is. You jump up, you twist and flip and spin around and give yourself about twenty chances to fuck yourself up pretty good. Way safer just to sit in the stands and watch. You might do a belly flop. Hell, you might crack your head open on the board.

"Greg Louganis—a gay man, by the way, *super* gay dude—Greg Louganis, one of the best divers *that ever lived*, he whacked his head on the board at the Olympics. The Olympics! It's a real and present danger. But what are you going to do? Either you're going to jump or you're not. And if you're going to jump, then just jump. Jump and get out of the way, you know? Get out of your own way.

"Man, I should have dived more high. I would have been unstoppable. Could have gone downstate. Still, whatever, all-conference. Pretty sweet. Pretty sweet.

"Hey, what do you guys want to do for dinner?"

7 Suggestions Floated for Dinner and the Reasons the First Six Were Shot Down

1. China Palace (Nate)—That place is nasty (Kyle). No, it's not (Nate). Whatever, we can do better (Kyle).
2. Sluggo's Sliders (Kyle)—Darren is a vegetarian (Nate).
3. Ichiban (Nate)—I'm sick of sushi (Kyle).
4. Namaste (Nate)—Just because Darren's a veggie doesn't mean dinner has to suck balls. Sorry, Zoey (Kyle).
5. Campus Pizza (Kyle)—Yeah (Darren). Cool, but let's go out (Nate). Yeah (Darren). Why, man? They deliver (Kyle). I don't know, Darren and Zoey are here, what's the point of staying in all night (Nate)? Yeah (Darren). Because I'm lazy (Kyle)? C'mon (Nate). And look, it cleared up (Nate). It is pretty nice out (Darren). We're going to go out later, let's just hang here for now (Kyle). No, screw that, I don't really feel like pizza anyway (Nate). Pizza sucks (Zoey). Yeah (Darren).
6. El Jefe (Nate)—Seriously (Kyle)? What (Nate)? We have two guests, including a lady, and you're going to eat Mexican (Kyle)? Oh, you're an asshole, man (Nate). You'll thank me later, dude, or at least these two will (Kyle).
7. Abu Adam (Nate)

247

3 Interjections Made by Kyle during Nate's Impassioned Monologue, the First after *"Eureka, Bitches!"* the Second after "No, You—You Brain," and the Last after "Get Out of Your Own Way"

1. Eureka in the house!
2. College is for thinking.
3. That's a metaphor.

11 Miracles Darren Wishes His Mom Could Perform While Speaking to Him on the Phone (Even Though She Called Nate, Who Immediately Tossed His Phone to Darren Like the Thing Was About to Explode)

1. Make dinner (spaghetti and red sauce, broccoli, and ice cream for dessert) appear.
2. Make two pairs of underwear, two pairs of socks, his Gap jeans, a couple of T-shirts (including the Paris one), and maybe another hoodie appear.
3. Get Zoey some clothes too. Whatever she wants.
4. Let him know how much he should be worried about Nate, if at all.
5. Give him just a general preview of any drastic steps that might be taken once Darren gets back home, a preview that makes it clear that there won't actually be any truly drastic steps.
6. Make Zoey want to kiss him. And drive him to school every morning. And quit smoking. And talk more like she did outside before that SUV showed up, because she has said exactly two words since they came back inside.
7. Promise him that if he gets drunk and/or high this weekend (which he probably will, he just has this feeling), it will be fine.

8. Make it so Darren and his dad already went to all the therapy sessions his dad is going to want him to go to with him to talk about being gay and whatever else.

9. Keep the sky clear like this for the rest of his visit.

10. Make Nate realize he should cut his hair, or at least shave. And study more, if he's not studying enough.

11. Promise Darren another five or six miracles at least, because there's definitely more stuff he wants, but it's hard to think of what they are when he's talking to her and trying to make sure she's not too worried or suspicious, which is pretty much impossible, even though she kind of sounds resigned to the whole situation and is probably relieved that Darren isn't talking the way a giant stoner would.

4 Different Things Darren Sort of Feels Like He Is with Regard to Nate and Zoey

1. THE LITTLE RED RIBBON TIED AROUND THE MIDDLE OF THE ROPE DURING A TUG-OF-WAR

There's an old wooden chair over by the window that Zoey's sitting in, which is pretty far away from the couch, where Nate and Kyle are hanging out. There's maybe enough space on the couch for Darren, but he winds up just standing in the middle of the room, about halfway in between everyone, hoping someone will help him figure out what to do next.

2. AN INTERPRETER

"Darren," Nate nearly moans from the couch, "will you ask Lady Z questions?"

"What?" Darren asks, rather annoyed. "What are you talking about?"

"You know," Nate says, nearly giggling. "Questions, about stuff."

Zoey is looking at a book, either choosing not to acknowledge what's going on or having suddenly lost her sense of hearing.

"Uh," Darren says, "why don't you ask her yourself?"

"Because you're her bud, man. You speak like fluent Zoey-ese, right?"

"Zoey-ese," Kyle adds, which is weird, because Darren was sure he was asleep.

"Zoey," Darren says, trying to sound friendly, "you speak English, right?"

Zoey looks up from her book, her brow a little wrinkled. With his hands and arms, Darren tries to apologize. Or maybe he just begs. She goes back to the book.

3. WHATEVER THAT THING IS THAT'S ACTUALLY BETWEEN THE ROCK AND THE HARD PLACE

"Darren, man," Nate says, "tell Lady Z that she's kind of rude."

"Shut up," Darren says.

"What? I'm just trying to make small talk with her."

"No, you're not."

"Lady Z," Nate sings. "What is your secret?"

Zoey looks up from the book and does not appear pleased. Darren uses his hands, arms, shoulders, and face to communicate something along the lines of, *I'm sorry, I don't know what to do either.*

Zoey puts the book down, walks to the bathroom, and shuts the door. She doesn't slam it, but she doesn't not slam it either.

"I forgot to put the seat down, Lady Z, sorry!" Nate says.

"Dude," Darren says, and walks over to Nate. "You gotta stop it, seriously."

4. A NEGOTIATOR

"Hey," Nate says, more or less ignoring Darren. "How about a little Rock Band?" Nate nudges Kyle in the ribs with his foot. Kyle groans. "Kylie Boy, how about a little Rock Band?"

Kyle sits up.

Darren doesn't say anything, just looks at Nate and waits for an explanation.

"You know," Nate says, "maybe she's one of those 'I sing because I can't talk' type ladies."

"Maybe she'd talk if you weren't one of those 'I'm a giant douche bag' type guys."

"Go ask her what she wants to sing," Nate says.

"She's in the bathroom."

"So go ask."

Darren walks over to the door. "Zoey. Zoey. Hey. What do you want to sing on Rock Band?" No response, shocking. "Zoey, c'mon, come out." Darren turns back to the couch, which is now empty, since Nate and Kyle are getting ready to rock.

3 Plastic Instruments Nate, Kyle, and Darren Play While Intermittently Trying to Convince Zoey, Who Came Out during Their Second Song ("Manic Depression," Jimi Hendrix), to Sing with Them

1. Guitar (Nate)
2. Drums (Kyle)
3. Bass (Darren)

4 Remarkable Events That Occur Before They're Done with Rock Band

1. Zoey actually agrees to sing. She doesn't announce this, she just gets up off the couch and picks up the microphone. The guys laugh and holler like this is some kind of huge victory.

2. They actually find a song she's willing to sing. Which takes a long time, because Zoey says, "Whatever," in response to the first eleven suggestions they make. At which point they just toss the little catalogue/booklet thing at her so she can decide.

"'Precious'?" Nate asks when she shows him. "What the hell is that?"

"The Pretenders," Zoey says quietly.

"Don't know it," Kyle says.

Zoey looks at Darren, who asks, "Is it hard?" Zoey shakes her head no. Darren says, "YouTube."

Everyone goes to Nate's room to watch it on his computer, which has all these ridiculous stickers all over it. The guys nod their heads and every once in a while check out Zoey, who may be mouthing the words and almost smiling.

They listen to it a second time and then go back to the game.

3. Zoey actually sings. At first she holds back, but then it's like she starts forgetting to hold back, to the point that Darren realizes that she's heard this song at least one hundred times, and if he hadn't been in her car before she probably would have been singing some of those other songs, and definitely not holding back. He wonders if this somehow has something to do with why she's such a fantastic driver.

4. Zoey goes a little nuts at the end. More than a little nuts, actually. Because near the end of the song there's this "fuck off" in the lyrics (which the Rock Band people didn't even include in their version), but that Zoey definitely includes. Then she includes it more than once. And in this way, that involves her kind of ignoring the fact that everyone else is still playing the song. The next thing Darren knows, she's just screaming. It's maybe a little bit the kind of screaming that singers scream in certain kinds of punk or heavy metal songs, but honestly, it's pretty much just her screaming.

Darren stops playing and watches her as she keeps screaming. There isn't all that much to see, because she's got her back to him and the rest of the band. But she's definitely still screaming. She's not screaming any words, and she's not shrieking, either, the way you might expect a girl to if you told her to scream. She's just screaming, really throaty, and like she means whatever it is she's screaming. Eventually Kyle and Nate stop playing, but she keeps going for another few seconds, which feels like a very long time under the circumstances. Darren feels really bad for her throat.

Then she stops. And turns to them. And throws the mic at Nate. She doesn't hurl it at him, but she definitely doesn't toss it at him either. Then she goes back to the bathroom.

"Cool tune," Kyle says after she closes the door.

"Damn," Nate says. "Lady Z can bring it."

"No lie," Kyle says.

A few minutes later Zoey comes out of the bathroom. Darren is unable to find any trace of what just happened on her face, including in her eyes, even though she looks at him and must know that he's looking for some sign from her that all that just happened.

Darren walks over to her and says, "Hey."

Zoey stares right at Darren for a few seconds, like she's trying to decide if she should punish him or something, but instead she says, "Your brother."

"I know, but he's all right, you'll see, it's just that—"

Zoey takes a step closer and whispers in Darren's ear, "He doesn't have a mark."

7 Arrangements Darren, Nate, Zoey, and Kyle Form during Their Nine-Block Walk to Abu Adam

1. Kyle, Nate, Darren, Zoey
2. Kyle, Nate/Darren, Zoey
3. Kyle, Darren, Nate/Zoey
4. Kyle, Nate/Zoey/Darren
5. Kyle/Nate, Zoey/Darren
6. Nate, Kyle, Zoey/Darren
7. Nate, Kyle, Darren, Zoey

4 Highly Valuable Possessions Darren Would Be Willing to Give Up So That They'd Be Heading to Hill Auditorium, Where Their Band (the Planets) Would Be Scheduled to Play a Sold-out Show, with Kyle on Drums, Nate on Guitar, Zoey on Vocals, and Darren on Bass

1. His good name
2. His left nut
3. His actual bass
4. The approximately $3,800 still remaining in his bar mitzvah account

30 Questions Darren Would Like Nate to Answer for Him If They Were Different Kinds of Brothers in a Different Kind of Situation

1. What do you think of Zoey?
2. Is smoking cigarettes that bad?
3. Is smoking cigarettes better or worse than smoking pot?
4. Should I smoke with you later?
5. Will I?
6. And what about drinking?
7. Are you going to be high all day tomorrow?
8. Are you high most of the time now?
9. You aren't getting such good grades, are you?
10. Should I go here (if I get in)?
11. Do you think I'd get in?
12. If I don't get in here, where should I go?
13. Wisconsin?
14. Did you know Dad was gay?
15. What do you think about Dad being gay?
16. Do you ever think you're gay?
17. Do you ever think I'm gay?
18. If I were gay, would I definitely know it by now?
19. Is Dad being gay going to be a huge deal forever from now on?
20. Is that why Mom is the way she is these days?

21. How would you explain the way Mom is these days?

22. Do you remember that Mom and Dad are divorced or do you sort of forget about it most of the time you're up here?

23. Do you think about the fact that I have two beds and two dressers and two rooms and two places to remind me that Mom and Dad are divorced?

24. Why did Maggie Block do that to me this morning?

25. Do you think Zoey's parents have any idea where she is?

26. What do you think about all her piercings?

27. Are you happy?

28. Will I ever be?

29. Will you make sure the rest of this visit is fun?

30. Are things always going to be this way?

4 Dinners Ordered at Abu Adam While Darren Starts Getting This Weird Feeling Like the Evening Is Getting Away from Him, Something That Is Not Helped by His Dad Deciding to Text Him, Even If It Is Just to Say, *Hope Everything Is Okay up There. I'm Sure You're Busy, but Let's Try to Find Some Time to Talk Tomorrow. Love Ya.*

1. Falafel sandwich with hummus and extra tahini, cherry Coke
2. Chicken shawarma sandwich, cherry Coke
3. Falafel sandwich with hummus, cherry Coke
4. Falafel sandwich with hummus, no tomato, cherry Coke

8 Words Zoey Says during the Next Ninety Minutes

1. Yeah
2. Okay
3. Eleventh
4. It's
5. Okay
6. No
7. Maybe
8. Whatever

10 Relatively Unboring Five-Minute Stretches from the Three Different Mostly Super-Boring Parties the Four of Them Attend

1. 9:48–9:53 p.m.

They get to the first party, which is being held in a reddish-brownish house not that far from Abu Adam. The person who opens the door (Trevor?) smiles warmly when he sees them, plus he walks like a marionette while going back into the party. Inside there are only eight or nine other people, just sitting on couches, except for a guy who's teaching another guy how to juggle. Some indie rock song Darren doesn't recognize is playing not too loudly, plus there's a big plate of undercooked brownies on a really beat-up coffee table in the middle of the room. When Darren is introduced to the guy (Vin or Von) teaching the other guy (Cooper) how to juggle, Vin or Von catches all three beanbags, smiles a lot with half his mouth, raises his eyebrows, and says, "Wow, Nate Jacobs's little brother," as if meeting Darren is the most important thing that's happened to him all day.

2. 10:00–10:05 p.m.

The guy (Cooper) who was learning how to juggle (but wasn't getting any better and didn't really seem to be paying attention to Vin or Von) gives up, goes to the kitchen, and comes back with a few cans of beer, which he places on the table not far from the brownies. Nate picks up two and throws one to Darren. Darren catches the can, opens it, and takes a sip. It's really nasty. Just kind of bitter, and maybe spicy, too. He tries hard not to register this on his face, but if Nate's silently laughing expression is any clue, he didn't do a good job hiding his disgust. Still, he forces himself to take another half-dozen sips before giving up, which Zoey seems to notice, looking at him over her own can while taking a sip herself.

3. 10:19–10:24 p.m.

After his third brownie Darren goes to look for Nate, who he finds in the kitchen holding a different beer and talking to a girl in a purple turtleneck, tight jeans, and Uggs. Nate says, "Kimmy, meet my little brother, Darren, a fugitive from the law."

Kimmy smiles a big, toothy smile and says, "A fugitive, really?"

Darren doesn't exactly say anything, just sort of makes a weird face at his brother.

"Well," Nate says, "not from the law, more like from our parents."

Kimmy turns to Darren. "Oh, really?"

"C'mon, tell her," Nate says.

So Darren starts telling her, and she actually seems interested in his story, which he realizes *is* pretty interesting, but he can't explain it in any way that will make sense if he leaves out the parts about kissing Maggie and his dad being gay, neither of which he feels like getting into while keeping an eye on Nate and Nate's second beer. So he just mumbles something about a girl. Kimmy starts asking him questions about this "girl" (she puts her fingers up to make the quotes sign for some reason), but Darren has no idea what to say, because he'd have to lie if he's going to make him and Maggie sound like anything more than just making out all of a sudden in the band room, and he's just not up to lying right now. Plus Maggie's like a distant second in terms of girls who matter to Darren right now.

A minute into his story, which isn't going anywhere, Kimmy, still smiling, turns to Nate and says, "I think your brother is hiding something from me."

Nate, pretending to be insulted, sort of slaps her shoulder and asks, "Are you calling my brother a liar?" Kimmy pretends to be even more insulted, makes a sound (something between "uh" and "oh"), and slaps Nate back on his shoulder. Darren wonders if there are any brownies left.

4. 10:41–10:46 p.m.

On the walk to the next party, Darren asks Zoey (who is already smoking) if he can have one. She takes a cigarette out of her pack, puts it between her lips (so that she briefly has two cigarettes in her mouth), removes the cigarette she was smoking, and holds its lit tip up to the unlit tip of the new cigarette (which remains in her mouth). Once the new one is lit she passes it to Darren. Then they walk in silence together, smoking. He feels like he's getting better at it, and that Zoey can tell.

5. 10:59–11:04 p.m.

At the next party (which is actually in two different apartments connected by an outdoor stairway that cuts the building in half), Nate jabs Darren and says, "You see that girl?"

Darren says, "The one in the dark green jacket?"

"That's the one," Nate says.

"What about her?" Darren asks.

"Do me a favor," Nate says. "When you start fucking people, don't fuck her."

Darren feels a weird smile come over his face, so weird it sort of hurts his entire head. "Did you . . . ," he tries to ask Nate. But Nate is already walking across the stairway and into the other apartment, where he and Darren get in line for beer.

Right when they get to a shallow red tub holding a stubby silver keg, the girl in the dark green jacket comes up to Nate and says, "Hey."

Nate says, "Hey." Darren smiles at her cute, round face and big brown eyes. She smiles back the way you'd want someone to smile at you if you were the new kid in the cafeteria looking for a place to sit. Before Darren is done admiring her smile, Nate hands him another beer (which is even more disgusting than the first one). Darren shrugs his shoulders for her and follows Nate back into the first apartment.

6. 11:20–11:25 p.m.

Nate (calling Darren a pussy as he swaps his empty cup for Darren's mostly full cup) sort of pushes Darren in the ass toward a bedroom in the apartment that has the keg. He also sticks out his elbow and hits Zoey, who was standing just down the hallway from them and staring at a poster of a painting by Picasso or someone. "C'mon, kids," he says, "let's go." But they're not going actually, they're staying, or just going into a bedroom.

There's someone in the bedroom, maybe the person whose room it is, because the guy is just sitting on a bean-bag chair and doing something on Facebook. Nate says, "Hey Matt, is it cool if we smoke up here?"

Without looking up Matt says, "Cool it is." Nate sits down on the edge of Matt's bed. Zoey and Darren stand. She drinks from a red plastic cup and tries to tell Darren something with her eyes. It might be something along the lines of *I told you so.*

The walls are half-covered with posters of the old parts of what must be European cities, except for one poster of John Lennon giving the peace sign in front of the Statue of Liberty. Nate has a lighter and a wooden pipe in his hand that actually has a wooden cover on top that he pivots to the side, revealing some marijuana ready to be smoked. Darren can smell the plant from about two feet away.

The pipe and lighter are extended to him as Nate says, "The time has come, young Jedi." Darren almost giggles, takes the two items, and places the wooden pipe in his mouth, uncertain how much of it he should put in. The lighter doesn't light at first. Once it does (despite the angle and proximity of the whole thing to his face), Darren can see the green plant catching and soon feels the smoke, too much of it, taking over his throat. Yanking the pipe out of his mouth, he coughs uncontrollably, sending smoke everywhere.

Nate says, "Dude."

Zoey takes the pipe and lighter from Darren, who can't stop coughing. His eyes are watering, but he can still see Zoey smoking with much greater success.

Nate, just before receiving the pipe from Zoey, asks his brother, "You okay, champ?" Darren continues coughing, but less. Zoey exhales a thick cone of smoke in Matt's general direction. Nate says,

7. 11:26–11:31 p.m.

"Ready to try that again?" Darren may not be ready but nods in the affirmative, receives the equipment, lights the lighter quickly, inhales a tiny bit, and immediately exhales. Nate says calmly, "Yo, Spazologist, this isn't the Special Olympics." Zoey smiles a brand-new smile and maybe even nods her head in approval. Nate takes the pipe and lighter from Darren and says, "Sorry, Lady Z, not to jump my place in line, but someone here needs a serious tutorial. Okay," he says. "How to smoke up in six steps . . . no, seven. Please pay attention:

1. Put the pipe in your mouth. Like so.
2. Light the lighter. Ta-da!
3. Inhale, *gently*.
4. Crucial: Keep the smoke in your mouth [he says this and the next step like he's a ventriloquist, opening his mouth just a tiny, tiny bit].
5. Optional, but pretty crucial, too. Swallow some of the smoke.
6. Exhale.
7. Repeat.
8. Be high.

"Eight steps, okay?" Darren nods and tries, pulling off steps #1–4 and #6 pretty well. He waits for Zoey, Nate, and now Matt to do #1–6 (and Nate, and maybe Zoey, look to be taking care of #8, too) before doing #7 himself. He still coughs, but not as much, probably because his throat is a total and 100 hundred percent disaster by this point.

After #7 is done a couple more times, Nate asks, "How we doing?"

"Okay," Darren says.

"Yeah," Zoey says softly, her small eyes smaller than normal.

"Cool," Nate says, and directs them back into the party. "Nothing about this on your status update, Mr. Cook."

"Roger that," Matt says.

"Bye," Darren says. "Thanks."

8. 11:32–11:37 p.m.

Nate, Darren, and Zoey stand in the stairway between the two apartments. Darren tries to decide if he is high, unsure how he would know. "Nate," he eventually says, "how do you know if you're high?"

"If you have to ask," Nate says with a small grin frozen on his face, "you're not." Darren looks at Zoey, who is leaning against a wall with her eyes closed. He can't tell if she's okay or not. Maybe he should check to see if she's okay, but maybe he only thinks to do this because he's high, since of course she's fine, it's not like she's having trouble standing up or anything, she's just leaning against the wall with her eyes closed, what's the big deal?

"Does it not work sometimes?" Darren asks Nate.

"Was that your very first time, D?"

"Yeah," Darren answers, but not embarrassed. Nate places his hand on Darren's shoulder and squeezes it a few times, which feels remarkably good.

"Sometimes," he says, "the first time is sort of like just downloading the getting-high app."

"Oh."

"Then you've got to smoke another time to actually use it."

"Oh."

"No worries, little man," Nate says, sipping on a beer. "The night is still young." Darren looks at Zoey. She clearly downloaded her getting-high app sometime before tonight's party began.

9. 12:09–12:14 a.m.

Darren uses his app, which he can tell because he's never really thought about his tongue this much before. It's so thick and heavy. Not to mention: Someone actually invented carpeting. How in the world had that never occurred to him before? He has an enormous urge to look at the mark on his arm, but he doesn't, because part of him is terrified it will still be there.

10. 12:47–12:52 a.m.

Sitting on a couch high, Darren tries to not listen to the music, which is loud and heinous (like Dubstep but somehow even worse), only you can't close your ears. Nate just returned from getting another beer, which makes that like eight or nine beers at least. The house, which took forever to walk to, kind of looks like Bryce Cummings's house back in Chicago, which means big and not old and filled with low ceilings and puffy leather furniture. Being high is okay, but maybe just because this couch is probably the ninth-most comfortable couch in the entire Western Hemisphere. Darren wishes there were brownies nearby, but there are so many people dancing, there's no way he could go check without losing his spot on the couch, which would suck so bad he can't even think about it.

"Nate," Darren says, leaning his head most of the way toward Nate but not turning it at all.

"Huh," Nate responds.

"Dad's gay," Darren says, turning his face to Nate. "Isn't he?"

Nate scratches the side of his beard with his thumb, "Probably trending on Twitter by now."

Zoey is standing against a wall on the other side of the room, and if Darren leans to his right he can see her all the way. She's talking to a guy with a ponytail, though Darren can't actually tell if she's talking herself or just being talked to. The guy in the ponytail is probably a dick, because he has a ponytail. Though he does have a Windbreaker and hiking boots on, so maybe he's only a pain in the ass.

Darren would like to watch TV or have a snack or go to sleep. There are two girls dancing about three feet from him, and he wishes they'd take him out to breakfast tomorrow morning and tell him what their majors are and how swell college is and act like none of them were at any of these parties tonight. They seem nice, especially the one in tights who keeps doing disco moves while giggling.

Nate slaps Darren's knee and leans into him. What's weird

is that it makes more sense for Nate to lean into Darren than the other way around, because Darren is bigger overall at this point. Even though he's younger and always will be. And less wasted.

"Girls will like it," Nate says.

"Like what?"

"Dad," Nate breathes into Darren's ear. "Being all gay and everything." Nate seems to be snuggling into Darren. "Girls dig guys with gay dads."

What Darren would really like is some soup. Butternut squash, the kind his dad makes so well. Which may or may not seem more fitting now that his dad is gay. Either way, Darren would obviously need to eat it somewhere other than this couch. So maybe just some hot chocolate. Something for his throat. Something to drink.

"Hey, man," he says to Nate. "Can I have a sip?"

He takes a sip, and it's still horrible, but it does make his throat not hurt so much. What he'd like is this couch, reruns of "Family Guy," and a tray with a bowl of his dad's butternut squash soup on it. Or the two dancing girls at breakfast. But not dancing anymore, just telling him that of course they were planning on ordering Mickey Mouse pancakes too.

The guy with the ponytail is standing much closer to Zoey than he was just a minute ago. Zoey nods her head, but Darren can't tell what this means. He hasn't seen Kyle for at least an hour. There is a chance they're actually not that far from Nate and Kyle's apartment, because Darren has a really bad sense of direction and it's not like he knows Ann Arbor or anything. He'd bet the girl in the tights is an English major. If he had to bet. She's not very good at dancing, but she still seems to be having fun, which Darren admires.

Zoey must get in trouble a lot, unless her parents don't care anymore, which would be even worse. His parents still care, and that's both good and bad news right now.

The guy with the ponytail puts his hand against the wall, on a spot less than three inches over Zoey's shoulder. If Darren could shoot lasers out of his eyes, he'd vaporize the guy and his ponytail, assuming he could open his eyes wide enough to shoot his lasers.

"Can we go to sleep now?" Darren asks his brother.

"Help me up," Nate instructs him.

They get up with great difficulty and bisect the dancing girls, who Darren already misses. Nate is turning away from Darren, who bumps into people on his way to Zoey.

When he gets to her, he takes her wrist and pushes up her sleeve, revealing some of her design. "I knew it," he says, without even looking at the face of the guy with the ponytail, whose face he'll probably never see. "C'mon, time to go home."

"Okay, bye," she says to the ponytail. And then, a few seconds later, she whispers into Darren's ear, "This planet's lame."

4 Surprises That Nearly Redeem Tonight

1. Right outside the last party, Nate says, his speech slurred, "Darren, you've got to get us home—take my phone and GPS us, bro." After a lot of back-and-forth, Darren gets the address and discovers that they're only four and a half blocks from his brother's apartment. Nate has his arm around Darren, who holds up the phone to monitor their progress, making him feel like some sort of commando leader.

2. Zoey hums a song behind them. Pretty loudly. Not one that Darren recognizes, but it seems like a pretty happy song. After crossing a street, Darren pauses for a moment to adjust his hold on Nate, who may be more asleep than awake. He turns around and looks at Zoey, who keeps humming her song. She stops humming, opens her eyes wide, bares her teeth, and then giggles. For less than a second, Darren is able to recall exactly what Zoey looked like at her seventh birthday party, which he now definitely remembers attending, unless being high and exhausted gives you the ability to fool yourself into remembering a bowling party with a bowling-ball cake and a birthday girl with pigtails.

3. Stopping yet again to fix his hold on Nate, Darren notices some nocturnal animal, probably a possum, awkwardly crossing the street near the edge of a streetlight's illuminated circle. "Zoey, check it out," Darren says, pointing at it with his elbow.

"Huh?" Zoey asks.

"Over there," Darren answers, pointing some more.

Zoey finally sees it and exclaims, "Puppy!"

4. An orange camping tent has been erected in the middle of Kyle and Nate's apartment. Kyle is sitting cross-legged on their couch next to a sleeping bag, eating a bowl of cereal and watching one of the *Lord of the Rings* movies. Darren and Kyle make eye contact. "It was with the sleeping bags," Kyle says, and shrugs his shoulders. "You're supposed to air it out every once in a while, so, I don't know, guess you're camping out tonight."

3 Fictional Creatures Nate Sounds like While Puking

1. Chewbacca
2. Frankenstein
3. The Hulk

15 Confessions Nate Makes to Darren While Trying to Get Comfortable on the Dirty, Cold, and Arguably White Tiling of the Bathroom Floor

1. I don't study enough.
2. I don't even know what my major is right now.
3. I didn't fuck that girl Brittany. Just fingered her.
4. I puked on Tuesday, too. No, it was Monday. Or Tuesday.
5. Fuck, I don't remember.
6. Mom is always mad at me.
7. Shit, maybe it was both.
8. They think my major's Psych, but what am I going to do with that?
9. I don't know what Dad is. Other than gay.
10. I don't know what I want to be.
11. Psych just teaches you how fucked-up everyone is. What's the point of that?
12. You're way smarter than me.
13. I was going to try to hook up with Zoey, but I won't now. Promise.
14. I'm a bad brother.
15. I hate my beard with puke in it.

5 **Messages Darren Quietly Calls Out to Zoey from inside the Tent to Check If She Is Still Awake on the Couch, Though It Looked Like She Was Out Cold by the Time He Left the Bathroom and Helped Nate—Who Darren Sure as Hell Hopes Is Done Puking—Get into Bed**

1. Zoey?
2. Hey.
3. Zoey.
4. Good night.
5. Zoey?

1 Visitor to Darren's Tent during the Middle of the Night, Who Announces Her Arrival by Softly Pushing Her Head into His Side like a Kitten

1. Zoey Eve Lovell

6 Things They Do

1. KISS

But not much on the lips. Zoey is all about Darren's ear. She seems to be inflating him through this orifice, even though she's not actually blowing into it. It's just that his left ear hears and feels everything her mouth and throat are doing, and they're doing so much. For instance:

2. BREATHE

Very loudly. Zoey must be struggling to breathe. She keeps holding her breath for long stretches, and when she finally exhales, right into his ear, the air is so warm and moist that Darren can feel not just his ear, but most of his head, neck, and left shoulder turn that shade of white-orange-red your mouth turns when you put a flashlight inside it in the dark.

3. HUG

But it's different than regular hugging. Because a regular hug begins and then ends. And even if both people are agreeing to have a very tight hug, like when his parents dropped him off at the bus for that camp back when he was twelve, even then it's just a three-part thing. You start hugging, you keep hugging, you stop hugging. But now they're hugging and re-hugging and trying to out-hug each other. They're not stopping. At first Darren holds back a little, because he's so much bigger than Zoey that even with her on top of him he wonders if he won't hurt her if he hugs her as much as he can (and wants to). But then he notices how the harder he hugs her, the softer and deeper her breathing gets inside his ear. It's like the canal running between his ear and his brain is an extension of her throat, like he isn't just hearing her breath or feeling her breath, he can feel the tissue down in her throat making the breath, like Zoey's throat and Darren's ear are now the same thing. And the harder he hugs her, the more this is true, and he wants it to be more true than anything has ever been true, so he squeezes her with all his strength and she squeezes him back and breathes some more.

4. PUSH

Select a thigh and push. They are each wearing just T-shirts (actually, hers is a tank top) and underwear, so Darren notices how she's both soft and hard down there. And the hardness isn't only bone, though he feels some of that, too. Actually it's soft and hard and warm and damp down there, because of the sweat and whatever else is happening. His boner would normally have exploded right away, but this is so not normal, or maybe he's still high or maybe he was asleep and dreaming when it all started or maybe he's listening to her breath climbing up the mountain of his thigh or maybe her throat is ordering him to wait and he has no choice but to obey.

5. FINISH

But not just stop. When it happens, it's like his body is telling hers everything that his mouth has wanted to tell Nate for the past two years, like he's getting rid of all this stuff he's wanted to get rid of for so long. He finishes in his neck and shoulders and the place where his ribs meet right above his stomach and not just in the one obvious place. Plus her breath, right at the end, it reaches up and finds this impossible spot between yes and ouch. Like she's not exhaling or not only exhaling, but finding a way, for the first time since he saw her again at North High last year, to speak to him without trying really, really hard *not* to speak to him at the same time.

There's no way in a million years he'd be able to put into words what she's telling him (in part because he's busy telling her a million things himself), but when she says it (and when she pushes the hardest, despite all their slipperiness, she's pushed so far) it's like meeting all the Zoey Lovells who Zoey has been between the pigtails-bowling-party Zoey and the extra-holes-in-her-face Zoey. It's like hugging all the Zoey Lovells there ever were and ever will be, and this is why she can finally just tell him something without *not* telling him it at the same time, which must mean that this is what she's telling him: *I'm Zoey, I'm Zoey, yes, I'm Zoey Lovell, yes.* So he tells her the same thing, and for the first time in a long, long while he's grateful to be Darren Jacobs.

6. PASS OUT

3.
FRIDAY,
SEPTEMBER 26

5 Months That Have Passed

1. May
2. June
3. July
4. August
5. September, at least most of it

7 Reasons Darren Suspects Today Is Going to Be Great, Assuming Today Is Opposite Day

1. His nose, sinuses, throat, and maybe lungs seem to be filled with about four pounds of phlegm for the second day in a row.
2. Rachel Madsen likely sent him between one and forty-three messages on Facebook while he was asleep.
3. A certain math test for which he is not particularly well-prepared awaits.
4. Therapy with his dad and Dr. Schrier at three p.m., oh joy.
5. Shabbat dinner with his mom and (probably/maybe/who knows) Nate.
6. Rachel Madsen is coming to visit today.
7. Still no Zoey.

7 Days Since Saturday, April 26, That Darren Hasn't Thought about Zoey within the First Four Minutes of Waking Up, Not That He Understands What Was So Special about Those Days, When He Was Definitely Thinking about Her Before Breakfast Was Over Anyway

1. Thursday, May 22
2. Tuesday, June 17
3. Thursday, July 3
4. Monday, July 21
5. Sunday, July 27
6. Friday, August 8
7. Monday, August 25

4 Objects the Crumpled Kleenex Overflowing the Small Wastepaper Basket Sitting Next to His Bed Could Be Said to Resemble

1. A cloud, of the cumulus variety
2. A snowy mountain range
3. A human brain, if something was really wrong with it
4. Cauliflower, maybe

7 Cons That Ultimately Outweigh the One Rather Obvious Pro in Darren's Deliberations over Whether He Should Stay Home from School Today, Which Is Only a Half Day Anyway

1. He'll have to deal with his mom more if he stays home, since she'll be working here most of the day, which maybe wouldn't be so bad, except she'll come check on him a bunch, and then he might have to lie to her if he's actually not feeling that bad.

2. Staying home might preclude the possibility of doing something fun later today, and even though he's not really sure how fun it's going to be, there's probably going to be something with Rachel happening.

3. He'd probably wind up feeling worse, physically, than he would if he went to school, since he is definitely at least a tiny bit sick, meaning if he stays home he'll just act like a genuinely sick person and then feel like one too.

4. His dad might somehow find out (it's not really clear how that might happen, and it's probably not likely, but if Darren has learned one thing since his parents stopped being together, it's that you're a moron to think you can predict what's going to happen with

them). But he (his dad) would want to somehow do something about Darren's health, which would probably involve offering to bring soup by, which in general Darren wouldn't mind at all. In fact, it wouldn't be the craziest thing for him to offer, since back when they were just a regular family, it was kind of official that his dad would make soup for anyone who was sick (this somehow being the one thing his dad was way better at cooking than his mom). And maybe his mom would be fine with that, but maybe she wouldn't, and so then he'd get to listen to half of yet another disagreement and/or argument between them, one that (like a bunch of others) he'd be kind of indirectly responsible for them having.

5. He'd be around whenever Nate finally woke up, which would be so late it would bum Darren out a little bit by adding more evidence to the "I think my brother is a genuine slacker" argument. Plus Nate would maybe do something to piss their mom off for whatever reason, like play really loud music or make a mess in the kitchen and not clean it up.

6. He's got his first test in Algebra II/Trig today, and Mr. Cowens made it pretty clear in his nearly amusing, definitely intimidating way that it will be a very bad idea to miss this test. (His exact words were: "You may miss this test, conditional on a death. Your own.")

7. Staying home from school would be almost like a trap in terms of obsessing about Zoey, which for a few weeks there he thought he was done doing, but somehow things changed. On Yom Kippur of all days.

2 Decisive Acts Darren Performs That Make It Official He Will Attend School Today

1. Showers
2. Gets dressed, and not in sweats

1 Fairly Prestigious Center of Higher Learning Nate Jacobs No Longer Attends

1. The University of Michigan

3 Items His Mom (Sitting at the Kitchen Counter and Listening to Some Dude Rocking Some Serious Classical Cello) Is Touching or That Are Touching Her

1. HER MACBOOK AIR

Darren's mom is pretty much sponsored by Apple at this point. She's got two huge Mac monitors in her office downstairs, plus within like a day of whenever it comes out she's always got the latest iPhone. She's on to her third iPad (two regular and one mini—the company she's consulting with apparently gives them to her), but she claims not to like them except for when she's traveling (which is a lot).

But she's most into her MacBook Air. Some of her relationship with the thing is obvious: e-mail, music (classical or super lame pop music), *Huffington Post*, and even Facebook (Darren quickly averts his eyes and scrolls down frantically whenever one of her updates appears on his page). But some of it's not: these crazy work-related applications and software packages, a bunch of which are just black screens with small, colored fonts that kind of scare the crap out of him.

Every once in a while Darren will get on her computer to do something fast (very fast, because she gets visibly nervous whenever there's another human being between her and the thing, and because she also made it kind of clear—nicely, but still—that if he accidentally did anything to any of those weird, scary programs running, let alone the computer itself, her maternal instincts might be seriously compromised). Anyway, when he gets on he'll do that thing where you press Command and Tab at the same time to switch applications, and he'll see she's got about fourteen of them running at once, including five or six with icons he doesn't recognize at all.

2. HER COFFEE MUG
Filled with about two-fifths of today's first cappuccino. His mom has been a coffee drinker since, like, forever, and she would always order fancy coffee drinks whenever they went into a Starbucks. But at home, back when his dad was still in the picture, it had always been just regular coffee (with milk). But then, right after his dad moved out and she rearranged the kitchen, she went and got an espresso machine from Bed Bath & Beyond.

She used it for a while, though she complained (mostly just aloud to herself) pretty much every time that she wasn't crazy about the thing. Until one day she brought home a much nicer machine that she got at one of those kind of fancy and super boring stores that sell kitchen stuff (Williams-Sonoma maybe). She read the directions like she was about to deliver a baby. But ultimately she wasn't crazy about this one either. She even invited some seriously hipster girl (Jess, who was kind of pretty but had an extremely deep voice) from the local non-Starbucks café to their house so she could show his mom how to make a real cappuccino.

Apparently what Jess taught his mom was that it might not be a bad idea to get another machine, because about three weeks later a UPS guy knocked on their front door with a box from Amazon that weighed a ton. She and Darren took the shiny, silver thing (made by some company called Pasquini) out of the box very, very, *very* carefully. Jess showed up about thirty minutes later and then the two of them (Jess and his mom; Darren went upstairs but left his door opened, who knows why) set up the machine and talked about it like there was a Rolls-Royce in the kitchen.

Twenty minutes later Darren heard Jess say, "What do you say we fire this baby up, Brenda?" Three minutes later his mom said, "Oh my God!" and laughed. She then said "Oh my God" three more times, emphasizing a different word in the short phrase each time. Jess, meanwhile, said "I told you" after each "Oh my God." Darren subtly rushed downstairs, where, thankfully perhaps, he found his mother sitting across the room from Jess and licking some foamed milk off her index finger.

Not to mention, his mom can make some pretty insane hot chocolate with the thing.

3. HER LULULEMON OUTFIT OF THE DAY
Which is these black tights that end around her calves and a green pullover. Actually the tights have a green line running down the sides, and the pullover has a black stripe or two.

Meaning it's an ensemble of some sort. She's got three or four outfits like this, all from Lululemon (the one time Darren actually said the name of the store out loud, he felt so stupid he promised himself he would never do that again).

She's wearing it because after she drops him off at school, she'll go to the local athletic club to do Pilates or yoga or something. She works out in the morning, because California is still pretty much asleep then. It's a different class every day, and it's definitely every day. Darren guesses she looks pretty good, but he sort of tries not to think about this too much, since it's kind of obvious why she must be working out so religiously. Even though, thankfully, she still hasn't mentioned going out on a date with anyone or anything like that.

But the other reason she works out so religiously is that she does a lot of things religiously now. Like keep the house insanely clean (with a huge amount of help from Dita, who comes three days a week) and put together a menu for the whole week on Sunday (and then do a huge shopping trip Sunday afternoon). She's even got this crazy, elaborate, color-coded, magnetic dry-erase calendar on the wall by the fridge that she's constantly updating (and yes, there's a matching one on her computer). And yes, she expects Darren and Nate to take a look at it each morning.

In fact, what's weirdest is that she's practicing religion a little religiously too, these days. Nothing too crazy. She's not like any of those Jewish women with the wigs and stiff black skirts he sees over at the CVS on Howard. But she finds a reason to go to their synagogue a couple times a month, stopped eating pork and shellfish (Darren could give a shit about pork, but no shrimp at home was a major bummer), and on Fridays when he's with her, they "do" Shabbat.

And yes, today is Friday and today he's with her.

4 Ways in Which His Mom Acknowledges (or Has Recently Anticipated) Darren's Presence This Morning

1. There's a bag lunch, apparently already packed, sitting by the toaster.
2. She looks up from her computer and (somehow without stopping to type) gives him a very warm smile.
3. She says (after stopping to type), "Good morning, sweetheart."
4. There's a bowl, a spoon, a folded napkin, a box of rice milk, and a box of Peanut Butter Bumpers set up on the counter next to her.

2 Words Darren Needs to Say for His Mom to Realize That He's Super Stuffed Up, Which Causes Her to Detach Herself from the Laptop and Go Upstairs to Her Bathroom to Get Him Some Medication

1. Good
2. Morning

4 Things Zoey Didn't Do on Saturday, April 26, All of Which Darren Laments, Yet Again, as He Shovels Cereal into His Mouth

1. WAIT IN THE TENT, OR AT LEAST THE APARTMENT, UNTIL HE GOT UP

When Darren woke up late that morning, aside from being really confused about what he was doing in a tent and trying to figure out whether he should continue wearing his only pair of underwear (part of which was stuck to a spot right below his waist), he pretty quickly noticed that Zoey wasn't in the tent or even anywhere in the apartment. Including, thank God, his brother's bed. He was so confused, he checked his arm about three times to make sure the mark was still there and that he hadn't just dreamed the past twenty-four hours. But he hadn't, so he went out into Ann Arbor to look for her, wishing he had thought to get her cell number at some point. Not that there had ever been a particularly natural opportunity to do that.

He walked around campus and down all the major streets he could find, even though he couldn't come up with a single good reason for her to be hanging out in any of the many places he looked. But around the time he was about to give up, he saw her sitting in a café with Nate's laptop. Darren felt a number of very different things when he finally found her, because he just really wanted to see her and had slowly been realizing while looking for her that he was pretty crazy about her, but what was she doing in a café and why did she have his brother's computer and how stupid was Darren to let himself get crazy about someone like her?

2. BE AFFECTIONATE OR EVEN JUST NICE WHEN HE FINALLY FOUND HER

Still, he went inside and walked up to her table and just looked at her until she noticed him, which took about four seconds. This seemed about three and three-quarters seconds too long. When Zoey finally looked up, she just said, "Hey." Not nice or mean or welcoming or dismissive. She just said, "Hey." She didn't say, "Oh, hi, I'm glad you found me," or, "I was about to come back to the apartment; I only left because I figured I'd make a lot of noise and wanted to let you sleep," or, "I was just thinking about you," or, "I know I shouldn't have taken Nate's laptop, but I'm writing my parents a long e-mail explaining everything to them, and I couldn't really wait any longer to do that." And she definitely didn't stand up to kiss or hug him or reach out her hand with that awesome ring on it and squeeze the mark on his arm, which Darren suddenly realized he wanted so badly for her to do that he thought he might start crying right there in the middle of the café.

So Darren asked (because it was one way to not mention

any of the stuff that really mattered right then), "Why do you have my brother's computer?"

Zoey just looked at the computer, shrugged her shoulders, and mumbled, "I don't know." If she had said it like she actually felt bad, that would have been one thing. But she said it pretty much the way she might have said, "Whatever."

Darren was now sweating, because Saturday was warmer than Friday had been and he had been walking a lot and because, for some reason, he sometimes sweats when he's hungry, and he hadn't eaten a thing yet and it was already almost noon. None of which was helped by the fact that there was about a third of a poppy-seed bagel on a plate next to Nate's computer.

"You want it?" Zoey asked him, but not really offering it to him. It was more like she was wondering, "If I let you eat it, will you promise to stop staring at it like it's a one-hundred-dollar bill or something?"

So Darren looked up from the bagel and right at Zoey, in particular that spot on her top lip, which, again, unless he had dreamed up the whole thing, had spent part of last night attached to his left ear, something that he knew he didn't dream up, because about an hour earlier, after removing his underwear, he sat down on the toilet in Nate's apartment and (with great effort) bent his head down toward his left thigh. Which unquestionably smelled like, well, it didn't smell like his left thigh had ever smelled before.

It was hard for Darren, at that particular moment, to

know if he loved Zoey. And not only because he wanted to scream and maybe even grab her shoulders and shake her. But he most certainly loved that spot on her top lip, and not in the way you might say you love some small, beautiful thing like a butterfly or a cool signature. He loved that spot on her top lip because during the previous twenty-four hours or so, it was the place he had been storing everything else he liked and maybe even loved about Zoey. Meaning when he looked at that spot on her top lip, he was sort of seeing a bunch of things, including all sorts of stuff you couldn't even see, like her decision to join him and how she drew on his arm and the way she sang when she finally let herself sing and her smell and the sound she made into his left ear at the very end.

But all she did was say—she actually said this—"Your brother's got problems." Darren must have made a face that demanded an explanation, so she turned the laptop to face him, which was open to Nate's e-mail. Darren, who was still standing, froze a little bit more, so Zoey said, "He's on academic probation or something."

Darren finally convinced his arm to move, which he extended to forcibly close the laptop, the shutting of which made more noise than he expected. This noise allowed him to say, "What the hell?"

And she at least looked right at him for a second, but then she turned away and reached up for the piercing that went through her eyebrow.

Darren said, "Zoey." Which he said because he was pretty sure he had never said it in order to get her attention as someone he had a special tie with, and because he wanted to say it the way he maybe would have said it at the beginning of a long sentence about how amazing last night in the tent was and how, if she wanted to be, he would be psyched if she'd be his girlfriend. So he sort of half said her name that way, but he mostly also said it the way he would say "please," as in: "Please don't." Or the way you would say "hey," as in: "Hey, asshole, I'm standing right here."

Just then his phone rang. Darren knew by the ring that it was Nate. "Yeah," Darren said into his phone.

"Dude, where the hell are you?" Nate asked.

"In a café, just down the street," Darren answered.

"Hey, did you take my laptop, you tool?" Nate asked.

"It's here, yeah," Darren answered.

"Okay, wanker," Nate said, "why don't you and my laptop come back so we can come up with a plan?"

"Sure," Darren said.

"Hey," Nate said, "if Lady Z is there, bring her with you."

"Okay," Darren said, and ended the call.

Zoey stood up, grabbed her bag, and said, "I'm going to the bathroom."

Just before she turned away she looked at Darren, really looked at him for the first time that morning, so that he knew last night had happened and that she liked it as much as he did and that she wished she weren't such an absolute, four-alarm freak and that she was sorry about the laptop and so please wait until I come back because maybe not everything is lost.

3. JUST LEAVE ONCE AND FOR ALL, RIGHT THEN

Zoey took a step toward the bathroom, but suddenly turned around, took two steps toward Darren, and hugged him. Really tight. Plus her fingers raced up to the back of his head, and the next thing he knew she had pulled his ear down toward her mouth.

He could feel her lips moving against his right ear, but they weren't kissing him, at least not at first. It sounded like she was saying something, or at least starting to, because about three times he could swear he heard actual syllables. Things like "pleh" and "dar" and "yuh." The whole right side of his body sprouted goose bumps and he hugged her tight, so tight he could feel her chest heaving a little bit. Or maybe it was his chest, because he really felt like he was about to pass out by this point.

Then she did kiss him, in the ear, her breath perfectly warm, and it felt so good that he figured everything would have to be okay now. Because how could there be a world that allows that kind of kiss to coexist with anything even a little bit painful, including especially the feelings you have for the person giving you that kiss?

4. RETURN

After she let go and went to the bathroom, Darren sat down, ate the rest of the bagel, and opened the computer. And read a couple of e-mails and closed the computer. And studied the top third of the mark on his arm and thought about where they'd go for lunch and used his index finger to pick up all the poppy seeds that had fallen off the bagel. He assumed every sound he heard was Zoey coming back, meaning he looked up eagerly every two or three seconds. Until after maybe four minutes, when he picked up the computer and walked back to where the bathroom was.

But the bathroom, which was right next to a door leading out of the back of the café, was empty. Even though he knew there was no point, he opened the door and looked out into an alley, which seemed horribly empty and clean.

And that was the last time he saw Zoey.

3 Surfaces Coated with the Color Crimson That Briefly Converge Just Before Darren Takes Two Pills from His Mom and Swallows Them

1. His mom's mug
2. His mom's fingernails
3. The pills

2 Messages Darren Reads or Rereads in His Bedroom
Before Grabbing His Backpack and Heading Downstairs

1. Facebook message from Rachel Madsen: *Morning, Sweet Stuff! Can't believe today is the day!! I'll text u the second I get to Krista's! So excited!!!*

2. Message from Zoey, written in black ink inside the back cover of that *When Things Fall Apart* book: *Darren, I had to go. I'm sorry. But I didn't forget about together. It'll happen. It will. And then we'll go somewhere far away. I promise. Just don't change. I'm serious. Don't. —Z*

11 Questions His Mom Asks Him during the Six-Minute Ride to School

1. How are you feeling?
2. You sure you're up to going to school?
3. You ready for that test?
4. Do you want me to pick you up after?
5. What do you have planned for this afternoon?
6. A girl from camp?
7. Does she have a name?
8. Would you like to invite her over for Shabbat?
9. For the challah: Breadsmith or Harvest Time?
10. With or without raisins?
11. Do you know I love you?

4 Causes Explaining How It Is That Darren Almost Doesn't Recognize His Mother When He Looks at Her One Last Time Before Getting Out of the Car

1. She's getting older. There are some new lines around (and especially below) her eyes that he noticed when he came back from camp. They're most visible in the morning, maybe because of sleep and maybe because she doesn't put on any makeup before she works out.

2. Her workout clothes just really don't look like something she'd wear. Until, like, a year ago, she never really wore work-out clothes that are so obviously workout clothes. In fact, his mom used to not care a whole lot about what she wore in general, and now she's the kind of person who does, even or especially when she's exercising.

3. She's still his mom and everything, but between all her traveling and all the time Darren spends at his dad's, well, he can just sort of tell now that sometimes when they (Darren and his mom) are together, one or both of them kind of forgets about the whole mother-son relationship they supposedly share. Because they share it less regularly than they used to.

He first noticed this once when he got dropped off back

at the house after five days with his dad. The packing up of his stuff (again) and getting dropped off (again) and just kind of preparing himself to switch parental gears (again) bummed the hell out of him, so maybe he sort of decided to ignore his mom for a while. Which he could tell she noticed, and could tell upset her a lot. So he tried, in the future, not to do that to her.

But then the weird thing is that even though she never does exactly the same thing to him, he can still tell (because sometimes she just sort of stares off into space, or takes longer to answer his questions, or goes down some e-mail rabbit hole for an hour when she said it would only take ten minutes) that she's getting a lot of practice these days living her life without any kids around. And so Darren can tell she's been gradually learning how to do that pretty well.

She probably had some kind of whole life without Darren before the divorce and everything, but all the stuff that's happened since must have given her no choice but to make her without-Darren life much bigger. Who knows, maybe Darren just notices things better than he used to. All he knows is that sometimes, like right now, he looks at her and kind of can't believe she's his mother. Not because he thinks his real mom is somewhere else, hiding or whatever. More because somehow the whole thing just seems kind of unlikely at this point.

Or maybe there's a simple physical reason. Because since when is her hair almost reddish? And how did her teeth get so damn white?

4. He's over five feet seven now, so he looks at her from a slightly different angle than before.

13 Faraway Places He'd Like to Go to with Zoey Once They Finish Their Task

1. Paris
2. Barcelona
3. Rome
4. London
5. Brazil
6. The Galapagos Islands
7. Costa Rica
8. Alaska
9. China
10. Thailand
11. Tokyo
12. Wherever they have safaris
13. That planet they first came from

4 Places Darren Spent the Rest of That Saturday Back in April

1. NATE'S APARTMENT

Darren tried to convince Nate to help him look for Zoey for a while, but Nate was exceedingly hungover and Darren eventually had to agree that if Zoey didn't want him to find her, which she pretty clearly didn't, he wasn't going to. Nate had to take a nap after being awake for only about two hours, so Darren just spent a lot of the day on the couch, mostly screwing around with Nate's guitar, staring out the window, and feeling a little like he might puke.

2. CHINA PALACE RESTAURANT

Just before they were getting ready to go grab some pizza, there was a knock at the door. It was their mom, who had flown into Detroit and rented a car. She didn't seem mad or anything; in fact, she was so calm that Darren and even Nate were sort of powerless around her. The three of them went out to dinner, where they managed to talk about not a single thing of importance. Somehow, no one so much as mentioned their dad, thereby making him the gayest, most prominent ghost that had ever haunted that particular Chinese restaurant. Right from there Darren and his mom drove home. Nate just walked back to his place.

317

3. HIS MOM'S RENTAL CAR

Almost as soon as they got on the interstate she started asking Darren tons of questions, all of which together told him in no uncertain terms that she was pretty pissed about the whole thing. But she stayed calm, even after he made it kind of clear that he wasn't going to give her any long explanations about anything.

Darren fell asleep before they got to Kalamazoo but woke up around New Buffalo. Without moving, he stared at his mom for a while in the strange, shifting light coming from the car's interior and the occasional passing car. NPR was on, but he could tell she wasn't listening. He asked, "When did you know about Dad?"

She turned her head toward him and said, "Morning, sleepyhead."

"When did you find out?"

His mom looked back at the road. "Do you remember when you and Nate went to see that movie on Christmas? When he was back from school after his first semester? We had sushi and then you went to see a movie. Some comedy about drug dealers, I think."

"Yeah."

"That's when."

Darren sat up and kind of rearranged himself. This mostly involved trying to do something about his underwear, which unfortunately was starting to feel exactly the way you'd expect underwear that you've been wearing for thirty-six hours to feel. He tried to remember that weekend. What his mom was like. What his dad was like. But he couldn't remember anything being suddenly different about them. Or really anything about that weekend at all. Jesus, how the hell did she remember what movie they saw?

"You didn't know before?"

His mom put some hair behind her ear. "Not the way I knew after that night."

"What does that mean?"

But she didn't say anything for another five miles. Darren almost repeated his question about ten times, but something told him not to. Eventually she said, "I knew your father—" Her voice caught for a moment and Darren could tell she was crying, or trying not to cry. He tried to figure out which, but the light kind of sucked. All he could make out was the weird way she was holding her mouth, so he looked down at his knees. "I knew that he was . . . that he found some men attractive. I knew"—she cleared her throat—"other things."

Darren was trying to scrape a stain off the knees of his jeans, which might not have been a stain at all but just some sort of shadow. "What other things?"

"Nothing."

"What?"

"Darren, honey, you'll need to ask him about the details

of his past. I don't—" She was definitely crying now. "I don't really want to; I shouldn't be the one to do that."

"So, what, he was gay and then wasn't and now is again?"

"Not exactly. It doesn't work like that."

"Well then, how does it work?"

"It's complicated."

"Is it why you got divorced?"

She turned the radio off, even though it was barely audible to begin with. "Yes, in the end. Yes. But it wasn't . . . It wasn't exactly why we first got separated."

"What are you talking about? He told you on Christmas. You decided to get separated in March, I remember. He didn't move out until April."

His mom blew her nose in this weird way of hers that makes absolutely no noise. "We decided to get separated in November. We—"

"You did?" Darren put his feet up on the dashboard.

"Don't put your feet there."

"It's a rental."

"Please don't."

He kept his feet where they were. "Why'd you wait so long? To have him move out? And to tell us?" Now she started crying more. Or at least louder. He put his feet back down. "Why?"

"We already knew it wasn't working."

"What wasn't working?"

"Darren."

"What? What wasn't working?"

"A million things."

"Such as?"

But she didn't answer. Now he could see that her cheeks were pretty wet, so for a few minutes he decided to leave her alone.

"So then why'd you wait?"

She blew her nose again. This time it made noise. "Bugs had just moved that summer."

"So?"

"And we wanted to let Nate move out first."

"Why?"

Nothing.

"Why?"

"So—" She exhaled really loudly. "So he could be gone. So he wouldn't . . ."

Darren turned the radio on. Found a rock station that wasn't too static-y. Turned it up a bit.

A couple minutes later his mom turned it down. "I'm sorry, Darren," she said.

"Whatever."

"I'm so sorry about all of this."

He didn't say anything.

When they crossed into Illinois, his mom tried asking him questions, this time about him and his dad. Darren wasn't exactly forthcoming. He just answered "I don't know" to most of her questions. But maybe it wasn't really a matter of his being forthcoming or not. Maybe he really didn't know. Not what he felt about his dad's announcement and not who he planned to tell and not if he thought him and Nate would ever really talk about it. He also didn't know what he thought about the fact that he would have gotten, like, an 11 percent on a multiple-choice test about his own fucking family and its history over the past two years, assuming someone gave it to him before Thursday morning.

The other thing he didn't know (not that she asked him about it—how could she, seeing as how she knew pretty much nothing about it) was what it meant that his dad's love (if that's what it could be called) for men somehow led (even directly, maybe) to Darren's love (if that's what it could be called) for this one particular, recently disappeared girl.

They were back in Chicago by this point, and there were cars everywhere on the highway. They weren't in a traffic jam, but probably couldn't go more than fifty, either. Darren kind of felt how it might be easier to make sense of all this in a quieter, less crowded place. Like Ann Arbor, if Nate was someplace else and none of this weekend had happened there. Because he felt how he had no choice but to try to make sense of all this overwhelming stuff. Even though he had a hunch that he wouldn't really be able to.

What's weird is that there was almost something satisfying in knowing this. That he had to try and fail to make sense of everything. And that he'd have to do this for a while. It was almost like his life had a point now, even if it wasn't exactly the kind of point he would have wanted it to have back before he thought much about his life having a point or not.

4. THE HOUSE

The second they went inside, Darren said, "I'm super tired. I think I'm going to bed." Which wasn't a lie, because he could barely even stand up straight anymore. His mom said, "Of course," so he gave her a hug and said good night. She kissed his cheek, held him by the shoulders, looked up at him, and almost smiled.

Darren's first priority, once he got upstairs, was to take a serious shower, because he felt beyond nasty by that point. But about two seconds after getting under the awesomely warm water, he turned it off in a sudden panic. Because of his arm, which luckily only got a little wet. He quickly grabbed his towel, carefully dabbed at some menacing drops clinging to his forearm, and actually breathed a sigh of relief when he saw that the design hadn't been ruined at all.

The next thing Darren knew, he was—despite being naked—on his hands and knees, rummaging through the cabinet under the bathroom sink. It took him a while, but he located a bag of cotton balls and a couple of rubber bands. Thirty seconds later, the cotton balls had been liberated from the bag, the bag had been pulled over his forearm (Darren used his teeth and fingers to rip open a hole in the bottom of the bag), and the rubber bands had been enlisted to keep the barrier in place. Though the bags and rubber bands would change, Darren would, with religious devotion, employ such a system all the way into June.

After his shower, Darren sat down in front of his computer and logged on to Facebook. Zoey had a page, including one with a picture of her that showed almost a full third of her face (but not the third with that spot on her lip). Darren just sat there opposite the screen and that picture for a few minutes. He maybe nodded off for a minute or two. Plus he kept staring at the design, which he would spend approximately seventeen hours in total doing during the next six weeks (by which time it somehow faded all on its own, despite his efforts to preserve it). Darren felt a little squashed by a vague conviction that being heterosexual, assuming the term does indeed describe him, isn't exactly a walk in the park, despite it probably being way easier overall than being gay.

Zoey had the privacy settings in place, so all he could do was try to add her as a friend. Plus send her a message. He wrote, *Zoey, Where are you? I'm back home, my mom*

picked me up. I hope you're okay. Please call or something.
And he left her his cell number. And, for some reason, his street address.

He wrote her once the next week and twice the next month. She never friended him, though. The picture of her there made him crazy, in part because her hair was all one length in it, which made her look even more beautiful.

7 Labels Darren's Schoolmates Might at This Point Assign to Him, Seeing How He Pretty Much Gave Up on Finding a Replacement for Bugs, Doesn't Really Talk Much to Anyone, and Usually Eats Lunch in Mr. Keyes's Office, Where the Two of Them Don't Really Talk a Lot but Just Listen to Old Jazz Albums Instead

1. Freak
2. Loner
3. Creep
4. Loser
5. Weirdo
6. Nut job
7. Reject

4 Experiences He Bets Feel Somewhat Like How He Feels Sitting in the Back of History Class as the Medication and His Respiratory System Battle It Out for Control of Darren Jacobs

1. Being really high at four in the morning
2. Floating in outer space
3. Deep-sea diving in one of those old suits that include a spherical metal helmet
4. Having your brain and sinuses replaced by straw but somehow not dying

17 Days That Passed Before Darren Found the Note Zoey Left Him, Which He Only Found When He Was Cleaning His Room (at His Mother's Request/Demand) and Dropped *When Things Fall Apart* in Such a Way That It Landed with the Cover Kind of Bent, Because Otherwise He Never Would Have Even Noticed It at All

1. April 26
2. April 27
3. April 28
4. April 29
5. April 30
6. May 1
7. May 2
8. May 3
9. May 4
10. May 5
11. May 6
12. May 7
13. May 8
14. May 9
15. May 10
16. May 11
17. May 12

1 Corporate Symbol Darren Feels a Bit Like Today

1. THE MICHELIN MAN

The guy that's made just out of those white tire-looking rings. Which is weird, because lately he's been feeling like less of a fatty. Even though he still feels like a bit of a fatty from time to time. But not Michelin-man fatty.

Must be the cold, or whatever this is.

8 Facts about Rachel Madsen and Darren's Possibly Ongoing Relationship with Her

1. THEY MET AT GREEN RIDGE CAMP FOR THE ARTS IN NECEDAH, WISCONSIN

After the whole thing in Ann Arbor, his parents (even though they were obviously divorced) still managed to agree that it was time to get a little stricter about stuff. Like how late he could stay up and if it would ever be okay for him not to answer his phone when they called to check in (it would not be) and that the time had come for him to wash that thing off his arm already (though Darren refused this last one). Plus, they basically just told him (his mom told him, but said both of them had decided this together) that he had to go away to camp this summer.

Darren put up a pretty big fight, saying kids his age don't go to camp, but still, he could tell almost right away there was no way he was going to win this one, because his parents had somehow anticipated this response and had, like, five names of kids he knew who did go. But at least they gave him a choice, so he chose Green Ridge, because its session was shortest and because he'd get to play music there and because it was really, really expensive.

As it turned out, the camp was actually all right. Most of the kids were kind of weird and nerdy, but being all alone together out in the middle of Wisconsin sort of made this not matter, kind of like how it feels during ensemble rehearsal, but times about two hundred. Darren was probably one of the coolest kids there, mostly because he really didn't give a shit about anything by that point.

2. SHE PLAYS PIANO.
She's pretty good, even if she's mostly into classical. Also, she has big green eyes and super straight light brown hair, and other than an extremely loud laugh that always makes her blush, she was pretty shy, at least at first.

3. THEIR RELATIONSHIP STARTED BECAUSE OF A VISITING CELLIST
One day after lunch, Jackson Yates, a drummer from his bunk, said, "Hey, man, I heard that Rachel Madsen thinks you're cute." The next night some big-deal cellist from New York flew out to give a recital, so Darren tried to sit near Rachel. And he could tell by the way she kept looking at him all the time that Jackson was right.

So then he went up to her at snack after the recital and asked her what she thought. She seemed really happy that he asked (she said the recital was *amazing*) and sort of glanced quickly over at a friend of hers, who smiled and disappeared instantly.

4. THEY HOOKED UP INSTEAD OF WATCHING *DRUMLINE*

The next night was movie night, because that's what Sunday nights always were. They'd show them some movie with a lot of people playing music in it, even if most movies with a lot of people playing music in it come across as really stupid to actual musicians. Anyhow, that Sunday the movie was *Drumline*, which Darren had seen parts of about twenty-five times on cable, and he was strangely kind of excited to have an excuse to see the whole thing straight through.

But then this girl Krista, the one who smiled at Rachel and disappeared, came up to Darren after dinner and said, "In *Drumline* tonight, when the main character makes a one-on-one challenge, go behind the piano building." Darren just looked at her confused, so she repeated her instructions and added impatiently, "Rachel will be there."

So he did as she said, in part because the movie turned out to be better if you didn't watch it straight through. Sure enough, Rachel was waiting behind the piano building. She even had a sleeping bag in her hand. She said, "Hi."

Darren said, "Hey." Then he started trying to think of things to say. But she just turned around and started walking back into some trees. He followed and they soon got to a small hill that was pretty flat at the top. Darren was still trying to think of something to say, when she started kissing him. Within about a minute they were down on the sleeping bag, making out. Unlike the times with Maggie and Zoey, Darren thought it might make sense not to go crazy all at once. So he just kissed her a lot, and he could taste how she had definitely brushed her teeth within the past ten minutes, probably more than once. Her tongue was almost too soft, but she licked his teeth a couple times, which he thought was kind of cool.

After about two minutes he figured it would be okay to touch her boobs, which were small and pretty hard. Two minutes after that he went under her shirt, and two minutes after that she sat up and undid her bra. Watching her do this (it was dark out, but the moon was almost full) definitely woke up his boner all the way, but he still managed to avoid humping her thigh for real.

5. SHE WASN'T SHY ABOUT EVERYTHING.

They kissed for a while, until Darren stopped to adjust his weight (the ground was hard and his left arm had pretty much fallen asleep). Then, just before they started kissing again, she said quietly (this may have been the first full sentence she ever said to him), "If you want to, you can kiss them."

She made her offer so politely that he almost felt like it would be rude to decline, not that he had anything against kissing her boobs. So he lifted up her shirt and saw her boobs, which were the general size of Hostess Ding Dongs (though rounder, of course) and (in the moonlight) incredibly pale. He started kissing them, especially the nipples, which seemed to be light brown.

Even though it was a pretty fun thing to do, kissing a girl's boobs after being invited to kiss a girl's boobs (not to mention licking and sucking them, which he wasn't officially invited to do but figured was probably allowed anyway), he mostly just noticed how much they tasted like soap, like she spent that afternoon diligently cleaning her boobs in the shower, and not the way actual women with giant boobs clean their boobs in the shower in movies (when the point isn't really cleaning them so much as looking extremely sexy).

Plus, he just wasn't getting the feeling Rachel was enjoying whatever it was he was doing to her boobs that much. It's not that she was suffering or anything, but the way she just lay there and played with his hair (slowly and gently and steadily) like nothing all that interesting was happening, even though he was kissing her boobs and everything, sort of reminded him of how she sounded on the piano, which was like she'd rehearsed a ton but just wasn't all that great in the end.

6. SHE ASSUMED THAT THEIR *DRUMLINE* RENDEZVOUS MEANT SOMETHING.

The next day at breakfast she came up to him with this sweet smile that made him realize she now thought he was her boyfriend, which seemed like a pretty reasonable assumption on her part, but that didn't excite him all that much. Still, he tried, because she was nice and laughed easily and let him kiss her boobs three out of the next four nights.

7. THERE WAS MORE TO COME.

The following Sunday (without any warning and when most everyone else was watching *Once*, which Jackson Yates said was pretty solid), she placed her hand on his boner (over his pants). A minute later he turned over on his back and helped her unzip his shorts.

It had never occurred to him how good he had become at giving himself a hand job or how bad someone else could be at it. The only way he enjoyed it at all was by reminding himself of what, in general, was happening, because the hand job itself was actually quite painful. Much too much friction, and a good bit of yanking, too.

8. BEING WITH RACHEL DIDN'T MEAN STOPPING THINKING ABOUT ZOEY. IN FACT, IT WAS KIND OF THE OPPOSITE.

It was at this moment, when he was sort of both trying and not trying to concentrate on what was happening, that he thought of Zoey. It wasn't that he had entirely stopped thinking of Zoey before then, but something about being in the middle of nowhere in Wisconsin with tons of new people had a little bit finally knocked her out of the center of his head, where she had sat stubbornly for the last couple months. But now she was back in a major way. Which doesn't mean he said a word to Rachel about her, or even really felt that he should.

And it also wasn't so much that he was thinking, *Wow, if*

I could replace Rachel with Zoey, this would be more enjoy-able (though it probably would have been), it was that—it was hard to make sense of it, exactly—he suddenly missed Zoey in a way that made him wish he could just fall asleep for a very, very long time.

The rest of camp, even though it included two much better hand jobs with hand moisturizer (Rachel's idea) and a pretty excellent jazz trio concert the last night, wasn't all that much fun, because (in addition to not really knowing what to do with Rachel or why he didn't like her more) he realized that as far as Zoey was concerned, Green Ridge Camp for the Arts was like an island prison. Wherever Zoey was, there just wasn't any way she was going to show up here.

10 Diversions Darren Explores While Killing the Last Twenty-Five Minutes of Mr. Cowens's Exam, the Results of Which Are Not Going to Be Pretty

1. Counting the number of *X*'s on the exam (twenty-seven)
2. Blowing his nose
3. Staring at the thin line of Megan Brougham's pink underwear that becomes visible whenever she leans forward to write an answer
4. Watching the clock until he's pretty sure he can see the minute hand moving
5. Using his pencil to trace the initials (*A.R.; D.D.; K.M.*) engraved in his desk
6. Closing his eyes and listening to the sounds of learning
7. Staring at his forearm, wishing the design was still there, and tracing out parts of it with his pencil from memory and wondering, yet again, just how likely it is that he will one day walk into a tattoo parlor with all the pictures of it he keeps on his phone and his hard drive and pay a professional to redraw it on his arm, permanently this time.
8. Observing Mr. Cowens as he tries to remove a stain from his tie, which, even spotless, would be an astonishingly ugly tie

9. Concluding, through the process of elimination, that no more than four people in this room (excluding Mr. Cowens) will ever have any use for the material covered in this exam

10. Envisioning possible scenarios involving Rachel later today

10 Albums Mr. Keyes Has Played during Lunch That Darren Hopes to Hear Again

1. Duke Ellington, *Money Jungle*
2. Bill Evans, *Waltz for Debby*
3. Joe Henderson, *Page One*
4. Wayne Shorter, *Adam's Apple*
5. Art Blakey and the Jazz Messengers, *Moanin'*
6. Horace Silver, *Song for My Father*
7. Herbie Hancock, *Maiden Voyage*
8. John Coltrane, *My Favorite Things*
9. Charles Mingus, *Mingus Mingus Mingus Mingus Mingus*
10. Miles Davis, *Cookin' with the Miles Davis Quintet*

1 Place, 1 Person, and 1 Idea, All Directly Tied to Zoey

1. THE PATIO

After math Darren goes down to the Patio. It's not his first visit to the place since he asked Zoey to drive him to the El way back in April. Closer to the tenth time at least, if Darren had to guess.

Because once a whole week had passed without Zoey showing up after the Ann Arbor thing, Darren thought he was going to die. But he figured if anyone knew what had happened with Zoey, it would be the citizens of Patiostan. He wasn't too eager to go down there, but he was even less eager to keep googling her name every day, just to see if she was dead or something. So he went down to the Patio in early May sometime to look for Derek Schramm. This was even before he found Zoey's note.

Derek was playing with a silver metal lighter, flicking it open and closed. Flicking it open somehow caused it to light. Derek flicked it open again, showed Darren the flame, and said, "No idea, dude. You should ask

1. GRACE PEARSON—

they were pretty tight."

But the next period was about to start, so Darren had to wait until after lunch, when he went back down there and found Grace, who had long silky hair but was kind of gross-looking in general. She offered him a cigarette, even though he hadn't asked for one.

"Do you know what happened to Zoey?" Darren asked.

Grace turned her head away from him quickly, looked around, and lit her cigarette. Then she exhaled her smoke really hard. "Her parents sent her somewhere."

"Where?" Darren asked.

"I don't know"—Grace turned back to him—"some kind of hard-core boarding school probably." Then she squinted her eyes, which seemed to Darren like a twitch maybe.

"How do you know?" Darren asked.

"She texted me, but just one time, real early in the morning before I was up, but then that was it."

"What did she write, exactly?"

Grace reached into her enormous bag, which hung open and seemed to contain about three hundred objects no bigger than a pack of cigarettes. She dug around in there for a while and eventually pulled out her phone. After pressing a bunch of buttons, she passed it to Darren.

Parents are shipping me to New Mexico crazy farm fuck me. That was all it said. The text had been sent at 6:32 a.m. on Wednesday, April 30. Just seeing her name on Grace's phone made his hands shake a little.

"Can I take her number?" he asked Grace.

"Go ahead," she said, "but don't bother calling. Wherever they put her, she probably can't have a phone there." Grace looked over his shoulder and maybe mumbled, "Oh shit." Then she took a drag and said, "That's how it was with Miles Fagen, anyway."

So at least he finally had Zoey's number. He texted her, pretty much right away, *Hey its Darren this is my number call if u can hope ur okay.* And every once in a while he would just look at her name and number in his phone. Her number has four sevens in it, which Darren likes.

He even went back down to the Patio a few more times the next week and the week after that, in part because he sort of convinced himself that a good detective keeps snooping around until he finds more information. And also because Grace would always give him a cigarette, and so sometimes he would smoke one by himself on the way home from the bus. But other than the second time he talked to Grace, when she sort of clarified a few things for him, all he found out was that she definitely has a twitch and that most of the people on the Patio are actually kind of nice. Meaning it was probably a good thing that the school year ended not much later, because otherwise he'd be an actual smoker by now.

Still, every once in a while, like today, he goes down to the Patio. Partly to check in with Grace and partly because even though he doesn't exactly feel like he belongs with the Patio crew, it's easier not to belong there than it is not to belong in all the other places at school he doesn't belong. Plus today is a good day to go down there, since his cold will keep him from wanting to smoke, which otherwise he'd really like to do. Plus Grace is always nice to him.

"What's up, Grace?" he asks, sitting down next to her on a cement bench.

"Chilling," she says.

Darren nods. He still hasn't told Grace about the note, he's not sure why. Even though he plans to. "Any word from Zoey?"

Grace smiles, looking almost a little disgusted. "Jeez, you're mental over her, aren't you?" He shrugs his shoulders and sniffles. "You totally are."

Apparently, today's the day. "She left me a note."

"What are you talking about?" Grace appears deeply skeptical.

"In Ann Arbor. Before she took off or whatever. She wrote it in this book that was in my backpack."

"A book," Grace says. "What kind of book?" He hesitates before answering, not ready to reveal that particular detail. "Never mind, what'd the note say?"

Darren wipes his nose on a part of his left sleeve just below the shoulder. "It was mostly personal stuff."

"Duh," Grace says. "But, like, what kind of personal stuff?"

"Just that she, I don't know," he tries inhaling through his left nostril, "likes me. Pretty much."

"Pretty much?"

"I don't remember."

"Liar. You've probably memorized the thing."

"Maybe." He smiles.

"You are a freak," Grace says, with approval and emphasis on the verb of being. "No wonder she likes you."

"But so you still haven't heard anything?"

"You know"—Grace takes out a pack of cigarettes and starts banging them against the palm of her hand—"you should

1. WRITE HER A LETTER,

like an old-fashioned letter. You totally should."

"And send it where?"

"Give it to her parents, they'll know how to get it to her."

The bell for the next period sounds. He's already late. "Have you done that?"

"Nah." Grace stands up, while her right eye slams shut. "Her parents seriously hate my ass."

2 Text Messages from Nate

1. *Come back here after yur weakass half day. We can jam rocknroll style.*
2. *Swing by super burrito. Just called in our order. Under the name Sergeant Jose Morales III.*

5 Claims Grace Made about Zoey and Her Parents the Second Time Darren Went down to the Patio, Some of Which Seemed More Credible Than Others, but All of Which Together Clarified Something Important for Him, Even If He's Still Not Sure Exactly What the Name of That Clarified Thing Might Be

The second time Darren went down to the Patio, he had a pretty clear goal in mind: find out what exactly was wrong with Zoey. Because people don't just take off to Ann Arbor, run away to who knows where from there, and then wind up in a hard-core boarding school, all for no reason.

Of course, asking someone that kind of question, especially if you barely know that someone, isn't the easiest thing in the world, so at first he just smoked his cigarette. Until he decided it was time to be bold.

"Grace," he said.

"Huh?"

"What," Darren said, and took a long inhalation, either because he was trying to stall or because he sort of sensed that this is something cool and courageous people do in movies when they're smoking and about to say something important. Only he didn't feel very courageous, and not all that cool, either. "Why," he started asking instead, "do you think they sent her away? I mean, I guess she took off and everything. But still."

1. "Yeah," Grace said, "her parents, they're pretty hard ass, you know?"

"Yeah," Darren said, even though he didn't.

2. "They told her, I don't remember when exactly, like a few weeks ago," Grace said, and kicked at something nonexistent with the tip of these ankle-high suede boots she was wearing. "It was after she burned a little hole into some fancy leather couch they have. Not even on purpose. They told her something like"—Grace put up the index and middle finger on each hand and said in some kind of weird voice that must have been her imitation of Zoey's two parents together, an imitation that was kind of hard to make out, because she was still holding a cigarette in her lips—*"one more thing, Zoey, and that's it."*

"One more thing?"

"Or something like that. You know, like she was out of warnings."

"But what'd she do before then?"

"I don't know, not that much," Grace said. Darren was pretty sure this couldn't possibly be true and sort of wanted to say as much, but he didn't want to sound like he was siding with Zoey's parents, so he kept quiet, half trying to figure out how to express his skepticism and half trying to figure out what else Zoey might have done to make her parents so mad.

No one said anything for a little while, so Darren just sat

there, scratching at his elbow, which had started to itch like crazy for no reason.

3. "Look." Grace started speaking again. "Her parents, they just decided, like a long time ago, that she's this problem."

"What kind of problem?" Darren asked quickly and quietly. Grace didn't answer. "I mean"—Darren felt the words coming out, wondering if he might want to stop them—"what's wrong with her, anyway?"

"What?" Grace said, making a face like he said something so stupid that it actually smelled bad.

"Nothing, nothing," Darren said, wishing he had a time machine that operated in ten-second intervals.

"Did you just ask what's *wrong* with her?"

"No, forget it."

"I mean, are you serious?" Grace said, her voice super pissed. With no time machine nearby, Darren resorted to shoulder shrugging as some kind of hopeless backup strategy. "What, like do you want to know if she has ADHD or is on meds or cuts herself or has to go to therapy nine times a week?"

"No," Darren said defensively, even though he wouldn't have minded knowing those things.

"Because that sure made everything better," Grace said super sarcastically.

"What did?" Darren asked, relieved that Grace was still talking to him.

"Oh, you know, every time they switched her to a new therapist so they could diagnose her with something else." Grace kicked at that spot again.

4. "Last year it was Oppositional Defiance Disorder. Yeah, right. Whatever."

"Oppositional Defiance Disorder." Darren had to say the words himself, though he made sure to sound like he was saying them with disapproval.

"How about," Grace said, her face freezing up for a moment, "how about My Parents Suck Disorder? Or no, how about All This Stuff Is Actually Making Things Worse Disorder? How about Why Can't Anyone Just Leave Me Alone Disorder? You know?"

"I Was Born into the Wrong Family Disorder," Darren mumbled, feeling some kind of new smile cut across his face.

"I mean, who doesn't have that?" Grace asked, and actually smiled.

Darren nodded.

5. "She's just Zoey," Grace said, sounding almost relaxed all of a sudden. "She's complicated, okay? That's it. Everyone's always telling her what she is. Especially her parents. Like that's going to help anything. You're this, you're that." Grace exhaled loudly through her nose. "She's Zoey, that's all. You know?"

He didn't know, but he sure as hell wanted to. Darren felt like he was done smoking and for some reason elected to separate his fingers until gravity could finally have its way with his cigarette. Though it wasn't surprising in general, there was something unlikely about the way the thing fell straight to the ground, where it continued smoldering even after he went off to continue his high school education.

6 Possible Scenarios Involving Rachel Today

1. Darren pretends or actually gets too sick to see her at all.

2. Darren gets dropped off at Krista's. They hang out there. A couple of other kids show up. Darren and Rachel sneak up to Krista's room. He gets an HJ.

3. Darren gets dropped off at Krista's. Rachel is so happy to see him, she almost starts crying. Darren feels kind of good to see her for some reason. She whispers in his ear that she missed him so much and really just wants to see him (and not Krista) this weekend. So he invites her over for Shabbat dinner. She accepts. It's nice. Her and his mom totally hit it off, even if Rachel isn't Jewish. After dinner his mom goes to synagogue. Nate disappears somewhere. They listen to music (he lets her choose) and talk about all sorts of stuff. By 10:24 p.m. Darren is no longer a virgin, and Zoey is in his life's rearview mirror.

4. Darren gets dropped off at Krista's (after Shabbat dinner, which Rachel didn't come to). Krista's parents are nowhere to be found, but about twenty-five other kids are. Krista's parents have a well-stocked liquor cabinet. By 10:24 p.m. Darren is sitting right outside the upstairs bathroom, listening to Rachel puke up deep-dish pizza.

5. Darren meets Rachel and Krista at Old Orchard Mall. The mall is lame, Krista is lame, Rachel is lame. She wants to hold his hand, which just feels stupid for some reason. He starts pretending that he is sicker than he is. Gets picked up. Spends the rest of the evening figuring out how to not have to see her again while she's in town, as well as how to officially (and finally) break up with her.

6. Darren meets Rachel and Krista and like eight other kids at a bowling alley. Rachel is nice but not that nice. After they return their shoes, Rachel walks him over to the air-hockey machine, where she tells him she has a boyfriend back in Minneapolis. They French-kiss one last time, who knows why.

3 Items on Nate's To-Do List for Today, According to Nate

1. Rock out a little bit with Captain BassMaster, a.k.a. Little Brother, a.k.a. D. Jakes
2. Look for a job. Hooray!
3. Something, anything, other than go to therapy with Dad

6 (or Maybe Just 4) Advantages to Having Nate Around

1. He makes Darren laugh a lot.

2. Sometimes they'll do stuff together on the weekends, like go bowling or see a movie or drive to some cool neighborhood in the city and just walk around.

3. About once a week or so Nate will come up to Darren and for no reason call him a "monster" or a "total beast" or an "imposing physical specimen" and then sort of force Darren to wrestle. Not exactly wrestle, more like grapple. Just their hands and arms and stuff. Which is somehow fun and sort of feels good, partially because Darren is definitely stronger than Nate overall at this point, even though Nate's hands are crazy strong.

4. They jam a couple times a week and will probably put Oblivion back together as soon as Nate finds a drummer who doesn't totally bite.

5. Nate makes it so Darren doesn't have to be alone with their mom or dad so much. Though this one can be a disadvantage, too, since Nate isn't a minor anymore, meaning he can totally ignore all the custody arrangements that apply to

Darren. Plus, Nate can be pretty difficult with both of their parents, meaning that sometimes it's actually better when he's not around.

6. In some ways, Nate is the one person in the world (maybe even including Zoey) who Darren most wants to be with, meaning when Darren heard that Nate had to leave U of M he was kind of psyched at first. And sometimes just having him around does feel good. But it's definitely pretty complicated, too.

Because, for instance, on the day Nate finally came home for good, he and their mom had about nine different fights, the last and biggest one of which was about some new "rules" she said that she and Darren now follow (even though Darren had never heard of them). When the fight was over, their mom left Nate's room, stormed down the hall, slammed her door, and didn't come out again until the next morning. Nate fell back onto his bed, put his pillow over his face, and shouted into it, "I fucking hate my life!"

Darren laughed a little when Nate did this, but when Nate removed the pillow and sat up quickly, Darren got a really good look at his face and somehow realized right away that it actually wasn't funny at all. And so having Nate around can also be a disadvantage, because the new Nate can be kind of lame compared to the old one.

4 Questions His Mom, Who's in the Middle of a Conference Call, Writes Out on a Notepad When Darren Comes Down to Say Hi to Her

1. *Feeling any better?*
2. *Dinner 6:30 okay?*
3. *Tilapia or salmon?*
4. *Want to invite anyone?*

4 Answers Darren Writes on This Same Notepad

1. *Not really*
2. *Sure*
3. *Tilapia*
4. *No*

2 Bits of Advice Nate Gives Darren about "the Ladies" While They're Tuning Their Instruments

1. You should rock that Rachel girl's world. Because it's pretty clear that honey is coming all the way from the Twin Cities for some sweet loving. Like how many dudes your age are there in Minneapolis, but she's still coming here to see you? I mean, c'mon.

2. You need to get over Zoey, man.

4 Supporting Points Nate Makes in Order to Convince Darren of Point #2, Which He Presents Using a Lettered, Not Numbered, Format

A. You guys were never even boyfriend and girlfriend.

B. She's not effing here anymore, my man.

C. She's totally mental.

D. If she were half as into you as you're into her, she would have contacted your ass by now. I mean, she might be at some therapeutic rehab boarding school for social dimwits, but it's not like they sent her to Guantanamo. At the least, she would write you. Think about it.

3 Reasons Why Nate and Darren Sound Kind of Awesome When They Jam Together

1. Nate has a pretty good voice, even though he does this weird falsetto thing from time to time. Which he can almost pull off, but it's still sort of unnecessary. Plus his guitar solos can kind of wind up all over the place. But even though he's not perfect, Nate's really good overall. He probably has more natural talent than Darren does. Darren practices a lot more, obviously, and is technically way better at this point, but that's not all that matters. Because Nate's definitely a natural performer. He could be a great front man someday, maybe because of his charisma or whatever, which makes up for the sloppiness and everything. Like if they ever were a real band and someone made a music video of them, then Nate would be the one on-screen most of the time. Which is fine with Darren, as long as that means they're an actual band.

2. Darren is a pretty excellent bassist at this point. In fact, playing the kind of songs they play together when they jam is super easy for Darren compared to the stuff the jazz ensemble plays. All he has to do is kind of focus on a steady rhythm, since the keys and chord changes are really basic. But he doesn't mind this, because the

steadier he plays, the harder it is for Nate to get lost when he goes totally nuts, which he definitely does about every other song. The truth is they sound their best when Nate is just about to get lost but doesn't. And so that's kind of how Darren thinks of his job when they're playing. Tie your bass-playing around Nate's ankle so he doesn't totally go off the deep end.

3. More than anything, Darren can tell that he and Nate have chemistry, probably because they're brothers. Whatever the reason, having real chemistry is huge. In fact, in some ways chemistry matters more than anything else when it comes to music. And so if they could just find a decent drummer, they might wind up being a pretty kick-ass band.

3 Commands Not Related to Music Darren Repeatedly Gives Himself While They're Jamming

1. Don't get over Zoey if you don't want to.

2. Remember that even though you weren't officially boyfriend and girlfriend, you did stuff that even some boyfriends and girlfriends don't do. Not to mention she pretty much said you are her match, as in her interplanetary match. And if she hadn't disappeared, which probably wasn't her long-term plan, you'd have a good chance of being boyfriend and girlfriend right now.

3. So just write her a letter already. Today. Otherwise how is she going to know, and how are you going to find out what she'll do once she knows? Because if Grace is right and Zoey really doesn't have a phone or a computer or anything, then she might have no idea you've been trying to reach her, and so maybe she's been dying to contact you this whole time but hasn't, since she thinks you hate her for how she left and everything.

8 Exchanges in a Brief Back-and-Forth Darren Holds with Himself Right After Saying Bye to Nate, Who May or May Not Actually Be Going Out to Look for a Job

1. Know what?
2. Huh?
3. What is she going to know if you write her?
4. I don't know.
5. Well, you better figure that out.
6. Leave me alone.
7. Seriously, what's she going to know?
8. Shut up.

3 Characters (2 Probably Fictional, 1 Definitely Real) Darren Thought about on Yom Kippur Just a Couple of Weeks Ago, the First Two of Which Are Then Maybe Responsible for Him Not Getting Over the Third

1. JONAH

It had been a couple of years since Darren had been to synagogue, even for the High Holidays. They used to go, but then they just kind of stopped for some reason. Like his bar mitzvah was some kind of terminal act as far as being Jewish goes. Only this year, his mom pretty much insisted. Nate refused, in an actually not-that-dickish way ("Look, Mom, I totally get you're really into this, but I'm just not, trust me. I promise to atone today. Seriously, I mean it, just not there, okay?"). Darren wanted to refuse, but in the end he couldn't. Because his mom more or less pleaded with him to come with her, saying stuff like, "It would mean a lot to me."

And just like he thought, it was painfully boring. As in physically painful. Darren and his mom sat right in the middle of their row, which was pretty close to the front, too, and whatever they were doing up there seemed pretty serious. But the seats were uncomfortable and the service just seemed to go on forever. After the first twenty minutes, Darren struggled to get his body to cooperate whenever the rabbi asked everyone to stand up, which seemed much too often. Not to mention the italics in the prayer book, all those stupid sentences he was supposed to read aloud with the nine thousand other suddenly Jewish Jews gathered there.

But his mom, man alive, she was way into it. It wasn't like she was swaying or crying or beating her chest or speaking in tongues, it was more that she wasn't at all distracted, like she was so on board with the Yom Kippur program that it didn't even occur to her to wonder what the point of the whole thing was. Darren had absolutely no idea himself, but he kind of realized he might make it lame for her if he got up and left. It had to end at some point. Meanwhile, Nate was probably smoking up at home and listening to some Indian music and reading about Buddha, which maybe wasn't all that ridiculous compared to this.

Just when he thought he was actually going to lose his mind, the rabbi, in his white robe, got up to give a sermon. He started talking about Jonah, and Darren, just as a change of pace, tried to pay attention. But he only lasted about two minutes, because there was something about how the rabbi was talking that made Darren wonder if he was, in fact, speaking English. But at least these two minutes were long enough for him to learn around where in the Bible the story of Jonah is.

So Darren grabbed one of the heavy copies of the book

version sitting in the shelf/pocket attached to the back of the pew in front of him. It took about five minutes to find the story, which he then skimmed in English. Weird stuff.

Jonah was kind of a coward, that was pretty clear. God said, "Go over there and tell the people something," but Jonah just went somewhere else. Then he got on this boat, at which point God kind of gave Jonah (along with everyone else on the boat) the old "you can run, but you can't hide" treatment. Meaning there was a big storm, with huge waves and everything. And at first, Jonah seemed to think, *Whatever.* Because while everyone else is freaking out on deck, he goes down inside the boat to take a nap.

At which point the other dudes on the boat are like, "Hey, what's with that guy?" Or something like that. They cast lots, not clear why exactly. But whatever the reason, Jonah (of course) draws the short stick. And they're like, "Yup, he's why we're all about to drown." So then Jonah, somehow deciding to stop being a little selfish bitch, tells them, "Toss me overboard." Why he suddenly started thinking about someone other than himself, who knows. But he did.

So they did, they tossed him overboard. And the storm stopped. Which would maybe seem like the end of the story, assuming some little ship came to save Jonah or something. Like, wouldn't God have made his point by then? Only then the whale showed up.

2. THE WHALE

Which was actually just a "big fish" in the version Darren read. The rabbi, Darren noticed, kept talking about "those three days." Meaning the days Jonah spent inside the whale. "Why three days?" the rabbi asked, really emphasizing his confusion about the whole thing. "Wouldn't, oh, fifteen minutes inside the belly of a whale be more than enough for anyone to get the point?" Some people laughed. "Only what was the point?"

Darren thought to himself, *Yeah, what was the point?* So he kept reading. The story got extra weird around that part. Darren decided to see if the rabbi knew, which of course he did. Or at least he pretended he did.

"Jonah runs from his obligations, from his duty, from his calling. Again and again and again. But the Lord catches him. Tracks him down. Then, rather than immediately return him to where he'd wanted Jonah all along, to do what the Lord wanted him to do all along, the Lord instead put him inside the whale, has the whale that the Lord *appointed* swallow him. So that Jonah can sit there and reflect upon the whole situation. *You will sit, Jonah, inside this briny muck, inside the dark, heaving, terrifying guts of this massive creature, until you get it. For three days. Because one day, even two days, will not suffice.*"

Somehow this made Darren chew on his thumbnail, which he realized maybe he shouldn't be doing, since there were people fasting all over the place. Darren kind of spaced out for a little bit, but then he decided to try to listen again, by which point the rabbi was talking about Yom Kippur.

"Because the point of this ritual, of this annual undertaking, is to sit inside the frightening space of that thing we're always running away from. Our community. Our family. Ourselves. Whatever it may be. But not today. Today we sit in our personal, custom-made whales. Because, in the end"—the rabbi paused, held out his hands to the congregation—"we cannot escape the things we must face."

3. ZOEY

It was the running-away thing that got him thinking of Zoey. Obviously. There were a million things that got him thinking of Zoey, so maybe that wasn't such a big deal. Cigarettes, nose rings, buses, his forearm, wooden stairs, planets, it was kind of endless. But running away wasn't just another thing. It was like number two or three on the list of things that got him thinking of her.

So Darren wondered if Zoey was maybe some kind of Jonah, not that he could figure out what that would mean, exactly. But so he wondered more what she was running away from, only he couldn't exactly guess, and not because he didn't have a pretty good idea based on the stuff Grace told him. Maybe drugs, or not being able to do drugs. Maybe her parents and how bad they appeared to suck. Or school, or friends, or maybe even her whole entire life. Maybe the details didn't really matter all that much. Because maybe all that mattered for sure was that she'd been sitting inside her big fish for a while now, assuming she really was stuck wherever she was stuck.

"Our fear . . ." The rabbi just wouldn't shut up. "Our fear is that the world might pass us by while we're inside the whale. That we might finally face this thing, only to find a changed world greeting us once we're spit back out. Shot through the blowhole. The truth is, we have no choice. The world is always changing. And so are we. We will find another self when the whale is done with us. And this is just as well."

Darren closed the Bible and put it back. He was tired. And hungry. He wasn't fasting, but he purposely had a really small lunch. He zoned out for a while. Counted bald heads. Only about ten minutes later, he thought about Zoey again. Or him and Zoey.

One good thing to do would be to be there whenever she got out of her big fish. He pictured himself waiting for her on the day she got back, like it would all be coordinated with her parents somehow. He'd be there, at the airport, or her house, maybe he'd even have flowers (or a towel, ha). Making him some kind of hero almost.

He wanted so badly for that to happen, for her to see him and know that he waited; it somehow made Darren feel like the whole world, now that Zoey wasn't in it, was his big fish.

Like he was in some kind of limbo too. But what was he supposed to face up to? What was he running from? And why did he suddenly think the whole Jonah and the whale story was anything but a bunch of bullshit?

It didn't make much sense. All he knew was that he needed Zoey to come back and he needed to see what would be then. And that him nearly getting over her was just being weak and stupid. Or in denial. He still didn't know what love was or if he was in love with her, but whenever he thought about her he felt something he didn't feel except when he did. In his stomach and around his eyes and sometimes in the tips of his fingers. He didn't know why, or what it all meant, or what he should do about it. But trying not to feel it, trying to make it go away, now seemed deeply uncool.

He turned to his mom, who looked beautiful and old to him. She noticed him staring at her, smiled, and patted his thigh.

23 Steps in Darren's Effort to Finally Write Zoey Lovell a Letter

1. Gets a piece of paper and a nice black Uniball pen.
2. Sits down at his desk.
3. Realizes he has no idea what to write.
4. Thinks about just writing, *Zoey, I don't know why, but I really, really like you. I maybe even love you.*
5. Finds himself unable to do that.
6. Feels a bit grateful that he's unable to do that.
7. Considers writing a regular letter. An update about his life and everything. But that's stupid, because why would Zoey give a shit about who he has for physics?
8. Sits there some more.
9. Chews on his pen.
10. Realizes this is why he hasn't written her a letter before. Because it's hard.
11. Gets a weird, maybe great idea.
12. Goes online and finds the lyrics for that song "Precious" Zoey sang on Rock Band.
13. Writes them out. Luckily, he's sort of good at writing capital letters (long lines at slight angles), so he starts the beginning of each line with one of those.
14. Stops in the middle, because he realizes the words don't make a whole lot of sense. In fact, the parts he

does understand seem kind of bitter and maybe even mean.

15. Wonders if maybe he should find a different poem. An actual love poem.
16. Gets back online and googles "love poems."
17. Within about ninety seconds feels intensely embarrassed to have even had that idea.
18. Decides Zoey would get why he chose "Precious," meaning the words themselves don't matter.
19. Finishes writing out the lyrics.
20. Adds, at the end, *I miss you a lot. I hope you're okay. Darren.*
21. Folds it up and puts it in an envelope.
22. Writes *Darren Jacobs* and his address in the top left corner, and just *Zoey Lovell* in the middle.
23. Last, puts a stamp on it. It's just one of those flag stamps. Too bad it's not something cooler, like a wildflower or a picture of outer space. Oh well, not everything can be perfect.

6 Highlights from among the Approximately Twenty-Nine Stupid Opening Lines Darren Involuntarily Pictures Himself Saying to Zoey's Parents

1. Hello, my name is Darren, and I have a letter for your daughter, Zoey. I would be forever grateful if you could please send it to her.

2. Hi. I'm in love with your daughter. Oh, and here's a letter for her.

3. Greetings. Do you believe that there's only one person in the whole universe who's meant for you, and that if you find that person, you can't let that person get away?

4. Howdy. Remember how when your daughter ran away to Ann Arbor, she did it with some kid from school? Well . . .

5. Good afternoon. A few days before you sent your daughter away, the two of us sort of rocked each other's worlds in an orange tent in an apartment in Ann Arbor. It's a night I'll never forget.

6. Here's the deal: If you told me right now where Zoey is, and even if it is all the way in New Mexico, I would seriously consider getting back on this rickety, piece-of-shit bike and just pedaling my stuffed-up ass all the way out to her. I would.

2 Rationales Darren Manufactures for Getting off His Bike and Locking It Up a Couple of Blocks Away

1. It'll give him a chance to stop sweating.
2. If her parents see his bike they will be less likely to accept his letter.

5 Features of the Lovells' House and Property Darren Notices as He Walks up the Driveway and Then along the Curving Sidewalk That Ends at Their Front Door

1. The house is built out of gray stones.
2. The roof is a very dark shade of black.
3. The lawn is well kept.
4. Except for some kind of weird, yellowish dead spot over by the two white wicker deer hanging out in the pie-shaped part of the lawn between the driveway, the house, and this sidewalk.
5. Holy crap, they have two wicker deer hanging out on their lawn.

7 Physical Manifestations of Darren's Nervous Energy on Display After He Presses Their Doorbell

1. Grasps his right wrist with his left hand (while holding the letter in between the index and middle fingers of his right).
2. Tries to sniff back up all the snot that kind of worked itself loose during the ride over.
3. Closes his eyes and shakes his head vigorously to check if he is, in fact, light-headed, which he thought he might have been when he was about to reach this spot.
4. Switches hands/wrists (but still keeps the letter between the tips of his right).
5. Quickly presses the doorbell again.
6. Counts to forty out loud.
7. Spins around with the intention of jogging or even sprinting back to his bike.

2 Clicks That Keep Him Standing Right Where He Is

1. The first one the door makes
2. The second one the door makes, which is a bit louder and higher-pitched than the first one

6 Types of Communications Darren Calls Upon, in Addition to the Letter Itself

1. VERIFICATION

The door opens maybe a foot. And some woman is standing there, partly visible.

Zoey's mom?

Whoever she is, she's wearing khaki pants and a dark blue cardigan sweater. She looks a little older than Darren's mom. Before he got to the house, he had tried to picture what she (or Zoey's father) might look like, but this woman just seems like some totally random woman. So much so that he can't remember at all what the woman he tried to picture only about five minutes ago in his head looked like.

Her hair is sort of dark blond and wiry, and a couple of deep wrinkles run from the edge of her mouth down toward her chin. She isn't pretty, but she might have been once. Most of all, she doesn't look anything like Zoey. Except maybe for her nose, which is small like Zoey's.

"Mrs. Lovell?" Darren asks, because maybe she isn't, maybe the Lovells don't live here anymore. Maybe Zoey didn't get sent anywhere but just moved to Houston or something and decided not to tell anyone, not even Grace. Maybe her family is in a witness relocation program.

"Yes," she says, kind of tired and maybe just a tad annoyed.

2. INTRODUCTION

"Hi, um, my name's Darren, I'm sort of a . . . a friend of Zoey's."

Zoey's mom, if that's who this really is, shifts her weight and blinks her eyes once very slowly but doesn't say anything. Darren can't remember any of the things he came up with to say on the ride over, probably because he hadn't considered the possibility that this particular woman would open the door.

3. INQUIRY

Eventually he just asks, and not because he thinks this is the smartest thing to say, "Is Zoey okay?" As soon as he says this, he suddenly has to swallow something, sniffle almost violently, readjust his feet, and let go of his wrist, which was getting pretty sweaty.

Zoey's mom, whose skin, Darren now notices, is pretty dark, almost black, in the area around her eyes, closes her mouth (which wasn't exactly open to begin with) in such a way that her thin lips almost disappear altogether.

4. CONFESSION

"I just . . . ," Darren continues. "I know she must have gone somewhere, but so I was worried."

"Zoey's fine," her mom says, but for a moment looks back inside the house (which is totally silent) when she says this.

Even so, Darren can see how the nostrils on her small nose got much bigger after she spoke, like she is very mad or very sad or maybe even both. Then the two of them just stand there for a moment, or maybe a few moments, until she says, "Thank you," and starts shutting the door.

5. REQUEST

"Please, wait," Darren says as politely as he can, and holds out the letter. "Would you give her this? Please."

Zoey's mom takes it but doesn't say that she'll send it. Instead she just closes the door, which then clicks a couple times again, only faster this time.

6. FAREWELL

"Okay, bye," Darren says to the door. Then he wipes his right wrist on the side of his khakis and walks slowly back to his bike. The leaves on one of the trees lining the Lovells' street are starting to change colors. Or maybe that tree is just sick for some reason.

4 Suspicions Darren Has about This Cold Medicine, Which Feels Like It's Kicking In Again Right as He Reaches the Third-Floor Landing in Front of Dr. Schrier's Office

1. This isn't actually cold medicine.
2. Whatever it is, I'm taking too much of it.
3. It might be a very bad idea to take too much medication or the wrong medication or too much of the wrong medication and then go to therapy with your dad.
4. I might just be sicker than I thought.

5 Relatively Innocuous Questions Dr. Schrier Asks Darren as Some Kind of Warm-up Round to Begin Today's Session

1. So how's school going?
2. Are your peers discussing college yet?
3. You're a bit under the weather today, yes?
4. Are you still enjoying having Nate back home?
5. Any plans for the weekend?

1 and Only 1 Type of Punctuation a Person Would Need in Order to Transcribe about 94 Percent of Dr. Schrier's Speech

1. ?

7 Physical Features or Mannerisms of Dr. Schrier's Darren Finds Himself Zoning Out On

1. His beard, in particular the way his mustache is way grayer than the rest of it (which is sandy brown)
2. His silver-framed glasses that are insanely out of fashion
3. The round ball of flesh that is the tip of his nose
4. The deep wrinkles running horizontally and vertically over his forehead
5. The way he rubs the end of his left thumb along the length of his index finger when someone else is talking
6. The slow, inconsistent rhythm at which he bobs the toe of his left shoe, which is at the end of the leg crossed over his right leg
7. How he occasionally lifts his chin a bit and inhales, as if the air just above his nose is better than the air below

5 Combinations of People (All Involving His Dad, Darren, and Someone Else) Discussed and Analyzed during This Session

1. HIS DAD, DARREN, AND DARREN'S FRIENDS (OR LACK THEREOF)

"I told Darren," his dad says to Dr. Schrier, "that he could tell me if—if my situation, my being gay, if that was placing constraints on his ability to make and develop friendships."

"You didn't tell me," Darren says. "You asked me to tell you. If it was."

"Okay. That's fair," his dad says.

"Constraints?" Dr. Schrier asks.

"Yes, constraints," his dad answers.

"Darren"—Dr. Schrier turns to him—"do you know what your father means by 'constraints'?"

Darren shrugs his shoulders.

No one says anything for a good five seconds. Darren, alone on the couch, blows his nose. His dad and Dr. Schrier, each in one of the armchairs that face one another, have some kind of elaborate conversation with their eyes and the angles at which they hold their heads.

"As best I can tell," his dad says, and then clears his throat, "you're spending a lot of time alone, Darren—"

"So?"

"Well, I would hope that—that you're not alone as much as you are because you feel uncomfortable with people knowing about me."

"What are you talking about?"

"If you're ashamed—"

"I'm not ashamed," Darren says, clearly annoyed. "I'm not."

"Okay."

"I don't care that you're gay."

"Okay," his dad repeats, sounding a bit hurt.

"Would you guys still be married if you weren't?"

"That's an impossible question, Darren," his dad says. "If I weren't gay I wouldn't be me, and so who knows what would have been."

"But you said that's not why you got divorced."

"Well, not exactly why. Not only why. But it's hard to say, I—"

"If you're not together anymore," Darren says, "then whatever. You can be whatever you want."

More silence for a while. Dr. Schrier writes something on his pad.

"Not being ashamed of having a gay father, who you did not know was gay until rather recently, this," Dr. Schrier says, "speaks to an unusually tolerant and mature son, wouldn't you say, Darren?"

"Whatever, I have no idea. I don't care. Not about that.

Maybe about the divorce and him being kind of a freak and—"

"A what?" his dad asks.

"Forget it."

"You said freak."

Darren says nothing.

"You think I'm a freak." Darren almost turns to his dad. "Why do you think I'm a freak?"

"Because."

"Because why?"

"Because of everything."

"Everything?"

"Yeah. How you talk now and all those books you have and that smell in your apartment—"

"The incense?"

"Whatever. And that little shrine or whatever it is in the corner of your living room. And that you keep asking me to come here so we can talk about how awesome it is that you're gay."

"That was hurtful."

Darren blows his nose.

2. HIS DAD, DARREN, AND NATE

"What about Nate?" his dad asks.

"What about him?"

"Do you . . ." His dad runs his hand over his bald scalp. "Do you enjoy having him back?"

"Dr. Schrier already asked me that."

"I know, I know. But truly. Do you?"

Darren crumples up the Kleenex and sets it down on the coffee table. "Sometimes."

"Sometimes yes, sometimes no?" Dr. Schrier asks.

Darren nods.

"When no?" his dad asks.

"What?" Darren responds, confused.

"Sometimes you're not happy he's back, is that what you meant?" his dad asks.

Darren shrugs his shoulders.

"When would be a time like that?" Dr. Schrier asks.

"You guys know."

"We do?" Dr. Schrier asks.

His dad smiles a bit.

"He should be at U of M."

"Why is that?" Dr. Schrier asks.

"Because he's twenty and smart and got in there."

"Perhaps he needs some time off," his dad says. "To figure out what he hopes to get out of his college years. To do some searching."

"Like you?" Darren asks.

"And what is that supposed to mean?" his dad asks.

Darren blows his nose and tries to clear his throat but fails.

3. HIS DAD, DARREN, AND DR. SCHRIER

"Darren, why do you come here?" Dr. Schrier asks.

"Because my dad asks me to," Darren says.

"But he gives you the option not to, yes?"

"Yeah."

"Nate, for instance, Nate elects not to come, correct?"

"So?"

"So, you don't have to come, but you do. So why?"

Darren doesn't say anything. Studies the fern on Dr. Schrier's desk. He suddenly wishes this fern was in his room at the house.

"Would you at all," Dr. Schrier continues, "would you want to come here without your father?" Darren looks at Dr. Schrier. "Would that interest you more or less than coming here with him?"

"Yeah," Darren says, and wrestles again with the phlegm in his throat. "Maybe."

He looks at his dad, who appears deeply satisfied.

4. HIS DAD, DARREN, AND ANOTHER HYPOTHETI-CAL MAN

"Darren," his dad says.

"Yeah?"

"How do you think you'd feel if I . . ." His dad looks at Dr. Schrier, who nods.

Darren looks back and forth at both of them, like he's watching a tennis match in which both players have agreed to cheat.

"If I brought a boyfriend home, how would you feel?"

"You have a boyfriend?"

"No, I do not. But if I did?"

Darren says nothing.

"It's just, I've begun to suspect I'm a serial monogamist at heart."

"A what?"

"How would you define that, Dr. Schrier?" his dad asks.

"A person who participates in a series of exclusive relationships?"

"A lot of men, Darren, like myself"—his dad quickly licks his bottom lip—"have numerous partners. Without any commitment."

"So?"

"That doesn't feel right to me."

Darren's phone vibrates in his pocket. He ignores it. As does everyone else, more or less.

"Not morally. I mean right, as in, it doesn't suit me."

There aren't any plants in the house. Maybe that explains something.

"What I'm getting at," his dad continues, "is that I started dating your mother when I was twenty-two. I had exactly one girlfriend before her, Catherine Parcell. She and I dated for the last three years of high school. I dated no one else. And so despite, you know, who I am now, I feel a strong urge to find a partner."

"Okay."

"And so I was wondering, how you, if I were to—"

"How the hell am I supposed to know?"

5. HIS DAD, DARREN, AND RACHEL

Darren's phone vibrates again. And then again. He takes it out of his pocket. Three texts from Rachel: *I'm here! Call me! CALL ME!!!* ☺ Darren sniffles and possibly smiles. Puts the phone down and looks at Dr. Schrier.

"Something urgent?" the doctor asks, possibly in jest.

"For her," Darren says.

"Her?" his dad asks.

"Yeah."

"Do you need to write her back?"

"Soon."

"Her?" Dr. Schrier asks.

Darren looks at his dad, not necessarily with approval.

"Uh-huh."

"Whoever she is, she's a lucky girl," his dad says proudly. Darren rolls his eyes. "What? She is. You're a catch, Darren."

"Ha."

"Not 'ha.' You're an amazing young man, Darren."

"Whatever."

Darren leans forward, grabs a few pieces of Kleenex, stuffs them in his pocket, and stands up. "I like someone else." He walks toward the door. "I've got to call her."

Darren shuffles down the stairs, wondering what he'd talk about with Dr. Schrier if it was just the two of them.

2, Possibly 3, Lies Darren Texts Rachel

1. *Cant call in an appointment*
2. *Awesome ur here*
3. *Will call soon*

2 Reasons Darren Declines His Dad's Invitation for Darren to Drive Home

1. This medication is really strong and messing with his head.
2. He doesn't want to drive, ever, so please stop asking.

6 Opinions His Dad Shares with Him on the Ride Home

1. Your willingness to share your sensitivity shows great courage.
2. I am certain Dr. Schrier admires this as well.
3. I believe we'll look back on these sessions and be grateful.
4. I am not as much of a freak as you may believe.
5. Everyone's a freak, Darren.
6. I have simply chosen to hide my freakishness less than most.

2 Questions Darren Badly Wants to Ask His Dad but Doesn't

1. Do you really think Mom's hiding her freakishness?
2. If so, what's she hiding?

2 People Who It Turns Out Aren't Feeling So Hot Today, Though the Second One Is Doing Way Worse Than the First (It Must Have Been the Sushi Rachel and Her Had on the Way Back from the Airport, Even Though, Luckily, Rachel Is Somehow Totally Fine, but, Oh My God, Krista Is Definitely Not)

1. Darren
2. Krista

5 Parts of a New Plan Darren Finds Himself Suggesting or Agreeing To

1. Rachel will leave Krista's place, because it's pretty clear she and her parents have better things to do than take care of a houseguest right now.
2. Rachel will come over to Darren's, since she doesn't really know anyone else in Chicago.
3. Darren and his mom will pick her up. Darren will drive. Maybe.
4. Rachel will stay for dinner.
5. And maybe even the night as well, though the relevant parents will have to discuss this one first.

11 Self-Directed Questions Darren Has Difficulty Answering While Driving Himself and His Mom to Krista's House

1. How do you feel about Rachel maybe sleeping under the same roof as you?
2. How do you feel about the likelihood of the two of you being alone under this roof for a couple hours after dinner, assuming your mom goes to synagogue and Nate takes off as well?
3. Should you have let Rachel know that dinner is actually Shabbat dinner?
4. Is this all some kind of sign?
5. Some kind of plan?
6. Why do you continue to fear turning left?
7. Can't you see that this green arrow has been installed at this intersection in order to facilitate and simplify just this very maneuver?
8. Who is this Rachel person?
9. And what about Zoey?
10. And why does this cold medicine make it feel like two small lead balloons have been inflated below your cheeks?
11. How many distinct and separate things are wrong with you at this very moment?

2 People and Their Respective Positions on an Invisible Spectrum Labeled "Degree of Knowledge Concerning Rachel and Darren's Relationship"

1. Darren—the left edge, which is for those who know just about everything there is to know
2. His mom—the right edge, which is for people who don't even know they have a relationship

4 Objects or Entities Darren Is Thankful Require His Attention during His Mom's On-Again, Off-Again Interview of Him (an Interview That Might Be Titled "So Who Is This Rachel Girl, Exactly? I Don't Remember You Mentioning Any Rachel before Today.")

1. The stop light at Church and Crawford
2. The shiny blue pickup truck pulling out in front of him
3. The police car driving ominously in the other direction
4. The squirrel with a death wish just a couple of houses from Krista's

5 Developments That Freak Darren Out a Little Bit to a Lot a Bit within Twenty Seconds of Their Arrival at Krista's

1. Rachel (bag in hand) is already waiting in front of the house with a man who must be Krista's father.

2. Rachel hugs Darren in a way (long and tight and unmistakably audible) that likely reveals to his mom (busy introducing herself to Krista's father, but more than capable of multitasking in this instance) that none of the information she acquired during their recent interview should be considered even remotely reliable.

3. This hug feels kind of good, especially for the part of him that is ill, as if Rachel contains healing properties.

4. And even though thankfully she doesn't try to kiss him (he had his "I'm pretty sure I have a cold" excuse ready, just in case), he realizes that he maybe wouldn't be opposed to such a thing, assuming his mom (and Krista's dad) were someplace else.

5. Someone (e.g., Krista, probably) moans from some-where up on the second floor, because a couple windows are open up there, who knows why.

1 Additional Development That Freaks Darren Out More Than a Little Bit and So Deserves to Be Mentioned Separately

1. Rachel has dyed her hair black. And cut it short. Holy shit. It looks really good. Really, really good.

3 Features of Rachel's Face Newly Framed by This Inviting Yet Daunting Hairdo

1. Her large green eyes, which now seem a little magical, like if she were capable of casting a spell, these eyes would probably get even a little greener right when she was doing that.
2. The wideness of her cheeks, which almost seem to be actively pushing out against the edges of her hair.
3. Her steady smile and the slight, slight gap between her two front teeth, because maybe there is some very interesting disagreement taking place between her smile and her hair, such that Darren suddenly doubts that he really knows Rachel at all.

7 Reasons Why Darren's Brain Is Malfunctioning

1. His mom clearly knows (he can tell by the tone of her voice and the little, barely contained grin on her face) that Rachel is not just "some girl."

2. His mom seems to approve (her voice is doing that "I will try to make you enthusiastic by sounding enthusiastic myself" and/or "I will help you think this is okay by sounding like I think it's okay" thing), as if she somehow knows that Darren isn't sure how he himself feels about their new, soon-to-be guest.

3. Rachel and his mom are totally hitting it off (chatting easily and laughing regularly), to the point that Darren (were he to get more sick himself or somehow just announce his refusal to participate in the coming visit) can pretty much picture them going shopping or taking a walk or just sitting in the living room drinking fancy espresso drinks and having a blast together.

4. A tiny little particle or two of something rising off Rachel has managed to burrow its way into the smell-interpreting part of Darren's snot-laden sinuses. Jesus, it's the first thing he's actually smelled today. It's one of those morning-dew, forest-after-the-rain scents that he loves for some reason. Dammit.

5. He's supposed to not kill them accidentally while guiding this two-ton machine through these deadly streets.
6. If Darren sneaks like a quarter-second look in the rearview mirror (while squinting his eyes in a way that is maybe dangerous and definitely stupid, considering he's driving), then he can nearly convince himself that Zoey is sitting in the backseat.
7. Only it's not Zoey, or not the Zoey he remembers, but a warm, friendly, funny, and extroverted Zoey, a Zoey other regular, normal human beings would approve of and know what to do with, a Zoey who probably wouldn't indirectly turn him into a smoker or disappear on him or break his dim-witted, gullible heart.

4 Lengthy Conversations Darren Somehow Has Instantly, Merely by Getting Caught Noticing the Intricate, Bewildering Expressions on Various Faces

1. The one with his mom right after they pull into the garage and she leans over to undo her seat belt
2. The one with Rachel when he walks back to the trunk with her to remove her bag
3. The one with his mom and Rachel in the kitchen, right after his mom asks Rachel what she'd like to drink and Rachel says, "Nothing, thanks, I'm fine," only his mom insists, so the two of them sort of volley this back and forth, faster and faster, until they somehow start laughing like this is absolutely hysterical
4. The one he has with himself in the bathroom mirror. He knew he shouldn't have looked up while washing his hands

2 Floors at the House Where Conversations Are Held within Fifteen Minutes of Their Return Home

1. DOWNSTAIRS

"Oh, darn," his mom says, checking a few drawers in the kitchen. "I need to go out and get some candles." Addressing Rachel: "We celebrate Shabbat." Rachel nods with her mouth open slightly. "Do you know what that is?"

"Yeah, of course," Rachel answers, and takes a sip from her iced tea.

"Can't Nate just pick some up?" Darren asks.

"Actually," Rachel says, "Darren, I don't think I ever told you this. Why would I? But one of my grandmothers, she was Jewish. I guess."

"Huh," Darren says.

"Really?" his mom asks, with what might be approval.

"Yeah, my mom's mom. But she died when I was only two, so I never got to know her."

"What a shame," his mom says.

Darren opens the refrigerator, looks for something.

"I guess it means that I'm technically Jewish." Rachel takes another sip. "Like, according to Jewish law, right?"

"Yep," his mom says. "That's how it works."

Darren blows his nose.

"Okay." Rachel smiles, and maybe clears her throat. "I

know this is going to sound weird or something," Rachel says, looking at Darren, "but sometimes I kind of *feel* Jewish. You know?"

"Not really?" Darren responds.

"Darren," his mom says.

"Like, in seventh grade, there weren't so many Jewish kids at our school, but I did go to Jordan Peltz's bar mitzvah. And . . ."

"Yeah?" his mom asks a few seconds after Rachel trails off.

"Nothing," Rachel says, dismissing whatever she was going to tell them with her hand.

Darren drinks from a carton of OJ.

"What?" his mom asks, to encourage her. "Darren, use a glass. You've got a cold. For God's sake."

"It's just, it's really weird." Rachel laughs. "But I felt, I don't know, kind of at home in the temple. Where the service was." No one says anything. "I mean, we don't go to church almost ever. My dad thinks religion is stupid. Sorry. And whenever we do go, it just feels like this weird place to me. But at his bar mitzvah, when they opened the—is it called an ark?"

"Sure is," his mom says with a smile.

"I swear"—Rachel blushes—"I got the chills."

She stops talking. Right before his mom says, "That's a wonderful story," Rachel looks down and puts some of her hair, painted black, behind her right ear.

2. UPSTAIRS

"Why won't you kiss me?" Rachel asks, sitting on Darren's bed.

"What?" Darren is standing by his dresser, maybe pretending to straighten the thing out.

"You haven't even kissed me once yet."

"I have a cold."

"So?"

"So you want to get sick?"

"I don't care about getting sick," Rachel says. Darren tries exhaling through his nostrils, with little success. "Your mom's gone."

"When did you do that to your hair?"

"You don't like it. I knew you wouldn't."

"No, I do."

"You don't have to lie."

"No, seriously, I do. A lot. It's cool."

"Really?"

"Yeah."

"Thanks."

"It just, it kind of surprised me. That's all."

"I know. Me too. My friend Carrie dared me. It totally freaked my parents out. Totally. And it's crazy, how people treat you differently when you look like this."

"Seriously?"

"Yeah. Like, I don't know, in public and stuff, you can tell people think, I don't know, like I'm some bad girl or something."

"Bad girl."

"I'm so bad."

Darren thinks about hopping up on his dresser, so he can sit there with his legs dangling off. But he's not sure he'd make it.

"Do you think you're going to keep it that way?"

"Maybe. At first, like the first time I saw it in the mirror, I freaked. I was like, 'Oh my God, how long is this going to take to grow out?' But now . . ."

"What?"

"You're going to laugh."

"What?"

"It's just—it's kind of fun to see if you can be someone else. You know? Not like I'm bad now, but still. Like everyone just always assumes I'm some goody-goody. Rachel Madsen, straight-A student, plays the piano all day, vice president of the Spanish club. Blah, blah, blah. So stupid."

Darren stops fussing with his dresser. "Yeah."

"Right?"

"Yeah, I think so. Just how people don't know the first thing about what other people are really like."

"But the weird thing is, it made me realize, like—this is even crazier, but I swear . . ."

"What?"

"It's just, I don't know if I know what I'm really like." Darren nods his head, sits down on the bed next to her. "You know?"

411

"Yeah."

They kiss for a bit. Unclear who started it.

"Do you have a girlfriend?"

"Why do you think I have a girlfriend?"

"I didn't say I think you do. I just asked."

"Do you? Have a boyfriend?"

"Not really. A guy asked me to homecoming. We've gone out a couple times. Tyler Kinsey. Supposedly he's an amazing soccer player. Like I should care. He's nice, but not my type, I guess. I think he might be stupid. I know that's mean, but I'm pretty sure it's true. He's kind of boring to talk to." She squeezes Darren's hand. "Okay, honestly, like to be totally honest, he wants me to go with him to some big-deal party next week, but I don't know."

"Are you going to?" he asks.

"What about you?" she asks. Darren doesn't answer, gets up, tends to his sinuses for a few moments. "You do, don't you?"

"I don't know. Sort of. Maybe."

Rachel nearly laughs. "What's her name?"

"Zoey."

"Zoey what?"

"Zoey Lovell."

"What's she like?"

"I don't know. I barely know her. I swear. It's kind of a long story. I actually"—Darren tries inhaling through just his right nostril—"I mean, I knew her and stuff, before camp."

"You did?" Rachel asks, her brow moderately furrowed.

"Yeah. But—but she doesn't even live around here right now."

"Did she move?"

"No. Her parents sent her to some kind of boarding school or something."

"Really? What'd she do?"

Darren rubs his nose with the back of his hand. "I think she ran away."

"No way."

"Probably some other stuff too."

No one says anything. Darren tries not to look at Rachel's hair. He fails.

"You're crazy about her, aren't you?"

"Maybe, I don't know."

"Why didn't you say anything? Back at Green Ridge?" Rachel asks this sounding more curious than hurt, which isn't to say she's not some of both.

"I don't know." Darren grabs some more Kleenex. "I probably should have." He blows his nose forcefully, which fails to alter the situation in his sinuses. "Sorry. I feel so dumb with this cold."

Rachel nods her head. "It's okay, I get it." Her bag, still unopened, sits up against the bed, next to her. No one says anything for a while. "I can ask my parents to switch my flight. Maybe I can still go back tonight."

"No, it's cool."

"No, it's not."

"You should stay."

"You're such a liar. You are."

No one says anything. Rachel plays with a zipper on her bag. Darren keeps scanning his room, like he's trying to figure out what kind of room it is now that she's in it. They look at each other every once in a while but then look away. There's a chance neither of them is sure how they're supposed to do even that at this point.

"I feel so bad for Krista," Rachel says.

"Yeah," Darren says.

More silence.

"Hey," Darren says eventually. "Can I play you something?"

"Sure," Rachel says, her voice really soft.

So he opens his computer and searches for the song.

"It's kind of stupid," he says.

"Play it," she says.

The song starts, and soon some guy is playing the saxophone, but so softly it sounds like something else. Or like the guy playing is hanging upside down from a hot-air balloon.

"That's beautiful," Rachel says.

"Right?"

"What's it called?"

"You don't want to know."

"Why not?"

"You'll laugh."

"No I won't."

They listen without speaking for a while. Darren breathes through his lips, which are quite dry. He closes his eyes, maybe in order to think about Rachel. When he opens them, she's looking at him, smiling. A nice chunk of late-afternoon sunlight is coming through his window and passing not that far from Rachel. All the dust specks illuminated inside it seem to matter somehow. Maybe Rachel is beautiful, maybe he could love her, maybe his life would be ten times better had he been born in Minneapolis, or in 1936, or whenever this song was first recorded. Like what if you don't have to be alone in your whale? Like what if that's the point? To find the right person to sit there in the whale with you.

When the song ends, Darren starts it over. He makes sure Rachel can tell he's doing this. She seems to swallow something when she notices this is what he's doing. He loves this song so much right now, it makes him a little sad. Like his life will never be good enough to deserve this as part of its sound track. The guy on the sax holds some of his notes for so long, bending them a bit at the same time. It makes you feel like you're riding in the hot-air balloon. Or that you *are* the hot-air balloon. That he and his saxophone are inflating. With helium, and something else, something that makes it feel really good and just a little bad to be filled up like this.

So Darren goes and joins her on the bed. There are easily ten thousand things he'd like to tell her right now, and another ten thousand he wouldn't mind asking her. But instead he lets some combination of gravity and desire and soft mattress bring their shoulders together.

And then they're kissing again, this time because of Darren. And then they're lying back on his bed. He's so much bigger than her, but she doesn't seem to mind.

"I missed you, Darren," she tells him. He didn't miss her, but maybe he should have. He could have sat alone in his room, listening to this song, wishing she were here like she's here right now. Instead he's wishing she's the one he can't get over.

The garage door starts opening. They sit up. They stand up. Just before they leave his room to go back downstairs: "'Day Dream.'"

"Huh?" she asks.

"That's the name of the song."

She takes his hand and leads him back downstairs.

4 Physical Components of the Verdict Darren's Mom Quickly Delivered to Darren on Her Way out the Door to Get the Candles

1. Shoulders raised
2. Eyebrows raised
3. Bared-teeth smile
4. (After lowering shoulders and eyebrows, and un-baring her teeth), the words "She's cute!" mouthed

4 Interpretations of These Components

1. The shoulders: something like, "Isn't this fun?"
2. The eyebrows: "Lucky you!"
3. The teeth: "Kind of crazy, but pretty neat, too!"
4. The mouthed words are more complicated. But if Darren had to guess, then he'd guess something like: "Though I'm certainly not focusing here on anything sexual, per se, I am pleased that this fairly attractive, rather wholesome, and probably well-behaved girl appears interested in you, and I strongly encourage you to be interested in her as well, because, let's face it, your social calendar has been awfully empty of late, and maybe this is just what you need, so I'm going to do my part to, you know, give you two some time alone, because, just between you and me, we totally have Shabbat candles, I just made that up!"

4 Questions That Nate Asks and Then Immediately Answers Himself Right After Being Introduced to Rachel Downstairs

1. You're the piano player, right? Right.
2. Hey, if I could unearth that old Casio keyboard we got like nine hundred years ago, would you be willing to rock out with me and the bro-ham? I'll take that as a yes.
3. How ya feeling about watching us be Jewish for dinner? Pretty psyched, I bet.
4. Guess how many jobs I now have? Zero!

14 Observations Nate Quietly Shares with Darren While Rachel Is in the Bathroom

1. Dude.
2. I can't believe the gods arranged home delivery for you.
3. You must have really suffered in some previous life.
4. I'm completely serious about that, by the way.
5. And the dyed-black hair, man.
6. It's like your stinking destiny to wind up with a girl who dyes her hair black.
7. Which isn't my thing.
8. But hey, different strokes for different folks and all that.
9. She's quality, I'm serious.
10. You can just tell.
11. Like right away.
12. You need not worry about my hanging around this evening.
13. Insane.
14. Totally insane.

3 Medical Supplies Darren's Mom Presents to Him upon Her Return, Along with Her Instructions

1. A red and white box ("Take a couple of these now, I don't think the others are helping.")
2. A green and blue box ("Take two of these before you go to bed, they'll help you sleep. Knock you right out.")
3. A travel pack of Kleenex ("These have aloe in them, so your poor nose doesn't end up raw.")

3 Bits of Dress-up Nate Is Wearing When He Comes Up from the Basement, Casio Keyboard in Hand

1. A black felt fedora
2. An oversize pair of yellow plastic sunglasses with purple lenses
3. A pink feather boa

3 Musical Acts Rachel (Now Wearing the Boa) Mentions to Nate (Still Wearing the Fedora) After He Asks Her, "So What Do You Listen to Other Than Classical?" While Darren (for Whom Everything Is Now Purple) Follows Them to the Garage and Helps Set Up the Keyboard

1. THE BEATLES

"The Beatles don't count," Nate says.

"Why not?" Rachel asks.

"Because everyone loves the Beatles."

"So?"

"Okay, fine, so what's your favorite song of theirs?"

"Favorite? That's impossible."

"Fine. Favorite two. Or three."

"Hmm. Okay. 'Penny Lane.' Uh, 'Martha My Dear.' And 'Lady Madonna.'"

"You like Paul."

"You don't?"

"What else? Someone else."

2. ELTON JOHN

"Seriously?" Nate says.

"Yes, seriously. What?"

"Nothing. Noted. Next."

3. JONI MITCHELL

"Right on," Nate says.

"I'm glad you approve."

"You like anyone who still exists?"

"I told you he was kind of a dick sometimes," Darren says.

"You won't like the current stuff I like."

"How do you know?" Nate asks.

"Because you're not a twelve-year-old girl."

"But you still are?"

"No comment."

"Meaning in spirit or something?"

"Darren, do you guys play here a lot?"

"C'mon, Rachel," Nate says. "You have to tell me."

"Sort of," Darren says.

3 Hugely Popular Musical Acts Nate Accuses Rachel of Liking, Only One of Which She Denies

1. Too embarrassing to mention
2. Worse than #1
3. This is one that not even Rachel likes

3 Chords Nate Calls Out and Starts Playing Over and Over Until Rachel (on Keyboards, Obviously) and Darren (Bass, Duh) Join In

1. G
2. C
3. D

4 Stages of Darren's Experience of Playing a Certain Mega Teenybopper Hit

1. Playing competently.
2. But still feeling like the distant point on their pop-music triangle. There's something Nate and Rachel are sharing that Darren can't really share with them. It might be a sense of abandon. As in, you decide to play some arguably stupid song you've told yourself to hate a hundred times, whether or not it deserves to be hated at all. But then you start playing it, and you realize it's kind of a cool song, or at least a very fun song to play.
3. Getting into it. Finally, because what's the big deal?
4. Only then remembering you hate it and that you maybe (no, you definitely) judge the crap out of people who do like this song. Making it so you can't totally give yourself over to the song right now, even though why not? Because what would be so wrong with just enjoying this song (and your rendition of it) for a measly three minutes? Who would care? Who would think less of you for it? Certainly not Rachel or Nate. They're having the time of their lives. And no one else is even here. Leaving only you. It's you who won't let yourself. You idiot loser.

7 Accoutrements Assembled for the Sabbath Meal

1. Two silver candlesticks
2. Two candles
3. One silver wine goblet
4. Some red wine
5. One ceramic challah platter
6. One poppy-seed challah
7. One challah cover, which says in reddish-orange Hebrew lettering on top, SHABBAT SHALOM

11 Physical Acts His Mom Performs Before Even Saying the Prayer for the Candles

1. Lights the candles
2. Places her hands over her eyes
3. Just stands there like that for maybe six seconds
4. Inhales deeply
5. Holds her breath
6. Exhales rather dramatically
7. Inhales deeply
8. Holds her breath
9. Exhales even more dramatically
10. Removes her hands
11. Smiles in a way Darren still doesn't understand

1 Person Darren Realizes Would Maybe Appreciate This Moment More Than Anyone, with the Candles Flickering and His Mom Standing There, Breathing Slowly, and Rachel Being Attentive and Respectful and Maybe Even Grateful, but Somehow in a Way That Isn't Obsequious at All, and Even Nate Looking Off to the Side Pensively, Like the Whole Damn Picture of the Four of Them Is God's Advertisement for Shabbat or Something

1. His dad

4 People Apparently About to Participate in His Mom's Little Pre-Meal Activity, Which Involves Answering the Question "What's One Good Thing—and It Can't Have Anything to Do with School or Work—That Happened to You This Week?"

1. His mom
2. Nate
3. Darren
4. Rachel

2 Participants Who Get to Go Before a Nice Little Argument Leads to His Mom Saying, "Forget It. I Try to Do Something Nice, Something Special, and This Is What I Get. Great."

1. HIS MOM

"Fine, I'll go," she says. "Hmm. I had a good week. Not great, but it was good. What to choose from? Had a nice coffee with Karen yesterday. No. Had a great talk with the new project manager at—"

"You said it can't have anything to do with work," Darren says.

"You caught me. I'm so awful. Okay. Hmm. All right, I know. You're going to laugh, or roll your eyes, you two. But so what? I met my son's friend Rachel. Who I didn't even—never mind. I met her, and well, you'll understand this when you're older, I was so relieved. No, that's not strong enough. I was so grateful, yes, grateful, at what wonderful taste he has in people. No, I mean it. Why are you covering your face, Darren? Do you guys remember, I'm sorry, Nate, but do you remember when Nate brought, what was his name, Ricky Dubrowski?"

"Rich, Mom," Nate says. "Rich Dubrowski."

"Ugh! I'm sorry, but ugh. I got so worried about you, Nate, when you brought him home. Of course, I can say that now, since that was the last time you did that."

"He was kind of douchey," Darren says.

"Whatever," Nate says.

"But so, it's just nice to meet you, Rachel. And have you as our guest."

"Thank you," Rachel says. "Thank you very much."

2. NATE

"Well," Nate says. "That was lovely and extremely embarrassing for around fifty to seventy-five percent of the table. So, my turn. Okay? Excellent. The best thing that happened to me this week is my mom reminding me I'm not in school, nor do I have a job, just before serving me a lovely Sabbath meal."

"Nate," she says.

"It's such a special time of week, when we take a break from all the zaniness of our many important academic and professional obligations."

"Nate."

"It feels so good to have someone remind you, as part of her new-and-improved observance of the Sabbath—"

"Nate!"

"Dude," Darren says. "C'mon, cut it out."

"Fine," Nate says, tearing off some challah. "I got tickets to see Wilco next month. D, you should come with. Their guitarist is insane."

5 Things Nate Offers Darren after Dinner up in Nate's Room While Rachel Helps Their Mom down in the Kitchen

1. MARIJUANA

Nate pulls open his underwear drawer and takes out an Altoids tin.

"You want some weed?" Nate asks.

"No, man," Darren says. "That's cool. I don't think she smokes. Plus my cold and everything."

Nate doesn't put the tin away. Instead he begins to prepare a bowl for himself, which, Darren assumes, he will smoke somewhere else sometime this evening.

2. ADVICE

Without looking up, Nate says, "I would like to strongly encourage you to . . ."

"To what?" Darren asks, leaning his head out the door, as if it's his job to make sure Nate doesn't get busted.

"To take advantage of the present situation."

"What does that mean?"

"Oh, I don't know." Nate stops what he's doing and says the next three words with slow emphasis, "You enormous moron."

"What?"

"What do you mean, what? Rachel. You. Empty house."

"What?" Darren approaches his brother. "What? So you want me to have sex with her or something?"

3. PROTECTION

"That's one option, and I have the necessary protection in this drawer right here if that's the path you choose."

"I'm not going to have sex with her."

"And why not?"

"Because."

"Because. Excellent reason."

"I'm serious."

"Okay, okay. I'm just saying, do not let this evening pass you by. She is, as far as I can tell, ready and willing."

"Whatever." Darren plops down on Nate's bed, a position that still affords him a decent view of the hallway.

Nate is nearing the end of his preparations. "And do not let thoughts of you-know-who stand in the way."

"Why not?"

"Because you're not dumb and she's not your girlfriend and she's not here and Rachel is and I can't even believe I have to explain any of this to you."

"And what if I like Zoey more than her?" Darren whispers loudly. "Then what?"

"Do you dislike Rachel?" Nate asks as he puts away the

tin. After closing the drawer, he rolls his chair over to Darren. "Is she unfriendly? Unkind? Unattractive? Uninterested? Unworthy? Un-ready to roll?"

Darren doesn't say anything.

4. A SCENARIO TO CONSIDER

"Worst-case scenario: You seize—no, wrong word—you *welcome* this opportunity with open arms, but you don't enjoy yourself. Then, at least, you know. But you do not, under any circumstances, let this just pass by watching some lame On-Demand movie."

"What, so I should just like use her or something?"

"Use her?" Nate buries his head in his hands. It may be a bit theatrical, but only a bit. "How would that be using her?"

Darren stands up. Checks the hallway. "Because I'm just doing stuff with her to do it?"

"D, she wants you to do it. It's like leasing with an option to buy."

"What the hell does that even mean?" Darren starts heading back toward the kitchen.

5. AN IDEA THAT MAY LEAD TO A BRIGHT MUSICAL FUTURE

"Hold on," Nate says.

"Huh?"

"You should get her to move here."

"Move here?"

"I mean, I know it's not happening, but we sounded good together. Am I right?"

"Yeah." Darren continues down the hallway.

"Her keyboards. Not to mention a female voice." Nate catches up to Darren. "I don't know why I didn't think of it sooner. The three of us, if I could find us a half-decent drummer, we'd get gigs no problem. But screw it, because regardless, we're going to have a band soon. I've been thinking about it. We're pretty good already, me and you, and with the right drummer, I mean, think about it."

"Yeah."

"I've been writing some songs—"

"You have?" They're on the stairs.

"I have. They're not ready yet, but they will be soon. And they're good. I mean, you and Mom might think I don't have a plan—"

"What are—?"

"But I figure we can get some weekend gigs, and then I can do something stupid part time, plus I met this guy last week, at Trey's, said they're looking for someone to do music reviews over at *The Reader*. Doesn't pay much, but it'll add up. College is bullshit anyway. In like twenty years, practically no one's gonna be going. Total rip-off."

2 People Who Are Gone within Thirty Minutes

1. Nate
2. His mom

5 Conclusions Darren Quickly Draws After Rachel, without Warning, Kisses His Eyes When They're Downstairs on the Couch

1. It's not particularly sexy.
2. But it's sort of mind-bogglingly kind.
3. No, it's loving—nurturing, even.
4. Something on her face says, *I want to care for you.*
5. She's kind of amazing if you stop and think about it.

6 **Articles of Clothing Darren and Rachel Quickly Put Back On at 8:47 p.m., Right After Darren Says, "Crap, I Think My Dad Is Out Front," but Before Hurrying Upstairs, Because They Were Watching a Lame On-Demand Movie in the Basement, at Least Officially They Were, but Then Someone Started Texting Darren, Who Ignored the First Couple Texts, for Obvious Reasons, but Then by the Third Sort of Had to Check**

1. Darren's pants
2. Darren's hoodie
3. Rachel's bra
4. Rachel's sweater
5. Rachel's pants
6. Darren's socks

3 Text Messages from His Dad That Darren's Phone Received between 8:18 and 8:46 p.m.

1. *You home? Hoping to bring something by for you soon.*
2. *On my way. If you're not there I'll just leave it by front door.*
3. *I'm here. You watching TV downstairs?*

2 Incomplete and Likely Misleading Introductions Darren and His Dad Make for Each Other

1. DARREN'S INTRODUCTION OF RACHEL TO HIS DAD

Darren's hand is on the front doorknob before he realizes that within about three seconds his dad will maybe somehow know what Darren was recently up to, and that's even if Rachel stays out of sight, which he's pretty sure he told her to do when they were rushing up the stairs, but maybe he only whispered it, who knows why.

"Hello," his dad (wearing a gray sport coat and peach-colored button-down) says after Darren opens the door.

"Hey," Darren says, stuffing his hands deep into his pockets, as if that might somehow conceal all the naughtiness he was recently participating in downstairs.

"How are you feeling?"

"Okay, I guess."

"Did you take something?"

Darren nods. "Yeah. Mom gave me some pills."

"Good. That's good," his dad says, and then raises a brown paper bag he must have been holding all along. "I made you some soup."

"Thanks." Darren takes the bag.

"My destined-to-be-FDA-approved chickenless chicken soup." His dad smiles.

"Cool," Darren says, hoping to say good-bye already. Only, his dad clearly notices something, or someone, over Darren's right shoulder.

"Hi," Rachel says, still a good distance away.

"Hello," his dad says, his smile now amused and curious.

Darren does nothing for maybe two seconds, hoping that somehow none of this just happened. Only here's Rachel, cheeks still blotchy and dyed-black hair all bent in the back, standing right next to Darren.

"Hi, I'm Rachel," she says very clearly. She actually extends her right hand to his dad, as if the thing hadn't been literally wrapped around Darren's pecker less than two hundred seconds earlier.

"Nice to meet you. Howard," his dad says. "Darren's father."

"I'm a friend of Darren's," Rachel says. "From camp."

"Oh," his dad says, as in, *Isn't that nice?*

"Yeah," Darren begins to catch up, "from Minneapolis. Only her, this other friend of hers, Krista, got sick, so she's—"

"Darren offered to put me up for the night," Rachel says, laughing.

His dad laughs. "Sounds great." Then he steals a glance at Darren, who, maybe because he was trying to be anywhere but this doorway, just noticed that the car idling in front of the house is not his dad's. The light isn't great out there, but someone's sitting in the driver's seat. A guy with a beard. In a sport coat himself.

2. HIS DAD'S INTRODUCTION OF RAY TO DARREN AND MAYBE RACHEL

His dad notices Darren noticing, so he turns around a bit to look at the car himself.

"Ray," he says to Darren. "A friend." Darren maybe lowers his eyebrows a bit or tilts his head, because his dad repeats himself. "Just a friend." Darren's eyes dart over to Rachel, who is still wearing the warm expression of a moment earlier, though it now appears a bit frozen and so seems warped as well.

"All right," Darren says, for whatever reason.

"Well, you two have fun," his dad says, and begins walking away. Then he stops and turns around, his face undecided about something. Darren takes a couple of steps toward him, feeling some blunt urge to get his dad to say whatever it is he may be thinking about saying. Only his dad just tips his head up at the mailbox affixed to the house's outer wall instead. "You forgot to bring in the mail."

"Oh," Darren says, turning around and grabbing it.

"Bye!" Rachel calls out.

"Nice to meet you," his dad says.

When his dad opens the car door, Darren gets a better

look at the driver. Definitely has a beard and glasses. Seems younger than his dad, though it's hard to be sure. They don't touch, but the car sits there for another five or ten seconds before driving off. His dad had Ray drive here, whoever the hell Ray is; his dad had him drive to the house he used to live in, and now he's telling this bearded guy about Darren, and maybe Rachel, too, and whatever it is he thought they were doing before he came by to deliver his fucking soup.

7 Questions Not Exactly Answered

1. "How long have your parents been divorced?"

   "My dad's gay."

2. "He is?"

   ". . ."

3. "Darren, are you serious?"

   "I think that might have been his boyfriend or some-thing."

4. "Are you okay?"

   "I think my dad has a boyfriend."

5. "When did you find out?"

   "I think he did that on purpose, have that guy bring him over. So I'd see."

6. "Do you want to talk about it?"

   "He does that kind of weird shit."

7. "What kind of weird shit?"

   "I'll be back in a sec."

5 Thoughts Darren Has While Peeing in the Upstairs Bathroom

1. Did the driver have glasses? Maybe he didn't. Definitely had a beard.

2. They were going out. At the least. That guy and his dad. And swinging by your old house to drop off soup for your son is definitely not the kind of stuff you do on a first date. Whether you're gay or not.

3. Rachel would *love* to talk to Darren about this. She'd listen like nobody's business. And then, whether or not their talk helped at all, she'd give him a chance to explore his heterosexuality with her. As reassurance or consolation or diversion. Or all three.

4. If Ray is who Darren thinks he is. If he is. Then what? If he is, if he is, if he is. That's as far as Darren can get with that thought. No, maybe he can delete the "if." But then that's truly it. Beyond that his brain just sort of shuts down. Like some appliance designed not to overheat and explode into flames. If he is, he is. He is if he is.

5. Oh right, the mail. Holding it in his other hand the whole time while he was pissing.

25 Letters Not Written in the Top Left Corner of the Third Envelope Darren Looks At, Which Is Addressed to Him (and Has the Words "Mailed from Belén, New Mexico" Printed over by the Stamp)

1. A
2. B
3. C
4. D
5. E
6. F
7. G
8. H
9. I
10. J
11. K
12. L
13. M
14. N
15. O
16. P
17. Q
18. R
19. S
20. T

21. U
22. V
23. W
24. X
25. Y

6 Sections of the "Letter" Darren Reads After Zipping His Pants Up, Washing His Hands, and Pacing Back and Forth in the Bathroom for a Full Minute

1. The date (September 14)
2. An absolutely amazing drawing of two forearms with that design on them, the hands attached to these arms holding each other, their fingers intertwined
3. Right below the drawing, in this cool block font, *"Having a mark means you're super special, but it kind of sucks a little too."* And then below that: *—Darren Jacobs*
4. The initials *ZL* in the bottom right-hand corner of the page
5. On the back, the sentence, *They asked us to draw a "fond memory."*
6. Under this sentence, *Zoey*

39 Extremely Urgent Questions Darren Would Like Answered ASAFP

1. Seriously?
2. That's it?
3. What the hell?
4. What does this mean?
5. Who the hell is "they"?
6. And did her putting "fond memory" in quotes mean that she doesn't really remember it fondly?
7. And doesn't she remember that we didn't even hold hands then?
8. Or ever, actually?
9. Does she think we did?
10. Did we?
11. Why did seeing my name written out by her make me feel like that was the first time I'd ever seen my name in my whole life?
12. How in the world does this get here the day I send her my letter?
13. And the day Rachel is here?
14. Is all this some kind of sign?
15. And if it is, what kind of sign is it?
16. Why didn't she include a return address?
17. Why didn't she tell me anything else?

18. Doesn't she realize this is like a form of torture?

19. Is she totally insane?

20. Or is this proof that she wants me to wait for her until she gets back?

21. Because she must have thought a lot about us holding hands while she worked on this, right?

22. But seriously, one lousy sentence?

23. When is she getting back?

24. And should I wait until she does?

25. Where the hell is Belén, New Mexico?

26. Should I write her back, even though I just wrote her?

27. What's going to happen now?

28. Who do I tell?

29. Should I tell anyone?

30. Rachel?

31. What would happen if I told Rachel?

32. Would that be mean?

33. Would she still want to fool around if I did?

34. Would I still want to?

35. Do I still want to?

36. What am I supposed to do?

37. Why isn't it obvious?

38. Or is it?

39. Why is my life like this?

10 Diversions Darren Calls Upon in Order to Delay His Exit from the Bathroom

1. Washing his hands, again.
2. Brushing his teeth.
3. Examining this one little, not-really-a-zit-yet zit that might be coming in on his chin.
4. Looking again at the rest of the mail, which is all clearly junk.
5. Washing his face.
6. Examining the two types of medication his mom brought him.
7. Performing some simple calculations.
8. Opening a box.
9. Taking two capsules.
10. Peeing again.

3 Forces Darren Surrenders To

1. RACHEL'S AFFECTION

When Darren finally opens the door and begins walking toward the stairs, he hears her say, "Over here." She's in his bedroom. So he turns around.

The room is dark, except for two candles. Not the Shabbat candles his mom lit before, but Shabbat candles all the same.

She grins, kind of sheepishly. "Am I like breaking a law or something? We can put them out."

"Who gives a shit," Darren says, unsure what, if anything, lies beyond his indifference. He's never seen his room lit only by candles. He has no idea if he likes it. He doesn't dislike it, that's for damn sure.

Rachel is by his computer. She presses a button. The song from before, the one he played for her, starts playing again. The lighting is absurdly appropriate. She comes over to him, her eyes all business. "How long until your mom comes home?"

"An hour, maybe. She'll text first." He's holding the mail. Meaning they're not exactly alone, him and Rachel.

"You know what the first thing I liked about you was?" Rachel asks between kisses, her voice accompanied by the sophisticated sounds of the Duke Ellington Orchestra.

"Huh?"

"Your name."

"My name stinks. It's stupid."

"No, it's not. I liked it. I saw it on a list of the bunks. *Darren Jacobs.* It seemed like, I don't know, like a kind name. I wanted to hug your name. I swear. I liked you before I saw you, Darren. Before I knew you at all."

She raises her mouth to his ear and whispers his name into it.

2. THE MEMORY OF HIS LAST DAY AT CAMP GREEN RIDGE

Darren estimates that about a third of the campers at Green Ridge cried the last day of camp, which wasn't really a day at all, but just breakfast and then getting on the buses. And though it was about a third overall, it was way more than half among the girls, definitely including Rachel. Because she might have been quiet when the whole camp was together, but this didn't mean she wouldn't cry, no siree. She was already crying the night before, when maybe only about 10 percent of campers (all girls) cried, and so she cried straight through breakfast and kept going when they all went outside where the different buses were waiting.

Darren hugged her a bunch that morning (more to comfort her than because he was all that sad to have to say goodbye to her). But after a while, around the time her face started to freak him out a little, because her eyes were puffy and her skin was red and splotchy, Darren just sort of decided that he would hug her some more but that they were kind of already broken up in his head, something he had been considering for a couple of days by that point, but that seemed sort of pointless with camp almost over.

Then there was this weird half-hour stretch during which the counselors had already told them they really had to get on the buses "now," but before everyone was finally on them (in fact, pretty much no one except some of the youngest boys got on a bus in the first ten minutes). Meaning camp was already over, but no one seemed ready to admit it. And even though Darren had a feeling that Rachel intended to be one of the very last people to get on her bus, Darren didn't himself feel like being a part of all this much longer, because there was something creepy about looking over at his bunk and knowing it was now totally empty except for the bed frames and mattresses.

So the first moment it seemed kind of reasonable for him to get on the bus, he took her hand, hugged her once more, and said, "I think I'm going to get on now."

She smiled this super weird smile for him, reached into her backpack, and handed him a letter in a purple envelope. "For the bus," she said.

"Okay," Darren said. "Thanks." They kissed one last time (a pretty good kiss actually, like her crying had done something to make her lips softer than normal), and he got on the bus.

Darren forgot about the letter until around Madison (he'd passed out almost as soon as he sat down, since he had stayed up pretty much the entire night before). Inside was a card with a drawing of fireworks printed on it. Rachel had written, *Once upon a time there was a girl. One day the girl met a boy. The boy made the girl very, very happy. But then the girl had to say good-bye to the boy. This made her very, very sad. The girl began to cry and could not stop. She cried for days and weeks and months until the land was flooded, until the water rose all the way up to her bedroom window. The girl built a boat out of her bed and sailed away. She sailed past all the cities and all the towns and all the villages, but still, she could not stop crying. She met a kind seagull, who tried to cheer her up. But it could not, so it flew away. She met a friendly otter, who tried to make her smile. But it could not, so it swam away. She met a funny turtle, who tried to make her laugh. But it could not, so it crawled inside its shell and floated away. The girl was left alone with her tears. Until one day another boat appeared on the horizon. The girl sailed toward it. It was the boy. He stepped onto her boat and wiped the tears off her cheeks. She stopped crying. His boat drifted away. They kept on sailing together, in the slowly receding waters, past the far horizon. The End. Always, always, Rachel.*

Darren, still just sort of half-awake, reread Rachel's story a few times, until he started wondering what would have happened if they were at a camp for creative writing instead of music, and if he would have come to like Rachel more instead of less if he got to see her read her stories, because her piano playing sort of bummed him out and convinced him that there wasn't really anything so special about her, but this story, even though it was pretty corny and everything, it somehow got to him anyway.

Because if he knew this about her before, who knows, maybe he would have cried when they hugged and kissed that last time, because he did almost start to feel something then but didn't feel like letting himself feel it, so instead he kind of whispered, "Okay, I should probably get on the bus. Bye."

3. DOXYLAMINE SUCCINATE

Kissing is an awfully strange activity when you think about it. Like of all the things you can do with your mouth, it's weird that you can do this, too. Did someone have to invent it first? Because have you ever seen animals kiss?

It must be the lighting, or the horn section, or how he can taste Rachel's mouth more than he could before (maybe because he brushed his teeth). All he knows is that kissing her right now, not that it's bad, not at all, but if they sat here softly tugging at each other's ears, that wouldn't seem any more bizarre to him than this.

Life would be a lot easier if you liked the same person who

liked you. Or at least liked the person who likes you the same amount that they like you. Assuming you're lucky enough to have someone like you in the first place. And especially if that person knows how to act with adults, and likes not just making out, but also most of the other stuff that people do with and for each other after they've been making out for a while. Because that stuff's probably pretty great when you're doing it with a person you like exactly as much as they like you.

His mom said he should only take the green capsules right before he goes to bed, since they're for nighttime. Plus it had only been about two hours since he took the other ones. But sometimes being awake is an enormous inconvenience. Like when girls keep giving you letters that won't leave you alone.

It's probably not fair to Rachel to concentrate on her hair, or find ways of encouraging her to stick to his ear. She deserves better. Though the weird thing is she's definitely really happy right now. Or pleased. But then later on, at some point, he's not going to be able to keep this up forever, whatever it is he's keeping up right now.

The truth is, it feels quite nice to have her pressed against him like she is. She's so warm. But not too warm. Not hot. If there was some way to convince her to fall asleep on top of him, the way he's going to fall asleep below her, it would be sort of perfect, at least in the short term.

Is she the nicest person ever? And if so, how can that possibly be not enough?

When he finally passes out in a moment or two, there will remain the question of where she will sleep. Definitely not in Nate's room. Because who knows. His mom might put her down on the couch, or even give her the office. It is Shabbat, after all. So maybe it's okay, then. Just letting himself say good night to her and this Friday already without actually saying it out loud.

Good night.

4.

SATURDAY, NOVEMBER 29

2 More Months That Have Passed

1. October
2. November, at least most of it

4 Regrettable Ways the Morning Greets Darren

1. His right leg is off the bed, with the attached foot fully touching the ground, something his right leg and foot have been doing in his sleep on and off for a couple of months now.
2. He has an erection, which he has been holding unconsciously, which wouldn't be so bad, except:
3. Sonny is sniffing it. Not licking it, just sniffing it, but still. Not to mention (and worst of all):
4. His dad's head is peeking through the door, a head that is saying, "Sonny, stop that, let him sleep!"

5 Physical Changes Darren Has Undergone since the End of September

1. Crept over five feet seven and a half inches
2. Crept below 180 pounds
3. Each foot now requires a size eleven
4. Has grown, depending on the quality of the lighting, between three and four new chest hairs, bringing the grand total to four or five
5. Could reasonably justify shaving his mustache region once a month or so

10 Lousy Aspects of Having Your Birthday on November 29, Both in General and Especially This Year and Last

1. It stinks having your birthday around the time of another holiday, even if Thanksgiving is a pretty good holiday in general. Because the holiday sort of sucks the attention and excitement away from your birthday. Sure, his parents would have a couple of days off to make all the arrangements for his party, but what good is that if half the kids you invited are going to be out of town? Plus, it wasn't that the laser tag party for his eleventh birthday was bad, it was that you could just tell that people were pretty distracted and kind of tired, since everyone had been going to bed super late the past couple of nights and had eaten about four hundred pounds of food over the previous seventy-two hours.

So then some years they would just push his party back a week or so to get it far away from Thanksgiving, but then it's not his birthday anymore. And don't even get Darren started on what happens at school, where all the stupid Thanksgiving excitement and assemblies also stand in the way of him getting the treatment other students get on their birthday. Too bad his birthday isn't in mid-February like Nate's.

2. And Nate is pretty likely to make Darren's sixteenth weird somehow. Overall it maybe hasn't been so great having him back home. He's high all the time, delivers pizza for La Luna's (excellent pizza, but still), and keeps finding these kind of gross and stupid girls to go out with and even sometimes bring home. Darren's pretty sure he has sex with most of them and then doesn't see them much after that.

Nate still fights with their mom a lot, mostly because she won't stop asking him to just please enroll at Oakton Community College and take a class or two. Nate's still extremely nice to Darren most of the time, but for some reasons it seems like he's chosen Darren as the person he's going to impart all sorts of supposed wisdom to, wisdom that doesn't seem much like wisdom to Darren.

So Darren just has this feeling that Nate is going to do something in honor of Darren's birthday, something that Nate will think is deep and meaningful and even revelatory (or at least undeniably awesome), but won't really be any of those things, but is going to require Darren to pretend that it is.

3. This isn't his first birthday since his parents split up—that was last year—but at least last year his mom was in California, which she apologized for about ninety-four times but which Darren was sort of grateful for. Since she was in California, he could just pretend that was the reason only his dad was at the dinner, even though he knew it wasn't. Which made last year's birthday kind of lame too, but probably not as lame as this one will be.

4. But this year he's not so lucky, partially because he almost was. His mom was supposed to get back from San Jose on Wednesday night, but there was a big storm in Denver, where she had a layover, and her flight got canceled. So she decided to stay in California a couple more days, since apparently computer people work pretty much all the time, including over Thanksgiving weekend. Now she's only getting in this afternoon.

This has, of course, totally screwed up all the arrangements and agreements his parents took forever to work out, like where Darren will sleep and who he's having dinner with and when they'll do the hand-off, arrangements and agreements that ultimately required Darren's involvement, since it's his birthday they're talking about here, and so a few times they just asked him, "What would you prefer, honey?" which was both considerate and totally stupid, because what he'd prefer is for his parents to be together and what he wouldn't prefer (in addition to the divorce) is for them to make him choose between them in any way, which they both sort of acknowledged right before asking him, "What would you prefer, honey?" but still, they asked him anyway.

So now, he can barely even keep it straight: He'll have

lunch with his mom and dinner with his dad (instead of the other way around), but it's not clear if and when a movie and/or bowling might happen (and he can't even remember agreeing to maybe going bowling; he has a feeling this was Nate's suggestion, who's been bowling a lot, too, who knows why) or how the hand-off is going to happen.

5. Actually that last part is untrue. The hand-off isn't technically going to be a hand-off. Because you don't hand yourself off. Today is Darren's sixteenth birthday, after all. And in addition to all the other complicated things planned today, he and his dad are going down to the good old DMV right after breakfast to take his driving test. That's right, Darren gets to take a test on his birthday.

And everyone just assumes he's excited beyond belief about this. But he's not. He's more scared than excited. Scared and worried. Scared and worried and annoyed. Because he's got enough stuff on his plate, in terms of his messed-up family and girl issues and school just kind of sucking hard, so why has the world decided that the additional responsibility of operating a massive, expensive, complicated machine is something he should be looking forward to? The truth is, he'd be very happy if they bought him a really nice bike for his sixteenth birthday.

6. And sixteen in general is just way more pressure than Darren feels like dealing with right now. Because this birthday is definitely the most important birthday between thirteen and eighteen, whatever the hell that means. But Darren can just feel that he's not up to (or is not even capable of) enjoying himself enough today to meet the expectations of the sixteenth birthday as some kind of tradition, again, whatever the hell that means. In other words, he just feels that it's going to be a lousy birthday, and would be even if it was only his fifteenth or seventeenth. The fact that it's his sixteenth will only make it worse.

7. Not to mention, some years his birthday would be on the day right after Thanksgiving, which his mom and dad would for some reason act like is the greatest thing ever, since, they'd say, what can you be more thankful for than having such a wonderful son? But he wouldn't be thankful at all, because the rest of the world doesn't care one bit that it's your birthday, meaning basically no restaurants are open that day, except the ones offering Thanksgiving feasts, meaning you have to have dinner at home on your birthday, which maybe wouldn't be so bad if Darren wasn't a vegetarian, because it's not like everyone else is going to agree to give up turkey in his honor, which, even when he did eat meat he thought tasted horrible.

8. Darren is going to try really hard to not eat too much today, because even though his body has sort of stretched itself over the last few months, he still feels like an oaf most of the time.

But there's no question that now that he spent the night at his dad's instead of his mom's, Ray is going to show up and make some insanely delicious breakfast for him. Which isn't the end of the world, obviously, but his dad also asked Darren the night before if (now that he'd be waking up at his dad's) it would be okay with Darren if Ray could come by early to honor Darren's birthday the way they do in Ray's family, which means singing to you and giving you your presents first thing in the morning while you're still in bed.

Darren doesn't mind the idea of getting presents first thing (he's less psyched about being sung to while still in bed), but still, does his lousy sixteenth birthday really have to start with his dad's now totally official boyfriend (who Darren somehow actually likes) singing to him first thing in the morning, all because Darren's parents got divorced and his dad is homosexual and met Ray and then it snowed ten inches in Denver?

9. Plus last year Nate came home for Thanksgiving, which was okay in general, only at dinner he started talking about colonialism and Native Americans and ethnic cleansing and how, in his words, "Thanksgiving is pretty much total bullshit when you stop and think about it."

Their mom (it was just the three of them; they went to their dad's on Friday morning) listened to why he thought Thanksgiving was bullshit, and then she said, "Well, that may all be true, but I think we still have plenty of reasons to be thankful."

Only Nate just said, "Yeah, I guess, like living in a society where it's okay not to give a shit about genocide." And so then they had a big fight that Darren heard most of from the bathroom. It wasn't actually his birthday that day, but whatever, now he likes Thanksgiving even less, though he's not really sure if he should. Either way, he's pretty sure it's now going to make his birthday even lamer.

10. And the truth is none of this would matter so much if Zoey lived here and he knew she was his girlfriend. But she doesn't and he has no idea if she is. She's something, at least he hopes she is. Well, at least they're in touch, even if it is in their weird way. Things would be way simpler if it were all or nothing with her. Instead it's something in between. Way closer to nothing than all, but enough of something to be something.

Not to mention Rachel, his other long-distance love interest. They at least communicate with actual words, but is this even a good thing? Because Rachel is somehow okay with anything and everything, including him being honest with her about Zoey and continually postponing his visit to Minneapolis.

Maybe having the right girlfriend would make his life better or maybe it wouldn't. But he can't know that until he has the right girlfriend. Which he for some reason thinks Zoey would be and for some reason thinks Rachel isn't. But maybe he's wrong. Wrong about Zoey being right and wrong about Rachel being not right. Or, even worse, wrong about the whole right-girlfriend theory in general.

Whatever the case, there's no way in the world he's going to resolve any of this today, meaning the supposedly new stage of his life his sixteenth birthday is supposed to somehow usher in isn't really going to be a new stage at all. It's just going to be more of the pointless suckiness and confusion that seemed to jam-pack the year that came to an end yesterday at midnight.

9 Dates of Communications between Darren and People Who Have Been or Still Are in the General Vicinity of Belén, New Mexico

1. SATURDAY, SEPTEMBER 27

Say what you will about Darren, but don't think he feels anything but right at home in the land of Google. Because the second Rachel left their house Saturday afternoon (turned out her parents weren't so crazy about the stay-at-some-boy's-house backup plan) Darren was knee-deep in the search engine. He started with "Belén New Mexico boarding school," and it took him a while, but eventually he found it: Savilleta Ranch Academy, "a therapeutic boarding school for troubled teenagers," which looked to be about nine miles from Belén.

Darren spent two straight hours reading basically every last word on their website. The overview, the clinical program, the academic stuff, et cetera. He even read about a dozen of these very long and pretty strange "letters" one of the therapists writes to parents and alumni on a majorly regular basis. Sample sentence: "The courage required to be weak, to be vulnerable, this is what we asked of them yesterday."

Of course the site said absolutely nothing specific (or even vague) about any of the kids there, but that doesn't mean Darren was left without potential material for filling in his admittedly still fairly sketchy picture of Zoey. Drinking, drugs, addiction, mental illness, crime, suicide attempts, the list was long and there wasn't a single place to hide inside it. As Darren reluctantly put the list together and asked himself just how many of them fit Zoey, he couldn't quite convince himself the details didn't matter. Even worse, he couldn't help but notice this part of him saying, "Dude, turn off the computer and forget the whole damn thing already. And yes, that means Zoey, too."

But Darren didn't. Or couldn't. Or just wouldn't. Because apparently there was some feeling in him for her that was bigger and/or prior to the contents of her disastrous list. Which was either a really good sign or a really bad one. Regardless, he started another search, which was way more complicated and desperate than the first, but he eventually struck gold with "spent challenging years Savilleta Ranch Academy." There it was, a link to a blog belonging to some guy named Ben Zwiren. His blog's called *The Other Side* and showed a picture of Ben, who looked kind of scraggily and high and/or wise. More important, it included a few essays by Ben, one of which mentioned that he "spent two challenging years at Savilleta Ranch Academy." Two years that ended in June.

So Darren sent Ben a friend request.

2. MONDAY, SEPTEMBER 29

Darren had no idea how to respond to Zoey's drawing. Part of him thought it gave him permission to write her a real letter, and part of him wasn't so sure. He was so mental about her by this point, and even more mental about just being mental about her, that he didn't trust himself to use actual words where she was involved. Not to mention, without knowing how she meant "fond memory," there was just no way to actually say anything without maybe sounding very stupid and even mean. All he did know was that he sure as hell loved that drawing, which kind of made him understand that whole "a picture's worth a thousand words" saying for the very first time.

But what about some songs? Some of the jazz he was now into obsessively? Who knows, maybe she just wanted them to send stuff to each other but not give each other updates about what was actually happening in their lives. Which was why she sent that drawing in the first place.

If those were the rules, he could be okay with them.

And songs were kind of what was happening in his life. To the extent that anything was. Like, how many hours was he spending in his room listening to these songs and copying all those CDs he got from the library?

Not to mention, he decided, it would be kind of cool just sending stuff without actual letters, because most letters people send each other are just a bunch of boring updates or dumb clichés. And Darren knew he could make a pretty good playlist, and would probably make her a bunch of playlists if she were here (and they were at least friends).

Plus, even though he wasn't going to be using words, the truth was most of the songs he'd include were either love songs or songs that feel kind of romantic to him. So in some ways he would be telling her what he thinks. And even if she didn't get that at all, so what? But he kind of had a hunch she would. Like she'd get it even if she didn't totally 100 percent realize she was getting it.

So he sent her a playlist with a bunch of old jazz tunes on it.

3. WEDNESDAY, OCTOBER 1
Ben accepted Darren's friend request.

4. WEDNESDAY, OCTOBER 1
Darren sent Ben a message: *Hey, I saw on your blog that you were at Savilleta Ranch Academy. A friend of mine is there. I think. Zoey Lovell. Do you know her? Is she okay?*

5. FRIDAY, OCTOBER 10
Ben wrote back: *I can't talk about other residents. Sorry, man. I can't even tell you if she's there or not. Confidentiality: serious matter there. Serious. But if she is there, good place. Hard place too. But very good.*

For a while Darren figured that was that. She was there or she wasn't, but this Ben guy was clearly not about to divulge anything useful, even though, if Darren had to guess, he totally knew Zoey, maybe even better than Darren. Which made Darren just about lose his mind. But right when he was getting ready to assume she didn't get his letter, or did but couldn't give a shit, and that the whole thing was, is, and always would be a very bad idea, then, on

6. SATURDAY, OCTOBER 25,
he got a letter from Zoey. Well, not exactly a letter. Another drawing. Rolled up in a tube. It wasn't totally clear what materials she used, some kind of weird paint. So maybe it was a painting. Whatever it was, the picture was mostly dark, though you could sort of see the ground near the bottom, which was definitely desert. But most of the drawing was of the sky, which she somehow filled with stars, like hundreds or maybe even thousands of tiny individual dots that were actually the paint or whatever it was being removed. Very carefully.

Because it was pretty obvious, looking at the dots, which weren't all the same size or at all evenly distributed, that she spent a ridiculously long time making each and every one of them. Darren could almost see her in New Mexico, sitting outside her cabin (or wherever the hell residents stay at Savilleta Ranch Academy, a cottage maybe?) at night, staring up at the sky, looking down at her picture, scraping away a super tiny spot, looking up again, and repeating this for like three nights in a row. Near the top left corner of the picture was a little white arrow pointing at one star. And just below that, the word, also scraped out of paint, "home." A capital Z in the bottom right corner, same technique. That was it.

Darren, sitting in the house, which was one of his two supposed homes, wrestled with an urge to commandeer his mom's car and drive straight to New Mexico, even though he didn't have his license yet and hated driving. Instead, on that same day,

7. SATURDAY, OCTOBER 25,

he wrote Ben again. Maybe because all the alternatives (his mom, his dad, Nate, maybe Zoey or even Rachel) didn't exactly seem like alternatives. He was so confused about who to contact and what to say, he did one of those usually foolish, impulsive online things, which in this instance meant writing this:

Hey man. Zoey sent me a couple things. Her artwork. I don't know what to do. I really like her. These things she sent, I don't know, I think she likes me. And maybe needs something from me. To help her, even. But what the hell am I supposed to do? Am I crazy to like someone there? Am I crazy to think she likes me? Am I dumb to wait? I sent her a playlist, but I want to write her a letter and just tell her everything. I mean, EVERYTHING. Should I? I know you don't know me and maybe don't even know her, but at least you know where she is. I think. Please help.

But Ben didn't write him back for a while, so he just sent her another playlist on

8. WEDNESDAY, NOVEMBER 5,

which she still hasn't responded to. And Ben hasn't responded either. At least, he still hadn't when Darren went to bed last night.

9. FRIDAY, NOVEMBER 28

But here it is, the first birthday present Darren gets today. A Facebook message from Ben, which Darren reads on his phone, in his bed, while waiting for his dad and Ray to come and sing to him.

Okay, she's there. She is. Really shouldn't be telling you that, but I am (don't spread it, SERIOUSLY). As for telling her everything (I mean, EVERYTHING): not something I recommend. Not right now. Whatever she's dealing with, it's pretty intense. They make sure of that over there. If you show up thinking you don't have some serious shit to deal with, then first thing, they help you see you've got that very, very wrong. So yeah, basic tenet of the program: You're not supposed to have a girlfriend or boyfriend while you're there. Which I can explain why another time if you want, but basically: Dealing with your shit in a serious manner is not possible when you're telling yourself your girl-/boyfriend is going to make everything okay. Which is what everyone thinks. Everyone. Ergo: bad idea. But she needs a friend right now. Be that for her. Seriously. Oh, and happy birthday (Facebook told me).

So maybe it's not actually a present, but the timing, well, Darren can't exactly ignore the timing.

17 Songs on the First Playlist Darren Sent to Zoey

1. "I Love Music," Ahmad Jamal
2. "Lucky to Be Me," Bill Evans
3. "Autumn Leaves," Cannonball Adderley
4. "Theme for Lester Young," Charles Mingus
5. "Day Dream," Duke Ellington
6. *"Fleurette Africaine,"* Duke Ellington
7. "All Too Soon," Duke Ellington
8. "Dolphin Dance," Herbie Hancock
9. "Naima," John Coltrane
10. "Say It (Over and Over Again)," John Coltrane
11. "Ceora," Lee Morgan
12. "My Funny Valentine," Miles Davis
13. "It Never Entered My Mind," Miles Davis
14. "I Loves You, Porgy," Miles Davis
15. "I'll Remember April," Sonny Clark
16. "Footprints," Wayne Shorter
17. "Infant Eyes," Wayne Shorter

11 Songs Disqualified from Inclusion on the Playlist Because Their Titles Were a Little Too Appropriate

1. "When Your Lover Has Gone"
2. "I Got It Bad and That Ain't Good"
3. "I Want to Talk about You"
4. "The Touch of Your Lips"
5. "I Fall in Love Too Easily"
6. "My Foolish Heart"
7. "You Go to My Head"
8. "You're My Everything"
9. "It's Bad to Be Forgotten"
10. "If I Could Be with You"
11. "Lover Come Back to Me"

3 Languages Ray (and His Dad) Sing "Happy Birthday" to Darren In (Actually, His Dad Only Sings the First and a Bit of the Last)

1. English
2. Portuguese
3. Spanish

5 Ray-Related Memories That Come to the Surface While Ray and His Dad Are Singing That Once Again Prevent Darren from Hating Ray, Even Though He Keeps Expecting to Really Despise the Guy and Still Sort of Wants To

1. The first time he tasted something from the Green Llama, which is this amazing vegetarian restaurant where Ray's the head chef. Just a little dumpling filled with sweet potato and who knows what else. The thing tasted so good Darren couldn't just say, "Whatever" to his dad, which is what he was planning on saying when his dad first demanded he taste the thing. Instead, "Holy shit, that's insane."

2. The first time he met Ray face-to-face (and not just saw him from far away and through a car window, like he did the night of the soup delivery). Which was sometime in the middle of October, about four days after his dad decided to tell him (at Dr. Schrier's office) that some guy named Ray was now his official boyfriend. Darren stopped by his dad's place on the way to school that morning (he'd forgotten his physics textbook there) and found some guy on the couch, drinking coffee and reading the *New York Times*.

Darren just stood there, right by the entrance, looking at this guy, who was sitting on the couch, looking back at Darren.

"Good morning," the guy said in this accent of his, because, it turns out, his dad is Brazilian and his mom is from Nicaragua (it might actually be the other way around).

"Hey," Darren said, probably not loud enough to be heard.

Darren was so uncomfortable, he thought the back of his head might split open.

Only just then the guy said, "Ray," nodded his head a bit, and raised his mug toward Darren, maybe to mean, *Yes this is awkward and perhaps unfortunate, but here we are, and look, we have survived this moment, so cheers.*

Darren didn't say "Darren," in part because Ray certainly knew who Darren was, but also because Darren was still more paralyzed than not. Though whatever Ray just said did allow Darren to resume breathing. And it was around then—after he remembered why he was there in the first place and that it was an otherwise regular Tuesday morning and that at some point he'd have to do something—that he noticed the music, which had been playing all along.

There was something about the rhythm that grabbed him. The song almost sounded like one of the songs ("*Recorda Me*") Mr. Keyes was trying to teach them, but not exactly. It made Darren kind of want to tap his foot, even though he realized he had no idea how you were supposed to tap your foot to music like this.

Ray noticed Darren noticing the song, pointed to the

speakers and said, "Novos Baianos." Darren didn't say anything, so Ray said, "That's the name of the group. You like it?" Darren didn't want to answer, so he just shrugged his shoulders, walked to his room, grabbed the book, and left, mumbling, "See ya."

3. About four days later, at their first official meeting, when something similar was playing. Ray said, "Darren, if you like, I can put some of this music on your iPod, if you like."

Part of Darren wanted to say, *Ray, if you like, I can push you off a cliff.* But he didn't, maybe because Ray made his offer in this way that made Darren at least feel like he might want to consider it. It's a hard tone to describe, but it sort of sounded like, "I know we're only having this conversation because your parents got divorced and your dad came out of the closet, but this music is, I swear, a gift from heaven, and it would make me really happy to share it with you, and just think, if you really like this music—and I'm confident you will—then the divorce and your dad being gay wouldn't be all bad, so, you know, it's up to you."

Or something like that.

So Darren gave his dad his iPod to give to Ray, who put this playlist with about fifty songs on it.

4. This one weirdly sunny and beautiful day in late October, when Darren decided to walk home from school. He put on

Ray's playlist, which he hadn't listened to yet. Pretty much out of principle he hadn't. As in, screw Ray and his maybe literally gay music. But then, honestly, Darren was having one of those days he'd been having more often than not this school year, when it feels like the sucky-to-bearable ratio was around seven to one. Meaning he was feeling a little desperate. Plus, at some point Ray and/or his boyfriend/Darren's dad was going to ask Darren what he thought. So he might as well at least get this little bit of homework out of the way.

But then something strange happened. The music was kind of amazing. Almost right away. So much so that Darren suddenly started wondering, right there on Dempster, if his parents hadn't listened to this music all the time when he was little, because most of it sounded strangely familiar. He could swear he already knew it. As if he had two different childhoods but had somehow entirely forgotten about one of them.

As he kept walking, and maybe faster than normal, he had this weird sensation. It was like the music was making his life feel bigger, much bigger, than it usually felt. Because there he was, walking down the same stupid sidewalk and past the same stupid street signs, watching the same stupid cars with the same stupid Illinois license plates driving by, but somehow none of these things bothered him. In fact, he walked right past the house, confused and maybe even a little happy, because he was almost certain the music was telling him that someday his life would be much better. And

Darren totally believed the music and didn't feel like an idiot for doing so.

The only bad part about all this was him knowing that he wouldn't entirely be able to hide this from Ray or his dad. Because he really wanted to just give Ray the finger in every last way, but now he couldn't.

5. Just two weeks ago, when he overheard the very end of this phone conversation his dad was having with Ray. Darren had been in his bedroom, with the door closed and his headphones on, which is how he spends at least 87 percent of his time at his dad's apartment. But then he had to go to the bathroom. When he got to the hallway he heard his dad's half of the call:

"Yes, I know."

"You're so right, Ray. You are."

"So smart. Of course. I'll just call over there in the morning and see if they'll go up to three twenty-five."

"Right." His dad laughed. "I'm sure it will turn out to be nothing."

Darren knew from the "go up to three twenty-five" thing that they were talking about real estate. But that wasn't the point, wasn't the thing that made Darren just stop right there in the middle of the hallway. Because there was something in his dad's voice. Like Darren almost wasn't sure it was his dad talking at all. So Darren turned around and quietly walked toward his dad's room instead of the bathroom and peeked in through the partially open door.

"I know. Amazing. You're amazing. You are."

"Thanks."

His dad sounded—what was it?—he sounded sort of relaxed and confident. He sounded like this version of his dad Darren hadn't heard in a long time. So long, he had sort of forgotten until just then that this version of his dad ever existed in the first place.

"We will."

"Yes, of course."

"Bye."

There he was, Darren's dad, hanging up the phone and facing the bed so that Darren could see the side of his face. He looked so happy. But not like "Yippee!" happy. So maybe it wasn't happy at all. But it was something good, something positive, something really positive, something so positive that it made Darren almost want to spend time with him. Almost.

And he's been sounding and looking that way more and more lately. Thanks to Ray, who's singing to Darren in Spanish at this very moment. Because that's how out of whack Darren's life has gotten: His dad's boyfriend seems as likely as anyone to make things better at this point.

4 Presents Darren Gets from His Dad (and Maybe Ray) for His Sixteenth Birthday

1. A $25.00 iTunes gift card
2. A gray zip-up hoodie lined with the stuff they make long underwear out of
3. These new, probably expensive earbud headphones that go right into your ears that his dad says might take some time to get used to but will sound a million times better than the lousy ones that came with his iPod
4. A small keychain in the shape of a *D*, made out of thin, dark metal wires woven together, with some kind of car key already on it

6 Reassurances/Encouragements/Explanations His Dad and Ray Give Darren After It Becomes Clear That the Key on Darren's New Keychain Goes to Ray's Infiniti G37

1. Don't worry, it's insured and so are you.
2. Your sixteenth birthday should be special.
3. Ray will take the train to work today. I will drive him to the station.
4. You're a good driver. If we didn't think you could handle it, we wouldn't have given it to you.
5. It's just for today. Seriously, don't get too used to it.
6. You're going to feel really cool in it. Trust us.

6 Features of Ray's Car Darren Can't Help but Like, Even Though He Wishes He Didn't, Because Then None of Him Would Want to Drive It

1. It's a coupe, which is sporty but not exactly a sports car. Which matters and is good, since Darren can't help but sort of assume that anyone who drives a sports car, especially if he's a guy, is a dick, like Mr. Krickstein and his I'm-a-dick goatee, who lives next door to the house and drives a Porsche and always looks at Darren like Darren smells bad.

2. The color and paint job are pretty killer. The exact name of the color is probably something ridiculous like Evening Smoke, but still, it's not gray or silver or black, it's somehow all of them. Plus it's both shiny and not.

3. It's a fancy car, but not a super fancy car, which, like sports cars, sort of means you're a dick, because Mr. Krickstein's Porsche is much fancier than Ray's car.

4. "G37" just seems like a good letter/number combination; Darren's not sure why.

5. The sound system, and he hasn't even turned it on yet.

6. The main curve from front to back, which is nice to look at.

5 Adjustments Darren Makes to Ray's Car While Waiting for His Dad

1. MOVES THE SEAT UP ABOUT TWO INCHES

Which is less than Darren would have guessed he'd need to move it up, since Ray is over six feet. And this makes Darren a little happy, because he's definitely getting taller, a realization that somehow almost has him thinking that this birthday might not be so bad after all.

2. TILTS THE REARVIEW MIRROR DOWN A BIT

At which point he sees a black Prius drive by, the same car his mom has. And there's something about how Darren's suddenly not feeling all the way cruddy has him thinking about just how much she's the opposite of cruddy these days. She got her hair done differently a couple weeks ago, and it looks really good. Plus she keeps talking about how her work is developing in very promising directions. And even though it's weird to him, she seems to think that keeping kosher and not checking e-mail on Saturday are super meaningful developments in her life. Thankfully, she hasn't even so much as hinted at having her own Ray hidden somewhere, but even so, Darren kind of gets the sense that she could find someone if she wanted to.

3. BRINGS THE LEFT SIDE MIRROR IN JUST A TAD
Which means that both of them, his dad and his mom, are doing better now than they were doing before the divorce. Maybe even way better. But so is Darren supposed to be happy for them about this? Should he even be happy for himself in some way, seeing how having happy divorced parents has got to be better than having miserable married parents? Which is pretty much what they were by the end, if he's going to be totally honest about it. And so does turning sixteen mean turning the age when you're just supposed to figure out how to be happy for other people even if their happiness means a little suckiness for you?

4. BRINGS THE RIGHT SIDE MIRROR IN JUST A TAD
But he can't help it. What's he supposed to do? He liked having the family together. And he didn't like the divorce. So whatever, maybe it's best for his parents that his dad finally admitted he's gay and that his mom got to start her new life before she was super old. But what Darren would really like for his birthday, more than this car or anything like that, is to get replacement parents, married (and, yes, straight, or maybe even just both gay to begin with) replacement parents who are actually just his parents from when he was around nine years old. That would be perfect.

5. TILTS THE STEERING WHEEL UP, THEN DOWN, THEN UP AGAIN

But apparently that's not happening, because here's his new and improved and officially gay dad, buckling himself in and rubbing his hands together.

"All righty! Next stop: DMV!"

Darren takes the car out of park and notices this part of him that wants to plow the car straight into the wall of his dad's apartment building. This part also wouldn't mind if Ray, and maybe even his dad (and mom, too?) were standing in between the car and the building.

So maybe it's not going to be such a great birthday after all.

4 Moving Violations Darren Wants to (But Simply Cannot) Execute (in Order to Purposely Fail the Driving Test), Since for Some Reason the Part of Him That Does What It's Supposed to Do Sort of Kicks the Ass of the Part of Him That Intends to Blow It, as If It Were God and Not the State of Illinois That Placed These Signs and Established These Rules

1. Running the stop sign at the corner of Lawler and Berwyn.
2. Exceeding the 40 miles per hour speed limit on Milwaukee.
3. Failing to signal while changing lanes on Central.
4. Failing to yield to a pedestrian at the designated crosswalk at Bryn Mawr and Menard.

1 Sign That the Troubling Impulse Darren Had Back in Front of the Apartment Building Is Still Lurking inside Him Somewhere

1. "You passed your driving test on the first try," his dad says, "and with flying colors at that!"

Darren turns right back onto Elston. It's a simple turn and there's basically no traffic, but the maneuver still gives him an excuse to ignore what was just said to him.

"And the weather's magnificent," his dad says. "Especially for late November."

"Mm-hmm," Darren says.

"I can't remember the weather ever being so nice on your birthday. The universe decided to give you a little gift. How considerate."

"Ha."

"It's your birthday, Darren. You're sixteen!"

"Yup."

"You're smart. You're handsome. You've got this *amazing* car at your disposal for the whole day." His dad does this sometimes. The gratitude roll call, or whatever he calls it. And he does call it something, something with the word "gratitude" in it. Probably picked it up at his "men's group," the creepiest gathering in the history of humanity. "And healthy, thank God."

Darren nods his head. They drive in silence for a while.

Ray's car is a very good car. The stereo is probably insane. He'll be able to check it out soon enough.

His dad makes some sort of awkward sniffling sound. They're at a red light, so Darren turns his head an eighth of the way around; his eyes can do the rest. His dad is crying. Not a lot, but he's definitely crying.

He wipes off the tears with the back of his hand. The gesture strikes Darren as unforgivably effeminate. "I'm sorry, I'm sorry," his dad says. "But Darren, you bring me so much joy. You're such a joy. I love you so much. I just can't—"

"Will you fucking stop it? For once?" It just comes out.

Then they're driving again, so Darren looks straight ahead. His dad will get out soon. Just a little bit longer.

5 Parking Lots Darren Turns into within Ten Minutes of Dropping Off His Dad and Enduring an Awkward Good-bye, Parking Lots in Which He Now Tries to Thwart the Freak-out Building Slowly and Steadily inside Him

1. Subway/cleaners
2. Shell gas station
3. Walgreens
4. The liquor store right next to the beauty salon, which has an electronic sign with red lights that keeps flashing: EYEBROW THREADING $5
5. Poochie's

5 Excuses Darren Has Recently Come Up With for Not Turning On His Cell Phone Most Mornings

1. No one really calls or texts him, and so it kind of bums him out to turn his phone on, watch it boot up, but then just sit there. So then what's the point of turning the thing on?

2. Pretty much the main reason he has a phone at this point is so his parents can check in on him, which is a pretty lame reason. But they don't tend to do this in the morning, plus he can claim he just forgot to turn it on if they do, and in that way be a little bit defiant without them knowing for sure if that's what he's being.

3. Nate is the main person who calls and texts. And sometimes it's still okay talking to Nate, because he can be pretty funny and Darren does like the sound of his voice, but a lot of times he can tell that Nate's just high because he's not really talking about anything, just sort of going on about something that happened at work or some band he's into or some show they should go see, even though Darren can't get into bars (Nate isn't twenty-one either, but his beard is getting thick enough that his fake ID works almost every time). Still, Darren hates actively ignoring Nate's calls, meaning that when he turns his phone on he's sort of saying to himself, *If Nate calls, you have to answer.*

4. He doesn't really like his actual, physical phone, either. For some reason the thing gets pretty warm after about forty-five seconds of talking to someone, so his cheek is almost sweaty by the time he's done talking to Nate. If he wanted one, he could probably get his parents to buy him a new one, but he doesn't, because:

5. He just doesn't really like cell phones in general. Sometimes it can be fun to text, but it's not like he ever thought to himself, *Wow, I'm so happy I have this phone.* Of course, if he had more friends, or even just a couple, or even just one he truly liked, who he couldn't wait to talk to, maybe things would be different.

5 Key Scenes or Sequences from a Documentary about Him and Zoey (*Muses in Love,* or Something like That) Darren Pictures While Hanging Out in the Poochie's Parking Lot

1. THE CONCERT

It'll open with Darren and his band playing before a pretty huge audience. Actually, not so much huge as just totally and utterly ecstatic. And it will be shot from the edge of the stage. It's not clear who else would be in the band. Maybe Nate, maybe not. The music would be kind of jazz and kind of rock, but not fusion and not any other kinds of jazz-rock hybrids, because most of those are pretty lame. It'll be something new and amazing that hasn't been invented yet, because the whole point—no, half the point of the movie is that this music is some kind of key development in music history.

And Darren's at the center of it, obviously.

So the opening is just an example of this music. No, it's more than an example, because this footage will be from some famous concert (in New York or L.A. or maybe even Chicago) that established the band and their music as a big deal. Like, about three seconds in—no, before the concert is even shown, when the screen is still black, it will say in white letters on a black screen, something like *March 24, 2021,* and then the name of some famous club in New York or wherever.

2. ZOEY'S FIRST INTERVIEW

And then right after a whole song, or most of a song, is shown, just to establish how awesome the band is and how totally mesmerized every last person in the crowd was, it will switch to Zoey being interviewed. And she'll say something like, "Did I know what I was capturing that night? No. How could I? No one could have. I just wanted to capture it, because I wanted to capture everything he was doing. That show was one of about twenty I filmed that spring. Because I couldn't get enough."

Of course, this will be a much older Zoey speaking. Maybe she'll even have a little gray streak running through her hair. Like, she might even be forty by then. But she'll still be beautiful, maybe even more, somehow. And she'll be sitting on a couch in their cool Brooklyn apartment. Or maybe on some porch with one of those L.A. canyons in the background, if that's where they live. It will just be Zoey talking, even though they'll still be together then. Because they'll interview Darren separately, because that's what you do when you're making a stellar documentary.

3. DARREN'S INTERVIEW

The parts with Darren, his interviews, will start with him looking through a scrapbook with Zoey's first drawings. But it won't be clear at first that it's Darren looking through it, because the camera will just be doing a close-up on the drawings. The first of which will be the letter with them holding hands, and designs on their arms. Then he'll turn the page and it'll be the second one, the one with all the stars at night. And then he'll turn the page again, revealing the one that arrived on the afternoon of his sixteenth birthday: the self-portrait, the one with the heavy shadow covering up half her face.

But not the spot on her lip, which is clearly the focal point of the entire drawing. And you'll see Darren pointing at it and him saying (while he sort of laughs in disbelief), "The amazing thing is, she didn't know yet how I felt about that spot. But she focused on it anyway." The camera pulls back and there's older Darren, his hair a little less crazy but still curly, some gray hairs here and there. A kind of noticeable potbelly, but who cares. Somehow not even Darren cares. There are instruments and mixing boards behind him, he's in some sort of recording studio. "Like she already knew."

And what showing these early drawings will make clear is that they're all by the same person, but a person who's getting way better at drawing from picture to picture. Later on in the documentary, gallery owners and other famous artists will look at Zoey's work and explain why it matters so much in fancy, technical art terms. But this scene is just so everyone can get a look at her first works, and learn when and where and why and for whom she started drawing.

And, just as a little extra bonus, one of the songs from the first playlist he sent her will be playing in the background.

4. THE EXPERT SPEAKS

Later on they'll interview some dude who's an expert on creative couples. Because there's an expert for everything. He'll be talking in front of a huge bookshelf, of course. And he'll just look crazily smart, with intense eyes and black-framed glasses and probably a beard or something. And it will say his name at the bottom of the screen, along with "author of" and then the name of some book that will make it clear he's an (maybe *the*) expert on the subject. And right away he'll be talking, excitedly, using his hands like crazy.

"There are, of course, no shortage of famous creative couples, creative pairs," he'll say. "Lennon-McCartney is probably the best-known example. But what's truly remarkable about the Jacobs-Lovell case is, well"—he'll laugh—"there are a number of remarkable features. One, the two of them worked, have worked, continue to work, and excel, in two fairly distinct fields. Jacobs in music, Lovell in the visual arts. For more than two decades now. Two, they each made truly astronomic leaps at around the same time, in their late teens and early twenties. Three, their work was, in many senses, *about* the other. Four, even after each was quite famous, they continued working in close proximity to each other, Lovell traveling with Jacobs's band, Jacobs writing and recording in a studio literally attached to Lovell's studio. And, most of all, five, they have been a couple, a *romantic* couple the entire time. And their relationship has survived!" The guy smiles and shakes his head. "There's truly no precedent for this."

5. THE HAPPY ENDING

Of course there will be a bunch of other stuff in the middle of the movie. But the best part will be near the very end, after all the history has been shown and all the experts talked to. It'll be in their house or apartment or whatever, which will be super cool and awesome (because obviously they'll be totally loaded) but without being too fancy or anything. Funky art on the wall, though probably not Zoey's stuff. Plus some pretty kick-ass furniture. Maybe they'll even have a kid or two; yeah, they probably will, but the kids won't be in the movie.

The point of this scene would seem to be the two of them somehow explaining how they've been able to be so creative separately while staying in love at the same time. Like maybe the filmmaker will even ask them point-blank at the beginning of the scene. But neither of them will answer the question at all. They won't even try, really.

They'll just be laughing, or giggling, even. Zoey will be really happy by that point. Will have been for years. Not all the time, because how can you be happy all the time, but she'll smile this great smile of hers a lot, plus she'll have this amazing laugh that Darren, the sixteen-year-old Darren, still hasn't heard.

But okay, the point is, they won't answer the question.

Instead, Darren will be playing a ukulele, trying to get Zoey to sing some harmony with him, but she's pretty bad with harmonies when it comes to singing. Of course, it won't matter, because the whole point of the scene is just to make it clear that they're still totally in love. Totally crazy about each other. Everyone else is trying to figure out their secret, but the two of them couldn't care less. And between their love and them not caring about the rest, it's sort of like anyone who sees the movie will be super jealous of them but will still like them anyway.

4 Voice Messages Waiting for Darren on His Phone

1. UNCLE CRAIG AND AUNT MARGIE

["Happy Birthday" sung in some kind of harmony that might be intended to be funny]. Craig: *Hi, Darren, we hope you have a sweet, sweet sixteenth, kiddo. We put something in the mail, but it might only get there Monday. Love ya. Eli! Come here and wish your cousin a happy birthday. Is he coming? Yes or no? Okay, well, looks like Eli will call you later. Have a great day. Bye-bye.*

2. HIS MOM

Happy birthday, sweetie! I hope you're having a wonderful, special day so far. I cannot believe you're sixteen. My God, my baby's sixteen. Unbelievable. Anyway, I'll be getting in around noon, I'll call you then. And I have a special present for you, and it's not a night at that motel near the Denver Airport, trust me. What a dump! Okay, I love you very, very, very, very, very, very, very much. Happy birthday!

3. RACHEL

Happy birthday to you, happy birthday to you, happy birthday dear Darrr-rren, happy birthday to you. OMG that you're sixteen. And boo that I'm not there. Or that you're not here. Completely unfair. So, okay, you won't believe this, or maybe you will, but I've been working on something for you. I better get it done by this afternoon. Just check your e-mail in a few hours. Okay? Okay. Oh, and remind me to tell you about Monica yesterday. Crazy. And check Facebook. Okay, okay, I know I'm rambling. Happy birthday. I miss you!

4. NATE

[Somewhat incoherent message delivered in a few different voices, including (probably): sultry female, generic foreigner, and urban gangster type]. *Good morning, Darren Jacobs, you sexy bastard. I'm calling to* [unclear] *you a happy, happy, happy sixteenth birthday. I'm getting so hot just thinking about what a man you must be today, oh God. And I thinky so many, so many* [unclear] *hug and kissah your face to tell you I'm loving you, so many!* [three to four seconds of unclear noises, definitely not speech, possibly beat-boxing] *Because, straight-up mofo, we's gonna bring it today to celebrate your motherfucking sixteenth, bee-utch! So call me. Love, your brother. I'm out.*

4 Text Fragments Delivered in Quick Succession

1. *Crazy idea. Any interest in picking me up at airport? Should get in at 12:17. Won't be too much traffic this time on Saturday. You can just GPS O'Hare from our house. Takes about 30*

2. *min. United flight 839. OK if you don't want to. I can take cab. Really. But thought might be fun on your 16th to do some driving. If you got license already. Sure you did. Will pay you $30 plus*

3. *tip. Seriously. And more time together then. Can take my car or Nate's. Text me if you can do it. Didn't check bags, so should be outside bit after 1230. Terminal 1. Just follow signs for*

4. *arrivals. The Dawg House on way home! Love you very much. Excited to see you. XO.*

10 Pros from the Pros and Cons Deliberations over Whether He Should Pick Up His Mom That by around #5 Have Already Overwhelmed the Cons

1. It will make his mom very happy.
2. Thirty dollars plus tip.
3. It's sunny, so the roads won't be a problem.
4. She said there won't be much traffic, either.
5. Plus, highway driving is actually easier overall than city-street driving, assuming you can merge onto it without crashing into another car and dying.
6. He'd be a moron not to take Ray's car on the highway while he's got it.
7. If he doesn't kill himself and/or destroy Ray's car, it might make him a more confident driver, which he'd really like to be.
8. It's not like he's got a lot planned today, other than heading over to the house to see Nate, so it's something to do.
9. She might even say it makes her proud, something that always embarrasses him when she says it, but he still sort of likes it when she says it.
10. The Dawg House.

4 Recurring Developments in Darren's Various Fantasies about Zoey (and Him, Too)

1. It becomes much easier for him to picture her talking freely once she gets to around age twenty-five.
2. She removes most of her piercings during college, which isn't to say he's sure she's actually going to college.
3. The older she gets, the happier she gets.
4. And the same with him, now that he thinks about it.

3 Reasons Darren Does Not Turn Right on Red at the Corner of Gross Point and Touhy

1. There's a sign that says, NO RIGHT TURN ON RED 7 A.M.–7 P.M.
2. Darren doesn't really like turning right on red even when it's legal, because if, for some reason, he doesn't notice a car coming that way, then he's going to get into an accident that will definitely be his fault (something that would be about three hundred times worse in Ray's car).
3. Screw the guy behind him.

1 Douche Bag Who Clearly Feels Differently about Darren's Decision Not to Turn Right on Red at the Corner of Gross Point and Touhy

1. The douche bag behind him, who honked quickly once, then waited maybe two seconds, then honked about five more times, with the last one going on for about three seconds. Plus, Darren could see when he looked in the rearview mirror, the guy is super pissed.

3 Forces Nevertheless Allowing Darren to Resist Any Urge to Turn Right on Red at the Corner of Gross Point and Touhy

1. THE LAW

   It's 12:12 p.m., dickwad.

2. THE PROTECTION PROVIDED TO HIM BY RAY'S INFINITI G37

   Big, metal. Doors locked.

3. DARREN HIMSELF

   He doesn't like to turn right on red, okay?

9 Transformations to the Scene at the Northwest Corner of Gross Point and Touhy by 12:14 p.m.

1. The light turns green for cars heading Southwest on Gross Point.
2. Darren begins turning right onto Touhy.
3. The car behind Darren drives around Ray's Infiniti G37 but still turns right (meaning he passes Darren *inside* the actual intersection).
4. The guy driving that car points at Darren and says extremely unkind things to him very loudly.
5. Darren raises his left hand and the attached middle finger.
6. The car once behind Darren pulls in front of Ray's Infiniti G37.
7. This car stops suddenly.
8. Darren slams on the brakes just in time.
9. The guy gets out of his car, which is some kind of Chevy, and starts walking toward Darren. The guy does not appear to approve in any way of anything Darren has done since around 12:11 p.m.

8 Physical Characteristics of the Guy Now Standing Just on the Other Side of the Driver's-Side Door to Ray's Infiniti G37

1. Five feet six, maybe five feet seven
2. Late twenties or earlier thirties, probably
3. A little heavy, or maybe just really stocky
4. Straight black hair, almost shaved on the side; plenty of hair product
5. Big red cheeks
6. Maybe Latino, could even be Asian, almost certainly not black, probably part white
7. Clean-shaven
8. Wearing a tan button-down shirt and a brown leather bomber jacket with three patches

8 Exclamations, All of Which Darren Can Hear Pretty Clearly Despite His Window Being Up, the Music Playing Kind of Loud, and the Other Cars Driving Past, One of Which Even Honks

1. Fuck you, motherfucker!
2. Flip me off again, c'mon! I fucking dare you!
3. Put your fucking window down, dick!
4. Fuck you!
5. C'mon out, bitch!
6. Learn how to fucking drive!
7. Faggot, in your faggot car!
8. Fuck you!

6 Strategies Darren Assumes in Order to Withstand This Guy's Onslaught, Which Now Includes Him Banging on the Window and Trying to Open the Door

1. Keep hands at ten and two on the steering wheel.
2. Quickly look to see that the doors are locked, but definitely do not relock them, for fear of accidentally unlocking them.
3. Otherwise just stare straight ahead.
4. Don't say a word.
5. Wait for the guy to go away.
6. Pray for a cop to drive by.

2 Exclamations Darren Screams at the Back of the Guy's Chevy Caprice as It Tears Off, Because for Some Reason the Guy Gave Up, but Not Before Telling Darren to Fuck Off One More Time and Punching the Window Kind of Hard (It Didn't Break, Thank God)

1. It's my birthday, you dick!
2. You fucking dick-fucker dick!

5 Reappearing Images from Various Nightmare Scenarios That Escort Darren down Touhy Avenue for a Mile

1. The guy yanking open the somehow-unlocked door.
2. The guy grabbing Darren right below the collar and dragging him out of the car in such a way that Darren pretty much falls to the pavement, except for his legs, which are still inside the car.
3. The guy kicking Darren in the chest and calling him a faggot.
4. The guy going absolutely bananas with a crowbar on the trunk and roof of Ray's car.
5. The guy climbing onto Darren, pinning his arms under his legs like they do on "The Ultimate Fighter," and then just whaling on Darren.

2 Consequences of Darren's Inability to Stop Imagining the Nightmare Scenarios

1. He's not really paying full attention to his driving.
2. He's definitely not paying any attention to the GPS lady.

4 Mostly Short-Term Commands Darren Tries to Obey from the Side of Touhy Avenue Just West of Dee Road, Where He Has Pulled Over

1. Calm the hell down.
2. Figure out how to get to O'Hare, since he definitely missed a few turns, even though the GPS lady could totally give a shit about the asshole in the Chevy and has already figured out a backup route.
3. Make sense of how it could be that he was driving completely fine even though he wasn't really paying attention.
4. Call his mom and let her know he'll be there soon, which he should have done back at Poochie's, and if he had, then just that little thirty-second delay would have prevented him from crossing paths with the dickface in the Chevy.

8 Factors Possibly Explaining His Mom's Failure to Notice That Darren's Voice Sounds Different, Which It Must

1. Her enthusiasm and excitement, because she's thrilled he's picking her up and can't wait to see him.
2. Her insistence on singing him a little snippet of the "Happy Birthday" song, even though he only listens to a couple of lines before saying (annoyed and impatient), "Mom."
3. It's pretty noisy on her end of the line.
4. Her dropping the phone at one point.
5. The quality of their phone connection in general, which isn't great.
6. Her interrupting him to ask, "So, are you up for the Dawg House?"
7. Her just sounding kind of distracted, which isn't so weird, considering she's getting off a plane or walking toward baggage claim or going to the bathroom or whatever she's doing exactly.
8. Him trying to sound normal, and possibly succeeding.

10 Responses Nate Has to Darren's Story and Subsequent Real-time Freak-out

1. Dude, I cannot believe Ray's letting you drive his car, that trusting, benevolent homosexual.
2. Never flip someone off when driving, my man, it's just not worth it.
3. Take a deep breath, birthday boy, it's all going to be okay.
4. And the faggot thing was pretty uncalled for, considering the situation.
5. That would have been totally killer if you had actually rolled down the window enough to tell him it was your birthday, cause there's a slight chance it would have made him realize what a huge cock he was being. Because how mean can you be to someone if you know it's their birthday, you know?
6. Let it all out. It's okay. Let it all out.
7. Yep, there's definitely no shortage of tough-guy dicks out there.
8. I bet you would have kicked his ass if it came to that. Because, who knows, maybe God gives you extra-awesome fighting skills each year on your birthday. Would be cool to test that one out in a safe environment.

9. Were you going to invite me to the Dawg House, weenus? Forget it, it's cool. I agreed to come in to help with the lunch rush and I'm already late. Chuck didn't show up again, the reject.

10. Exploit the Infiniti for me, okay?

4 Extended Silences in Darren's Conversation with His Dad, Who Calls Right Before Darren Starts Driving Again

"Hey."

"So, how are you enjoying the car?"

"Uh, it's okay."

"Wonderful. Listen, how would you feel about . . ."

1.

"Huh?"

"I'm supposed to see Dr. Schrier today."

"And?"

"And I thought perhaps you'd like to join me."

"Today?"

"Yes, today. At two thirty. I realize it's not the first thing most people like to do on their birthday, but . . ."

2.

"But what?"

"Your anger, Darren—"

"What?"

"You had an outburst in the car, which I can understand. But an outburst is still an outburst."

"What's that supposed to mean?"

"Just that it wouldn't be the worst idea in the world to talk about it. That's all. And today is—"

"No thanks."

"You sure?"

"Yep."

"Okay, I understand. But can I count on you to come with me on Tuesday? It's been a while since we've met with Dr. Schrier."

3.

"Darren?"

"Yeah?"

"Did you hear me?"

"Yeah."

"Well?"

4.

"Can we talk about this later, Dad?"

"Sure, I suppose it can wait."

"Cool. Talk to you later."

2 Alerts Darren's Phone Now Displays

1. MISSED CALL FROM RACHEL M
2. VOICE MAIL FROM RACHEL M

2 Additional Requests Darren Makes of His Phone Before Hitting the Road Again

1. Please tell me about the weather in Belén, New Mexico. (*Okay, it's forty-eight and sunny.*)

2. Please send this message to Ben Zwiren via a certain popular social media site: Well, so what should I do? Because I've got to do something. (*Message sent. Anything else, sir?*)

5 Indications That Darren May Not Be Fully Over the Incident at the Corner of Gross Point and Touhy

1. He really, really wants to hug his mom.

2. He's more or less losing his mind trying to figure out where he should or is allowed to momentarily park Ray's car, since there are about nine thousand other cars coming and going (not to mention about forty thousand people all over the place, including a bunch who think they can just cross wherever), and in some places the cars are two deep, but then there's also this enormous man and his mustache and fluorescent green vest who may be a cop walking up and down the passenger pickup area making it pretty clear that if you park your car for too long or in the wrong place that you and your car will go straight to jail.

3. His mom is about to see Ray's car, which means he's going to have to explain this to her or just watch her react, and she may not like it for whatever reason, meaning he's a moron for not mentioning it over the phone.

4. When he finally stops the car and removes his right hand from the steering wheel to put it in park, Darren

notices a nice little band of sweat where his hand had been.

5. He really, really doesn't want to hug his mom, even though he does.

6 Spots on His Mom Darren Has Been Able to Look Straight at When Hugging Her over the Years

1. Her waist
2. Her tummy
3. Her breasts
4. Her shoulders
5. Her nose
6. Her forehead

8 Deviations from Their Standard Hugging Protocol

1. Darren begins it with one foot on the street and the other up on the curb where his mom was waiting. Midway through the hug he lifts up the other foot.
2. His mom says, "Ooh, sweetie, it's so good to see you!"
3. He squeezes her pretty tightly, tighter than he intended to.
4. He sort of pulls away when he senses this, but his mom hugs him even tighter, so he settles on a tightish embrace, which feels kind of good, actually.
5. His right hand is holding his new keychain, which holds the key to Ray's Infiniti G37.
6. His mom also sort of hums and says into his neck, "Happy birthday."
7. Near the end, when he's pretty ready to be done hugging, he tilts his head back and rests his chin on the top of his mom's head, sort of just to see if he can (he can).
8. The hug lasts nearly five full seconds.

4 Surprising Things His Mother Says Right After He Tells about Ray's Car, Which Together Suggest That Something's Up

1. She looks at the car and says, "Wow, what a beautiful car. How generous that he let you have it for the day." She says this without any sarcasm or bitterness. In fact, Darren almost swears she's for the first time sort of realizing and even being happy about the fact that Ray is the kind of guy who would let his boyfriend's sixteen-year-old son drive his forty-thousand-dollar car.

2. So they get into the car and Darren turns it on, and of course he forgot to turn the music off, so Milton Nascimento just picks up where he left off. Darren is mortified, but before he can grab his iPod she says, "No, no, don't turn off the music! I like it. What is that, some sort of Latin something? Look at you, Mr. World Beat!"

3. She even does this weird dance move, raising both her hands to shoulder height and snapping. Plus she bites her bottom lip. All of which is more embarrassing than her discovery of the music itself.

4. Around the time they get back on the highway, she starts talking again, really, really quickly. "Can I confess something? I am so looking forward to the Dawg House. I was

almost even thinking about saying, Screw it, what's so bad about a cheeseburger? How much could God possibly care? But then, it is Shabbat, and maybe the whole thing with the weather and that rotten hotel in Denver, maybe that's what I get for traveling on Shabbat, which I promised I wouldn't do when I could help it. But who cares? The Dawg House, here we come!"

11 Sources of Darren's Presently Ambivalent Stance on the Dawg House, Even Though Overall He's Hardly Bummed about Going There for Lunch

1. There's a huge doghouse on the roof, with the head of a dog sticking out. Plus the dog is holding a hot dog in his mouth that is probably the size of a canoe.
2. It's spelled the Dawg House.
3. The food is pretty great, but obviously heavy and greasy, so sometimes you feel gross after.
4. You can order from your car and then eat in it too, which was super exciting when he was a kid, but then sometimes it seems like they'd screw up the order that way, plus then when you're done you're just already sitting in your car that smells like hamburgers and feeling kind of gross.
5. So now they eat inside, which means ordering at this big window between the dining area and the kitchen that is somehow a little depressing, but then eating in a little room where the walls are covered with articles about the Dawg House, some of which are actually pretty interesting (and together make you feel kind of lucky to be eating there).
6. All the sandwiches have ridiculous names, like Dognation, Dogology, and Ridogulous, which Darren loved

a lot when he was younger but now seem a little silly to him.

7. Obviously, they serve a ton of meat. And it's not that Darren really cares so much that people eat meat (it would be better if people didn't eat so much of it, but whatever). Still, sometimes (not most of the time, just sometimes) he does have trouble not thinking about how much meat people are eating at a place like the Dawg House when he's there. Plus, not surprisingly, Darren used to eat meat himself, and the Dawg House might be the place he can most remember eating meat, like he can nearly taste it again when they go inside, which isn't such a good thing.

8. But so at least they have a solid fish sandwich, which most burger/hot dog places don't have.

9. All the sandwiches come in these boxes, where they just dump the fries on top of the sandwich, which, like the names, Darren used to be a bigger fan of than he is now. Not to mention all the garbage.

10. His family used to have this tradition of stopping at the Dawg House on the way back from O'Hare (assuming they didn't get in really early in the morning or really late at night), which was an awesome tradition. Because going to the Dawg House at the end of a trip was a great way not to be too sad about the trip being over, plus his parents could use the promise of

the Dawg House (or the threat of no Dawg House) to make sure Darren and Nate behaved on the flight back. And so maybe his mom and his dad would say that it's still a tradition (after all, it's hardly a coincidence he's about to eat there with his mom after picking her up at O'Hare), but Darren's not so sure, and not just because his parents are divorced. Because Nate's also pretty old by now, to the point that it's not clear the family would still be taking trips together even if his parents weren't divorced.

11. The milk shakes. Yum.

Members of the Jacobs Family Who Have Ever, in the History of Visits to the Dawg House, Suggested Taking a Walk by That Park over There After Eating

5 Comparisons His Mom Makes between California and Chicago during the Start of Their Walk

1. "People don't do as much walking around here, probably because of the weather," she says. "Even though it's pretty warm today, at least for Chicago in late November." She's talking super fast. Maybe it's the huge Diet Coke she just had.

2. "I know we just ate at the Dawg House," she says, "and don't get me wrong, it was absolutely delicious, but it's hard to argue when someone says that most people out west have healthier lifestyles than people here. You can see it the second you step off the plane."

"Pretty much all Americans are fat," Darren says. "I heard people in Texas are fattest."

3. "Though the leaves are wonderful," his mom says. "Even if the trees are mostly bare at this point. Nothing like that out in San Jose. You look out your window, and there's no way to know if it's February or August. Kind of weird if you ask me."

Darren would marry his milk shake if such a thing were possible.

4. "I mean," she says, "I could see how you'd miss the seasons, even the crummy ones."

"I hate February," he says. "Except for Nate's birthday."

She might grab his hand. Which, back when he was much younger, she used to do all the time whenever they walked. He would maybe, maybe, *maybe* let her.

"I know you probably couldn't care less," she says, "but I've gone to this really cool synagogue out in Palo Alto a couple of times. It's like they get it. You know? I think you'd be impressed. Like they realize you can't just keep doing the same things over and over and expect people to care."

"Well, it couldn't be any more boring than Beth Emanuel."

Now she's walking fast too. Maybe it was the huge coffee she was drinking when he picked her up.

"Look at those birds," she says, pointing at some tree near a creek. "I mean, how do they know to fly south? Incredible."

Darren removes the lid of his milk shake and tips the cup back to try to get a last sip or two.

5. "You want to hear something amazing? About an hour from my work, in Santa Cruz, which I can't believe I haven't taken you to already—so awesome, there's a place the monarch butterflies come to every year. On their migration. I haven't seen it myself, but I hear it's amazing. We'll have to go."

"Can you stop talking about California already?"

"You're right," his mom says. "I'm sorry, but it's just . . ."

And then she sits down on a bench they were passing and pats a spot next to her.

So he sits down. And she turns to him and shows him her reassuring smile. Which was always, always, always reassuring until about two years ago, when it started being reassuring only about half the time. This time is definitely one of the times it is not reassuring. At all. In part because it's clearly smaller than normal, plus what's with the goddamn lip gloss, and most of all because her eyes are sort of sad somehow.

She turns away and doesn't say anything. Then she squeezes his hand, which just feels weird out here. Says, "Honey, I . . ."

19 Colors Darren Watches Drive Past on the Street about One Hundred Feet Away, Rather Than Say Anything or Even Look at His Mom

1. Silver
2. Brown
3. White
4. White
5. Blue
6. Maroon
7. Blue
8. Red
9. Yellow
10. Gold
11. Red
12. Silver
13. White
14. Black
15. Greenish blue
16. Green
17. Red
18. Black
19. White

4 Announcements His Mom Makes over the Course of about a Minute

1. They want me to join the company, instead of just consulting.
2. They want me to head a new division.
3. They—they asked me to move.
4. They asked me to move out there.

10 Simple Verbs Darren Demonstrates Once His Mom Finishes with Her Announcements

1. Tilt (back the cup in order to get one last sip out of his milk shake)
2. Crush (the cup in his hand)
3. Throw (the cup toward a large garbage can about fifteen feet away)
4. Stand (up)
5. Walk (toward the garbage can)
6. Bend (over)
7. Pick (up the crushed cup, which hit the side of the garbage can and landed on the grass nearby)
8. Drop (the cup into the garbage can)
9. Return (to the bench)
10. Sit (down)

18 Questions Darren Asks, Though Not Necessarily Because He Wants to Know All That Much More about This Whole Thing

"Darren, do you understand?"

1. "Do I understand what?"

    "What I'm telling you."

2. "I don't know, what are you telling me?"

    "It's not clear?"

3. "What's not clear?"

    "What I said before."

4. "About what?"

    "About my work."

5. "What about it?"

    "That they offered me a full-time position."

6. "So?"

    "So, do you understand what that means?"

7. "Do I understand what it means about what?!"

    More silence. More cars passing.

"Darren, I'm sorry about this," she says. "I'm sorry this is happening on your birthday. It wasn't my plan, I promise. I'm sorry."

Cars tend to pass in clusters of the same color for some reason. Maybe that means something.

"They're starting a new division," she says, "which, with a company of this size, basically means starting a new company. It's going to be based a lot on developments that came out of what they acquired from me in the first place. And they want me to head it. In fact, they said they may not even launch it if I decline the offer."

Darren looks at her but doesn't say anything.

"It's for a lot of money. A lot. A lot more than I ever thought I could make, even after I started learning what people make out there. But it means no more consulting. It means I'll have to go full time. Out there. I'll have to move. I haven't accepted it yet. But they want an answer by the sixth. I asked them to give me until after Christmas, but they said, with the operating budget for next year and everything, they need to know by the sixth."

Finally, she looks at him. "That's the deal, honey."

Darren's lack of milk shake right now feels like some sort of war crime. Like someone should contact Amnesty International.

8. "How much will you make?"

"A lot."

9. "How much is a lot?"

"A little more than four hundred. Thousand," she says. "That doesn't include bonuses. Plus I'll get some stock options."

10. "So when would you move?"

"They'd want me to start on Monday the fifteenth. To get in a couple of weeks of full time before the division launches in January. So I'd probably go back out on the tenth. But I'll be off completely until then."

11. "What about the house?"

"Your father and I will work that out. If he thinks there's any point in putting it up for sale, that's what we'll do. Otherwise, we'd rent it until the market turns around."

12. "And what about Nate? Where's he going to live?"

"That's up to him. Move in with your father, get his own place, I don't know. He said he might be thinking about enrolling at UIC; he could get a place in the city. He knows we'll support him as long as he's in school."

13. "Would you come back here still?"

"Of course. Of course."

14. "How often?"

"I negotiated a Friday and Monday off every month for

the first year. So at least once a month. Because there's MLK Day and your spring break, when I thought maybe you could come out. When I find a permanent place for myself, you'll have your own room in it. Of course."

15. "So what, then I'd just live with Dad?"

"Yes. You'd live with your father. And if he wants the house, I'd consider it."

16. "Does he know?"

"Yes, he knows."

17. "Do you want to take it?"

"Yes, I do. Very much."

18. "Are you going to?"

No response for too many seconds.

"It's an incredible opportunity, Darren," she finally says. "And not just for me."

2 Letters Spoken in Monotone by Darren as He Stands Up to Head Back to the Dawg House

1. O
2. K

1 **Word in Portuguese Darren Now Knows After Asking
Ray the Meaning of It, Because It Seems to Be in about
Every Single Song Ray's Ever Given Darren, Including
"*Tristeza e Solidao*" (as Sung by Monica Salmaso), Which
Comes On about Ninety Seconds After They Get Back in
the Car and Sounds So Good That Darren Finds Himself
Trying to Crawl inside Her Voice, Which He Nearly Does,
Even Though Her Voice Isn't Simply Making Everything
Better, Not at All, in Fact It Might Be Just the Opposite**

1. *Coração* (which sounds sort of like "korasow" and
   means "heart")

4 Days in Addition to Today Darren Is Now Crying about, Even Though He Didn't Actually Cry on Any of Those Other Days

1. BUGS'S LAST FULL DAY IN CHICAGO

Bugs's mom, Andrea, is pretty much always in a good mood, and she loves to plan special days and stuff like that. So the last day before they moved, even though they were obviously pretty crazy with all the moving stuff, she put together a special day for Bugs and Darren. She had her sister, Bugs's aunt Bonnie, take them up to Six Flags, which was pretty awesome, obviously, but then even when that was over, the day wasn't. Because instead of just dropping Darren back off at the house, they drove to Andy's Frozen Custard, where Bugs's parents and Darren's mom met them. Which made the custard sort of the official good-bye custard, like the rest of the day wasn't a good-bye at all.

And even though both their moms were talking about when they'd see each other next, making all sorts of plans and acting all happy, Darren started feeling almost how going to Six Flags was like some kind of trick. Because Bugs was moving, meaning that having a great day with him only made that worse. So he barely ate any of his custard (and not only because he ate a mountain of crap at the amusement park) and instead just sat there trying not to show Bugs that he was sort of mad at him for moving, even though he knew it wasn't Bugs's fault.

2. THE DAY OF THE PASSOVER SEDER, FRESHMAN YEAR

His dad finally moved out of the house in mid-April of Darren's freshman year. Meaning for Passover, which fell in late March that year, they were almost still a regular family (though Nate was already at Michigan). Plus, Darren didn't yet know that his dad was gay, meaning it was still pretty easy to wish or just decide that things could somehow be how they used to be.

His family, even though they definitely were not very religious at all back then, used to host the Seder a lot, which a little bit annoyed Darren, because he doesn't really like the holiday all that much. He'll admit that the idea of it—all that slavery and freedom stuff, and the having to remember it— he'll admit that that's pretty important, and so he can understand why they'd make a holiday out of it. But he hates matzo and sitting at the table forever waiting to eat and most of the songs, too.

But his dad would get pretty into the Seder, to the point that for a bunch of years, instead of just telling the story about Moses and being slaves (like it says you're supposed to), he had everyone act it out or make up a song about it. Which was actually pretty awesome the first couple of times they did it, especially the second year, when there were costumes, too. But then, after maybe the third or fourth year of finding creative ways to retell the story, Darren just got the feeling that they were only still doing it because no one was willing to admit it wasn't that fun anymore, and so maybe they should go back to a regular, boring Seder.

Anyhow, freshman year, his parents decided to have the Seder with just the family, as opposed to inviting over relatives and friends and stuff. Even though everyone already knew his dad was moving out soon. Or maybe it was because of that. Whatever—the point is that it was only going to be the four of them. But then, pretty much at the last minute, Nate said he didn't want to come home, because of exams or something, which even Darren knew was a big fat lie.

His mom cried for most of the afternoon, plus his parents had all these horrible almost-arguments in what used to be their room (his dad was sleeping in Nate's room), the door to which was definitely closed (but Darren could still hear how they were having entire conversations in these weird loud whispers). Darren was hoping they'd either just cancel it or at least check to see if they could still accept the invitation from the Waxmans. But then around five o'clock his dad (like there was nothing strange about it) set the table for the Seder, putting out the matzo and the Seder plate and all the other crap, even though he only put out three places for actual people.

And as bad as that was, the actual Seder was much worse, to the point that even right now, as bad as everything feels, there's just no way he can really think about that, especially the part right after the Four Questions, when his dad leaned over and kissed his mom, who had started crying again for at least the fifth time that day and then kind of spastically pushed his face away.

3. ZOEY'S LAST FULL DAY BEFORE GETTING SENT AWAY

And Darren doesn't even know a single thing about it. He can remember a little bit of what happened to him that day, because it was only a few days after he got back from Ann Arbor, and his parents were still treating him differently, but that's not even the point. Because when he saw that last text message, the one Grace showed him a month or so later on the Patio, and saw that it was sent at 6:32 a.m., he just got this sense for how totally nuts things must have been for Zoey by the end.

Because that last full day must have been the day when her parents finally found her or when the police brought her home or even when she just showed up back at home in the same clothes she had been wearing since Friday. And even though Zoey was definitely kind of responsible for whyever her parents decided that the only option left was telling her at six thirty in the morning that she was going to

New Mexico, he still bets she felt like that wasn't even an option, like her life was just sort of over at that point.

4. A WEEK AGO IN DR. SCHRIER'S OFFICE

Darren's had three sessions alone with Dr. Schrier. The first two were totally useless. Because Darren pretty much decided in advance that he wasn't going to even come close to talking about anything important. The reason being that he was only going to Dr. Schrier's in the first place to get his dad to shut up about Darren going to see Dr. Schrier (even though, of course, going to see him a couple of times didn't exactly appease his dad once and for all).

But the last time Darren was there, who knows why, he just started talking. It started with stuff about Rachel, and why she annoys him, but why he sort of likes her anyway. Because everything about Rachel kind of confuses him, so he figured, isn't the point of therapy to talk about stuff that confuses you? And maybe Darren was just tired, but Dr. Schrier started asking Darren questions and doing that thing with his thumb and index finger, until the next thing Darren knew, he was talking about almost everything. Everything but Zoey, in fact (who Darren felt like he should protect from Dr. Schrier). The point is, once he started talking, he couldn't really stop.

And after about a half hour Darren could tell that all this talking wasn't actually helping, but still, he couldn't get himself to shut up. Like his mouth was one of those closet doors in cartoons, the kind that when some characters unknowingly open it, he or she gets buried in an avalanche of shoes, clothes, tools, tennis racquets, picnic baskets, bowling balls, fishing rods, etc. And until Darren kind of cleared everything away, he wouldn't be able to shut the door, or his mouth, again. And you had to talk about stuff to clear it away. Or something like that.

But so eventually Darren started talking about Mr. Keyes, who knows why. Maybe because Darren sort of started sensing that all the other stuff (his mom, his dad, Nate, his lack of friends, and even Rachel) might be almost dangerous to keep talking about. So he sort of intentionally changed the subject to Mr. Keyes.

"I've been eating lunch a lot in Mr. Keyes's office."

"Mr. Keyes?"

"The band director, I told you."

"Yes, Mr. Keyes. Of course. What about him?"

"Well, he's got a ton of old jazz albums."

"Yes?"

"The covers are pretty cool."

"How so?"

"I don't know. They just are. Like, they're kind of the guys who invented being cool, you know? Like, people in 1870 or whatever, they didn't know how to be cool yet. Or even that you could be."

"But now—"

"And he lets me choose what we're going to listen to."

"And do you?"

"Yeah."

"And then?"

"So then we listen to an album and eat our lunches."

"And you enjoy that?"

Darren nodded but didn't actually say anything. Just pictured himself eating from a brown bag, and Mr. Keyes taking some Tupperware out from this little fridge he has plugged in near the corner of his office. And that's it. Because Mr. Keyes, exactly not like Dr. Schrier, never asks Darren anything, except maybe something musical. That's really it.

Because if Mr. Keyes ever did ask him anything, while they were sitting there chewing silently and listening to Thelonious Monk, it would probably be something along the lines of, "Hey, Darren, why it is that you, an almost-sixteen-year-old in a building packed with more than its share of almost-sixteen-year-olds, are choosing to spend a majority of your lunch periods with a thirty-eight-year-old failed jazz pianist listening to music recorded half a century before you were ever born?"

Around then Darren realized, back in Dr. Schrier's office, that he wasn't breathing so great. And definitely couldn't talk. So he just looked down and nodded for Dr. Schrier.

Luckily, their session came to an end just then. Dr. Schrier lifted up his nose and took one of those deep inhalations of his. Then, closing up the pad he had been taking notes on, he said, "How about we pick up from here next time? What do you say?"

3 More Questions, Not All Spoken Aloud, Asked Not That Far from the Corner of Gross Point and Touhy

1. Rubbing his shoulder, his mom asks, or maybe just says, "Honey, why don't you let me drive?"

2. "Because Ray didn't say you could drive his car today, did he?" Darren screams at her. "No, I don't think so."

They drive on for a few more miles. João Gilberto's "*Águas de Março*" comes on. Just him, whoever he is, or was, on a guitar. If Darren ever followed a religious figure, he would have to sound exactly like this guy. Calm, accepting, and just a little optimistic.

3. Can you not know a language and understand it at the same time? Like this is Darren's useless superpower.

There's some other place where this song makes perfect sense. Where you're not weird for liking it.

Then it ends and it's just the two of them again. "I need this," his mom says, pretty much under her breath. "I need a new beginning." She speaks so quietly. But he can tell, she means it as much as she's ever meant anything. "I deserve a new one, Darren." She means it so much, he feels like she couldn't possibly want her son, the one she used to call "my baby," to know she can want something for herself this badly.

1 Offer of a Very Special Present

1. "Darren," she says when they're sitting in the driveway. The car's off.

"Yeah?"

"I had an idea for a special present for you today."

"What?"

"It's going to sound, I don't know, wrong now."

"What?"

"Like I'm trying to bribe you to be okay with everything."

"What?" He's losing his patience.

"I thought, I thought we could buy you a car today. A car that would be yours."

Why is everyone determined to give him a car today?

"What kind?"

"I don't know. Nothing fancy. Nothing like this. But you deserve something special."

"Thanks," he says. Stares at the steering wheel for a moment or two. "But can we talk about it later?"

"Of course, honey. Of course."

2 Awkward Displays of Affection Resulting from Darren's Effort to Show Some Gratitude, Because He Knows He Should

1. A hug seriously compromised by the car's armrest.
2. A kiss on his mom's cheek, which he wasn't going to give her, then was, then wasn't, then did.

2 Unsolvable Puzzles Darren Confronts While Kissing Her on the Cheek

1. Are you really supposed to kiss it full-on, the way you would someone's lips? Because there's something about the angle that sort of makes that impossible unless the other person is holding out their cheek to the side so you can come at it straight-on.
2. What, exactly, are you supposed to do when your mom not only doesn't make everything better (like she did, effortlessly, for the first fourteen and a half years of your life), but also actually now makes things worse (and maybe even much worse)?

3 Details of the Present Scene That May Account for the Surfacing of Unsolvable Puzzle #2 at This Particular Time and Place

1. Darren is sitting behind the wheel of a fancy car, which he has just driven 29.7 miles without so much as scratching it.

2. His mom has recently switched fragrances, which he gets a pretty clear whiff of when his nose briefly stops about an inch from her ear. The smell, objectively speaking, is probably really pleasant and bright, like it's soft and sharp and even airy all at the same time. But it doesn't smell anything like his mom.

3. Though he closes his eyes for most of the hug/kiss, there's this moment (just as the armrest drives into his ribs) when he gets a look at her hair against the backdrop of the fancy leather headrest, and the unfamiliar combination of colors (hair = maroon, headrest = dark gray) has him wondering where he is and who, exactly, he's hugging and kissing on the cheek.

5 Differences between Most Regular Meals and the One Nate Is in the Middle of When Darren and His Mom Get Home

1. Most regular meals, including regular meals of pizza, don't include one person eating an entire extra large with ham and pineapple (which, Darren's pretty sure, Nate doesn't even like) straight from the box.

2. Most regular meals of pizza aren't eaten with the box of pizza resting on one of those insulated pizza delivery bags, which looks like it's still holding at least one other pizza.

3. Most regular meals are not washed down with sips taken straight from a two-liter bottle of Sprite.

4. Very few if any regular meals are eaten bare-chested while wearing a La Luna's shirt pulled almost all the way off, so that the collar is now stretched over the crown of your head and the rest of the inside-out shirt falls down across your shoulders and back, almost like a cape.

5. Most regular meals are not eaten while sitting on the kitchen counter, which would probably break a rule, not that "no sitting on the counter" was ever presented as an official rule.

4 Observations Shared by Nate Before Anyone Else Speaks, the Last Two of Which Only Darren Hears, Because His Mom Shakes Her Head in Disbelief, Throws Down Her Purse, and Goes Upstairs After Nate Finishes #3

1. It's the birthday boy and the weary traveler. Greetings and salutations.

2. I know you both just rocked some Dawg House action, but I've got to say, this Hawaiian pie is pretty tasty, if you're interested. I never would have ordered it myself, of course, but I might have to rethink that going forward. We could pick off the ham.

3. Ricky's an asshole, I'll tell you what. Always finding some reason to bitch at everyone. Treats us like slaves. But this'll show him. Sure you don't want a piece?

4. I believe there will be some rocking and rolling today. I truly do.

6 Things That Had to or Still Have to Happen for the Accidents, Nate and Darren's New Band, to Get an Actual Paying Gig

"Ready for some birthday glory?" Nate asks Darren after he comes back up from the laundry room, wearing a new, regular T-shirt.

"Huh?"

"Remember how we said we shouldn't keep it a secret anymore?"

"You mean about the Accidents?" Which also includes this guy Mike Kaminer on drums. He's not bad.

1. Nate found him on Craigslist. At first Mike, who's twenty-two and finishing up at DePaul, was not particularly psyched by how young Darren is. But he shut up pretty damn fast once he heard Darren play.

"Check it out, Birthday Man. What time is it?"

Darren looks at the oven clock and feels a weird pit in his stomach. "Quarter to three."

"Cool, we still got some time."

"What?"

"You remember Jordan Weiss?"

"From Temple?"

"Yeah."

"What about him?"

2. "I ran into him last week at a show. That alt-country piece of shit I told you about. He was there. Going to Northwestern. Smart cock.

3. "Anyhow, his parents are in Norway or some such shit for the next three weeks. Something to do with his dad being some kind of world-class heart surgeon."

"Yeah, so?"

4. "So he's having a serious, serious party next weekend, up at their place in Glencoe. Like he is planning on getting a professional DJ. That kind of party."

"Are you going to go?"

"Man, D, you're such a Grade A idiot sometimes."

"What?" Darren says by way of defense.

"So I said to him, don't get a lame-ass DJ. DJs suck."

"Not all of them do."

"True. True. But a good band, a good live band kicks the shit out of a DJ. Am I right?" Nate stops talking. Gives Darren a long look. Raises an eyebrow. "Do I really need to spell this out to you, little brother?"

Darren figures it out. "No way! We're playing his party?"

"Maybe. We're maybe playing his party."

"What do you mean maybe?"

"So I said to him, 'How much are you paying for your shitty DJ?' And he says, 'A grand.' So I say, 'I can get you a good, no, I can get you a *great* band for half that—'"

"We're getting paid?!"

5. "Don't shplooge your pants just yet. Nothing's for sure. But I got him to agree to give us an audition."

"What, like, to see if he wants us?"

"I believe that's what people have auditions for."

6. "And if he likes us—"

"Then the Accidents play his house party next week. And get paid. Happy birthday, my man."

Darren nods his head. Smiles. Stops smiling. Looks back at the oven clock. "Hey, when do we need to leave?"

"An hour, little less. I told him we'd be there at four. Why?"

Darren's maybe doing some math in his head, which keeps him from answering at first. "Uh, nothing. Just curious."

7 Lies Darren Tells Nate in Order to Escape from the House for about a Half Hour

1. I'm gonna run over to Best Buy. Dad got me a gift card for there.
2. No, it's cool. I'm only going for a little while anyway.
3. Plus I need to put some gas in the car.
4. And maybe I should get it washed.
5. Okay, I made that stuff up. There's this girl.
6. Just some girl.
7. Forget it, I'll tell you later.

2 People Likely Talking on the Other Side of the Door That Darren, Breathing Kind of Heavily from Racing up the Stairs, Knocks on Thirteen Minutes Later

1. His dad
2. Dr. Schrier

1 Request Darren Makes of His Dad Before Even Really Bothering to Respond to Their Surprised Greetings

1. "Hey, do you think I could just talk to Dr. Schrier alone? Just for a bit."

2 Unequal Halves from the Beginning of a Conversation

1. "Hey, Dr. Schrier, sorry—I'm sorry about that, but thanks, you know, for being cool about this, because, I don't know, man, things are kind of crazy. Like, crazier than normal. I mean, can you tell me—what do you do when it feels like, when it feels like . . . Shit, I don't know, when everything seems all screwed up and out of whack and everything? Everything. Because, seriously, it's not even that everything's bad; it's like, I swear, it's like I can't even tell if things are bad anymore, you know? That's how out of control everything is. I mean, I haven't even told you a quarter of everything. Not even a quarter. Because there's this girl Zoey, and, shit, sorry, I don't even know where to start with her. But I probably should start. Plus my mom . . . Maybe my dad already told you, because I guess he knows. She just dropped this fucking— Sorry, she just dropped this bomb on me. Today. My birthday. It's my birthday. Right? Like, what the hell is up with that? Today is my birthday, which, I don't even know if that's good or bad in the first place, but she tells me today, I'm sure you know, my dad probably told you. Plus this guy, this guy Ben, who I know from Facebook, he admitted that Zoey is where I think she is, but that I shouldn't tell

574

her everything. About how I feel. But does that mean I can't tell her other stuff? About my mom. For example. And maybe my dad, who—I'm sure he told you—I was kind of a dick to before. Even though, no, I was definitely a dick. But still, I don't know, like, who the hell am I supposed to tell everything to? Because Nate, I can't tell Nate. So, I mean, what the hell?"

2. "Darren, would you like to sit down?"

3 Dates Darren Has Agreed to Return to Dr. Schrier's Office, Which He Now Leaves Only Ten Minutes after His Arrival, Feeling, at the Most, 14 Percent Better

1. December 10
2. December 21
3. January 6

4 Requests Darren's Dad Makes in the Stairwell outside Dr. Schrier's Office

1. "Darren, would you stop? C'mon, please don't pretend you don't see me standing right here."

"Okay, sorry. It's just—"

2. "Whatever. Why don't we go back inside? Dr. Schrier and I weren't discussing anything all that important before you arrived. We could talk about what happened—"

"I can't. Sorry. Nate arranged this audition for our band, and we got to be there pretty soon, so I really can't right now. Seriously. I'm late already."

3. "Okay. Fair enough. But can I ask you to set aside some time for the two of us to talk? Before tonight, I mean. Will you do that?"

"Do what?" Darren is already descending the steps, albeit slowly.

4. "Will you call me? When you get a chance? Because I really think we need to—"

"Sure. Yeah." He's already at the bottom of the stairs. "I'll try. Bye."

6 Pieces of Equipment Nate and Darren Somehow Manage to Pack into Ray's Car, during Which Time Darren Says "Be Careful" about Thirty Times

1. Nate's guitar
2. Nate's amp
3. Darren's bass
4. Darren's amp
5. Nate's mic
6. Nate's mic stand

16 Buttons and Dials Nate Touches Before Darren's Even Backed out of the Driveway

1. Stereo volume
2. AM/FM/SAT
3. Cursor down (for satellite radio)
4. Cursor up
5. Enter
6. Destination
7. Route
8. Map
9. Info
10. Zoom in
11. Zoom out
12. Back
13. Seat warmer
14. Seat angle
15. Passenger-side light
16. Passenger-side window

4 Bits of Praise Nate Has for the Infiniti G37

1. Holy shit, these are good speakers. Whoa.
2. Very user-friendly. Ergoriffic!
3. Smooth ride.
4. Whatever the gay version of "pussy magnet" is, this is it, no doubt. Cock magnet?

3 Main Streets Darren and Nate Pass Before Nate Asks, "Dude, What's Up? Someone Die or Something?"

1. Dempster
2. Church
3. Golf

2 Rather Huge Updates about Their Parents Darren Has Given or Is Now Giving to Nate

1. That their dad is gay, back in April.

2. "Mom's probably moving to California in about two weeks."

"What the hell are you talking about?"

"They want to hire her or something."

"Who does?"

"XR Systems, I guess."

"XR Systems doesn't even exist anymore. They got bought by—"

"Right, Cloudmarket, and they—"

"No shit. They want to hire her."

"Yeah."

"Good for her," Nate says. Darren doesn't say anything. Turns onto Ridge. "Well, welcome to the new economy, I guess."

"You're going to have to live with Dad. Though he might get the house back or something."

"Should have seen it coming."

"I guess."

"Our mother's a motherfucker."

Darren almost laughs.

"Hey, you okay?" Nate asks.

Darren shrugs his shoulders. Nate pats the right one. "Don't worry, Little Man, we're about to rock the shit out of the Weiss Plantation."

7 Public Spaces the Weisses' Living Room Is Big Enough to Be

1. A restaurant
2. A library
3. A clothing store
4. A medical clinic
5. A yoga studio
6. A kennel
7. A morgue

3 People Already in This Living Room

1. JORDAN

Darren probably hasn't seen him in three years at least, but he looks pretty much the same. One of those strawberry-blond guys who'll never need to shave.

2. BASHA

Or something like that. She's wearing a light patterned skirt with tights on underneath. This room and the attached living room sort of feel like a hotel lobby, with sofas scattered everywhere, but she prefers sitting on the floor.

3. DRAKE

Or something like that. Crazily tall with long, wavy, blond hair. He keeps disappearing into the kitchen.

7 Reasons Darren Can Tell That the Three of Them Are All Super High

1. The place reeks.
2. One of the fourteen coffee tables boasts a pipe,
3. a bong,
4. some rolling papers,
5. a lighter,
6. an ashtray, and
7. a couple of tiny plastic bags filled with what even Darren can tell is marijuana.

10 Reasons Darren Only Half Pays Attention While Jordan Introduces Nate to a Bag Filled with Something Called "Sour Haze"

1. It's supposedly like the fourth-strongest strain of weed in the whole universe.
2. Darren might wind up trying it himself, but he can't decide just how bad of an idea that would be.
3. Nate is 100 percent going to try it, which won't be that big of a deal (he's high about 75 percent of the time they play anyway). But if he's way higher than normal because of it, then who knows.
4. Where the hell is Mike?
5. From the kitchen Drake screams, "Ah, crap, I burned the goddamn walnuts again!"
6. Even though no one is laughing, Basha says, maybe three times from her spot on the floor, "Don't laugh. The Haze is some serious shit."
7. His mom's moving to California.
8. The way he burst in and then ran out on his dad.
9. Ben Zwiren's Facebook message.
10. Today's Darren's sixteenth birthday.

9 Additional Developments That Contribute to Darren Not Really Knowing How to Respond to the Pipe Filled with Sour Haze Making Its Way around the Room

1. Mike shows up. He doesn't give a shit one way or another about the Haze, just asks for a beer. Jordan obliges.

2. Drake brings out salad. In separate bowls for everyone. "Drake makes the *best* salads," Basha announces.

3. Jordan brings the pipe up to his mouth, lights it, inhales, and then, three seconds later, says, "Holy shit."

4. Drake does and says something similar.

5. Basha does and says something similar.

6. Nate receives the the pipe from Basha.

"Hey man," Darren says to him, trying to be discreet. "Aren't you going to tune up or something?"

Nate points at his head. "Gotta tune this up first." Then he takes a long hit, causing his eyes to sort of deflate down into his expanding smile.

7. Nate presents the pipe to Darren.

"No, I'm good," Darren says.

"Good is good," Drake says. "But better is better." For this observation, Jordan rewards Drake with a hand slap.

8. Basha sits on the floor with her legs spread way out to the sides. Somehow her entire torso is flat against the rug in front of her. She may be purring.

9. The pipe makes its way back to Darren once again.

"D," Nate says, his smile suggesting absolute permanence, "trust me. It's stellar. Try some. Just a little."

So Darren does.

5 Possibly Fluctuating Spaces Darren Is Suddenly Super Aware Of

1. THE ONES BETWEEN DARREN AND THE REST OF THE WORLD

Darren can't stop noticing all these infinitesimal spaces just outside of him. These spaces aren't necessarily any bigger than before, but they can't be ignored, either. They're absolutely real.

2. THE ONE BETWEEN HIS FINGERS AND THE BASS STRINGS

Meaning that even when he plays, his fingers aren't fully touching the strings. Or maybe that's wrong. Maybe they are. Touching. Maybe it's just that his skin, as a layer separating him from the rest of the world, his skin is like a *thing* he can't ignore right now.

Shit, what if he can't play? There's no way he'll be able to play. Mike will be pissed. He can't look at Mike. Mike looks like he belongs in the military. Mike doesn't like him. Mike's pissed he's in a band with a high schooler and has been looking for an excuse to let this be known. To make a scene. At this very audition, for instance.

3. THE ONE BETWEEN MIKE'S FIST AND DARREN'S FACE

Shit, Mike's going to hurt Darren, isn't he?

4. THE ONE BETWEEN DARREN AND NATE

Darren puts down his bass, which he's been holding for who knows how long without doing anything more to it than depressing a couple of strings against its neck. Then he somehow walks all the way over to Nate, who's enjoying his salad on a couch the size of a small swimming pool.

"Hey," Darren whispers, certain everyone can't believe he's got the gall to whisper to someone in front of the whole group. "I don't think I can play."

"Why not?" Nate asks, chewing and unconcerned.

"Too high," Darren says. "I'm way too high."

Nate sets his salad down on the coffee table. Puts his arm around Darren, who's now awkwardly hunched over the back of the couch. "Close your eyes," he says.

5. THE ONES BETWEEN THE UPPER AND LOWER PARTS OF DARREN'S EYELIDS

Darren closes his eyes and quickly notices the laser light show going on somewhere inside them.

"Check it out," Nate says. "You're going to play just fine. You're going to play better than fine."

"But what if I don't? What if I can't?"

"It feels like more is going on than normal right now, am I correct?"

"Yeah. So much more."

"And that you can't focus."

"Not even a little."

591

"But check it out, Little Man, you're actually just focusing on more. Focusing just as good as normal, only on more stuff. Meaning, you'll be playing great while, I don't know, finally understanding what syncopation really is or what it means that Mom is going to be getting all intimate with Bill Gates's weenie in six months."

"Shut up."

"Right, sorry. He lives in Seattle."

"Seriously. Say something else. Now."

"Your dad—"

"C'mon, Nate. Stop messing with me."

"Just remember to breathe."

Darren inhales and leans into his brother.

"Will you try?" Nate asks.

Darren nods that he will. He can hear Basha purring. Of course it sounds sexual. How could it not?

5 **Genres and Subgenres of Alternative Rock the Accidents Might Be Said to Play, Though It Should Be Pointed Out That Nate Thinks Those Kinds of Labels Are "Total Pointless Bullshit"**

1. Indie Rock
2. Post-Punk Revival
3. Garage Rock Revival
4. Jangle Pop
5. Power Pop

3 Members of the Accidents and How They're Performing Right Now

1. MIKE
Rocking extra hard.

2. DARREN
Whoa, Nate was right. Somehow Darren's fingers are listening to his brain. Incredible.

Mr. Keyes talks about "being in the pocket," which is kind of another way of saying "being in the groove." Darren's in the deepest pocket in world history right now. Like, imagine a pair of pants the size of the Willis Tower, a pair of pants 1,451 feet long. Darren and his bass are straight-up taking a leisurely stroll around the pocket of those pants. It's so big, he was able to invite Mike and his whole drum set to come inside and join him.

3. NATE
And that's a good development, because even though Darren has no idea how Nate figures into the whole pocket thing, it can only help him. Because Nate is definitely on Planet Nate right now. There are only three people in the audience, but you'd never know it from Nate's performance.

5 Additional Half-Baked Analogies That Might Explain the Musical Dynamic at the Heart of the Accidents' Audition

1. Darren and Mike are the cake and Nate's the frosting.
2. Darren and Mike are the trampoline and Nate's the acrobat.
3. Darren and Mike are the canvas and the frame, and Nate's the paint. Or the painter.
4. Darren and Mike are the chairs and the table. And the plates and the silverware. And the glasses. And Nate's the food.
5. Darren and Mike are the rules. And Nate's the game. Nate's playing the game. And winning.

5 Places Drawing Darren's Attention While He Plays

1. THE COUCH
Drake's nodding his head like the Accidents are steadily convincing him of their stance on an important, controversial topic. Jordan, meanwhile, has closed his eyes. Every once in a while he crimps up his entire face.

2. THE CARPETING RIGHT IN FRONT OF THE COUCH
They got Basha up off the floor. She's not exactly dancing, but she is most certainly moving.

3. THE STAGE, MEANING THIS ONE CORNER OF THE ROOM
The hilarious thing is that Nate is messing up pretty regularly. Not super bad. But he's singing a verse he already sang. Plus he was supposed to be using a capo for this whole song, but totally forgot. Luckily Darren was able to adjust the key for himself. And luckily Mike doesn't know the difference. Plus they were supposed to play this song third, not second.

Good enough for rock and roll. That's what Nate would say, since he says it all the time at home when he's screwing up.

4. THE INSIDE OF HIS OWN CRANIUM

Darren wonders if it's this easy for other bassists. Just keeping the beat and not worrying about anything else. Or maybe Darren just likes being responsible for something pretty straightforward. In this case, the rhythm.

Maybe it's not so hilarious, actually. The amount Nate is messing up.

Look at them. At Jordan, Drake, and Basha. And Nate. Have people ever thought they were cooler? Maybe they are cool. Maybe Darren's cool too. Because people can decide pretty much anything, and anyone, is cool. That's how cool works.

But, honestly, they're kind of idiots, too.

That's not nice.

No, but they are. Like, they really look stupid right now. You can just tell Basha is the kind of person who totally means what she says, only everything she says makes zero sense. And Drake. The guy looks like Big Bird.

Is Jordan flunking out of Northwestern? Maybe. Probably. Who cares? And this stupid house. Who needs a house this goddamn big? A house half this big would be too big. And Jordan's going to trash the place while his parents are off in Oslo or wherever.

And the Accidents are going to provide the sound track.

Sweet.

Plus, honestly, this music, it's pretty whatever. Any music you can play this sloppily and not have anyone care, or even notice, there's something wrong with it. Or with the people who like it. Mr. Keyes would tear his hair out if they just made up some key on the spot.

And then there's Nate. He really thinks he's going to be a rock star. Maybe he's good enough for the Sour Haze crowd, but at some point he'll have to get serious. Good luck getting him to practice like Darren tells him he should. "You've got to do your scales, it'll help with your solos." That's what Darren tells him. Nate says, "I get better at soloing from soloing."

Whatever, man, whatever.

5. DARREN'S POCKET, HIS ACTUAL POCKET

And Darren's endlessly annoying phone won't stop vibrating in his pocket. His real pocket, that is. Probably his mom calling to remind him that Legoland is in California.

8 Displays of Affection Shared by Those Present After the Accidents Finish and the Applause Stops and Jordan Yells, "Hell Yeah! You Guys Are Sick!"

1. Hug (Nate and Jordan)
2. Fist bump (Darren and Mike)
3. Fist bump (Darren and Jordan)
4. High five (Nate and Mike)
5. Hug (Nate and Basha)
6. Double fist bump (Nate and Drake)
7. Double hand squeeze, half hug (Darren and Basha)
8. Hug (Darren and Nate)

3 Post-audition Activities Undertaken by the Various Members of the Accidents

1. Mike taking apart and packing up his drums
2. Nate hunkering down on the couch to smoke a celebratory joint with Jordan and friends in order to seal the deal or something
3. Darren setting out for the bathroom. Not that he has to go to the bathroom. Pulls out his phone on the way. There's been a lot of activity.

6 Exact Quotes Taken from the Voice Messages Darren Listens to While Meandering around the Weisses' House, Which Seems to Just Keep Going and Going

1. HIS DAD
Your mother called, asking how I'd feel if you slept at her place tonight instead of here. I said it's up to you. Let me know what you think. I'm fine either way.

2. HIS MOM
I went ahead and asked your father if he would be okay with you sleeping here tonight. He said that was fine with him as long as you're okay with it, so if you're okay with it, let's plan to do that. Okay?

3. HIS MOM
Okay, just trying to get ahold of you. Hope you and Nate are having a good time. I'll—forget it, never mind. Just please call when you get a chance. And don't think I forgot about the thirty dollars and tip I still owe you.

4. RACHEL
Okay, my present to you today is not giving you permission to not talk to me today! Oh my God, that was so selfish. Sorry! But please call, please! And you better have gotten my e-mail.

5. HIS DAD

Since it looks like you'll probably be spending the night at your mother's, I thought maybe we could go downtown to the Green Llama for dinner instead of getting sushi up here. I know Ray would love to spoil you a little more today, and your mother said she actually had someone down around there she's been meaning to have coffee with for a while, so she could just pick you and your brother up straight from the restaurant afterward. And then you guys could actually just meet us down at the restaurant around seven thirty. Let me know what you think.

6. HIS MOM

Hi, honey. I want to apologize for today. For me breaking the news like I did. That wasn't fair to you on your birthday. I'm sorry. We do still need to talk about the whole thing, though, and soon. But okay, I suppose it can wait a day or two. I love you.

2 Objects Confounding Darren, Who Is Thankfully Way Less High Than He Was an Hour Ago

1. His phone. Which is actually pissing him off. Not just the messages and all that, but the actual phone. Because how did everyone (as in, everyone in the whole damn world) just agree that it was a good idea to haul these things around all the time? They're like little monsters or something.

2. And why do the Weisses have a jukebox in their laundry room?

2 Family Members to Whom Darren Texts the Message

We'll Be at Green Llama at 730

1. His mom
2. His dad

4 Conversations, Only Three of Which Actually Take Place, and None of Which Go All That Well

1. Eight seconds later his phone rings. His dad. An impossible call to ignore in light of the timing.

"Hi," Darren says, sitting down on the landing of a flight of stairs he somehow didn't walk up to get to the second floor, which is the floor he's on. Unless there's a third floor.

"How's your day?" his dad asks.

"Fine."

"Enjoying the car?"

"It's nice, yeah."

"Great. Well, I wanted to be sure you're okay with the arrangements for tonight."

"Yeah. Sure. Whatever."

"I just —"

"Didn't you see my text?"

"Yes. Of course. But it was rather terse."

"It's a text message, Dad."

"Okay, okay. I just wanted to check. And see how you're doing." Darren is now lying down on the floor. When he tilts his head back he still can't see the end of the hallway.

"I'm fine, Dad."

"I mean, I was rather surprised when you showed up at Dr. Schrier's like you did."

Darren says nothing.

"Though I was pleased to see you turning to him for help. Assuming that's what you were doing. He said nothing to me about what you told him, of course."

"Of course," Darren says, with no discernable emotion.

"And you're not angry about anything?"

"Like what?"

"Well, like about what you said to me in the car this morning."

Was his dad always like this? Darren can no longer remember for certain, though he doubts he was. Either way, there's some troubling chicken-egg something here, as far as his dad is concerned.

"Dad, c'mon, please. Not right now."

"Well, Darren, it's just, I'd just really like us to talk through this, however briefly, before dinner tonight. Otherwise, otherwise it may just cloud everything." Darren closes his eyes. Tries to remember to breathe like Nate said. It's not working. "If you want me to drop it, I will, but—"

"What do you want me to say, Dad?"

"There's no need to raise your voice like that, Darren."

"Seriously. What do you want from me? You're kind of weird sometimes, Dad. You are. It's true. And I don't know what you want me to do about it, because—"

"You don't need to do anything, Darren. All I need from you is for you to—to . . ."

"What? Do I have to say that I'm glad you're gay? That it's awesome? That nothing could make me happier? Is that what you mean? Is that what you're waiting for? You're gay, Dad, I get it. You're gay. I'm okay with it. I am. I swear. And Ray's a cool guy. He is. Like, way cooler than you, in fact. Like, ten times cooler. But okay, what else do you want from me? Do I have to ride the float at the next parade with you? Do I have to say I'm proud of you? Do I really have to like it? Is that what you need for me to say? That I'm psyched you finally found the right guy to fuck from now on?"

Extremely awkward silence.

"I see."

"Dad, shit. I . . ."

"I'll see you at dinner, Darren."

"Sorry, Dad. No, don't. I'm sorry."

"No, it's okay. It's good you were able to say that. But I think I should get off now."

And he does.

2. Eight seconds later he calls his dad back.

"Hello."

"I'm sorry, Dad. I didn't mean that."

"Darren, there's no need to lie."

"I didn't."

"We'll get through this."

"I'm sorry."

Silence.

"Dad?"

"Yes."

"I'm trying."

"I know you are. I know this is hard."

"I love you, Dad. I do."

"I know, Darren. I know. I love you, too."

"So then, can—"

"I'll see you at dinner, Darren. Good-bye."

When you're in a weird place, or maybe just a bad place, and you recently had a couple of weird conversations, or maybe a couple of bad conversations, it's impossible to know if you're high still. Because being high means being not normal. And everything is so far from normal right now that Darren can barely even remember what normal's supposed to mean.

So maybe the Sour Haze is responsible for Darren being stuck to this floor like he is. Or maybe it's not.

3. Darren stares at Zoey's number. Maybe she'd understand. Maybe, while she's busy fixing herself, she could fix him, too. Whatever, might as well try. Only, before he can make the call:

"Darren!" Nate screams. "Hide-and-seek is over. Get your ass down here."

4. "I'll tell you what," Nate says after closing the trunk on Ray's car about ten minutes later. "When they write the history of the Accidents, that house is going to be like ground zero."

"They loved our shit," Darren says.

"You want to know why? Because it was the opposite of shit."

The day is winding down.

"We rocked absurdly hard," Nate says.

"Yeah," Darren says.

Where the hell did the sun go?

"Can you believe it?" Nate asks. "I mean, can you effing believe that shit?"

"Hey," Darren says, "why'd you play 'When You Were Young' in G instead of C?"

"What?"

"You played it in the wrong key."

"No I didn't."

"Yes you did. You forgot to put on the capo."

"Shit, you're right. But so what? It sounded fine, right?"

"Pretty much."

"Pretty much?"

"Yeah, pretty much."

"Yo, what's the dealio?"

"I don't know. It's just, I had to like figure it out on the spot."

"And you're a beast, so you did."

"And it's 'I can't take you apart,' not 'I can't take you to heart.'"

"What are you talking about? I didn't sing that."

"Yeah you did, it's in the chorus. You sang it that way like four times."

"Man, listen to you. Haters gonna hate."

"I'm just saying."

"What?"

"That, I don't know, we can do better."

"Better? Are you kidding me? Didn't you feel us getting drenched in the multiple orgasms blowing up all over that room?"

Darren doesn't say anything.

"This is about Mom, isn't it?" Nate asks.

"What? No."

"It is, man. She pooped on your birthday cake with her high-tech master plan. Even the Haze couldn't help your stunned ass."

"What, like you don't care that she's moving?"

"Not really. Far away but making mad bank. Kind of ideal if you ask me."

"She's not going to give you anything if you're not in school."

"Yeah, right."

"She's not. She told me."

"Whatever." Nate extends his right hand. "My turn to drive."

"You just smoked up again," Darren says.

"And? Give me the keys."

"Ray didn't say you could."

"Oh, you're such a puss job."

"He didn't."

"Must I remind you that I was, until about four hours ago, a professional driver?"

"So?"

"So," Nate says, "there is no way in the world he explicitly told you not to let me drive. Am I right?"

"Sorry. You can't."

"D, man." Nate takes hold of Darren's hand. "Don't forget, he's going to be my gay stepdad soon too, you know."

"Shut up."

"Make me, weenus."

"You can't drive."

Nate's other hand gets involved in the struggle. "Give me the keys. Now."

And then, just like that, they're on their way to the ground.

10 Potentially Iconic Black-and-White Photographs That a Professional Photographer Would Be Capable of Capturing from the Jacobs Brothers' First Physical Fight in More Than Four Years

1. Nate tackling Darren
2. Darren putting Nate in a headlock
3. Nate driving his right knee into Darren's left thigh
4. Darren pressing Nate's face into the grass just north of the Weisses' driveway
5. Nate elbowing Darren in the ribs
6. Nate freeing himself from Darren's headlock
7. Darren tripping Nate
8. Darren climbing on top of Nate
9. Darren pinning Nate's right arm under his left knee
10. Nate bending Darren's left pinkie back

1 Additional Conversation

1. "Ow!" Darren more or less screams. "Let go!"

"Get off me."

"Let go."

"Let me drive."

"No."

"Fuck you."

"Fuck you."

"Just to the lake."

"No."

"C'mon. It's only like two blocks from here."

"You're a dick."

"I know. But you shouldn't care so much."

"You dick."

"Just to the lake."

"Fine."

"So get off of me."

"Let go of my finger."

"Fine. On three."

"One, two . . ."

Darren rolls over next to Nate. They lie there, breathing loudly.

"How the hell did Haze make you so angry?" Nate asks.

"Blow me. It didn't."

"Bullshit. We just rocked and you're shitting all over it."

"You need to get better."

"And you need to lighten up."

They lie there silent for a minute or so. Darren stares up at the sky through the empty trees. Why do they make it so hard to become an astronaut?

"Hey."

"What?" Nate asks.

"Did you ever think how if Dad . . ."

"What about him?"

"If he admitted he was gay all along."

"Yeah?"

"If he did that, we never would have been born. You know?"

"And you think I'm too high to drive."

"I'm serious. Think about it. Like, he had to be in the closet, or whatever, for us to even happen."

4 Parts of a Story Nate Tells Darren While They Sit on a Large Stone Near the Shore of Lake Michigan

1. "You know, the summer we moved up to Skokie, right before I started kindergarten, we went to the beach one day. Back when we lived on Belden. It was probably on a Saturday like today. Except it was the summer, so it was warm and there were a million people everywhere. And there was this street performer. He was doing the one-man-band thing. Bass drum on his back, cymbals between his knees, some kind of horn under his armpit, the whole deal. And I was mesmerized. Could have watched him forever, because he couldn't just play all the instruments at once, he could play entire songs and it sounded good; I remember how good it sounded. It was the most amazing thing I had seen in person in my entire life.

"But then I don't know what happened. At some point he must have finished, and I look around but don't see Mom or Dad. I search for them all over the place but can't find them anywhere. And I was scared, but, I don't know, at some point, I swear, I was like, 'Okay, they're gone forever I guess, time to figure this out myself.' I swear I thought that; I swear I wasn't that worried. I had a quarter in my pocket, because Dad gave me one earlier in the day to get a gumball, but the machine was broken, so I just kept it. I looked along the trail and found a couple of pennies—I didn't know how much things really cost back then, but I thought that I could probably find enough coins to last me for a while.

"And then there was this guy selling pretzels, this old guy with a thick, bushy mustache and a really thin face. He must have noticed me wandering around by myself, because he called out to me and asked in some weird accent, 'You lost, son?' So he gave me a pretzel and had me sit down on this wooden stool he had next to his stand. He said, 'We wait here for them. They come soon. I am certain.' And I'm telling you, I was sure they were gone forever, and I wasn't happy about it or anything, but I was like, 'Okay, there's this guy and he gave me a pretzel for nothing and is letting me sit here. I could do this tomorrow, too; I'll be okay.'

2. "Eventually, of course, they found me. And they were freaking out, crying and pretty much hyperventilating, especially Mom, who was wearing you in that baby carrier they used to have. She hugged me, just smothered me, with your legs dangling in my face. And I was glad to see Mom and Dad, relieved I guess, because I knew living by myself was going to be hard. But, I don't know, I was mostly thinking, 'Okay, that was some kind of test, and I passed it, because if I had to, I could be okay on my own.' You were literally tied to Mom, but I was surviving on my own; that's how I felt then.

3. "And so that's the deal, you know? Because even if it didn't really happen then, it's what happens. It's going to happen. At some point you're cut loose. At some point they leave you somewhere and don't come back. Pretty much, anyway. And so the key thing about growing up is just coming to terms with that, you know? And I think that's why I'm okay deep down with everything, because I figured it out at such a young age, so things just don't faze me the way they do other people. Everything is going to be okay, even when the worst thing seems to happen.

4. "I'm going to get my own place and just, you know, say whatever to Mom and Dad, which, the sooner you can figure out how to do, the better, trust me. It's not like they were the worst parents or anything, but at this point they're doing us a favor with all the divorce bullshit and her lame-ass California and Dad being whatever the hell Dad is at this point."

3 Overdue Communications That Take Place After Nate Goes to Piss

1. Darren checks his e-mail while walking toward the water.

Something from Travelocity. Almost deletes it, figuring it's spam. But decides to open it instead.

Rachel bought him a ticket. To Minneapolis. December tenth to twelfth.

Maybe if he commits to eating better and exercising regularly he could still become an astronaut. Or maybe regular people will be able to go into outer space in the future, though he sort of doubts it.

2. He calls Rachel.

"Is this the birthday boy?"

"Hey."

"You're lucky it's your birthday, Mr. Impossible to Get Ahold Of."

"Sorry. Crazy day."

"What happened?"

"Later. Forget it."

"Hey, did you get my e-mail?"

"Uh-huh. Yeah. Thanks. Thanks a lot. That's—"

"Were you surprised?"

"For sure."

"We're going to have the best time. Hopefully it won't be freezing here already, even though it probably will be. I don't how we're going to fit in everything I've planned. And you won't believe it, but that cellist, the one who—"

3. "Rachel."

"Yeah?"

"Um."

"What?"

"Can we . . ."

"Huh?"

"Nothing."

"What?"

"Forget it."

"Tell me."

"Rachel, do you think, I mean . . ."

"What?"

"Can we just be friends?"

". . ."

"I'm sorry. Shit. I know that's, like, crazily lame, to say that. 'Can we just be friends.' I can't believe I just said it. But look, I mean it. I do. I want to be friends. You're great. I just—"

"Oh my God. I'm so stupid—"

"No, you're—"

"I can't believe I bought you a ticket. I can't believe I act—"

"No. Don't say that. Don't. Please. You're, like, I don't know,

619

you treat me way better than anyone I know. You do. Way better than I deserve. I have no idea how I would have made it through the past few months without you. I'm totally, one-hundred-percent serious. Like, I owe you for that. And I really do like you a lot, seriously. But I feel like a dick pretending that—"

"Stop."

"No, I mean it."

"Okay. I get it."

"So can we still be friends? Can we?"

"Darren. Stop."

"Rachel, look, you might be my only friend. Who I can actually talk to."

"Great. Fabulous."

"But . . . I think I'm not meant for you. Or the other way around. You know, in that way. I don't know if I even believe in people being meant for each other. But maybe I do. Please be my friend still."

She's crying.

"Please."

"I should go, Darren."

"Okay. Sorry."

"Bye, Darren. Happy birthday."

And do they have rockets that don't ever return to Earth? Would his odds be any better if he told them he'd be willing to go on one of those?

7 Sentences Ben Zwiren Has Recently Sent to Darren

1. Can I give you some advice?
2. Don't ask people for advice.
3. Advice is overrated.
4. You're the one who's got to figure out what you should do.
5. So figure it out and then do what you should do.
6. Okay, yeah, I guess that was advice, but you know what I mean.
7. Good luck, man.

10 Fingers That Intertwine as Part of the "Mountain Climber's Grip" Darren Initiates to Lift Nate up off Their Rock, This Grip Being Something the Jacobs Brothers Have Employed and Celebrated for Years

1. Darren's right thumb
2. Nate's right thumb
3. Darren's index finger
4. Nate's index finger
5. Darren's middle finger
6. Nate's middle finger
7. Darren's ring finger
8. Nate's ring finger
9. Darren's pinkie
10. Nate's pinkie

2 Members of Storied Brazilian Duo Who Escort Them Down into the City

1. TOQUINHO
Darren drives. Competently. Better than competently.

2. & VINICIUS
"Say anything about the music and you walk the rest of the way."

"Me?" Nate asks. "What would I say? You're your father's son, what's so wrong about that?"

"You're such a douche bag sometimes."

"You say that like it's a bad thing."

They drive on for a while.

"Damn," Nate says. "These guys are good. Have you been intentionally hiding this shit from me?"

"Maybe." Darren might actually be smiling. "Maybe."

5 Signs That It Wasn't a Particularly Good Idea for His Parents to Drive Downtown Together, or Even Be in the Same Place at the Same Time Ever Again

1. They're both clearly waiting for Darren and Nate, but his mom is in her car, while his dad waits just inside the restaurant.

2. When Darren and Nate walk up, his dad exits the restaurant and his mom gets out of the car, so that soon the four of them are standing more or less in the same place. And Darren is certain he can feel a genuine electrical charge of some sort running between his parents, who both look remarkably unlike the people they looked like when they were still married only eighteen months earlier. But it's not an electrical charge like the kind people talk about when they're in love or attracted to each other. It's like some kind of short circuit or live wire the two of them form. Darren can feel it in his legs, to the point he's grateful to be wearing shoes with rubber soles.

3. His mom was definitely crying in the past ten minutes, and it's possible his dad was as well.

4. When his dad, trying to smile, welcomes Darren first by asking, "How was traffic?" Darren for some reason steals a look at his mom before answering. And she's trying to smile too but is doing an even worse job of it than his dad, because no matter what he says to his dad, he'll be greeting him before his mom, or because the person who gave birth to him is not going to be joining them for his sixteenth birthday dinner, or because in two weeks she's going to be living two thousand miles away.

Or maybe because of all those reasons.

"Fine," Darren says, looking right into his father's soft eyes, trying to say "fine" in a way that also might mean, *I'm sorry about what I said on the phone before, and I promise never to say anything like that again, but that would be a way easier promise to keep if you at least tried to hide your freakiness just a little from time to time. Not the gay freakiness, which isn't freaky, seriously, it isn't. Just all the other stuff. But so, I don't know, if you could just be a little patient and a little less weird while I figure that out and what to do about it, that would be great.*

There's a chance his dad understands. A chance.

5. Hugging each of them feels like some kind of test or performance or both, and the only way he feels like he can pass the test or get approval from the audience is by making sure neither hug is anything special, which means just sort of squeezing both of them really briefly, which in both cases means kind of underhugging his parents, both of whom were clearly expecting and maybe even needing more.

And then he just stands there, in between his under-hugged parents, who each place a hand on one of his shoulders at precisely the same moment. Like they had choreographed the thing before his arrival. His shoulders, they begin to smolder. As does everything in between.

43 Ingredients of a Fight That Ignites All at Once, Such That Darren Isn't Sure Ten Seconds Later If This Is Exactly How It Started, but It More or Less Went Something Like This

1. Mom: So I'll pick you guys up around nine thirty.
2. Dad: Why doesn't he just call you when we're finishing up?
3. Mom: How about ten o'clock, then?
4. Everyone:
5. Mom: Ten thirty?
6. Darren: Uh.
7. Mom: Look, call me when you're ready to be picked up, okay?
8. Dad: Brenda, why don't I just drop him off with you once we're finished? Where are you going to be?
9. Mom: Whatever, Howard. Do what you want.
10. Nate: Ridiculous.
11. Dad: Nate, please.
12. Nate: Dad, please.
13. Dad: Please, Nate, I'm asking you.
14. Nate: And what, exactly, are you asking me?
15. Mom: Cut it out.
16. Nate: No, I want to know. Tell me.

17. Mom: Nate.

18. Nate: Tell me.

19. Mom: Nate. Cut it out!

20. Dad: Please don't yell, Brenda.

21. Mom: Are you serious?

22. Dad: Yes, Brenda, I'm asking you, please don't yell.

23. Mom: You need to grow up. You do.

24. Nate: And you need to move to California already.

25. Dad:

26. Mom:

27. Darren:

28. Mom: You know he quit his job today? You know he can't—you can't even hold a job as a fucking pizza delivery boy!

29. Dad: What happened?

30. Nate: It was a shitty job.

31. Dad: What happened?

32. Mom: Tell him, Nate.

33. Mom: Go ahead, tell him.

34. Dad: Brenda, stop.

35. Ray: Howard? What's going on here?

36. Nate: Well, hello, Ray.

37. Mom: Tell him, Nate!

38. Dad: Brenda!

39. Ray: What is this? You can't—

40. Mom: Ray, this doesn't concern you.

41. Dad: Brenda, stop!

42. Ray: Howard.

43. Nate: Hey, Ray. Could I ask you to, uh, fuck off for a few minutes?

5 Perspectives from Which Darren Feels He's Witnessing This Fight

1. That of a mute stranger.
2. That of a five-year-old immigrant boy unable to understand anything but everyone's tone of voice.
3. That of an otherwise healthy person who just finished having open-heart surgery but is presently waiting to have his chest closed back up.
4. That of an invisible sixteen-year-old.
5. That of a person slowly backing away from the scene.

4 Storefronts Darren Walks Past Until He Can No Longer Hear Them

1. Bryon's Liquor
2. Suds Coin Laundromat
3. Saturn Café
4. Fifth Third Bank

10 Numbers Darren Dials Manually

1. The
2. Numbers
3. In
4. Zoey's
5. Number
6. Which
7. He
8. Memorized
9. Long
10. Ago

4 Rings Darren Hears

1. The first
2. The second
3. The third
4. The fourth, but only in his head, because someone actually answers before this day can get any worse

1 Finally

1. "Hello?"

"Zoey?"

". . ."

"Zoey?"

"Darren?"

"Yeah."

"Hi."

"You answered."

"Yeah, I'm home."

"Home?"

"Yeah."

"Like, Chicago home?"

"Yeah."

"For how long?"

". . ."

"How long are you here for?"

"My flight's in a few hours."

"Oh."

"They let me come home for Thanksgiving."

"From Savilleta?"

"What? Yeah. How did you know?"

". . ."

". . ."

"Why do you have to leave so soon?"

"Visits aren't supposed to be more than two days."

"Oh."

"It was a big deal they let me. And we're not supposed to see, you know, other people."

"..."

"I..."

"..."

"..."

"What?"

"I got your messages, Darren."

"So did..."

"And your letter."

"..."

"And your playlist."

"I got your drawings."

"..."

"You're an incredible artist."

"Thanks."

"You are."

"..."

"I didn't take your drawing off my arm for a month."

"I shouldn't have... I'm really sorry about... Ann Arbor and—"

"Zoey."

"Yeah?"

". . ."

". . ."

"Can I see you? Tonight?"

"I . . . Darren."

"Huh?"

"We're not supposed to."

"I know."

"It's just . . ."

"Ben Zwiren told me. I know."

"You know Ben?"

"Sort of. Yeah. He told me."

"The program I'm in. I'm mean, we're not supposed to."

"To what?"

"You know."

". . ."

"Have boyfriends."

"I know. I'm not—"

"You don't know."

"What?"

"What happened."

"I don't—"

"Why they sent me away."

"I want to see you, Zoey."

"I'm a fuck-up."

"I really want to see you tonight."

"And I'm trying not to be."

". . ."

"Darren, I'm sorry."

". . ."

"Sorry."

". . ."

". . ."

"Zoey?"

"Yeah?"

"It's my birthday."

"Today?"

"I'm sixteen."

"Happy birthday."

". . ."

". . ."

"It's been a shitty birthday."

"Sorry."

"A super shitty birthday."

"Sorry."

". . ."

". . ."

"Zoey, my life . . . I don't think it could be much better than yours right now."

"Darren, you—"

"No, I mean, it's a mess. I'm a mess."

"I'm sorry."

". . ."

"..."

"I'm going to be there in a half hour, Zoey."

"Darren."

"Will you sneak out for me?"

"Darren."

"Please? For me?"

"..."

"..."

"Darren."

"What?"

"I've been working hard."

"Okay."

"To not be like I was."

"That's good."

"So, I can't."

"..."

"..."

"What if I promise to help after?"

"..."

"To help you keep working and stuff."

"..."

"And you'll help me."

"..."

"And then I'll wait until you're ready."

"..."

"I'll wait. I promise. As long as you need me to."

". . ."

"Please."

". . ."

"For me."

". . ."

". . ."

"Okay."

"You will?"

". . ."

"Will you?"

"Yes."

"I'll be there soon."

"Hurry."

"I will."

"Wait, Darren."

"What?"

"I missed you so much. I'm so sorry I—"

"It's okay."

"Hurry, please."

"I will. I promise. I will."

3 Things Darren Does Before Walking to Ray's Car

1. Walks back to the fight, which is ongoing. Ray has disappeared. His three family members are speaking all at once, each of them at a volume located precisely halfway between talking and screaming.

2. Says, "Hey." Says it again. Says it a third time. Actually, he screams it this time.

They all stop and, still heaving, look at him. Everyone's expression is some version of *Where'd you come from?* or *What are you doing here?* or *Oh, right, Darren's part of all this too.*

"You want to know what I want for my birthday?" Darren asks. "You want to know? I want to be somewhere else right now. With someone else. I"—he looks into the restaurant, at all the people calmly eating their delicious vegetarian dinners, people who look totally normal and not insane—"I love you guys, I do, I mean it, but I can't . . . I can't." He digs his hand into his pocket and feels for his keys.

"Dad"—he looks at his father, and ignores the muscles in his own neck that seem determined to swivel his head over to his mom—"if you want . . . if you want, I'll go to Dr. Schrier's with you every week until I graduate. I'm serious."

"Darren," his dad says, "that's not necessary. We can just—"

"So whatever is. Whatever's necessary. We'll do that. I will. Okay? I promise."

Then he lets those muscles do their thing.

"Mom," he says to a wet and shiny face that apparently belongs to her. She runs her sleeve over it. "I'm okay." He's trying so hard to mean it. "I'm okay." Maybe saying it over and over will eventually make it true. "I'm okay if you have to move. I am. So go. It's okay. It'll be okay. I'm okay."

He has to close his eyes. It's the only way he's going to make it through this.

"Nate."

"What, D?"

"You're my only brother. You know that, right?"

"Duh. Yeah. So?"

"You're my only big brother. Okay? The only one."

"Yup."

"Right? The only one."

"Yeah," Nate answers quietly.

Darren opens his eyes. Looks back into the restaurant. Where he won't be eating tonight.

"Look," he says, turning back to all these people with whom he shares every last bit of his genetic material, for better or for worse. "I need to go see someone. I'll come back. I promise I will. But"—he swallows—"don't wait up."

3. Hugs them, like he means it.

6 Great Things about Lake Shore Drive

1. The way it curves gently.
2. The park it cuts through.
3. The lake that sits on one side.
4. The buildings facing it on the other.
5. How it's exactly the right place to drive when you're listening to Bill Evans play "Lucky to Be Me" all by himself. Like somehow the whole thing turns the car into a time machine.
6. And the way all that makes it possible for you to believe, even for just a moment, that maybe, just maybe, you could be happy living in this part of this planet after all. Assuming Zoey feels more or less the same.

14 Ways This All Ends, for Now

1. He pulls up in front of Zoey's house, and there she is, stepping out from behind the garage and rushing toward the car.

2. He unlocks the door and she hurries inside. "Go," she says with some urgency.

3. He drives. Drives past two or three houses. But can't stop wanting to see her, to really look at her. So he pulls over. And there she is, sitting right next to him.

4. Zoey Lovell.

5. The piercings are all there. Her hair is shorter. Closer to some version of normal. And her face, it's hers, but new as well. Different. Like it's open now, like it's opening up right now, just for him. Thankfully, the spot's still there. She's beautiful. But in a way that makes the word seem hopelessly inadequate.

6. "This is bad," she says.
   "No it's not."
   "You don't know."
   "What don't I know?"
   "Pretty much everything."
   "So tell me everything."

"This is going to set me back. I don't know how far back."

"I'll wait."

She looks down. Considers something for a few seconds. Smiles.

7. He takes her hand. That still wears the ring. Thank God she kept the ring. He lifts her hand and kisses it. He actually does this, and somehow it doesn't feel ridiculous at all.

8. They kiss, on the lips. Maybe for the first time ever.

9. "Drive," she says. "Just drive."

10. There are laws against sixteen-year-olds driving at night, against sixteen-year-olds driving with passengers under the age of twenty-one. And there are probably additional laws against sixteen-year-olds with passengers under the age of twenty-one crossing state lines at night. But she told him to drive, and he needs to get past the city and all its lights.

11. With one hand he drives, and with the other he holds her hand. His parents used to do that. He'd watch them from the backseat.

12. She talks. She talks a lot. She tells him things. All sorts of things. And that list, the one from the website, the one with nowhere to hide, she recalls a lot of it for him.

He just holds her hand. There are things from the nightmare list that make him want to pull away. Not want to, but almost have to. But somehow he doesn't.

Maybe because her list, it somehow matters and doesn't matter. It's Zoey and not Zoey at the exact same time. Sure, now he knows for certain what he only sort of knew before, but he also realizes, he finally gets it, just listening to the sound of her voice, that there are a million other, better ways to know her. And those ways have nothing to do with an update or a confession or anything like that.

He tries telling her this with his hand and how he drives and the precise way he says almost nothing back to her. So she keeps talking, gradually making one thing incredibly clear to him: She's trying to undo her list, to write another list. To not have a list. To be Zoey without a list.

13. Maybe everything would be better without all these horrible, endless lists. But maybe they're unavoidable and the point is just to find someone to share yours with. Or someone to write some new and better ones with. Maybe that's the point of the whole thing: Find the right person to write your lists with.

14. And assuming it is, here's how he'd start:

6 Things to Do Right Now

1. Drive for hours with Zoey Lovell.
2. Get off the highway at a random exit somewhere in Wisconsin.
3. Make a few turns until you're driving down a road no one's ever even bothered to pave.
4. Get out of the car at the edge of a massive, silent field.
5. Stand under the stars with her.
6. Realize that this planet isn't so bad after all.

ACKNOWLEDGMENTS

I wrote the first draft of this book in fifty-one wonderfully manic and optimistically impulsive days. Seven drafts and almost three years later it reached its final form. Many people helped along the way, and I'd like to thank them.

Dan Shere and David Levin offered useful notes, friendly encouragement, and reliable enthusiasm. Joel Grossman demonstrated, repeatedly, what unbridled excitement for this book might look like. Noam Hasak-Lowy was Noam Hasak-Lowy throughout, which is no small thing. James Mignogna let me know what needed to be known, at least by this book's future readers. Josh Radnor inspired me to think twice about the words I use. Sara Levine, in addition to being a valuable local ally, encouraged me to reconsider the form of these very acknowledgments.

Stephen Barr agreed to tell me what it really was like. Robert McDonald provided crucial, insightful, and honest criticism on a late draft. Ezra Garfield, Emily Downie, Hannah Chonkan-Urow, and Ariel Hasak-Lowy agreed to take on additional homework and, after completing said homework, delivered smart, cogent, and vital feedback late in the game. Ariel Hasak-Lowy gets mentioned twice because she, in fact, read it twice.

Elizabeth Gerometta and Genevieve Buzo, whom I still haven't met, unearthed the absurdly elusive title.

The team at Simon & Schuster did all manner of wonderful things to transform this from a messy file on my lonely laptop to an actual and rather snazzy-looking book that now lives out in the great big world. Jessica Handelman (cover genius); Hilary Zarycky (interior design virtuoso); Christina Pecorale, Victor Iannone, and the rest of the sales team; Carolyn Swerdloff, Teresa Ronquillo, and Lucille Rettino in marketing; Faye Bi, Michael Strother, Katherine Devendorf, Sara Berko, Mary Marotta, and Mara Anastas (commander in chief)—thanks to all of you for giving my writing such a warm home.

Simon Lipskar, my original and future agent, convinced me, however effortlessly, that "writing is writing," thereby diffusing at least one stubborn source of self-doubt.

Dan Lazar, my present and future agent (I know, it's complicated), helped this often-convoluted writer find his place within a readership he often assumed couldn't possibly want to have anything to do with him. Dan also provided reliable wisdom and steady guidance. And I remain grateful to him for having a master plan, even if it hasn't quite worked out yet.

Liesa Abrams—my genuinely brilliant, astoundingly diligent, and endlessly thoughtful editor—opened this door and explicitly invited me to walk through it. She more or less demanded that I write the way I wanted to write all along, at a time when I was beginning to wonder if that was even a remotely good idea. Though I wrote all the words, it was Liesa who figured out (again and again and again) how to make this peculiar book accessible at the same time. In about six distinct ways, this book wouldn't have happened without her. Last and far from least, she found a way to bridge the personal and the professional without compromising either.

Taal Hasak-Lowy is my patron and my best friend. I would like to thank her for agreeing, all these years later, to be number one on my list.